Love
by the
Numbers

BY

KARIN
KALLMAKER

Bella
BOOKS

2013

Bella Books, Inc.
P.O. Box 10543
Tallahassee, FL 32302

Printed in the United States of America on acid-free paper
First published 2013

Editor: Katherine V. Forrest
Cover Designer: Judith Fellows

ISBN 13: 978-1-59493-318-9

PUBLISHER'S NOTE

Other Bella Books by Karin Kallmaker

Acknowledgment

Twenty-Six, by the numbers, might be the gallons of Diet Coke drunk during this book's creation, or the number of late arrivals for school pick up because I was lost in Russia, or even the number of times I cursed the book's very existence. Twenty-Six is probably the number of times I've read it already, start to finish and found one more typo. Twenty-Six, or thereabouts, is the number of times my patient publisher asked how the book was coming along, and a mere fraction of the number of times she wanted to ask—her forbearance is much appreciated.

To my family and friends who have found me too often distracted, and apt to launch into non sequiturs about women who turn out to be fictional, and who have finally accepted this state of mind is what passes for my normal I say thank you.

To those family and friends who have not noticed these proclivities I say bless you.

Many thanks go out to Facebookers Georgi, Beth, Jackie, Jacky, Jane, Kerstin, Eileen, Minna and Karen for suggestions of places Lily and Nicole should visit.

Far more than Twenty-Six is the number of readers who have expressed their support and encouragement over the year it took for me to write this book. While I know that I will stop writing only when they pry the keyboard out of my cold, dead hands, nevertheless, it is the support of readers that makes me know that any day is a day that I can write and what I write will be read. Every note and every kind word led to sentences, paragraphs and chapters in this book and I hope that the respect and love I have for my readers shows in every page.

Twenty-Six and all the candles have no Wicks.

About the Author

Karin Kallmaker's nearly thirty romances and fantasy-science fiction novels include the award-winning *The Kiss That Counted*, *Just Like That* and *Above Temptation* along with the bestselling *Substitute for Love* and the perennial classic *Painted Moon*. Short stories have appeared in numerous anthologies and collections. She began her writing career with the venerable Naiad Press and continues with Bella. She was recently honored with a Golden Crown Trailblazer Award, recognizing her more than twenty years of writing for lesbian readers.

She and her partner are the mothers of two and live in the San Francisco Bay area. She is descended from Lady Godiva, a fact which she'll share with anyone who will listen, though she admits you'd have to pay her a lot to get on a horse, naked or otherwise.

All of Karin's work can be found at Bella Books. Details and background about her work can be found at www.kallmaker.com.

CHAPTER ONE

"I have worked for some first-class asses in my time, but you are the queen of them all!" Firecracker finger snaps punctuated the last three words. "I told Damon to shove this job and I only came back today for my stuff. I am out of here!"

Nicole Hathaway watched Eric snatch up a notebook and the satchel that he had left on her office side chair after his precipitous departure yesterday afternoon. There was little point in saying anything. She would be glad to see him go. Given his heightened respiration and exaggerated physical gestures, he would slam the door on his way out.

"If they found you murdered in your bed they'd have to question the entire state of New Hampshire and parts of Vermont! If I were you I wouldn't walk across the Quad, honey, because someone is surely going to drop a house on you!"

The door was slammed so hard the transom above it popped open, allowing her to hear the thick wooden echo resounding the length of the deserted hallway. She also heard the tinkling of his aggravating ringtone. He'd be fine—all the sympathy he could want at his fingertips, and in seconds, from his four or five hundred nearest and dearest friends.

She glanced at the time on her phone display: 9:07. No doubt she would hear from her publisher by the end of the day. She turned her attention to final edits of the Human Cognition course syllabus for the semester that began in less than two weeks. It would be needed when the powers-that-be of the University of Central New Hampshire got around to appointing someone to fill in for her sabbatical. Classes began next week, but the lack of an instructor for them wasn't her problem.

When her cell phone rang forty minutes later, she closed her document and answered. She only needed to give peripheral attention to her publisher's first two sentences. They would be almost word for word identical to the last time he'd called about the same matter.

When Damon paused for breath, she said, "He believed himself to be a standup comedian. Upon learning I don't watch much television, he felt it necessary to deliver a daily update of his most recent viewing. I don't know anything about real or pretend housewives. I don't intend to visit the Jersey shores. I don't wish to dance with any stars. He was upset when I asked him to stop his audible punctuation and unhappy when I informed him that I was not a studio audience and did not applaud on demand."

Damon's normally cultured tone was flat. "That was the third assistant I've hired—"

"May I remind you that Twitter, Facebook and blogging case histories were not my idea? That social media isn't my definition of social? Going on a speaking tour was not my idea either." She also hadn't asked for the voluminous correspondence but that at least could be handled remotely and usually with form letter answers from Damon's publicist staff. There was no need for someone to babysit her for public appearances.

"As you remind me every time we talk. So I will remind you that your involvement in social media and publicity travel is in your contract as long as we pay for the expenses. We are, so you must."

"You told me it was a formality and there would never be money allocated for a publicist and travel. We never discussed that I would have to deal with an assistant." Let alone someone who would disrupt her blissfully quiet office every day by demanding banal social interactions, and who would accompany her the first time the possibility of extensive travel on her own presented itself. She wasn't interested in details about hotel A versus hotel B, and which rooms had which views. If she was going to travel she wanted to be visible for her required engagements and utterly invisible the rest of the time.

"Neither of us anticipated that *Love by the Numbers* would be an Oprah 2.0 book."

She drew in a deep belly breath and slowly let it out. Oprah book clubs in major US cities were on the itinerary for most of October. "No, I never thought anyone would call the book 'the *I'm Okay, You're Okay* for the new millennium.'"

"Some authors would see it as success, not punishment. You leave for London the day after tomorrow. You've succeeded in driving every assistant away."

"Two quit and one never made it here. Lack of map skills is a problem with the educational system, not me."

"You drive them away," he repeated. From the background noises, she thought he might be in a taxi. "Nicole, enough games."

"I don't play—"

"Officially, I consider your persistent ruination of all my attempts to make this tour go smoothly to be courting breach of contract. If you don't go, we keep a lot of your money. Another assistant is on the way. She will arrive tomorrow morning. Her name is Lily Smith. You can huff and puff all you want, but you will not drive her away."

She held back a childish retort. He truly had no idea how much she wanted to travel by herself. She would hope, like assistant number two, that this Lily Smith creature never materialized.

After a chilly leave-taking on both sides, she set her phone on her desk. The phenomenon known as *Love by the Numbers* was temporary—it was a fad. Her academic research, meant for other researchers, had gone inexplicably viral. It was "Chicken Soup for the Romantic," the review in *O Magazine* had gushed. She accepted this. Her own prediction was that the furor would only last another eleven to twelve weeks before being replaced by some other fascination of the moment, just in time for the holidays. Or it would be supplanted by the cottage industries people were establishing based on her book. The woman in Michigan who claimed to be able to implement a relationship-scoring formula based on fingerprints instead of DNA would probably do very well for several years, especially when the digital fingerprinting was a fraction of the cost of DNA screening. In the meantime, the travel required by those regrettable clauses in her publishing contract lasted from late August to the first week of November.

She planned to make the absolute most of the disruption. Her private agenda was of no concern to anyone else. That was what *private* meant.

She went back to her syllabus and then turned her attention to a study that she'd been asked to peer review on meta-awareness and the effect of observation on frequency of social media use. At lunch she made her usual trip to the student union for the salmon salad and a short stint in the sun to boost her vitamin D and support the flow of oxytocin. She estimated the temperature as seventy-one or seventy-two—average for a summer day in New Hampshire. By the time she walked back to her office, however, she could feel the damp of impending afternoon rain in the air.

The rain had made good by the time she shut down her computer and a light steady sprinkle misted her office window. She picked up her helmet and pack and wheeled her bike slowly out of her office. The cleats on the bottoms of her biking shoes clacked on the cold marble floor.

The empty hallways of summer were always welcome. When students were present they resented that she brought her bicycle inside the building when they couldn't, but students were naturally resentful due to both their age and the strictures of academic rules. Six years as a student in these hallowed halls, two years obtaining her doctorate at MIT and another six-plus years spent teaching, conducting studies and publishing the results meant she was allowed to bring her bicycle indoors. That was how the academic life worked. It had also provided her an adequate office where she could enjoy solitude every day from eight thirty to five.

Many of her colleagues didn't darken their office doors for more than an hour or two a week and then only when classes were in session. From this fact she deduced that none of them lived with anyone like her mother.

The light humidity of late summer dampened her skin as she pushed through the doors leading out of the Herman J. Hathaway Science and Industry Building. She cast a glance at her great-grandfather-by-adoption's statue proudly guarding the courtyard. The statue had been commissioned by the estate to grace the building Hathaway had funded, and featured him holding a sextant and calipers. That he'd never finished high school was, she supposed, beside the point. Even his detractors admitted his ingenuity and community service were a credit to New England practicality and compassion. His millinery and textile fortunes had been inarguably crucial to putting the University of Central New Hampshire on the road to its small but mighty reputation in cognitive sciences research. She had earned her tenured position with hard work, but she supposed most of her colleagues assumed it had been a foregone conclusion—she had the Hathaway name. There were those who would add, only inside their reserved New England minds, that she might have the name but she didn't have the blood, obviously.

Pedaling as quickly as possible through campus to the main gates that would let her out onto Daniel Webster Highway, she anxiously eyed the thick, dark clouds that were pouring over the mountains and blocking the sunlight from the unsettled surface of the lake. The lightly misting clouds overhead were child's play by comparison. She would have to increase her usual pace.

Heavy drops were spattering on her helmet by the time she reached the long driveway to the house. She spotted Kate rocking in the porch glider, one hand on her large belly. If she went on tour she would likely miss her sister's delivery, but her mother's obsessive readiness rendered her own presence unnecessary.

Though she was already tired of answering people's questions and hearing their tedious anecdotal stories of how their own lives proved or disproved various *Love by the Numbers* hypotheses, the idea of being on her own for weeks and weeks would take her breath away if she thought about it more than she already did. No matter what her mother had to say about the propriety of it all, it *was* a business trip. There were no colleagues going to the same conference to suit Indira Hathaway's repressive notions about safety for her elder daughter, but her mother had ceased objections when Nicole had explained that her publisher was providing a travel assistant. Now that all the plans were made and she had no assistant—if this Lily Smith creature never arrived, that is—her mother would be truly torn between her lingering notion of what a proper, unmarried, well-bred Indian daughter should do and the waste of a great many nonrefundable travel tickets. Knowing her mother, the idea of wasted money would tip the scale.

Kate would have simply announced she was going, told her mother to expletive-off and left. But with a baby on the way, her unmarried, unemployed sister was going to need to live at home for the next several years. She might finally learn that a little finesse kept the volume level down.

There was a bright flash of lightning as she mounted the last steep stretch to the garage. The humidity had increased and she had negotiated both weather and wet roads without getting soaked to the bone or falling. Why did her publisher think she needed help coping with the vagaries of travel? She was perfectly capable of navigating a timetable. She had mastered the Boston transit system while going to MIT and was certain that trains and airports all over the world could be similarly conquered. Annual academic conferences in the US and Canada had not proven difficult to reach. Her mother had taken her to visit their family in India twice, though both times she'd scarcely been allowed to breathe without permission. Being only English-speaking and raised as a Christian hadn't helped her fit in either. Her experience with cars was limited but she could certainly drive a rental vehicle from point A to point B. After all, people spoke English everywhere and she wasn't afraid to ask questions.

It was as if Damon thought she couldn't manage the social interactions by herself, even though social currency and the predictability of behavioral exchanges were her area of expertise.

She could adequately introduce herself to a book club chairperson, or a bookseller, or even the radio and television hosts who were going to interview her.

Having someone by her side every waking hour would subject her to more juvenile humor, narcissistic tantrums and behavior expectations like those of the unlamented Eric, and it would rob her of any chance for other...pursuits.

She quickly dried her bike and helmet before hurrying across the breezeway to the house to let herself into the mudroom.

"Your shoes will be wet." Her mother's clipped tone, half due to her lingering Malayalam accent and half to her quick and decisive nature, carried easily from the kitchen. "Put them near the fire."

She made no answer—there was no point in reminding her mother that her elder daughter was thirty-two and possessed basic common sense, just as there was no point in saying that she didn't care for the vindaloo she could smell bubbling on the stove. She would have happily acquired her own dinner had she known the menu. She could easily afford to do so, and would have dissembled about having a dinner meeting with a colleague to avoid the lecture about wasting a perfectly good meal of wholesome food. An evening of sighs and ill-temper wasn't worth it at this point. She'd take an antacid before they sat down.

After shucking her damp, grit-spattered clothes and slipping into comfortable jeans and a blouse, she stepped out onto the porch to listen to the hissing rain.

Kate looked up from her paperback. There was a sly edge to her tone as she said, "Vindaloo. I know how much you love fucking vindaloo."

Nicole waited to see if a reprimand for Kate's language would be forthcoming from the kitchen. There was none, which continued to confirm her long-held theory that their mother's exceptional hearing extended only to Nicole's voice. Kate, a very pretty topez-blonde with skin a natural deep caramel a beach volleyball player would envy, had always been an American girl, a modern girl. No arranged marriages, no father's brothers trying to dictate her future. Their mother had not despaired of Kate's casual ways until Kate had arrived home four weeks ago, another college abandoned, still single and nearly five months pregnant via a liaison with a married professor.

The resulting maternal breakdown had been epic.

Nicole wasn't unsympathetic to her mother's distress, but what did her mother expect when Kate had always gotten everything she wanted by either flattery or pouting? Nicole had still not ascertained whether she herself was now in better maternal standing—she was also unmarried, and nearly eight years older than Kate. She had refused all attempts to marry her off to a relative from India, which was what the uncles on both sides of the family tree believed right and proper. It didn't matter to them that Nicole had been born on American soil, and adopted at age four by a placid American businessman who'd fallen hard for the young, exotic widow with a child. Nicole's blunt, repeated refusals had not endeared her to any of her Indian male kin. They, in turn, chastised her mother and it all rolled downhill, back onto Nicole's plate.

"I won't have vindaloo for several months." She glanced at her sister. "You'll have to eat my share."

Kate's reply was predictably foul, and Nicole watched the rain dancing on the driveway while she planned how to broach with her mother the topic of traveling alone. Contrary to her childhood fears, her mother did not read minds. And that was a good thing. She was going on this speaking tour. She would have the privacy she required.

All that was left was making her mother like it.

***

Nicole smiled with what she hoped was sufficient gratitude for her heaping plate of rice and vindaloo. It was the only dish her mother made spicy to the point of pain. Memories of previous vindaloos had already set her tongue to tingling, proof of the cognitive-neurobiological connection.

Her mother carefully replaced the ladle in the heavy ceramic crock that had served so many curries that the inside was stained yellow by turmeric and saffron. "I had a phone call from Betty Creedy."

Indira Hathaway was a magnet for gossip, and it wouldn't surprise Nicole to learn that her mother already knew about her assistant's departure. Nicole had received a call once about winning a prestigious research award, and immediately called her mother with the news only to discover that her mother had already heard it at a garden club meeting from a department secretary.

In any discussion with her mother patience was better rewarded than curiosity. She gave her attention to her dinner. The pork, potato, peppers and carrot curry had been her stepfather's favorite dish, and Nicole had heard many times about the marvel of her mother's vindaloo, so wonderful that he had married her.

She cut into a carrot, hoping to spread the mild flavor into the searing heat of the curry sauce and spare her taste buds. It never worked but she never stopped hoping it would. It would seem that her mother's vindaloo brought out a form of mental illness.

Kate, who had patted her stomach and said in a wan voice, "Just rice for me," asked the obvious question. "Why did Betty call you?"

Nicole took a big bite of carrot, winced and chased it with rice.

"Nicole's latest assistant apparently left something behind when he checked out." The hawk-like brown eyes turned to Nicole. "Did he leave, Nicky?"

She knew it was foolish, but when her mother called her *Nicky* she felt like the child who had once believed her mother could see through walls. A foolish childhood fear, she reminded herself. "Yes, he left. He was inappropriate to the job."

"Who is going to go with you on this tour, then? You cannot travel alone. It isn't right."

There was no point yet in mentioning the possibility of someone new arriving in the nick of time. If that fell through her mother would be even more upset. The best long-term strategy was to win the important point that she could travel on her own.

Nicole knew better than to make a flat declaration. That was Kate's style. It worked for Kate, or so Kate thought. This conversation would follow their predictable pattern.

She soothed with, "Mom, I'm very sensible." She expected her mother to next fret and predict mayhem and scandal.

"I don't know what I would do if you were harmed. What will our family say?"

She ventured a gentle point of fact, knowing she'd be chastised for her disrespect. "Our family in India has no spy here. They won't know your unmarried daughter is traveling by herself unless you tell them."

"Maybe these are the old ways, but your blood is pure Indian, as is mine. I respected tradition and I am happy and blessed even though I have had the sad misfortune to bury two husbands. Each left me a daughter and I am comfortable in my means. All because I listened to my father when he told me to marry *your* father. My father also agreed to let me marry dear Robert."

Nicole did not remind her mother that Robert Hathaway had overcome objections to his American nationality by arranging work visas for a dozen or more family members over the years. His generosity had included air tickets and start-up money for their burgeoning small businesses. Her mother was very close to being a bought and paid for bride, and such were the revered old ways. But she didn't say any of that because Robert had done it for love. Based on the tone of her mother's voice when she said his name, and her happier demeanor when he'd been alive, Nicole believed her mother had returned his feelings. He had been the only father Nicole had ever known and she still missed him.

It would also be unproductive to point out her mother's hypocrisy in insisting adherence to Indian customs for women when her mother was the one who had decided little Nicole would speak only English and then join Robert's church. She understood that her mother had been intent on reducing the impact of being "other" in a very white community. It had worked, up to a point.

Around a hearty mouthful of rice Kate said, "Mom, Nicole is thirty-two, and she's American. Born here, raised here—her DNA is red, white and blue. When are you going to let her have a life?" She gave Nicole a sour look. "When are you going to actually speak up for yourself? Or do you enjoy being perfect?"

"There's no point to pushing water," Nicole answered her. Kate's support, as usual, came with a heaping helping of criticism.

"Your sister is now famous. Famous! The whole world can see her name and picture at Huffington Post and Amazon. She's in Wikipedia. And there will be news from all these famous places she is going, and they can find her on Google and there she will be, single and traveling by herself." Her mother concluded with her habitual, weak gesture of helpless confusion.

"Mom, the publisher is trying to find another assistant. But if they don't I'm still going or it will cost me a lot of money and the publisher a lot as well." There, her best card was on the table. She would see the world, more of it. And be less perfect—fine, if that's what Kate thought she was. Kate had no idea how less than perfect she had been in college and since, away from their mother's watchful gaze.

She supposed she proved her mother right. Away from scrutiny, she had misbehaved. Spectacularly, by her mother's standards. Nicole tried to smile her way through a bite of vindaloo, though her eyes watered. Pearl onions soaked up all the heat from the chilies and ginger. Her ability to accurately taste sours and bitters would be compromised for at least the next two hours.

There was a long silence punctuated with fitful sighs. A small, steady breeze from her mother's continual shaking of her head stirred the steam still rising from the vindaloo.

Toward the end of the meal her mother said, "I suppose my independent daughter isn't interested in the names of her cousins in London."

It was the expected olive branch. "I am interested. I could meet them for tea," Nicole answered. If that was all it took to put an end to the objections, she could handle it. Besides, if they were her age, they had no time in their lives for tea with a stranger. She'd pick someplace inconvenient to transit at the worst time of day and the cousins would decline. Issue solved.

Kate finished her rice and rose awkwardly. Nicole realized that the baby was suddenly showing a lot more. Kate's hands were swollen. "I'll be right here. Pushing a basketball out my cervix." She picked up her dish and a few stacked plates and waddled to the kitchen with their mother following quickly after her.

Since it wasn't her night to help with the dishes she went to change into her gym clothes. Tonight was her last chance to have a good workout before she left—tomorrow night would be stressful and rushed with packing—and she needed to claim the contents of her gym locker.

The long hallway that led to her end of the house echoed with rain drumming on the roof. She passed Kate's open door and didn't have to look in to know it was a mess. Clothing would be strewn across the bed, and a pile of empty coffee mugs and soda cans would be stacked at the end of the dresser. It was hard sometimes to believe they were half-sisters.

By the time she reached her own door the aromas from dinner were distant. The house's two wings rambled, and her portion had perhaps been added on for a not much liked mother-in-law in the hopes of keeping her away from the rest of the family. There was a bath with a shower, space enough for two large wardrobes in her bedroom, and her own sitting room that looked out on the long garden. She liked her view of the apple trees, the lone maple at the end and the rows of trellises covered with the climbing roses that were her mother's pride and joy. The last of the blooming season's petals were dusted over the white gravel walk like pink and red polka dots, rinsed off the plants by the rain. Likewise, the planter boxes were speckled with purple petals from the rhododendrons.

She would happily work in this lovely room but for her mother's constant interruptions. She'd tried it once for a few days one summer and her mother had found a pretext every hour to knock on the door. She knew her mother was lonely in spite of her involvement with a number of community groups in town, but it wasn't a void she could fill every day. She'd gotten nothing done because her mother didn't think that reading or tapping at a keyboard was a kind of work that couldn't be interrupted. After three days of continually broken concentration, she'd gone back to her little office on campus. Her productivity there was impressive enough to have drawn half-humorous rebukes from some colleagues and frequent suggestions that she consider "getting a life."

She had a life, which she was under no obligation to justify to anyone. It was busy, productive and…useful.

She quickly changed into boy-style gym shorts and a worn long-sleeve UCNH T-shirt. She'd cut the sleeves back just above the elbow and it was her favorite. By the time she returned to the living room, Kate had turned on the television and clicked over to one of the celebrity gossip programs that added no value to the world, at least that Nicole could see.

"Must you?"

Kate scratched her nose with a prominently extended middle finger. "I must. Besides, it's your only contact with the outside world."

"Sorry, but I'm off to the gym."

"Then what do you care?"

"My niece or nephew could absorb that drivel in utero."

She ignored Kate's second one-finger salute and escaped the din of the television program, which had gone from salacious dismay over a rocker's drug overdose to a weepy red-haired heiress surrounded by microphones.

The drive to the gym was through wet streets and around double-parked tourists clogging the Daniel Webster in the vain search for parking near the restaurants. The facility was actually one town over in Center Harbor, which gave her just enough distance that she was unlikely to cross paths with anyone in her mother's circle of acquaintances. She'd been avoiding parental radar since she was sixteen and supposed that some day she ought abandon the habit. She was no longer a teenager. But right now it was just... easier. Quieter. Simpler for certain aspects of her life to stay off her mother's view screen.

She signed in and headed past the weight room where the evening grunt-off between steroid divas was underway, in spite of the prominent sign that read, "As a courtesy to others, keep noise to a minimum." She could be on the Stairmaster with headphones playing Pink and still be able to hear the guttural *unh* and *gee-ezh* followed by long, exaggerated exhales.

She started with simple yoga stretches then moved to the elliptical machine and finished with hard cardio on the stairs. Then, because it would be so long before she had access to the equipment again, she braved the male zeitgeist of the weight room and did a full upper body workout. The gym was her safe place and no one paid her any attention as she flexed and strained.

Here, she rolled up the sleeves as far as they would go. Her mother would have a conniption if she got a good look at her biceps and abs, but she loved them. She'd honed the long, lean lines and loved the feeling of power and control. At the gym she wasn't Robert Hathaway's adopted daughter, not a professor, not a beleaguered daughter with an overprotective mother, not a first-generation American living her part of the Indian diaspora. At the gym she was just another body, looked over and overlooked based on how she moved, how much she lifted, how long she sweated.

The last arm curl complete, she mopped her face and neck on her way to the shower stalls. A quick rinse later she wrapped herself in her towel and surveyed the contents of her locker. She wasn't confident that if she left something in it that it would still be there months later. She would take it all home—it wasn't that much. Besides, the most valuable thing in the locker she was taking on the trip. It always traveled with her.

Dressed in fresh shorts and a faded red T-shirt, she glanced around the locker room before pulling the black leather jacket out of the locker's depths. Butter soft, with square shoulders, the sleek cut was exactly what a virtuous, perfect, obedient daughter and staid scholar did *not* wear.

She couldn't help herself—she slipped it on, loving the way it melted onto her shoulders and encased her hips. She felt strong in the jacket. The scent of the leather triggered memories of the music, the lights and the heat of the last dance before graduation. She'd known then that future trysts would be scarce, and that night she had lived like it was her last. As far as her subsequent encounters were concerned, that had been mostly true.

She kept the jacket on as she headed for the door, telling herself that she was about to embark on a long, stressful change to her routine, and the endorphins that the jacket released would bolster her resilience. She stopped at the counter to put her membership on hiatus. The twenty-something blonde who had helped her several times in the past gave her a second glance this time. Or rather, she gave the jacket a second look.

"You're all set, Nicole," she said, her fingers tapping on her keyboard.

The jacket was the symbol of how she successfully bifurcated her life between her public face and her sexual necessities. She was taking it with her and would wear it—unaccompanied by any assistant—in cities where it was a passport to meeting other women like her. On occasion, as she did now, she indulged herself in the whimsy of blaming the jacket for what she said and did. "Actually, I prefer Cole."

The young woman smiled, looked at the jacket and finally her gaze traveled up to Nicole's face. "Cole," she repeated. "It suits you."

"Thanks. See you in a few months."

The slow smile didn't really mean anything, but Nicole walked away satisfied by it. It wasn't an invitation she would ever pursue. It was too close to home and gossip reached her mother at speeds that defied all physical laws. Cole's dalliances had always been and were going to be far from home, quick and anonymous. Just the way she liked them.

CHAPTER TWO

After spending a frantic night packing what little was left of her possessions and the following day loading them into her Uncle Damon's hired van to be taken to the storage locker, Lily Smith had told herself she really could leave the country for weeks and weeks and not have to worry about anything. She had nothing left to worry about.

She glanced in the rearview mirror of her rental car and realized she could no longer see the skyline of New York City. Just like that, it was gone. She was on her own. Only the future ahead, she told herself. As the miles clicked off the built-in navigation system, she tried to focus on the next few days, but she kept checking the rearview mirror as if New York would suddenly reappear—or a pack of paparazzi would zoom into view in pursuit of Lillian Linden-Smith, celebrity miscreant. It was a bitter mix, feeling glad to have escaped from the only place she'd ever called home.

Look on the bright side, Lily. You could take advantage of Uncle Damon's spur-of-the-moment offer of a job because everything else you owned of value was sold in the auction. Visiting the storage locker gave you the chance to get your travel gear. Voltage adapters are expensive and now you don't have to buy a new one. You kept the Givenchy travel collection. Wasn't it great that you refused to sell the Kors little black dress, the Manolos and the two pairs of Bruno Maglis? No matter what being an "author assistant" means, you won't be an embarrassment. It all worked out for the best.

Her inner cheerleader finally got tired and she was no less anxious. After crossing into Connecticut she considered the best place to take a break. It was much later in the day than she'd planned. Last night, with no place else to go after the dealer took the last of her furniture, she'd collapsed in Uncle Damon's guest room and slept hard for the first time in what seemed like years. She'd woken up this morning with the vague feeling of having been crying, but after a brisk shower and the pleasure of making eggs for herself and Uncle Damon that he'd praised for being "as good as David's," she'd been in a more positive frame of mind. Even though David had passed away more than five years ago, the house still had his laughter and serenity, and she had soaked it up.

But the escrow officer who was supposed to take her keys from her had been delayed, making her start from Manhattan later than she had planned, especially after the time it took to secure the rental car. On the plus side, Uncle Damon had insisted on giving her an advance against her first couple of paychecks, and a small personal loan to pay down her credit card so she had some emergency funding should she need it. He'd been a little miffed that she hadn't told him just how desperate her financial straits were. One minute he'd been treating her to dinner and the next offering her a job. It was a relief to have those financial cushions. Her bank had been the last stop on her way out of New York.

She willed herself not to look in the rearview mirror. *There's nothing back there for you.*

The humidity dropped as she drove north and east through small town after small town. The cooler air was fragrant with the aroma of fresh sod and moss as she passed rolling pastures. The leaves were nowhere near turning but she could imagine how beautiful the landscape would be when reds, golds and coppers massed on the hillsides. Someday she might come back this way, maybe with someone special to share the sights.

It occurred to her that she could actually think about having a "someone special." That would mean, potentially, telling someone about her parents, and about hiding in her condo for a year and a half in fear of being recognized. Or about being judged, by the media at least, a financial swindler and criminal. How did one bring up, in a casual conversation, that one had an arrest record, or that perfect strangers felt justified when they swore or spat at you?

A cool, quiet roadside park beckoned. Alone in the parking lot she left the car radio playing a public radio broadcast of Beethoven's *Pastoral Symphony* and enjoyed the lunch Uncle Damon had made for her. His "little of this, little of that" turned out to be sliced pear, a lovely wedge of brie, a tart kosher pickle and cream crackers. For at least those few minutes she felt calm. Finally, she could focus on exactly what she'd undertaken. Uncle Damon had said the author was unpleasant. He'd only given Lily one stricture: she couldn't quit. Since the job was a godsend, she had no intention of failing.

So she didn't have to worry about money for a few months—what a relief. In addition to now having some resources on her credit card, another credit card from Uncle Damon's little publishing house would be waiting for her in Edinburgh on Monday. Her priority, after she reclaimed the packet of tickets and itineraries from the difficult Dr. Hathaway, was updating the air tickets to her own name. If she had a smarter phone she could probably take care of that right now.

Duh, she thought. Glad to find her mind could focus more clearly, she clicked open her cell phone and called Uncle Damon. After assuring him she was safely on her way and more than halfway to Meredith, New Hampshire, she made the case for needing better technology at her disposal.

"A laptop? Of course you need a laptop. I should have thought of it." She heard him call out to someone, then he came back on the line. "Lupe—my assistant—will see about ordering one from a store where you're headed."

He went away again, then returned after a muffled conversation. "She says there's an electronics store in Meredith. I'll give her your number and she'll keep you posted."

She thanked him and hung up with a deep breath. There, she told herself. Your brain isn't fried, just rusty. There was nothing inherently difficult about this job. It needed attention and forethought. After living day to day for the many months since the scandal had broken, thinking about next week and next month was finally a possibility.

Her final hurdle, however, was developing a working relationship with the famously boorish Dr. Hathaway. She'd had professors like that at Wellesley—brilliant and utterly without social graces. Some of them hadn't had social graces to begin with. Their neurons fired a little bit differently than most people's and their empathy was sometimes on a time delay. There, but slow to surface.

But there had been a few profs who simply dispensed with the niceties because it was easier for them that way. One professor in particular had it all worked out through a social exchange diagnosis that he could be an insensitive asshat and if you minded, it was your fault. When a student had told him she had breast cancer, his response had been, "Why should that matter to me?"

Lily's jaw still dropped every time she recalled it, not to mention his subsequent diatribe about the inherent manipulative nature of compulsory compassion. She didn't relish the idea of working with anyone who approached that level of asshattery.

Back on the road, and finally able to tune in several choices in music, she flipped channels between Gotye, Christina Aguilera and Florence and the Machine. The upbeat music and peaceful highway continued to improve her mood throughout the afternoon.

Though New Hampshire's sapphire lakes and emerald mountains should have already prepared her, she gasped when she caught first sight of the large, richly blue Lake Winnipesaukee. Green-crusted islands, some with large homes just visible between the trees, were dotted across the surface. Deep fingers formed large bays and there were almost as many small craft on its surface as moored at the numerous docks.

Daniel Webster Highway skirted Meredith Bay and would lead her into the heart of Meredith. She rounded the first corner into the town to find the roadside filled with food stands promising apples and peaches, shaved ices and fresh lemonade. In the lazy summer afternoon light, the water looked inviting. She envied the people out on their water skis, but noted they were all wearing body suits. The snow-fed lake was probably a few degrees above freezing. Given the crowds sunning on the lakeside beach and playing in the water, that was how New Englanders liked it. Not that New Yorkers weren't a tough lot. They just tended to think New Englanders took things to unnecessary extremes.

The rental car GPS warned her she was approaching Dr. Hathaway's home. Nearly five o'clock was much later than she had planned. At first she thought she was being directed into a bed-and-breakfast called The Lakeside House by mistake, but the building turned out to be a large private residence. The classic saltbox two-story main building had two one-story wings. The driveway was lined with blooming rhododendrons of lavender and scarlet. Somebody kept a beautiful garden.

Her tires crunched on the gravel as she slowed to a stop. It was a large house for the single loner that Uncle Damon had described. She'd had no time to even buy a copy of the professor's book and wasn't sure what she looked like. She realized that a young woman was sitting on the porch so she got out of the car with a brisk air, gathered her handbag and hoped her businesslike shirtdress that had served as her standard courtroom attire wasn't overly crumpled from the long drive. She'd chosen her Magli stilettos to add several inches to her petite height and because they boosted her confidence.

"Dr. Hathaway?" she asked as she mounted the three shallow steps to the cobblestone porch, even though she was guessing the woman was too young and fair-skinned to be the Indian-heritage professor.

The pretty blonde shook her head. "Not by a long shot."

Lily realized then the woman was very pregnant and roughly her own age. "Am I in the right place to find her?"

"Yes, but she won't be home for another half hour or so. You could set your watch if you like." She changed to a nasal, mechanical tone. "When you hear the bicycle bell the time will be five-a-thirty, exac-ta-lee."

"I see." She held out her hand such that the woman didn't have to rise to shake it. "I'm Lily Smith from Insignis Publishing."

"Kate Hathaway, Nicky's sister." Her hand was swollen and dry. "Are you a new assistant? I didn't know Nicky was getting another one. Does Nicky know she has a new victim?"

"A pleasure to meet you." Diplomacy 101 suggested that Lily would not need to understand Kate's reasons for being snide about her sister to a stranger, so it was best to appear as if she was unaware of any undertone. She was spared from further pleasantries by the opening of the front door.

A much older woman in a beautiful purple sari over soft green petticoats looked at her curiously. Kate and the woman shared the same nose, mouth and chin, though Kate's skin was several shades lighter.

"I apologize for arriving unannounced," Lily said. Uncle Damon had given her a sketchy version of Nicole Hathaway's bio and knew she was Indian by lineage and American by birth. This must be her mother, she thought, taking note of the simple gold cross at the woman's throat. "I'm Lily Smith from Insignis Publishing. I'll be accompanying Professor Hathaway on her tour. I understand she isn't available yet."

"I am Indira Hathaway." She offered her hand and Lily met her gaze. After a quick handshake, Mrs. Hathaway stepped back, holding the door open for Lily. "Welcome to our home. Please come in. My other daughter will be home very soon. May I offer you tea?"

She smelled what had to be dinner. Her timing was awkward. "I really must check into my lodging for the night. I could return later this evening. Around seven or seven thirty?"

"Please come in," Mrs. Hathaway repeated. "Join me for a cup of tea and please stay for dinner."

"It's not vindaloo," Kate said from behind them.

Lily froze for just a second before she realized that Mrs. Hathaway's glacial stare wasn't aimed at her. "I couldn't impose."

"It is no imposition at all. Please, be our guest for our evening meal."

She hadn't been to India since her exchange program stay of two months when she was a high school junior. From what she remembered, though, the repetition of the offer meant it was genuine. It would be rude not to accept and she had no reason to alienate Dr. Hathaway's family.

She nodded. "In that case, I'd be honored." It was the truth when she added, "It smells delicious."

"We're having spiced chicken. Are you a vegetarian?"

"No, though I really should be."

"Don't be ridiculous. You're already too skinny."

"Welcome to the house of joy," Kate muttered.

The interior was all wood paneling and tweeds from New England with vibrant artwork and ceramics from India. The cultural clash was surprisingly lively—she liked it. It reflected the strong personality of the woman who was leading her not to the sitting room but to a delightfully old-fashioned kitchen. There was even a huge open hearth at the far end, though its function appeared to be decorative in this era.

"My daughter did not mention that there was someone on the way to accompany her. I am very relieved." Mrs. Hathaway set two delicate teacups on saucers next to the stove where a kettle was already simmering. "Do you have a favorite tea?"

"Darjeeling, if you have it. But I'm not picky." Lily knew that Uncle Damon had told Dr. Hathaway she was on her way, so why had she not told her family?

"I do have it. Have you had a long journey today? Would you like to freshen up?"

"I would love to freshen up. Thank you," Lily said fervently.

"Certainly. Kate, please show our guest to the powder room."

The now taciturn Kate led her back to the foyer and gestured at another door. Lily used the few minutes to gather her wits. Brushing her hair, though nothing would improve the cut, and a fresh application of powder and lipstick all helped hide how tired she was. She didn't know why she was so nervous. Well, if Mrs.

Hathaway was anything to judge by, Professor Hathaway would be formidable.

The tea was well steeped by the time she returned, and she carried her cup and saucer into the sitting room in the wake of her hostess.

"This is a lovely home."

"It's been in my husband's family for many generations. I and my daughter Nicole have lived here since my Robert brought me home from our honeymoon. That's nearly thirty years ago now."

"If I may ask, I hope I'm not being rude, but what part of India are you from originally? I can't place your accent—but then I don't know enough of them to be sure of anything, Mrs. Hathaway." Lily inhaled the earthy aroma of her tea, hoping it would restore some of her flagging energy.

"You must call me Indira."

"That's a powerful name."

"It is. I have always liked it." Indira sipped her tea with a reserved smile. "I was born in *Keralam* province."

"In the south? I was told it's lovely there. I stayed in Chennai for two months when I was in high school. It was one of several exchange programs I was in. I wish I had seen more of India, but it is such a large country."

Indira's reserve faded and they were quickly discussing why the literacy rate in Kerala was so much higher than the rest of India. Indira was an avid reader of biographies and they found common ground in John Adams. She didn't enlighten her hostess that she'd decided to read biographies of American presidents, in order by presidency, during the long months of self-imposed isolation. Library books were free. So far she'd made it to Taft.

Indira excused herself for a few minutes to tend to dinner, and returned in full interrogation mode. Lily answered questions about her schooling. The word *Wellesley* brought a smile to Indira's lips, but it made Lily nervous. Questions about her family, her parents, her own job history were inevitable. Yes, she had completed her undergraduate degree, but hadn't yet chosen a master's program. She was spared explaining the interruption in her schooling by a timer sounding from the kitchen. Indira hurried away again, after assuring Lily that she needed no assistance.

After a moment, Kate, who had been sitting on the other side of the room, excused herself. "I'm not running away. It's just that the glider on the porch feels better to my back." She gestured at her belly.

Lily smiled. "When are you due?"

"Just after Halloween." As Kate moved slowly toward the front door a trilling bell sounded from outside.

She couldn't help but look at her watch. It was five thirty on the dot.

Kate glanced back and caught her noting the time. "Told ya."

***

The nondescript sedan in the driveway might belong to the new assistant, Nicole thought. Darn it anyway. It had been foolish to hope Damon's plan would fall through. She skirted the car easily, wishing the newcomer had decided to show up tomorrow morning at the college. Her bike tires had skidded on an unexpected puddle and she'd fallen. The mud smearing her left side was not the impression of competence she wanted to make, and it was beyond all reasonable expectation that her mother would let her quietly slip back to her bedroom to clean up.

Sure enough, within seconds of opening the mudroom door she heard, "Nicole, we're in the sitting room. Please come and meet Lily Smith."

In spite of being self-conscious about her appearance she was taken aback by the sitting room tableau.

Her mother, animated and all smiles, was perched on the edge of the sofa. The assistant sat next to her, sipping tea from the good china.

Tea, before dinner. Tea, in the good china.

The hands so adroitly balancing the cup and saucer were delicate, the shapely legs were crossed, and the high heels were the kind of stylish ones that Nicole had never *ever* wanted to wear but Cole had always found…intriguing.

The woman was setting her saucer on the side table and rising to her feet. Brassy blonde, perfect makeup, manicured nails, shimmering crystal earrings, green eyes.

She couldn't be any older than Kate and the top of her head scarcely reached the height of Nicole's shoulder.

They shook hands and exchanged names.

"Lily has agreed to stay to dinner," her mother said.

"Perfect." Nicole hoped any oddness in her demeanor would be put down to the mud. "I really must go change. I had a tumble off my bike."

"And yet you still got here on time." Kate, coming in from the porch, was giving her a look like she was in really deep trouble about something.

"I'll be back as soon as I can. Don't wait dinner on me."

"Of course we can wait." Her mother waved her away as she turned back to Lily. "When you were in Chennai did you ever try kootu?"

"I loved it." Lily Smith's voice was light and edged with humor. "I preferred the kind with all the greens and lots of black pepper."

Their voices faded away as she reached her bedroom. So the new assistant had been to India? That accounted for her mother's beaming approval.

She jumped when Kate spoke from behind her.

"You are so screwed."

She turned in her open doorway to give Kate a puzzled look.

"She wrapped Mom around her little finger in five seconds flat. You don't stand a chance."

"I don't know what you're talking about."

"I know, you don't need anyone, ever. Did you see her shoes? If those aren't real Bruno Maglis, I'm not pregnant. Though I haven't a clue what happened to her hair. Looks like a beauty school dropout soaked it with bleach and then cut it with a butter knife."

"What do her shoes have to do with Mom?"

Kate laughed. "You're so stuck with this one."

Shaking her head, Nicole left Kate to her ravings. She stripped off her slacks in the bathroom and examined the damage. The road rash was minimal—just a light scrape. Dirty water had soaked all the way through her bra on one side so a quick shower was mandatory.

She was away longer than she meant to be but by the time she returned to the sitting room she felt more human. She hoped her simple black slacks and plain white blouse would be sufficient to balance whatever Kate had meant about the assistant's shoes.

"I don't know a thing about chess," she heard the assistant saying. "My uncle taught me to play Go. We haven't played in some time, but our matches were epic—to us, at least."

Her mother said, "I used to play Go, but I can't find a well-matched player. My late husband always played chess with Nicky. She is playing a game by correspondence with a colleague in Seattle."

They were getting along so well that Nicole bypassed the sitting room and went instead to the dining room. If the good china was out, they were eating at the big table.

It was curious, she thought as she set the table, that when she tried to look at Lily Smith she couldn't focus. The simple crystal teardrop necklace was eye-catching and the turned back cuffs her of dress sleeves encircled shapely arms. Her eyeliner was amethyst, which brought out the green irises, but the more Nicole thought about it, the more she knew she hadn't a clue about the shape of her nose or mouth, or a sense of her entire face. It was—ridiculous thought—as if she were afraid to look at the woman.

Knowing they would be in close quarters on the road was the likely cause of her reluctance, she decided. Her mother's concerns for propriety aside, traveling with a man had not been the least bit threatening. Well, traveling with a woman wouldn't be either. There was nothing about Lily Smith that pinged her gaydar, and Nicole felt that hers was exceptionally accurate. She had made a study of the cues and signs of other lesbians to avoid giving out any of her own. It was a decision that had made sense when she had known she would not marry and settle down as her mother desired, and she had seen little more ahead of herself than the grind toward tenure and the repetition of research, publish, teach.

Cole's encounters in college were a long time ago, and the subsequent anonymous liaisons at conferences had been few and far between. The leather jacket and all that it represented, now packed inside her locked suitcase, was her outlet. She'd had no reason or temptation to risk the status quo with her family, or her colleagues, not when that aspect of her life was so neatly contained.

Of course the world had changed all around her ever since, but she hadn't felt the need to keep up. This trip, away from all her expectations and limitations, would allow her opportunities for the quick connections with women she couldn't help but crave. Cole would get what she needed. But she would return as Nicole.

The irony of the author of *Love by the Numbers: How Your DNA Forms Receptive Relationships* not being the least bit interested in a relationship of her own wasn't lost on her. Irony, however, was an emotional construct that created a false need to find resolution.

She heard Lily Smith's husky laugh followed by her mother's unmistakable titter and tried to school bitterness from her expression. Instead of the ease of simply putting on her jacket and visiting a club as many nights as possible, she was saddled with the epically feminine Lily Smith. She would have to make sure that Ms. Smith didn't think being a travel companion meant familiarity. They had nothing in common.

***

"This is truly delicious," Lily said, and it was the truth. The spiced chicken was rich with fennel, cinnamon and ginger, and the coconut-apple-pecan compote was perfect to complement it. If this was an example of a casual meal, then Indira Hathaway was an excellent cook. "Thank you so much for letting me share this meal with you."

Indira beamed. "What lovely manners you have. You are a credit to your mother, I'm sure."

She shook her head at her hostess. "I wasn't being polite. This is wonderful. I haven't had a home-cooked meal in years. I mean, one that I didn't make for myself."

"A girl like you—"

"Here we go," Kate said.

"A girl like you," Indira repeated with an arch look at Kate, "cannot possibly be single."

"I am. No prospects either."

"You're embarrassing her, Mother."

Nicole's expression was fixed in lines of too-polite interest. Lily was disconcerted that Nicole had yet to meet her gaze or attempt to draw her into conversation to break the ice between them. For the most part, the good professor—younger than expected—was simply listening. Lily hoped Nicole had missed her slight twitch at the mention of her mother.

"It's quite all right," Lily said automatically. It was as good a time as any to practice her vague responses to someone who asked about her private life. "I've been very busy since leaving college."

"How is it you have traveled so many places? Please help yourself to more of anything."

Lily immediately spooned out two more dollops of the tangy-sweet compote. "My parents believed in travel. When I was in high school I was an exchange student for two months during both my junior and senior years. On other occasions I spent time with relatives who had homes in other countries."

She returned her attention to her food, hoping she'd seemed forthcoming enough to forestall questions about her relative's names, her parents' occupation, how they had died...

"My mother is right that you have good manners," Kate said. "You haven't asked about the baby's father. I can't go anywhere without people asking when I'm due and what sex my husband and I want for the baby. And touching my stomach, which drives me nuts."

"It's not an unnatural question," Nicole commented. "You're going to have to get used to people saying the baby takes after the father, or somesuch."

"It might not be an unnatural question, but you don't have to satisfy their curiosity just because they ask." Lily realized she sounded as if she was rebuking Nicole, so she added quickly to Kate, "Strangers actually touch you? In nine-tenths of the world, that's rude."

"Really?" Nicole sipped from her water glass.

"Here we go," Kate said.

Nicole continued as if Kate hadn't spoken. "Ninety percent of the world's cultures frown upon unwanted touching of a pregnant woman's belly? Or did you mean ninety percent of the world's population? In India, it's considered good luck for a woman to touch a pregnant woman's belly, and that would be nearly a half-billion women—roughly—right there. So you probably didn't mean population."

Lily gave Nicole a faint smile. Might as well stand her ground from the outset. "I was estimating the number of societies—roughly—that frown upon unwanted touching."

"Is this something you've made a study of?"

"Yes." Their gazes finally locked. Lily kept hers as guileless as possible. "Extensive."

"A curious area of study."

"When you travel it's a good idea to know the cultural mores of your host country. I'll brief you when we travel to each new destination. Everything from ordering food, if tipping is expected. Avoiding cultural condescension. That sort of thing." She tacked on a bright smile and scolded herself for her attitude. This was a job, a good job. Uncle Damon had told her she couldn't quit, but that didn't mean she couldn't get fired.

Nicole continued to meet her gaze. Like her mother, she had deep brown eyes and a definite ascetic hook to her nose. She was thin, much the way Lily would think someone who biked daily would be, and her thick, straight hair wasn't more than an inch or two past her earlobes.

"How useful you will be. Perhaps I could simply have access to your guides to study them myself."

What a distant, chilly smile, Lily thought. She might look like her mother, but she doesn't have half of the personality. She tapped one temple. "All in my head. And I can always use my phone to find out if there's any current civil unrest."

"There's an app for that?"

"The CIA World Factbook."

One eyebrow lifted, just slightly. Lily had no idea what the woman was thinking.

Kate said, with a snarky smile, "It'll be good for you to have someone with you who can read a map."

"Kate, if your point is that I'm not well-traveled, then you could simply say so. Sarcasm is a waste of time."

Indira said to Lily, "They've always been like this. Sisters."

"I don't have any siblings," Lily shared. The byplay between Kate and Nicole was enlightening—Kate brought out a less guarded streak in her sister. She had no problem believing that Nicole could be scathing when she wished to be. She pitied her students.

"And your parents?" Indira glared at her daughters as they subsided into silence. "They are living?"

"No, sadly, I lost them both some time ago." She forestalled the expression of sympathy by adding, "That's why I'm so grateful to join you tonight. It's been a while since I've spent time with a family."

"And you two do nothing but bicker," Indira said to her daughters.

"I hadn't noticed," Lily said.

"Now you're being polite." Nicole set down her fork. "There's no need. We were, in fact, bickering."

"I'm not saying that you weren't." Lily could arch an eyebrow too. "I refuse to acknowledge it, which is quite different."

"Are you in the habit of denying that something exists?"

"Yes." Lily gave her the sweetest smile she could manage.

Nicole smiled back, for the first time. It reminded Lily of the Cheshire Cat. But all Nicole said was, "I see."

Had she made some kind of behavioral science faux pas? No matter. She turned her attention back to Indira. "This dish is so fragrant. I love that about Indian cuisine. What's your secret?"

**

Later that evening, after Lily checked into one of the motels on the main highway, she reflected on the undertone of the evening's conversation with the dear professor. Nicole had seemed always ready to spar, which Lily didn't understand. She was definitely not the kind of personality she'd ever seek out for a friend—too sure she was right about everything.

Over dessert, Lily had realized why her reaction to Nicole had been prickly. It wasn't just that Nicole was arrogant and distant. Her cold brown eyes reminded Lily of one of the prosecutors who had grilled her for hours about her knowledge of her parents' business dealings. So certain of facts, so quick to accuse. The prosecutor had brought out Lily's sarcastic side, which had only gotten her into more trouble. Nicole Hathaway touched the same raw nerve.

Well, she couldn't quit, and only Uncle Damon could fire her, so she would have to find the best frame of mind to get through it. She was living almost free for a few months and maybe when she returned home the scandal junkies would have found someone new to stick on a Pinterest.

Nevertheless, it was best the good professor learn right away that Lily was perfectly aware when someone was trying to make her feel inadequate. Picking at a casual comment like whether it was appropriate to touch a pregnant woman's stomach—that had been condescending. The dear professor had no idea exactly how well trained Lily was in certain things.

She wearily brushed her teeth, hoping she didn't fall asleep before she was actually in the bed. She looked at the dark half-moons under her eyes and sighed. Academic snobbery was nothing compared to the acid bites of wealthy people with nothing else to do but belittle each other. Professor Dr. Nicole Hathaway, Ph.D., PITA, might think her expertise in behavioral science made a formidable weapon in a battle of wits, but Lily had been schooled in bitchery by the best.

Those few years when her parents had seemed to have money to burn, they had spent lavishly on clothes and trips. Finally, they were on equal monetary footing with so many cousins, aunts and uncles. Her college breaks had been filled with weeks at Martha's Vineyard, skiing in Whistler, bargain hunting in Thailand, beach volleyball at Bondi...

Sometimes it all seemed like a dream. But then so did her studies—world literature, public policy, economics, sociology, world religions—they all seemed far, far away from a dining room making barbed conversation with someone who clearly didn't welcome her but whom she was supposed to help. All those months she'd been cooped up in her condo, afraid to step outside, she'd watched a lot of television. Smart people who lacked basic social graces made interesting detectives and might be useful to save the day when world crises threatened, but who wanted to spend three nonstop months in their company?

It was childish and not a good omen that she fell asleep thinking, *Bring it on, bee-yatch*.

CHAPTER THREE

Nicole parked her car in the faculty lot and battled an early morning wind as she carried two empty boxes to her office. She would have normally chosen jeans and a sweatshirt for what was going to be dusty work, but instead she was in slacks and a blouse and trying to ignore the fact that Kate's comment about Lily Smith's shoes had made her examine her own penny loafers with a more critical eye. They suited her. There was nothing wrong with them. Just because the shoes Lily Smith wore made her calves look sleek and her legs unnaturally long was no reason to change her own attire. Still, she hadn't wanted to look casual. It would set the wrong tone.

There was also Kate's insinuation that the shoes had something to do with how their mother had received Lily. That made more sense. By the end of the evening, Lily could have been the yellow-haired daughter her mother had always wanted. Kate was far closer to the American beauty ideal than Nicole, but Lily had them both beat. She was aware that her mother loved them both, but she had long conceded that her mother had fallen prey to valuing all the things of her adopted country as better than the country of her birth—except for the advice of the menfolk. Lily could probably be notoriously promiscuous and her mother would still find her charming. But then her mother wasn't alone in the tendency to forgive pretty blondes more readily than others for their bad behavior.

You're getting off track, she warned herself. It wasn't as if Lily Smith was capable of bad behavior from the looks of her. For someone only a little older than most of Nicole's students, she was so...*correct*. Not in a perfunctory or studied way, but as if it was programmed in her DNA to say the right thing, use the right spoon and wear the right shoes to make her legs look...like they did.

She would, someday, make some man the perfect Stepford Wife. And this trip, and all its opportunities, would be overshadowed by a Barbie clone who believed she could bluff her way through life. The assertion from Barbie-Lily that she knew exactly what percentage of world cultures frowned upon unwanted touching had been ridiculous. Her tone had been more than a little bitchy, actually. Three months of constant contact weren't going to be easy.

She calmed her erratic thoughts with a slow, deep belly breath. The oxygen had the desired effect of slowing her respiration and relaxing the muscles across her shoulders. She made one trip to her car, laden with files, and deliberately didn't think about how Cole was going to get in and out of her hotel room at night in her leather jacket without Lily Smith seeing her. Maybe she should just give up on the idea of visiting the Cat's Paw in London.

Her thighs clenched at the mere thought of what might happen if she did go out. Google Maps had shown the club only a short walk from the hotel. Her palms were damp on the file folders. It's a perfectly natural human response, she told herself. The sexual urge was an evolutionary survival trait. There was no reason someone she knew had to see her having that response. Certainly not the straight and proper Lily Smith.

She slammed the trunk closed. She knew she was most comfortable when she was in control of a situation. Cole was always in control, and that's all she was contemplating. Compatible liaisons, a few hours only, in London. And Frankfurt. And New Orleans.

Back at her desk she made herself focus on data tables, raw results and subsequent conclusions. With this peer review finished her colleague at UCLA could publish his study results on perceived hunger when presented with different visual and olfactory cues.

As she circled a column of statistical variances and noted that no bottom limit was stated in the conclusion about aroma, color palette and cognitive dissonance, she heard the light *tap-tap* of high heels in the hallway outside. That was probably her nanny now.

***

Fortified by a hearty bowl of steaming oatmeal with local maple syrup stirred into it, Lily made her way from the visitor's parking lot to the science building.

They'd agreed upon nine fifteen. It was nine thirteen when she turned the knob on Dr. Hathaway's door. The orderly office was no surprise, and she admired the view of the college common that was just visible from the window above the bookcase. Nicole, wearing the same style of no-nonsense black slacks and a simple blouse as she had last night at dinner, glanced up with a borderline frown and indicated an overstuffed manila file pocket on her desk.

"Everything I have that's related to the trip is there."

"Thank you," Lily said automatically. Though not invited to do so, she sat down in the side chair and pulled the folder toward her. The woman had no manners, fine. "I'd like to sort through this and ask you relevant questions, then I'll go elsewhere to make phone calls about changing names on the tickets I'll be using."

"That would be best," Nicole answered. "I plan to complete this review by this afternoon, but it will take focus."

Well, that do-not-disturb sign was plain enough, Lily thought. After a glance at the number-encrusted papers spread out on Nicole's desk, Lily studied her own paperwork. She worked quickly in silence, matching tickets against the itinerary and glad to see that only air tickets were assigned by name. The rail passes wouldn't be tied to a person until they were first used. The hotel reservations were in Insignis's name. There was less to worry about than she had thought, but still a lot to do before they drove out of town later today.

She was about to bring up the schedule of their departure when her phone chirped. She excused herself to take the call outside in the hall.

"This is Lupe, Damon's assistant. We have a laptop for you."

"Fantastic. You're a miracle worker." She wrote down the store name and address, repeating it back.

"I gave them a credit card and authorized it for four hundred more than the laptop so you can get accessories, spare batteries, other software. It was nice to work with a small store—they were very helpful and when I said it was urgent, they started installing software for you."

"It's a different world here," Lily agreed. "Thank you again."

Pleased, she tucked her notebook back in her bag. Returning to Nicole's office she said, "I have an urgent errand to run. It may take me an hour or so."

"Beekman's is just past the main intersection, on your right." Nicole finished writing something on one of her documents.

She hadn't realized she could be so easily heard and added *eavesdropper* to her growing list of Nicole's faults even as she chided herself for the childishness of having a list. She pushed all the tickets and slips of paper back into the folder and gathered it up. "Thank you. See you in a little while."

She got a nod in return. It wasn't that far to traipse back to her car, and the sun was warming up the morning. Her thin sweater was finally able to keep her warm. She hoped Nicole wasn't put off by the splashy peacock feather pattern—she was going to be seeing a lot of it in Lily's mix-and-match travel wardrobe.

The electronics store was right in the middle of town as Nicole had said. The moment she explained who she was she was whisked to the rear of the small store by the owner. His geniality kept her smiling even as she realized that the big screen TV at the front of the store was playing the so-called legal program with that woman,

Merrill Boone, who had made Lily the unrelenting focus of her investigative speculations.

Though Lily focused on the owner's explanations about the various add-ons she had available, she could hear that honey-sticky voice promising the latest update on a missing cheerleader and an exclusive, case-breaking interview with the girl's mother's boyfriend. He'd been cleared by the police, Boone reported. But, she asked, with her steely gaze, did he know more than he'd told her in yesterday's interview?

Lily wondered how many people realized Boone couldn't move her eyebrows more than a fraction. Botox had its side effects. It had also apparently frozen her heart.

Nerves twanging, Lily almost didn't recognize the sound of her own voice coming from the speakers. Good lord—it was the footage from her perp walk, as they'd hustled her in for her official arrest.

Even as her gaze told her she had lost weight since then, her ears could easily detect the tears in her voice as she gasped out, "No comment." New York's finest hadn't exactly kept her out of reach of the photographers.

With a visible startle she returned to what the owner was pointing out on the laptop's screen. Battery indicator. Did she want a spare battery? She agreed to one as she shook her hair into her eyes. It hurt, seeing herself before the hatchet job. She supposed that her long red hair had seemed luxuriously indulgent to the thousands of people so eager to hate her. It hadn't helped that the morning talk shows had immediately found a stylist to contend that she had a dozen hair extensions. Then they'd paraded a fashionista who'd identified her handbag as Givenchy. That she'd been released on bail a mere six hours later had been an outrage to all the victims, according to Merrill Boone.

That saccharine-and-steel voice—Lily hated it. It was that exact voice that had asked her, microphone in her face, if she had a comment on her parents' suicides. She hadn't given Boone the satisfaction of knowing that she had been the one to tell Lily how her parents had died. Right now the Boone on television was telling her audience that Lillian Linden-Smith had dropped out of sight. Scandalously, law enforcement refused to comment. They probably didn't even know where she was.

Because the case against me was dismissed, Lily wanted to wail. *They're not tracking me because I'm innocent.*

She was going to get away from all of this and eventually she would let her hair grow out and go back to its real color. It felt silly to mourn for it. But it had been her unassailable asset—one hundred percent hers. In the lineup with wealthy cousins who'd had noses, chins and ears touched up by surgeons, and who enjoyed hairdresser trips every other week costing what some people spent on car payments, her naturally luxurious hair had canceled out the little bump at the top of her nose, the blight of her thin upper lip and the distracting uneven line of her jaw. She hadn't even realized she had such noticeable flaws until mingling with women who offered the names of their plastic surgeons the way an investment banker might offer a stock tip.

She was profoundly grateful when someone changed the channel. She left forty-five minutes later Wi-Fi ready, wireless add-ons enabled and, happily, a dozen public domain books loaded that would help pass the time. The around-the-world adventures of Phileas Fogg and Passepartout seemed a must-read, given her assignment. She'd not read much Charles Dickens or Jane Austen and now seemed a good time to dive in.

The centerpiece of her acquisitions, though, was a GPS unit with worldwide maps. The box claimed it could locate itself within five feet, find any address in the world, and would switch to a pedestrian mode if walking to a destination. Since she'd already gotten addicted to the unit built into the rental car she was certain she'd like having it to rely on.

The visitor parking lot was only a little more crowded when she returned, and she was acutely aware that one person she passed gave her a long, quizzical look. When she'd woken this morning she'd wondered what Indira would have said if she'd known who Lily was. There were a couple of times that she thought Kate was looking at her oddly. They were nice people, she thought. Sure, Indira was a little intense but that she cared about her daughters wasn't in doubt. While she'd been growing up she'd known other kids had moms who cared like that and she'd envied them, sometimes. It was easy to want what you'd never had.

Refusing to respond to either of Nicole's two moods—chilly or annoyed—she gave her a cheerful greeting and explained that she needed a Wi-Fi connection.

"The student union has Wi-Fi." Nicole's expression was wooden. "You may find their lunch offerings to your taste as well."

"Do you mind if I text you with questions?"

"Not at all." Nicole rose. "I'm ready for lunch so I'll show you the way."

Surprised by the offer, Lily accepted. They left the building and passed a statue of a man who had the same last name as Nicole. Confused, Lily promised herself a visit to the university's website to read Nicole's bio in-depth.

The campus was lovely. Nowhere near the size of Wellesley, it was still spacious and the greenery was lush. Oak trees surrounded the commons and tall hedges lined the walkway to the student union. She loved living in Manhattan, but the cool, clean quiet here was soothing. There was probably a very different energy when students were present.

She spotted a table near an electrical outlet and headed for it after buying a cup of coffee. Though she kept her gaze on her laptop as it booted up, she was aware that Nicole had paid for her lunch and taken a few steps toward a table near the window—probably the one where she ate every day. Lily could almost see the calculation taking place as Nicole weighed her habitual behavior against the social construct of having someone she knew already seated at a table with more than enough room for her as well. She wondered if Nicole would be surprised at just how much behavioral science Lily had studied in preparation for a master's program in International Relations.

She hoped, someday, to get that master's degree. She hoped, someday, to get back to her dreams.

Nicole had turned in her direction. "May I join you?"

"Of course. This will be more efficient. I already have a question."

Nicole settled with her tray containing a small salad and cup of vegetable soup. "Go ahead."

"I don't want to bother you with all the possible combinations of hotel lodgings. Do you have a set preference? Did anyone else ask you about that?"

"Do you mean in regard to what's outside the window, how many beds, minibars and such?"

"And such."

"They asked, but I don't know what was secured."

It was like pulling teeth. "Well, tell me your preferences and I'll review them. It will make check-in less stressful."

"I don't care what's outside the window. One assistant was ecstatic about a balcony in Edinburgh, but..." She shrugged. "I like having tea when I wake every morning, but I have an electric kettle and a travel mug so I really don't require much in the way of amenities. My needs are simple."

Lily nodded. "And you'd prefer rooms that were nonsmoking?"

"Absolutely. Is that difficult in Europe?"

"No, not anymore. But it does depend on where you are. Only the large chains have nonsmoking rooms in Russia, it seems. It matters to me as well."

For once Nicole looked a little less certain. "I'm most intimidated by the idea of Russia. The lack of cognates in the signage, for one thing."

"Our destinations, Moscow and St. Petersburg, are very cosmopolitan. If it helps, I speak a little Russian."

Nicole blinked at her. "Really?"

Vexed that Nicole was surprised that she might actually have a relevant, useful skill set, but worried that she'd revealed too much, she rushed to explain. "I have relatives whose ties to the country date back to before the Revolution. My parents thought it might be a good idea for me to learn the language."

Lily could feel some heat in her cheeks and hoped Nicole didn't notice. After extensive lessons as a child, which had made clear she had a knack for languages, she'd finally met her very wealthy great-aunt, for whom she had been named, at her estate in Germany. She'd spoken a total of three sentences to the woman. The exercise had not resulted in a shower of gifts and treasures and she'd always felt as if she'd failed her parents somehow. She hadn't understood until the end how bitterly her parents resented their famous name and empty bank accounts, and the lengths to which they would go to keep up with their wealthy relatives. Most assuredly, if Great-Aunt Lillian Von Smoot were still alive, she would have nothing to do with the scion of the now notorious Linden-Smiths.

Fortunately, Nicole didn't seem to notice Lily's agitation and she quickly went down the list of cities for their first ten days to see if Nicole had any particular issues or thoughts about each.

"I know we'll be busy, but if I'm going to be in Dublin, I'd like to see Ashtown Castle or the gardens."

Glad that Nicole wasn't going to insist on just the overtrod tourist sites, Lily nodded. "I don't know anything about that, but I'll find out what I can. Walking tours and the like?"

Nicole had finished her sparse meal and was studying her empty bowl. "Daytime, yes. I'm not much of a night owl."

"Noted. Thank you. I think I have all I need for now. Would you like me to be at your house around four thirty? We must be on the road by six, earlier if possible. It's not that long a drive to Logan, but the travel sites warn about not trying to board international flights in under two hours."

"That sounds fine. The length of my mother's goodbyes will expand to fill the time available."

At least your mother cares that you're leaving, Lily wanted to retort. She'd once returned from a weekend with a school friend—a long ago, unconsummated first crush—to find that her mother hadn't realized she'd even been gone for two days.

She told herself there was no fixing the past. She settled in for the next hour, bookmarking and organizing the online information, creating a calendar grid—apparently no one had done that yet—with their commitments, reservations, already acquired travel vouchers and more notes about each city.

She finished up their first week and decided to get a salad. It proved a diverting break as the cashier who helped her was very buff, very cute and Lily's libido suggested the bumps under the muscle shirt were nipples with rings. She'd never been with a woman who had pierced nipples. Libido suggested perhaps it was time to live on the wild side. She told Libido to hush up and retreated to her table, sure her face was as flushed as certain other parts of her felt.

It was, however, a relief to discover that those parts of her were still alive and ready for action. She supposed, out of all real and fake factoids offered about her, she was grateful none had ever suggested she was a lesbian—no doubt they would have added *lesbo* to the list of notorious traits for "The 1% Rich Bitch." Now, apparently, Merrill Boone was going to go on claiming Lily had gotten away with her parents' Ponzi-scheme fortune. That lawyers had drained her of everything but suitcases and travel wear, used skis and some photographs, weren't facts Boone cared about. That every dime that had come to her from her parents' estate had been seized by the court was also irrelevant along with the fact that Lily had been completely ignorant of her parents' business dealings. Distant as they were, they had still been her parents. They had told her everything was suddenly coming up roses for them and she had believed it.

By the time the clock turned to four she had finished up most of their international travel plans. She would work on the United States and Canada at night. The oversized Prada handbag she'd chosen for the trip had room for the packets of rubber-banded material and the sleek little laptop. High fashion had its uses.

It was nearly half-past four when she rolled into the driveway at the Hathaways' house. Kate was rocking on the porch, looking even more pregnant and uncomfortable. In response to Lily's greeting, Kate said, "I just want the drugs and a C-section at this point, and I have almost three more months."

Eyeing Kate's narrow hips, Lily didn't envy her. "How far is it to the birthing facility?"

"Meredith General—just ten minutes. I don't know how pioneer women did that whole work in the field, squat, have the baby and then make lunch thing."

"Lack of options?"

Kate cracked a smile. "No little spa on the prairie."

A late-model all-wheel drive came up the driveway and passed the house. Nicole didn't respond to Kate's wave.

"I pity you, you know."

"It's going to be an exciting trip," Lily said truthfully. "I love travel and while it's hectic, there should be time to see parts of the world—and someone else is paying for most of it. What's not to like about that?"

"You have to put up with Nicole. She's such a moody shit."

Lily was curious about the strife between the sisters, but didn't want to elicit gossip—at least not outright. "Why would you tell me that?"

Kate lifted an eyebrow. "Fair warning?"

"I'm sure my experience of traveling with your sister will differ from your experience of life with her. It's impermanent, for one thing."

"Lucky you—okay. Don't get me wrong. She's not an evil person. But she hasn't got a warm-blooded, spontaneous bone in her body."

Kate's comment was close to Lily's own thoughts. She glanced out at the garden to keep herself from gracing Kate's belly with a meaningful look. Her tone neutral, she said, "Spontaneity can have a downside, perhaps?"

"Not for me. I always wanted children. I've just never wanted a husband."

Lily wondered if Kate realized she sounded like some of the women she'd known in college. Interested in families, but not interested in men, and some not interested in women either. The cute cashier had made her realize just how long she'd been celibate. It wasn't as if she'd been burning the candle at both ends at Wellesley, but she hadn't lacked for interesting dates and the occasional overnight experience. She'd quickly found that when the money went, so had the sorority sisters and friends. There hadn't been anyone special, but those friends she might have kept after graduation she supposed she'd pushed away. Everything had hurt.

San Francisco, she thought. Surely there was still a lesbian bar or two or three in San Francisco. And New Orleans—based on what classmates had said about Southern Decadence, there was no end to the delightful treats one could find there all year-round, she was sure. The professor wasn't a night owl so Lily supposed she might find herself with many evenings free. Why wait for San Francisco at the end of the trip?

London. Tomorrow night, Libido suggested.

"Shall we load the car?"

She hadn't heard Nicole's approach, and the question jolted Lily out of her reverie about loud music and cashiers with nipple piercings. Libido, her inner temptress, had bad timing as usual. She felt heat in her cheeks, but turned to fuss about opening the trunk. The calculating, dour Professor Hathaway was the last person with whom she'd ever share her fantasies.

***

"Do you have the kettle? Did you remember insect repellent?"

Her mother's agitated questions were wearing on Nicole's nerves but she reminded herself they were a manifestation of maternal concern. "Mom, I have everything I can carry. What I don't have I'll buy. I'm sure the inestimable Miss Smith will take care of me."

"You are very lucky. She has been everywhere."

Normally Nicole would have pointed out that Lily couldn't have possibly been *every*where, but sparring about it wasn't going to calm the situation. Her mother would begin to cry the moment she saw car keys. That would be better than acceding to any request to open her bags again. She'd left them locked all day to keep her mother from exploring the contents—her mother had little concept of personal privacy if she was worried Nicole had forgotten to pack socks. At this point she didn't want her mother to find the jacket.

Her thoughts were distracted by the view from the kitchen window of Lily fussing with her cases. At the moment only the lower half of Lily's body was visible as she reached into the depths of the trunk. The emerald-hued skirt was drawn tight against the backs of her thighs. The black patent high heels looked just as uncomfortable as yesterday's stilettos that had so impressed Kate. They were certainly equally...ornamental.

Lily put one knee up on the bumper, nearly disappearing into the trunk. One of the pumps dangled loosely from her toes, exposing the smooth arch of one foot.

Kate hauled herself up from the porch rocker, blocking the view. Nicole realized she hadn't been breathing. Her mother seemed to be waiting for some kind of answer, but Nicole had forgotten what they were talking about. Lily emerged from the trunk, her hair tousled over her face.

Her mother repeated, "You're lucky she's been everywhere."

"I'm sure that'll be a big help." Kate was leaning against the car now, and whatever she said made Lily laugh. Lucky Kate, who could always make a room laugh with a quip. Lily shook the hair back from her eyes and headed toward the house with a small bundle of clothes.

Her mother grew even more mournful when Lily appeared in the kitchen doorway. "Nearly ready to go?"

"I'm afraid so. I was just going to change in the powder room, if you don't mind. We'll be sleeping on the plane." She indicated what looked like a pair of jeans and a cotton shirt, plus black Mary Janes like the ones Nicole had hated as a girl, probably because her mother had described them as what a "good girl" wore.

At her mother's nod, Lily went in the direction of the powder room, and Nicole gave a quick rethink to her own clothing. She'd be better off in jeans as well, but if she changed she ought to do it by swapping what she had on with items from her suitcase. But she didn't want to open up her suitcase and risk her mother finding the jacket. Talk about a conversation she didn't want to have just before she left, and with the perfect Lily Smith as an onlooker. She'd live with dozing in her slacks and blouse.

Once Lily reappeared, more casual but still possessing an unshakeable elegance, their departure went rapidly. On the porch Nicole hugged Kate as best as her belly would allow. "Please do everything the doctors say."

"I will. I promise not to kill Mom too."

"At least not until I get back." They shared a look that said neither of them meant it.

As Nicole gave her mother another hug she heard Kate say something about Lily's jeans and Lily answered with, "You'll be back in them soon."

"Michael Kors? Not a chance. I'll be wearing mom jeans," Kate said, but her pout was quickly erased by a package that Lily handed to her.

Over her mother's "Be safe, take care, be safe," mantra Nicole heard Lily explain that she'd seen it at Beekman's and thought of

Kate. A small plush toy labeled "Baby's First Laptop" emerged from the wrapping. Kate laughed and thanked her. Her mother promptly let go of Nicole to admire the gift and Nicole was able to escape to the car.

Well, wasn't Barbie-Lily a thoughtful person? Every nuance in social balance, she was *perfect*. For a moment Nicole missed the finger snaps and pop culture chatter of Lily's predecessor.

Ten miles from home she still couldn't figure out why she was so annoyed. Deep breathing didn't help either.

CHAPTER FOUR

It was an odd sensation to be sitting next to a passenger Lily hardly knew, let alone a woman with whom she would spend many unbroken hours. The last few days had been so rushed that she was just settling in her mind that she would see dear Dr. Hathaway every day for the next several months. It was quite the road trip, after all. Lily supposed that in a movie there'd be an upbeat pop song in the background as they hit the road with the setting sun at their backs and infinite possibilities in front of them.

Instead the car was quiet and Lily wasn't sure how to broach the idea of maybe listening to the radio for the two-hour drive—she wasn't sure she wanted to find out that Professor Hathaway couldn't abide anything but baroque string quartets or would roll her eyes over a sappy love song that rhymed "shy guy" with "two ply." She herself was a bit of a sucker for sappy love songs.

Just when the silence reached an unbearable point the sound of chirping birds filled the car. Nicole answered her phone.

"I'm already on my way to the airport. I was very clear about the deadline, and I'm not taking any new peer reviews during my sabbatical. I have a full slate."

Lily kept her eyes on the road and tried not to make it apparent that she could hear both sides of the conversation. There was no way to avoid hearing it. Something about a study with new data and a publication deadline and owing someone a favor.

"Your favor to the Doctors Gunn and Harris doesn't have anything to do with me," Nicole answered with no discernible strain or heat in her tone. "My time is completely booked. You'll have to find another reviewer."

There were more garbled protestations. Her tone flat and intractable, Nicole finally said, "You shouldn't have implied to them that you could commit me to their review. If we'd had this conversation ten days ago it might have happened, but it's impossible now." She listened, then cut the other person off. "*You* missed my deadline and that doesn't make *me* a pain in the ass, Clement."

Lily had a little bit of sympathy for Clement, but it was clear he wasn't going to get what he wanted. Nicole would not emotionally engage at all. After a few more increasingly testy exchanges Nicole hung up.

"People aren't used to you being unavailable?"

"I suppose not," Nicole answered. "But they should be used to the fact that my schedule is booked early for peer review and I don't make exceptions." She pushed her phone back into her satchel. "Other researchers complete their evaluation of data they've gathered and then need peers to check it. Without ego, I can safely say that I am sought after to do peer review."

Lily nodded. She had no trouble believing that Nicole was very good at finding other people's mistakes and challenging their conclusions. "It does amaze me when people don't follow guidelines and then expect an exception, just for them. And if they don't get one, everyone else is being a pain."

"I *am* a pain in the ass," Nicole said, her tone matter-of-fact. "They appreciate it when I'm putting their data to the test, but don't when I can't figure out how to add three or four hours to my work day to accommodate their needs."

"Is peer review work going to be what occupies your evenings?" Lily decided it was safe to pass a slow-moving truck on the two-lane highway.

"Yes, and catching up on a good deal of reading."

"I acquired a number of good reads," Lily admitted. Belatedly she realized she really ought to read the book she was helping to promote and ask Nicole questions so she could learn to answer the most obvious ones. *Duh.* She hoped her chagrin didn't show in her voice as she looked for a safer topic. "I've never read the original Sherlock Holmes books."

"Appropriate reading for London."

Surprised at the note of approval, Lily glanced at Nicole when she was safely back in her own lane. Nicole was looking out the window and said nothing more.

The GPS estimated their arrival at Logan Airport in one hour and thirty-seven minutes. Lily would have given a lot for a sappy love song.

***

At least she didn't chatter, Nicole thought. She wanted to suggest some music, but Lily seemed to be a little white-knuckled as they drove, and she wasn't sure the distraction would be welcome. No matter. She rustled in her carry-on bag and came up with the first paper she was going to review. They wouldn't occupy all of her evenings, but the work did need to be done.

It seemed like only a few minutes had passed when she realized Lily was turning toward the airport. A low, slow-moving passenger jet crossed overhead.

"Idiots," Lily muttered as she swerved around a news truck that was partially blocking one lane at the first terminal. People with cameras and cables were filming a man with a microphone who looked very calm. "It's probably just for a weather report."

"It hardly seemed like a crisis."

Lily muttered something that Nicole didn't catch, then said, "Why don't I drop you at the curb so you can go ahead and get started with your check-in. I'll drop off the car—it might take a while. I'll meet up with you at the gate."

Nicole agreed and added, "I'll text you if there's any trouble." As she watched Lily drive away she belatedly wondered if they should have stayed together. But Lily seemed very competent at what she did. Still…

By asking a few questions she found her way to the check-in line and was pleased when her large suitcase came in under the weight limit. Fifteen minutes later she was slipping off her loafers, proffering her boarding pass and walking through the scanner. Her mother had warned her that her skin color and Middle Eastern features might attract incorrect assumptions about her nationality and net her heightened scrutiny from the security personnel, but every stage felt impersonal. The impassivity of the screeners, coupled with the bristling technology, failed to instill feelings of either safety or intimidation.

As she left the security area for the short train ride to the terminals she heard some kind of hubbub break out. Quickening her pace she was glad it had nothing to do with her.

***

"You have a crappy haircut and so far, so good," Lily repeated to herself. She could have kicked herself for mistakenly exiting the car rental shuttle one stop too early, which forced her to walk past the camera crew still recording some kind of report. She was just being paranoid. No one was paying any attention to her.

Her bags weighed and checked, and the penalty paid for being several pounds over on the larger one, she headed for security. She felt lightheaded—it was sinking in, that she'd be out of the US for just long enough to perhaps be able to pick up a life again. She could even pretend, for a little while, that none of it had ever happened. Her parents could be still alive and still their usual distant selves. She could be taking a break from college, on her way to one of the diplomatic internships she'd hope to secure.

It was a pretty dream, but before she could become truly euphoric she heard someone say her full name. She caught herself before she looked around.

"I'm sure of it—it's that Linden-Smith bitch."

It was a man's voice, joined by another, deeper male voice. "Traveling first class on everyone else's money, I'll bet."

There was a short silence and Lily moved closer to the front of the security line. She didn't think it was someone in line—the voices sounded too far to her left. She showed her passport to an impassive agent, who passed it under a bar code reader before handing it back, and prepared for the flurry of shoe removal, laptop exposure and liquids checking. Rounding the queue and picking the line that seemed shortest, she didn't realize that it brought her all the way to her left again, separated from the unsecured area by tall plexiglass panels. Abruptly, two men pressed up against the barrier.

"It is you! Hey! How's it working out for you? You got away with it!"

Her startled glance took them to be businessmen, probably the kind of people who never made scenes but were making an exception for Lillian Linden-Smith because Merrill Boone kept flashing her picture and insisting Lily had gotten away with financial murder. She ignored them at first, then found enough bravado to pretend she hadn't a clue why they were gesturing at her. She desperately hoped Nicole had long since moved on to their gate.

"Hey—she's skipping the country. That one there! She's wearing a wig," one of the men persisted. He gesticulated at one of the security agents and a discussion ensued, louder by the sentence, about creating a disturbance.

"She stole millions," the other shouted. "She destroyed my family!"

She heard a resounding thud just as she crossed under the body scanner. She jumped and glanced back in time to see that one of them had succeeded in dislodging a panel of plexiglass. A security agent had tackled him and another was warning his friend to step back.

She said nothing. Kept walking. Got her shoes back on, made sure her laptop was back in its bag, followed the yellow line to the stairs to the terminal train and hoped that the look on her face was one of disinterested incomprehension.

The brief ride let her heart rate settle back to normal, though she could feel sweat dripping down her back. There were no uniformed agents waiting for her at the terminal stop, and fortunately, Nicole was at their gate, looking comfortable as she drank what smelled like a chai tea. Lily parked her luggage and murmured she was going in search of coffee, but her first stop was the restroom. She stood in a stall, hands over her face and quelled the shaking that threatened to turn over her stomach. She hadn't been this frightened since an awful encounter on the subway. After a man and a woman in business suits had followed her from car to car, bumping into her and all but knocking her down with their briefcases—and never once actually looking at her or saying a word—she'd fled at the next stop and walked into the first hair salon she'd come across. Since then she hadn't been recognized as much. Was it going to be like this boarding every flight, crossing every border, though? Someone shouting she was in disguise and had no right to leave? Would it take plastic surgery to erase her face from people's memories? Why couldn't someone else do something really evil to take everyone's mind off her?

She gave her cheek a mild slap. That kind of thinking was bad Karma. No way was she wishing there would be a murdered child or a missing teen to take the heat off her. She was not going to let all the loss and fear she'd already endured ruin her perspective at this point.

Deep breaths, she told herself. *Baby steps.* Turn over the new page and start off by being nicer to the professor. Well, that would be easier if the professor had an ounce of warmth in her soul.

Feeling a little more composed she acquired a mocha and then made a short stop at the book kiosk. The pickings were slim, but there was only one book she wanted. When she rejoined Nicole she said, "Will you sign this for me?"

Nicole looked at the book and then raised an eyebrow. "Really?"

"It's good practice. You're going to be doing a lot of it." She felt her cheeks redden, then added, "I have to admit, I haven't had a chance to read it. I hope you won't mind if I ask you questions. I don't want to sound like an idiot when people ask me about it. If I answer the easy questions you can stick with the hard ones."

Nicole pulled the book over to her lap and opened it to the first page. She poised her pen, then set it down. "Will people expect me to sign it *Dr. Nicole Hathaway Ph.D.* or simply *Nicole Hathaway*? Or some further variation?"

"What are you comfortable with?"

Her upper lip curled slightly, Nicole answered, "I'm not comfortable with any of it."

Uncle Damon had explained at length about how Nicole had resisted going on this trip. Lily wondered how much of the journey would be done before Nicole stopped complaining about a situation many people would envy. "How about your name, no titles, and then below that, the city and date?"

Nicole picked up her pen again, signed as Lily suggested and handed the book back. "I'm told it's interesting, though I'm surprised anyone would take it for light reading."

"Are you suggesting I use it as a sleep aid?" Lily strove for an innocent expression and was pleased when Nicole smiled ever so slightly.

"It might prove useful for that, yes."

Nicole's smile was actually nice when it wasn't aloof, Lily thought. "A point of etiquette for social introductions. Should I encourage people to call you Nicole?"

"I prefer Dr. Hathaway."

"It's certainly appropriate," Lily agreed. "But if you're pressed into a social dinner and the conversation isn't as formal, I meant would you prefer Nicole or Nicky?"

"Only my mother and Kate call me Nicky."

Lily wondered if she'd offended—suddenly Nicole's eyes were darker. "Nicole it is then."

Lily was surprised when Nicole blurted out, "I prefer Cole, I mean, not from strangers, even over cocktails. But, I mean…"

Dr. Nicole Hathaway Ph.D. was stammering? "A nickname?"

"From college."

"Shall I call you Cole?"

"Yes, that's fine." The aloof smile was back.

"It suits you," Lily said, then turned her head because while her first thought was that the homophone *coal* fit Nicole's acerbic and moody humor, her second thought was that *coal* also described Nicole's smoky eyes. The tingle of quick heat that shot down her spine and settled in her groin set off alarm bells and *INAPPROPRIATE* flashed on the view screen behind her eyes.

Physical reactions of that nature were right out of bounds, Lily scolded her inner self. Libido, dressed in a French maid outfit, answered that she'd better look into all-girl clubs in London, then, because those eyes weren't going to get any less attractive.

CHAPTER FIVE

"England swings like a pendulum," Lily quipped as they joined the queue for a cab outside their international terminal at Heathrow. More passengers were arriving in droves, all laden with suitcases and children.

Frowning through the edges of a headache, Nicole said, "We could be anywhere." She coughed as a bus passed them. The exhaust was heavy under the overhang and all the surfaces seemed covered by black grit.

"Anywhere? Really, Dr. Hathaway? With the signs in English and the cabs almost all hackney black?"

She hadn't slept much on the plane and it was irrationally distressing that Lily was fresh as the proverbial daisy. Every time she'd opened her eyes to acknowledge that she still wasn't asleep Lily had been across the aisle and slightly forward of her, face completely relaxed, head propped by a clever wrapping pillow and not quite snoring. Nicole had watched, amused, as the businessman next to Lily had given all the cues of needing to get out of his seat but Lily had slept through them. He'd waited nearly an hour to gently shake her and then had apologized profusely. When he'd returned he'd tried to engage her in conversation, but Lily had replied pleasantly and promptly gone back to sleep.

Watching Lily and her effect on men did provide wry amusement. At deplaning, Lily had fielded three offers of assistance with lowering her carry-on from the overhead bin, including from her seatmate. Lily's solution had been to get it down herself while looking pointedly at an elderly woman in front of her, then at the woman's bag in the overhead. The seatmate had missed the cue, but another eager helper hadn't, and immediately offered his aid to the old woman. He had visibly puffed up when Lily gave him a dazzling smile.

The social exchange of roosters and hens—it was amusing to watch it happen instead of seeing the behaviors categorized in rows of data tables. Still, she'd have rather spent the night in her own bed, not wide awake in an airplane. Lily had excused herself on the way to claim their luggage and returned from the restroom with her face scrubbed and glowing, makeup freshly applied. The bump in her hair she'd gotten while sleeping was gone. By comparison, Nicole felt oily and rumpled. Her eyes had been replaced by bits of pumice.

"I wasn't being literal. I was commenting on the generic nature of urban industrial grime."

"I know," Lily answered. She could not have been more cheery. After a glance at Nicole's face, she added, "When we get to the hotel we'll find some tea."

"Tea and a nap."

"The nap is probably not going to happen." Lily stepped forward as the last party in front of them boarded their vehicle. "Our rooms may not be ready before we have time to do more than freshen up and leave for the Artful Reader. Also, it's highly advised for travelers to stay awake until local sunset at least, to more quickly adjust to the time change."

"Isn't that an urban myth?"

"No, not at all. Scientific research and everything—" Lily surrendered her larger suitcase to the cabbie. "Thank you. We're going into the Regent's Park area."

The same predictable pattern unfolded again as Nicole watched the burly, fortyish fellow fall instantly under Lily's spell. Was it the perfect manicure, the dainty accessories, the general prettiness or a combination of all three? Her luggage was handled like porcelain, the door opened with a genteel, "miss?" To be fair, her own luggage was likewise treated with care and it only amused her further that she was invited aboard the cab with "ma'am?"

"Now where exactly are you staying, miss? My dispatch will send me around the construction."

"Is there a big project underway in London?" Nicole had been long lectured by her mother about cab drivers taking detours to run up the meter.

Almost in unison both the cabbie and Lily answered, "There's always construction in London."

The route out of the airport proved the truth of it as they detoured and crisscrossed past backhoes, cranes and crowds of mostly men leaning on trucks and vans while piledrivers thumped the ground nearby. A few miles along the expressway the landscape began to show more green and there were patchy breaks in the murky high fog.

She supposed if she weren't so tired it might seem more magical, but at the moment there wasn't much to differentiate this part of London from south Boston. It was supposed to smell different, she thought. That's what the travel books said. Right now, England smelled like every cab she'd ever been in, including those in India.

"The train would have taken you almost right there, but I'm glad of the business," the cabbie was saying.

"This will be faster. At least that's the plan." Lily leaned forward to be heard past the glass opening between the driver and passenger area. "We have tourist rail passes."

"That's the smart way to go, once you're here. We can't buy those, but they're beauts for tourists."

The cab driver happily answered Lily's questions about the weather forecast and then current West End plays while Nicole turned her gritty eyes to the landscape again. She just wanted to sleep. So much for trawling through the girl bars. Awake all those hours on the plane she'd done little work and spent far too much time wondering what had possessed her to tell Lily to call her "Cole."

She woke with a start when the cab's engine was turned off. Disoriented, she saw a long street of white three-story row houses, none any different from its neighbors but for small signs next to the front doors. The one they were stopped in front of said "Queen's Park Inn."

Lily was smiling at her. "You got in a good nap—we hit some traffic. So about forty-five minutes."

"I feel better," Nicole admitted. "But groggy."

"Tea. There's a nice stall just that way. Edgar gave me a quick tour around the blocks. We can get some sandwiches in hand and relax."

Edgar was all smiles as he carried their bags up the three steps to the hotel door. He thanked her for the "lovely chat" and drove off in the direction of the business district Nicole could see at the distant end of the street.

Traveling in India had given her enough perspective to know that by American standards the lobby was small, but not as tiny as it might have been. Still, with the two of them and their bags, the floor was nearly covered. The clerk was promptly helpful and delivered the good news that they would be able to get into their rooms early, around noon.

Nicole belatedly adjusted her watch forward five hours. It was almost ten. Some tea and a sandwich sounded good. Then, regardless of Lily's advice, she was going to have a hot shower and a nap. Lily wasn't the one who had to entertain an audience at four.

***

A shrill, unfamiliar ringing broke into Nicole's sleep. She knocked the phone receiver off its cradle, then managed to get it to her ear.

"Cole, I let you sleep as long as possible, but you have to think about getting up now."

"Okay," she mumbled. It felt nice to be called Cole but she couldn't think of whose voice was on the line. It wasn't her mother or Kate. They wouldn't call her Cole either.

"Now. I'll hang up, but I'm calling back in two minutes."

"Okay."

There was more shrilling what seemed like immediately. She didn't remember putting the receiver back. As she answered she felt a jolt of "I've overslept" adrenaline.

"I'm up now," she told Lily, then she went to her tiny bathroom to get an idea of how bad her hair was. What had she been thinking, going to sleep with it still wet?

Fortunately, only the left side was sticking out and a wet comb with smoothing gel tamed it. She knew some Indian women went to great lengths to add some kind of curl to their hair but she liked the simplicity of the heavy strands. Though she could grow it much longer, she liked it cut above her shoulders so that it didn't tangle in the collars of her shirts and was nearly free of care.

A few minutes later she was in her habitual white blouse and dark slacks. The day had been somewhat muggy but she picked up a thin purple sweater nevertheless. In New Hampshire one did not go anywhere, at any time of the year, without a sweater at hand. She would have to break the habit as they traveled to more southern latitudes.

She met Lily in the lobby and saw that Lily too had felt the need for a sweater. That it was cut to mimic a jacket made it very stylish, and it fit snugly over a sleeveless white dress patterned with lively light and navy blue stripes. Kate would probably be disappointed in Lily's footwear—simple black sandals that fit her small feet well, the heel height half that of the shoes she'd worn at dinner that first night.

Lily led the way from the lobby, saying, "I've got a cab waiting. We should just make it. The Artful Reader is between Leicester Square and Piccadilly Circus. It's a large store with a lecture space, and it's well-known for lecture series and appearances. They were one of the first bookstores to feature J.K. Rowling, before anyone had really taken notice of the first Harry Potter book."

She continued to narrate the likely audience, clearly having spoken to the bookseller while Nicole had slept. "The good news is that their customers are well-versed in signing up in advance if they want to be sure of a seat, and there were over seventy sign-ups. That's just amazing these days." After a pause, Lily said, "You're frowning."

"I'm don't know what I expected, actually. Seventy does seem like a lot."

"You're a blockbuster. I got an e-mail from the university in Edinburgh—their hall has sold out. That's two hundred. They were considering moving you to the largest space they have." She cocked her head. "It's hard to imagine what it really all means. Going viral in today's world can mean lots of Web views and likes and shares and Tweets. In your case, it means lecture fees and books being bought, reviewed and talked about."

"I am still surprised by it all."

"It's time to enjoy it," Lily said. She turned her head away, obviously to keep in view a church that was probably older than the United States. "I hope you don't mind, but I booked a table at a restaurant I went to years ago—spending some Insignis expense account funds rather liberally, I'm afraid. You said you were open to most cuisines. This is soul food."

"In London?"

The church out of sight, she turned back to Nicole. "I know—it's a cross of American southern and Welsh country."

"Whimsical."

"It is!" Lily's entire face was alight, like a child thinking about a future piece of cake. "When I was there I had barbecue lamb ribs with a leek and potato cake, and cabbage that had been seasoned like collard greens. It was scrumptious."

Nicole's stomach growled loudly. Lily laughed. Suddenly it didn't seem the least bit odd to be in the back of a London cab while buildings she was sure she'd seen in movies flashed by, sitting next to a glamorous, poised woman and anticipating a lovely meal together.

With a jolt she reminded herself that Lily was her nursemaid and that her desire to smooth the path in front of Nicole was her job. The smile, the glow—they were for the city and the food. Maybe she wasn't as studied and pre-programmed as she'd seemed at first, but nothing had changed.

Perhaps after a good meal she would find the energy to slip out later and look for companionship focused on more basic needs. Lily, effortlessly collecting male hearts every step of the way, might well be repelled if she knew who Cole really was. Nothing had changed, she repeated to herself. Then she spent the rest of the cab ride wondering why she was dwelling on something that didn't matter.

They were greeted by the bookstore owner at the door. A bubbly woman in her late forties, she bustled them to the back of the store, chattering about the large crowd and brisk sales of the print copy of the book. The buzz from the room where events were held was just like that from a lecture hall. This audience might be mostly adult, and mostly women, but she'd spoken at conferences full of colleagues with no issue. She knew her material as always. There was nothing different about the situation, so her racing heart and suddenly dry mouth were inexplicable. Her fight-or-flight reflex was thoroughly engaged.

Lily's hand was suddenly on her forearm, just firmly enough to be bracing. "Dr. Hathaway, would you like water to drink while you're speaking?"

The owner immediately pointed out the pitcher and glass under the lectern.

"That'll be fine," Nicole said.

Lily gave her arm another squeeze, then said in a low voice, "All they have to believe is that you've been here before."

"But I haven't."

"It's a metaphor."

Nicole digested that information. "Give me a moment." She turned her back to the room and took a long, deep breath. The oxygen quelled her anxiety. Stage fright wasn't unusual, she supposed. Only unusual for her.

"What a great crowd." Lily smiled at the women nearest them, then gave Nicole's arm yet another little squeeze before letting go.

"It certainly is." The little bit of patter helped calm her nerves and Nicole felt a wave of relief. It was going to be okay.

***

Lily faded to the back of the room as the bookseller introduced Nicole to the crowd. Every seat was filled and more women stood at the back with Lily. Once she was sure that the microphones were working, that the crowd was settling and Nicole's look of shock had been replaced with an air of confidence, Lily let herself relax.

The crowd was mostly women and very mixed, with a significant number of darker faces present. Most of those looked to Lily to be of Middle Eastern heritage. She wondered if these women, in addition to being intrigued by the book's subject, saw Nicole as a role model.

The bookseller was wrapping up general announcements and starting on Nicole's credentials. It was dreadfully dull, Lily thought, but necessary. Nicole was a scientist, and that meant lots of alphabet soup, professional society accolades and published papers. She wondered if Nicole would be open to adding something more personal at the end—even a mention of where she lived. She had found the world over that anywhere else was exotic to someone. Lake Winnipesaukee had exotic in every syllable.

Nicole didn't smile. Lily was starting to think the frown was habitual. She wondered if Nicole would change if she rewarded smiles with chocolates. Her face transformed when she smiled—there was humor there, but deeply buried. All in all, Nicole was an enigma. Even living in a beautiful place like Meredith on one of the lake jewels of New England, earning a living in the field of study she obviously cared about, in the embrace of a loving family, and now enjoying a tremendous amount of fame and no small amount of money—none of that seemed to make Nicole the least bit happy. It was as if a key ingredient were missing.

Lily didn't want to be stereotypical and presume the missing piece of the puzzle was the very thing Nicole was talking about: life with somebody special. It seemed far more likely that the good professor didn't put stock in emotional constructs like "happiness." She only studied people who did.

Lily had learned the hard way that happiness mattered to her. She'd had too many days when she hadn't cared if the sun came up or she ever got out of bed. But it finally felt as if those days might be behind her. She could even think about finding a somebody special herself. But for the foreseeable future her chances of that were slim and none. Libido took that opportunity to announce that Somebody Special for a few hours would not be unwelcome. During Edgar's turn about the blocks around their hotel she'd spotted a bar called the Cat's Paw sporting a rainbow flag in the window. Libido had thought of little else ever since.

Nicole was trying to put energy into her opening remarks, but her exhaustion was obvious to Lily. On the other hand, Lily felt energized. No one would recognize her here. She could go out to eat, not hide her face—hold her head up. She felt alive for the first time in so long. So maybe it was a bit manipulative to plan to fill Nicole up with good food and then deposit her in a warm, comfy hotel room and hope she didn't hear the quiet open and close of Lily's door later in the evening. Even if all she did was dance like no one was watching, it would be fun.

She focused as Nicole transitioned from appropriate thanks to the bookseller and a general thank you to the audience for having come to the event.

"I hope that none of you came here today to find the magic solution to the difficulties of navigating uncertain social waters in today's dating environment."

Oh dear, Lily thought.

"Contrary to the popular belief, my book is not about a magic fix-all formula that will lead to finding the perfect life mate."

Uh-oh.

"Scientific method allows us to find common events in a group of subjects and to analyze the likelihood of their repetition throughout a larger unspecified population."

She blew out some air. She knew that Uncle Damon hadn't hired her to be Nicole's publicist, but as Nicole went into more and more detail about exactly what hopes and dreams wouldn't be solved by her book, Lily was dying by inches. She watched the faces in the packed room fall into disinterest.

Finally, after several minutes, Nicole switched gears and discussed several case studies. There was a palpable change in the audience. The background on the couple with fifty-six years of happy marriage brought smiles. The case of the widow, in her second of two twenty-year-plus marriages, whose first husband's DNA sequence had been available because of his participation in an earlier medical study, drew looks of surprise because the sequences that empowered social cognitive and reactive abilities were similar to those of her second husband, who was of a different race. The remarried widow herself described the two men as different in temperament and intellectual interests, but she was equally happy.

Nicole seemed unaware of the changes in her audience, but the final portion of her talk picked up a lot of steam when she discussed the vast DNA data that could be gathered about a single person, the impossibility of capturing, storing and manipulating that data for seven billion people which then led to the misconception that there was, therefore, no pattern to it, and therefore no reason to attempt to understand it.

"A massive amount data that we can't study is not the same as chaos. What seems a bewildering network of infinite unpredictability could be predicted if we had the tools to do so. Many, many people are working on exactly this challenge, not the least of whom are building massive social networking sites that substitute analyzing DNA with click patterns and nexus substantiation."

For the first time, Nicole smiled. "Until we have a super-computer we can access in our individual brains, we are, unfortunately, at the mercy of anecdote, experience and instinct to evaluate the situations we encounter. In excess of seventy percent of the study participants already accepted that their DNA made them more compatible with certain professions, places to live and foods. All of our research confirms that finding a life mate is no more mysterious than that."

It wasn't a great closing but the audience applause was more than polite and a queue quickly formed for Nicole to sign books. Lily joined her at the table and expedited signatures by chatting as she opened books to the right page before handing them to Nicole.

Thirty minutes later the room began to clear and fifteen after that they were thanking the bookseller and her staff for inviting Nicole to appear. As they left the staff was resetting the room for a lecture that evening by a popular memoirist.

Standing on the bustling street Lily asked Nicole, "How does it feel?"

"I can't tell at this moment if I'm numb because I'm tired or trying to process a new experience. When is our dinner reservation?"

"I made it early—six. It's seven or eight blocks from here. We could get a cab."

"I would prefer to walk." Nicole glanced at Lily's shoes.

"I can make it in these and I brought along this clever GPS box." She produced the slim unit from her purse. "It'll have us turning the right corners to get there. I would welcome a walk. Tomorrow morning I've promised myself time in the fitness room."

"Tonight's dinner will be welcome," Nicole said as they fell into step. "But I would prefer in the future to eat lightly."

Given Nicole's general fitness and slender frame, Lily wasn't sure she had a lot to worry about, but she did understand the concern. "I hear you. I don't want to get home with a waist that doesn't fit in my clothes."

The sun was partially obscured by a high layer of fog and brown air. Lily slipped off her sweater and liked the warmth on her shoulders. It felt wonderful to be outside and she didn't even flinch from her reflection in shop windows they passed. She'd let the awful color grow out. People would forget about her. It could happen.

Dinner was relaxed and delicious, though being persistently cheerful was tiring. Nicole seemed as charmed by the mash up of cuisines on the menu as Lily was, but would lapse into long silences. Lily let herself remember the mostly happy meal of her last visit, when two cousins had agreed to take a chance away from the usual five-star eateries with fawning waitstaff. They'd all had a good time. Jenna and Kirsten hadn't spoken to her since the scandal, the thought of which she put out of her mind. She was moving on.

***

It's nerves and exhaustion, Nicole told herself. She stood in her hotel room dressed in black denims, a white A-shirt and her leather jacket. But for some laugh lines and a simpler, shorter hairstyle, she looked exactly as she had going out to the women's bar near MIT. However, unlike those days, her hands were shaking and she was weak in the knees.

Dinner had been delicious. Lily had chattered a bit, but also seemed at times happy to lapse into a more or less comfortable silence. She'd asked some questions about the book, but not in any depth, and then they'd talked about their own visits to India, some recent movies and if they wanted to see a play the following night. Nicole didn't consider herself much of a drinker, but the bottle of simple red wine they'd agreed to share by way of celebration had left a good glow.

Looking at herself in the mirror and thinking about the silk and warmth of a woman's thigh, feeling that against her fingertips, about hearing the quiet and profound intake of breath in her ear as she touched…Shivers ran down her arms.

She quelled the weak knees by telling herself it was time to text her mother. A quick note saying they'd arrived safely and the first event had gone well was quickly composed and sent. But her mother, her life, everything about Dr. Nicole Hathaway Ph.D. was very far away. The freedom that Cole wanted was right in front of her—she had to grab it with both hands. She sat on the edge of the bed and envisioned pulling a woman down to her and finding their way to mutual nakedness. Her heart was racing again, her palms were damp. Her mouth was watering.

She closed her eyes and lay back on the bed, her mind washed over with possibilities and fantasies. She needed a moment to just breathe.

***

The Cat's Paw leaked bright flashes of crimson light into the night and pulsated with a low grinding beat. The line of eager partygoers along the wide sidewalk stretched across several more storefronts, all of which were dark and shuttered. Lily sighed as she took it in. She was ready—in every way—to join the party, but the thought of a long wait in a line was sapping her energy.

At least she was dressed appropriately for the crowd. A little black dress could literally go anywhere. Seamed black stockings and her Manolo stilettos testified to her willingness to dance. Cash and her hotel key card were slipped inside her bra which left her unencumbered by a purse. But it would all be for naught if she couldn't get in the door.

She remembered the first time she'd gone clubbing with Jenna and Kirsten. The exclusive night club in New York had had a line around the block and a bouncer who could have snapped any of them in two with one hand. As they'd approached she'd wondered how much of a tip it would take to get past the bouncer's enormous scowl, but the other two girls had breezed past, certain they would not be impeded. Time and opportunity being scarce, Lily gave herself a shake and thought, "Work the Manolos."

Deep breath, head up, shoulders back, eye contact steady. With a sexy step just short of a runway walk, she approached the tall, multi-earringed woman to raise an eyebrow at the rope barrier, and then blew her a kiss for removing it from her path. A brief hand clasp transferred a tip, which was quickly pocketed. She heard some grousing from those waiting to get in, and she knew it wasn't fair that wearing some people's monthly salary on her feet and a dress fitted to her in a designer salon was allowing her to cut the line.

She supposed another night she might be in a fair mood. But tonight, still a little tipsy from the wine with Nicole, being fair in the politics of clubbing wasn't on her agenda. She was inside the door. There were women everywhere. That was all that mattered.

She melted onto the dance floor, oozing between other dancers until she was close to the center. She was happy to dance alone if need be. But it was only a matter of minutes before a cute black woman in a white halter top, miniskirt and Nancy Sinatra go-go boots joined her. They danced in step for a while, tried a few touch moves and then moved apart when other women cut in. The floor was increasingly crowded and a lot of accidental contact was being made with everyone around her.

After almost an hour of feeling so liberated and free that her feet didn't seem to touch the parquet, Lily realized the hand on her hip and the body pressed against her from behind, keeping time with her steps, wasn't accidental. She twisted and turned and found herself in the arms of a woman in plain jeans, a white T-shirt and leather biker boots. Her bleached white peach fuzz hair looked soft and touchable, but she knew enough from her short time on the college scene that one only touched a butch's hair when invited to do so.

They didn't speak and their mutual contact, closer and closer, was agreed to with half-smiles and slow looks. In the flashing club lights the woman's blue eyes looked like a night sky full of twinkling stars.

A slower paced song moved them even closer together and Lily didn't mind in the least that they settled with the other woman's firm thigh between hers, moving suggestively like many of the other couples around them. It felt freely wanton. It was exhilarating.

She was considering inviting the woman back to her room, and equally considering the fallout if Nicole should hear anything— vigorous, when the woman pulled her close and said in her ear, just over the music, "Would you be interested in having a drink? We can take them into the alley if the bar is too crowded."

Head swimming and feeling like liquid from the waist down, Lily pulled Blue Eyes's head down so she could answer. "We can skip the drinks."

At the bar's rear exit, her companion paused. Looking searchingly into Lily's eyes she only said, "Yeah?"

"Yes," Lily said clearly. "I'm not in town for long—"

"I'm about right now."

Part of her couldn't believe she was going to go through with it. For all of Libido's urgings, she'd never done this before. Right now, she just wanted to wipe away the past. She had no one to answer to but herself. "Me too."

"The ground out here can get a bit mucked." Blue Eyes bumped the door open with her shoulder and said, "We don't want those pretty shoes of yours to get dirty."

Lily put her arms around the woman's neck and her heart raced as two firm hands under her ass allowed her to wrap her legs around the slender hips.

With a half-purr, half-growl Blue Eyes said, "That's going to be perfect."

She shuddered at the cool wall at her back and moaned as one finger traced the line of her panties along the inside of her thigh. She was swollen and so needy that for a moment she felt a tremor of fear.

"Say yes again, sweetheart. Let me."

With a hissed intake of breath, Lily managed to say, "Yes. Please."

Two fingers slipped past the elastic of her panties and teased, making Lily realize how wet she was. Her legs shook.

"Right here, sweetheart?"

"Yes please." It seemed the right thing to say. Lily pressed her cheek against the other woman's, sure that her own gasps of pleasure and want were welcome. She was dizzied by the other woman's deep groan as she slipped inside.

"Sweet and easy, unless you want it different."

Lily wasn't sure what she may have moaned, but fingers continued to trace her nerves, tease inside and out, play with her, then push in hard enough to make her breath catch. She ground back in increasing abandon, told herself to stop holding her breath, to let it happen but it never seemed like it could be easy—until it was. She clutched desperately at the other woman and finally cried out.

"That's it, so sweet," her companion was murmuring. "I have you. You're not going to fall."

After several heartbeats she realized they were moving in slow rhythm to the club's throbbing drum beat. She couldn't help but laugh softly. The other woman seemed to have no difficulty continuing to hold her up. "Well, clearly I needed that."

"You seemed to." She could hear a smile in Blue Eyes's tone. "I'm glad I was there for you."

"This isn't my usual scene, but I've lacked other options," Lily said. "But, um…what about you?"

There was a gentle nuzzle at her ear. "My girl and I have an understanding. She knows I'm here. She's okay with it—really. You're actually…foreplay."

Lily blinked. It seemed like she ought to be at least disquieted by being "foreplay" but all she really felt was an urgent desire to sleep. There were plenty of things she'd never agree to in a relationship, like having sex with other people, but it wasn't her place to judge anyone else who might think those things were okay. Besides, with her legs literally wrapped around a stranger she was not exactly standing on high moral ground. The only right thing to say seemed to be, "Thank you."

"My pleasure." The strong arms tightened around her. "And thank you. I'll be thinking about the hot American femme at the Cat's Paw for quite a while. How long are you visiting?"

"Just until the day after tomorrow." Lily felt herself blush. Was she a hot American femme? The wonder and simplicity of being admired washed over her. After being emotionally pummeled and physically fearful for so long it seemed miraculous to be seen as desirable.

She was gently carried across the alley and the other woman set her down as they reached the bar door.

"Do you mind if I have a name to call you, sweetheart?"

"Lily."

She got a wide smile. "Perfect."

"And you?"

"Wendy."

Lily grinned back. "That's shorter than 'hot English butch' so thank you."

"I'm Welsh, actually. Safe journey, love," Wendy said. She kissed her lightly at the corner of her mouth and faded back into the club.

The street back to the hotel was just at the end of the alley, so Lily turned in that direction. She could go back in the club and dance some more, but why? To make it look as if she'd been there for more than what had just happened? Her legs were wobbly, she knew she was smiling—what else mattered?

It wasn't until she tiptoed past Nicole's door that she wondered exactly what the staid professor would have to say about anonymous sex behind a nightclub. Maybe it was something a nice girl oughtn't do. On the other hand, there were a whole lot of people who didn't think she was the least bit nice.

She and Blue Eyes were both free to consent, so what was the problem? Libido was really quite pleased. But Libido's boring twin, Circumspect, was wringing her hands as she moaned, "An alley? Did it have to be in an alley?"

The bed was soft, warm, so welcoming. She would wrestle with her conscience tomorrow.

CHAPTER SIX

"Good morning, Cole. Did you sleep well?" Lily was stirring milk into something that looked like it might be oatmeal.

Nicole nodded and reached for the teapot already in the center of the smallest table in the tiny breakfast room. She'd already had a cup in her room, but more was needed. She'd slept well, all right. She'd slept just fine, deeply, for nine hours. She'd woken up with the zipper of her leather jacket imprinted on her breastbone and her left leg asleep.

Her first night of freedom and she'd slept through it. Her own frustration made Lily's cheer all the more annoying.

"Fine, thank you. When do we have to be at the next bookstore?"

"Ten—we need to leave in about an hour. I have a mad proposal, if you're interested. How about after the signing we dash for a train to Brighton, look at the seashore and walk around a festival?"

Nicole raised an eyebrow. "Wouldn't that take all day?"

Lily's eyes were gleaming with enthusiasm. "Yes, it would mean no theater tonight. I couldn't find a play that had tickets that didn't cost the same as an ounce of gold. But our rail passes are good for any destination and the festival is women's music. Plus there's a valley that has a regular sightseeing tour that sounds interesting. The weather report is terrific for the beach. Brisk, cool and very sunny."

"How long is the train ride?"

"Just about an hour, give or take, and they run until almost midnight in both directions."

Nicole wondered if "women's" music meant the same thing here as it usually meant at home. Did Lily know that they'd be in a largely lesbian crowd if it did? For the first time she wondered about Lily's politics. "It might seem unusual that a woman my age has never been to a beach," she admitted. "Except at a lake."

"It's not the same thing. Well, physically it's the same concept. Flat bit of land next to a body of water. You've never been to the ocean?" Lily's tone hid her surprise, but her wide eyes showed it.

"Not the ocean. New Hampshire is landlocked, and I never joined the groups that would go to the Cape for the holidays or to celebrate the end of the school year. I had obligations at home."

Nicole had heard all about Provincetown and the women's beaches, but her fear was such at the time that she had been irrationally convinced a photo would somehow, through the vagaries of Karma, find its way to her uncles or her mother or her thesis advisor and her doctoral committee. She'd exhausted her rebellious energy against familial destiny by studying a science that had no certain career prospects. Her mother had flatly forbade continuing her education through a doctorate but Nicole had done it anyway. For several years the waters between herself and her mother had been very rocky.

Now she was far too educated for the pool of suitors either uncle offered, and both had expressly blamed Nicole when they'd been faced with daughters demanding the same opportunities as their American cousin. Thousands of miles away she was a bad influence, and none of them even knew about Cole's pursuits. Kate's initial choice of a career as a dancer had also been blamed on Nicole's bad example. Nicole had been a teacher for nearly five years before her mother stopped referring to her job as a stopgap until something better—like getting married—came along. The book's success had further eased the pressure to "secure her future."

Your elemental truth hasn't changed, she told herself. Emotionally you are happiest when left alone. Your sex drive is manageable and need not run your life. Your intellect is challenged every day. Inertia is a basic law of physics, and no worse an influence than any other. Why was she revisiting any of this?

She said to Lily, "I was going to go to a conference in Miami, but it was canceled by a hurricane. I've never felt compelled to make a beach a specific destination."

"It's okay if you don't want to," Lily said. "There are so many things to see here in London as well. Of course. We could do the London Eye and see the views. Walk across the Thames, go to the Tower. And the British Museum is phenomenal—it takes days to see it properly. I suppose it is a little strange to get to London and promptly leave it for Brighton."

It sounded to Nicole as if these were all things Lily had done before. "Tomorrow there's the morning radio call-in show, yes?" At Lily's nod, she added, "I have tea with relatives at two. We could squeeze in something between those two appointments, couldn't we?"

"Where's the tea?"

"My cousins suggested a shop near Trafalgar Square."

Lily bounced in her chair. "The National Portrait Gallery—I've heard it's a treat for historians and it's just a block or two from Trafalgar. Not that far from the hotel."

"Then let's do that tomorrow, something very London. The gallery and Nelson's Column will do nicely. After tea we have the train to Edinburgh?"

"Yes. Why did they book a train versus a plane?" Lily smiled at the server as she delivered their breakfasts.

"I have no idea." Her spinach omelet looked acceptable.

"It was quite smart, actually. When you add early arrival time to a flight and the time to get to any of the airports from here, the train isn't a lot slower—about five hours and it's at least four by air. There's more room, there's Wi-Fi, there's quiet cars for people who want to work or read." Lily's eyes were unfocused, as if she were consulting a timetable written inside her forehead. She gave her head a little shake and added, "And the route I've heard is quite beautiful, along the coast for much of it."

She couldn't help her curiosity. "Have you traveled in the UK before?"

"Yes, but never to Scotland." With an odd smile she added, "I haven't enjoyed Wales either though I've heard the people are friendly." She paused to sip her tea. "There's no time for that for us, unfortunately. Before, I was in a group. They were mostly interested in shopping. I had the same kind of rail pass we have now and sometimes I headed out on my own. They found it very strange that I took a train two hours each way to go to the Roald Dahl Museum."

She was so young, Nicole realized. In spite of the infinite poise, she was a fresh-faced girl eager to see the world. An innocent. An innocent with long, sexy legs.

Appalled at where her thoughts had wandered, Nicole said, "So after the signing we'll go to Brighton." They might get back late, but the Cat's Paw would still be open.

"Terrific." Lily grinned at her as she waved her phone. "I have a train schedule app that seems to work so we won't get stranded."

They finished breakfast with more general talk, and Nicole was amused to see that Lily had cleaned her bowl of every last morsel of oatmeal. Travel made her hungry, apparently. Perhaps she had indeed spent time in the small fitness room earlier. Whatever it was, it had given her a glow.

***

The whoosh of the train doors opening let out an hour's worth of stale air and Lily immediately smelled the ocean. Brilliant sunlight poured down onto the train platform. "Hard to believe that just a little bit ago we were in that crowded bookstore."

"It was very warm in there. But the turnout was good."

She hoped that Nicole didn't find her eagerness to come to Brighton too bold. Music on an open stage, some local sightseeing— both good reasons to visit the seaside town. She was doubly glad for having suggested it when they'd left the stifling bookstore and discovered that the London afternoon had turned sticky and hot. The cool sea breeze was already refreshing her. Making their way out of the train station they waded into the exodus of other passengers from the crowded train.

"This is no small local festival," Nicole said.

"I guess not." They were surrounded by women, women everywhere, all shapes and sizes, some in leather, some in lace, some even in drag, but most in summer-at-the-English-beach attire: shorts, cute little shirts and big thick sweaters. Glancing down at her own business casual skirt and hose and the most practical of her high-heeled shoes, she added, "We're not exactly dressed for it, I guess."

Nicole's gaze was following a pale young woman in a skimpy bikini and a covering drape that was translucent enough to see the enormous goose pimples on her arms. "We're not the only ones."

"You're at least in pants." Nicole seemed to have an endless supply of black slacks and white blouses. Her daily footwear appeared to be variations of black loafers and black socks. The lack of variety made life easy—and it wasn't as if it didn't suit her. The tidy, buttoned-down look combined with Nicole's serious demeanor created an aura of expertise. Lily supposed if a woman wanted to be taken seriously in a field dominated by men she had to take "sexy" out of the equation. Given her mother's and sister's feminine flair, the lack of makeup or jewelry beyond simple gold studs was possibly just Nicole's attempt to declare her own style. Bottom line, Dr. Nicole Hathaway, Ph.D., looked exactly like a professor of neurobiology and bio…bio-whatever. Lily supposed that was the whole point.

She did envy the light New England tweed jacket that had been far too heavy for London, but was perfect for the strong breeze coming off the ocean. "I should have brought my jacket instead of this sweater."

"I'm sure we can find you a sweatshirt." Nicole's head turned to follow a willowy woman sporting a thick, long sweatshirt that declared *Brighton* in glittery letters. If she was wearing anything under it, it didn't show.

Lily feigned horror. "I couldn't possibly. I'd go over weight on my luggage." With a palm-dampening flash, she wondered what any of these women would think if they knew about the tryst in the alley behind the Cat's Paw. Every time she thought about it she got a trilling sensation in places that she couldn't even name.

She searched Nicole's expression for signs of disappointment that the festival was a large crowd, but Nicole was completely shuttered. Unable to see over the crowd, Lily followed in step along a narrow street and through a small park. The way abruptly opened up as women broke in all directions to stream across the broad boulevard, cordoned off from automobile traffic, that separated the beach from the restaurants and trinket shops.

She glanced at Nicole and waved an arm. "The English Channel!"

Nicole's smile was almost wry. "So I see. It's quite large."

Lily pointed. "Next stop France. Or is it Belgium?"

A stocky woman in biker boots paused long enough to casually redirect Lily's arm. "That way's Belgium, love. You can't see it from here." She moved Lily's arm again while Lily laughed. "That way is all France. And that way is my wife's bakeshop. Best pasties in town." She flicked a card into Lily's hand and winked. "Combo special for the festival and some of your pence goes for the local shelter today."

The woman eyed Nicole and then glanced again at Lily. Lily realized suddenly that in her eagerness to experience the music and the outdoor celebration she'd plopped herself and her charge right into the middle of a huge lesbian event. She could see the woman considered the two of them a couple and she didn't know how to set that right.

Fortunately, Nicole was gazing toward the beach. After all, she'd never been to one before. What about a beach full of girls?

Did Nicole find it strange to hear a woman say "my wife"? It gave Lily a happy little thrill.

Lily waved a thanks to her guide. She glanced at the card for the location of bakeshop. Maybe they'd stop in.

Recalling the visitor's map she'd looked at online, she drew Nicole to their right. "Well, this is a huge event. I don't know if the sightseeing tours will be running."

"Where would they take us?"

"There's a valley with old ramparts and on a clear day like today you can see the Isle of Wight. Devil's Dyke—there are open-top buses there and back and it's got great views, the book said." Lily had to stifle a laugh. If Nicole were a friend she'd have added, "But we can just stay here and see the dykes." But she had the feeling that while Nicole might get the joke, she wouldn't be amused. "Do you want to do that? Or wander here—there are a lot of booths and it looks like the main stage is up the beach that way."

"You should feel free to do as you like. I am capable of enjoying myself on my own."

Lily wasn't sure how to take the comment since Nicole wasn't giving out any emotional cues. Was she regretting that they'd made the trip? Or did she just want some Nicole time? Well she wasn't going to turn down time on her own either.

"How about I go see about getting a tour and I'll text if there's any issues. Otherwise, meet back at this spot at...five? And take it from there?"

"That sounds fine. Good heavens!" Nicole blinked at a sign in a nearby window. "Does that really say corn and tuna pizza?"

"I'll have to give that a try," Lily said.

Nicole brought her gaze back to Lily and finally she was smiling. "You do that. I look forward to your analysis."

She left Nicole window shopping, whipped out the handy GPS that she'd already programmed and quickly found the stall to buy a ticket to Devil's Dyke. There were a number of women queuing up and they were all making gut-groaning but usually funny puns about dykes, the Dyke and devils. Glad she was on her own, Lily joined in and had a delightful tour, clued in to most of the jibes and ribald comments. As rowdy as the group was, they all fell into a happy silence when they crested the Dyke and looked across the river-threaded landscape of Sussex. There were so many shades of green and gold that it would take a master painter to capture them all, Lily thought. She knew the cheap camera she'd splurged on at the shop next to this morning's bookseller wouldn't do it justice, but she took a number of photographs anyway.

She felt so far away from *everything*. The sunshine made her nose and cheeks tingle, while the wind whipped through her hair, chilling her to the bone. She didn't feel the least bit self-conscious when a good-natured woman with a thick Cockney accent offered to put an arm around her to keep her warm. It was simple, nothing more meant than a kind woman-to-woman gesture, and it made bruised and raw places inside her ease.

She abruptly thought of Nicole, and wished she had come along. Something about Nicole was wound tight and knotted hard—all work and no play made Nicole dull, that's for sure. Maybe a walk on a beach and some music would help.

***

Eye contact had always fascinated Nicole. How and why people made eye contact had both sociological and neurobiological causes and conjoined her two favorite subjects. Socially, lack of eye contact might indicate a superior/inferior relationship between two people, but it might also be simple safety reflex. Don't look the predator in the eye. Instead, look for an escape route.

The other explanation could be that one person was attempting to deceive the other. Attempt to deceive also explained lack of eye contact in the neurobiological sense. Deception took focus and averting eye contact allowed for more attention to the deception.

Though she tried to focus on the empiric subject matter, an increasingly strident inner voice asked her, *And so which is it, Nicole? Why are you wandering through a huge crowd of lesbians and not looking any of them in the eye?*

Social conditioning? Did she feel inferior because she didn't have rainbow earrings, a labrys tattoo or piercings in places other than her ears?

Was she trying to deceive all of them, trying to hide from their recognition? Was she deceiving herself? After having kept her professional, personal and sexual lives completely separate, why did this venue bring out...uncertainties?

From cluster to cluster she moved, observing the greetings to newcomers—squeals of recognition plus hugs and kisses. A tang of salt hung in the air as a mournful ballad of lost love streamed from the main stage. The sky was crackling blue with the occasional scudding cloud. The beach was mostly small pebbles with grit that got into her shoes so easily that she understood why nearly everyone was barefoot. She finally took off her shoes—it was an odd sensation to be dressed for business and yet have cold sand between her toes.

Purple, pink and yellow banners snapped in the brisk wind over the rows of food and craft booths. The shops on the other side of the boulevard were a mix of quaint, historic and tacky, just like their tourist counterparts in Meredith. Turning 180 degrees she studied the ocean. The distant horizon was limned in silver under the bright sun. Nearer to shore the gray turned to a faded green broken by lines of whitecaps spitting spray into the air as the wind whipped them to shore.

She saw the town, the beach, the sky. She studied everything except the lesbians. Cole did not know how to fit in here. Nicole should be at ease. There was no threat to Nicole on this beach... so why was her heart seemingly missing beats? Why was her respiration threatening to rise?

You have two choices, she told herself. Stay and confront the stimuli and discover why it is triggering a fearful response, or leave and remove the stimuli. But she couldn't leave without Lily. How could she explain to Lily that she'd seen the lesbians and retreated?

She wanted to be back in her quiet office where students trembled to enter. Where colleagues might not like her but clearly respected her. Where her mother was near but still far away, and she never *ever* had thoughts like these. She wanted walls to hide her from the bright, burning light. But she couldn't go back to that world right now, and had only herself to blame. Honestly, she chided herself, where was Cole when she needed her? Did Cole really only have control in a bar when the music was loud and the lights were low?

She made herself continue her stroll, knowing that the heightened chemical activity in the brain triggered by physical movement often spurred insights. Well, Dr. Hathaway, as any therapist would tell you, analyzing this situation through an academic construct was just another way to keep emotional distance. If Cole could not exist in the light of day, in a non threatening place like this, she'd have to admit that Cole was a construct of convenience to meet lesbians for sex. The very idea filled her with confusion, which was an emotion she liked even less than fear.

"Sorry mate!"

The apology was ringing in her ears before she felt the cold liquid soaking through her jacket and shirt. She swung round to find a pair of aghast women, wide-eyed and digging in their beach bags for tissues.

"Look what you did, Watty!"

"Did not, you fell over your own feet."

"You bumped my elbow."

Nicole's protests that she was fine were ignored. She was mopped with tissues and given advice on laundering her jacket interspersed with offers to buy her a beer. She was going to smell like a brewery later.

"I'm all right, really."

"You're a bit posh for the beach," Watty pronounced. Her large, dark eyes were prominent in a slender face and Nicole found herself smiling.

"I am. I wasn't expecting the crowd."

"Woman Fest is huge!" The other woman, larger in every way, gestured at the crowd with what was left of her beer as she stuck out her other hand. "I'm Carleen. If you were looking for ladies, this is the place."

They shared a sticky handshake. Nicole nearly said that she wasn't looking for ladies. Which she wasn't, because that was Cole's function and… She chose a more palatable truth. "I was hoping to hear the music."

"This is too far back from the stage. This is cruising and hook-ups, which makes sense because this is where the beer's for sale. Let me buy you a beer."

Still protesting that she didn't need one, Nicole found herself propelled toward the booths. She managed to convince Carleen she would be happy with a lemonade and they worked their way out of the crush of the queue.

"Let's go up toward the sta—" Carleen wheeled around to look at her. "What do we call you?"

"Cole," she answered. For a moment she couldn't breathe.

Watty had already downed half her lemonade. "Like Newcastle?"

"Like short for Nicole."

Feeling a little dizzy, she was drawn by her merry companions in the direction of the performance stage. They paused occasionally to browse through a vendor tent of hand-crafted earrings, carved wood and some beautiful artisanal fabrics. After they reached the edge of the booths they stepped around, over and sometimes directly through thickets of women on blankets and beach towels enjoying picnics, books and occasional hot-and-heavy making out.

She had to forcibly avert her eyes from the occasional bare breast. In her hunger and arousal she felt no more evolved than Pavlov's dog.

The low-key acoustic duo had been replaced by a full-scale rock band with a singer belting out a done-me-wrong song about picking up the pieces. Reaching a space just big enough for the three of them, Carleen and Watty plopped down. She looked at her black slacks, a fine gabardine, and wished for jeans. There was not really any other choice. Seated, she found herself again in the sea of women, not a shape, size, color or age unrepresented. The music battered at her ears while the glittering shimmer of sunlight and laughter battered at her brain. It was exhausting to keep it out.

She realized that Watty and Carleen assumed she was a lesbian, even if she wasn't sporting pro-gay shirts like theirs. Watty's was the more restrained, with a small appliqué of a rainbow-hued woman runner on her polo's chest pocket. Carleen's T-shirt could be read from 200 feet: BIG LESBIAN SHIRT.

"It's a party," Carleen suddenly said. "You can't cry at a party."

She lifted an eyebrow. "I wasn't aware I looked sad."

"Don't pay her mind," Watty said. "She thinks if you're not smiling you must be depressed."

"Do not."

"Do too."

She was reminded of her own bickering with Kate. She had a feeling the two were friends, not a couple, not that it mattered to her.

"So let me guess where you're from," Watty said. "Toronto?"

She shook her head. "Due east of there—New Hampshire."

Watty nudged Carleen. "She's not Canadian."

Carleen shrugged. "She sounds a lot like a Canadian, but an American is okay."

Nicole was inspired by the upbeat "Yes I Am" now rippling across the crowd to say, "Melissa. We gave the world Melissa Etheridge."

"I'll see your Melissa and raise you Catherine Jenkins." Carleen processed her blank stare. "You don't even know who she is! You don't watch *Dancing with the Stars*? A show you stole from the BBC?"

"I don't," she admitted. "I actually don't watch much television."

Watty pointed a thumb at herself. "Computers, sort of. What do you do?"

"I'm a professor and researcher in the fields of cognitive neuroscience and biopsychology." It occurred to her that she might have said she was a writer.

Watty blinked at her. "You look familiar, but I don't know why."

Nicole thought about not enlightening her, but Carleen abruptly said, "Oh! You're that love doctor."

She laughed—nothing, she felt, could be farther from her reality. "No, not quite."

"But you wrote that book, which I read, by the way. I loved the case studies, they were like short stories about real people who figured out how to be happy."

"I remember now," Watty said. "DNA seems more reliable than astrology. Though Carleen couldn't be more of an Aries if she tried."

"I should hope my research is more grounded in science than astrology."

"I like astrology because it feels right," Carleen said.

"That's called intuitive validation."

"Right." Carleen looked as if she were trying to add large sums in her head.

The band switched to an even higher energy song she didn't recognize and she wondered what Lily would make of it. She glanced at her watch. Given the maze to get back to the boulevard from where they were, she thought she probably ought to make a start to the agreed upon meeting point with Lily. Not that she was running away from more revelations or two pleasant women who called her "Cole" and saw her without the protective layers of degrees, research and awards Dr. Nicole Hathaway had worked so hard to procure. Not running away—she was keeping to a schedule, that was all.

She stayed through one more number, and when the show stopped to allow bands to change, she took a friendly leave and wished them a fun evening. When she finally reached the boulevard and spotted Lily's bright peacock-feather patterned sweater she felt a wave of relief. She quickly re-donned her shoes and felt more like herself.

"It was great, Cole," Lily called as soon as they were in comfortable earshot. "You should have come with me."

"The beach is an education," she allowed. She wished she had told Lily to keep calling her Nicole. It would have helped.

Lily brushed her wind-knotted hair out of her eyes. "How did it feel to walk in the surf?"

"I didn't do that."

Lily's eyebrows shot up.

"No one was doing it, so I presumed it wasn't the time or place."

"Oh." She blinked her green eyes, which, in Nicole's opinion, were altogether a more pleasant shade of green than the ocean. "Are you hungry? Shall we try out the pasty shop? Or there's a tearoom around the corner that didn't look very crowded. Most people are on the beach, I suppose."

"How about the tea shop? Especially if there's a restroom."

"Loo, remember?" Lily corrected. "I will certainly be happy to visit the loo. This wind is getting to be something else. If I got an umbrella maybe I could be Mary Poppins!"

Lily danced on tiptoe ahead of her, feigning holding an umbrella as the wind buffeted them both. She looked joyous and at ease, while all Nicole wanted to do was close her eyes and cover her ears. Maybe, she thought desperately, the confusion and uncertainty was the predictable and simple outcome of her introverted nature being hyperstimulated.

Yes, she thought, that explained everything.

CHAPTER SEVEN

"You don't have to come with me to the tea with my cousins. It will be very dull. You could stay here, then meet me at the station." Nicole turned from her study of a highly romantic Georgian painting of young never-to-be-queen Charlotte with a Belgian king. She hoped Lily did join them but it seemed only polite to give her the chance to decline.

"I love the setting of an opera box. It's very innocent, somehow." Lily's head was tipped to the side as she also studied the work. "I don't mind. But be honest, do you want me to be there? I won't be offended if you say no."

"I would be happy if you were. I don't know them at all, and if you were to imply we had to be someplace after a proper amount of time has elapsed, even if it's not time yet to leave for the station…"

"Say no more. I take your meaning, guv'nah." Lily winked. "We have to leave by three fifteen at the latest. Three would be better."

"Which is only an hour for tea." She glanced at the vaulted ceiling of the National Portrait Gallery, replaced after the original was destroyed by bombs in World War II. She admired that time and care had been taken to carve and paint it like the original but using a lighter, more mildew resistant wood. Sentiment tempered with practicality—it was clear that the New England sensibilities she had grown up with had not drifted that far from their British roots.

In spite of the fact that she found the portraits fascinating she fought a yawn. After dinner in Brighton they'd wandered the booths again and sat listening to the headline acts. Lily hadn't seemed at all uncomfortable in the very lesbian crowd but Nicole hadn't been able to relax. She wasn't ready to see or be seen. It wasn't a decision she'd come on this trip to make and she was grateful Lily spoke only of the music.

They had just missed one train for London and didn't reach the hotel until after one. She hadn't slept well again, and rising early for the radio program hadn't been easy. She didn't want to waste time meeting Rajesh and Priya but her mother would be very disappointed if she bowed out. "We can spend another ten minutes here, can't we?"

Lily gave her an indulgent smile. "Nine minutes, and then I get out my whip."

After a few more minutes, and admitting that there was simply not enough time to even peek at the collection that focused on Victoria, they left the gallery and Lily led the way. At the tea shop, with a quaint *The Trafalgar Rose Tea Room – Scones & Crumpets* sign over the door, Nicole paused at the reception, but a very slender Indian man, no more than thirty, enthusiastically waved to her from a nearby table.

"You're Nicole," he said as he rose. "I recognized you from your picture. I am Rajesh Ansari. This is my sister Priya."

A fine-boned woman, perhaps three or four years younger than Rajesh, rose to shake her hand. Nicole introduced Lily, who immediately murmured, "It's a pleasure to meet you."

Rajesh helped both of them into their chairs, and Lily filled the awkward pause with an observation about the much cooler weather of the day than yesterday. Nicole was glad to be spared a response of much more than a nod and a smile.

When the waitress stopped to take their order, Rajesh demurred to Nicole. "My American cousin will decide."

"I think we want to have a traditional tea," Nicole said. "When in Rome…"

"As long as that means strawberry jam and clotted cream with scones or Sally Lund bread," Lily added brightly. She batted her eyelashes at the server, who laughed.

"It sure does, love."

Lily grinned back. "It's been a while since I've had it."

"That so?" The server tapped her pen on her tablet and gave Lily what Nicole thought was a rather cheeky smile. "Then I'll have to make sure it's good, won't I?"

"I'm easy to please."

Rajesh laughed as if Lily had told the most amazing joke and Nicole realized she was watching yet another man fall under the spell of the wide smile and dancing eyes. It was tediously predictable at this point. She had an irrational urge to tell Rajesh to put his eyes back in his head.

Merriment subsided, Rajesh gestured at Priya. "My sister is studying at Dickson Poon."

Nicole wondered if that was a school where they taught women not to speak unless their brother said it was allowed. "What subject are you studying, Priya?"

"Law," Rajesh said before Priya could answer. "Lily, have you graduated from college? You're…twenty-four? Twenty-five?"

"Thereabouts."

"Rajesh," Priya admonished. Apparently not the model of decorum, she poked him with the butter knife. "You're asking a lady her age. That's rude."

"Forgive my curiosity."

"There's nothing to forgive." Lily's smile was exceedingly pleasant without giving away any emotional cues. Nicole decided she didn't like it much.

The waitress delivered their teapot and set out delicate china cups.

"I was indeed being curious, Priya is right."

Lily's smile softened as she glanced at the waitress. "Will all the crusts be cut off our sandwiches?"

"Of course." The waitress gave Lily a steady look. "Any other requests? I'm very flexible."

"That will work for me, but thank you for the offer."

Nicole tore her gaze away from the sparkle in Lily's eyes. "Are you specializing in any kind of law, Priya?"

"She had some idea of working in immigration, but there's no money in that," Rajesh said.

Nicole kept her gaze on Priya, waiting for an answer.

Priya rolled her eyes at her brother. "Immigration is definitely my field. I am concerned with issues of social justice."

"What do you hope to achieve after your studies?" Nicole asked. She was aware that Rajesh had asked Lily another question but she ignored it. Priya was turning out to be an interesting conversationalist, and she didn't need to watch Lily make another conquest to know that it had happened.

***

Ensconced in adjoining seats in the comfortable "quiet" car of their train, they were thirty minutes out of London before Lily asked, "Are all the men in your family like that?"

"I haven't met them all." Nicole glanced over at Lily. "I'm sure there are some that aren't. I believe he is what some of my students would call an 'asshat.'"

Lily laughed. "I'm not surprised he's unmarried. He won't find many modern women who want to be talked over and so obviously measured for suitability as a wife."

The parting had been amusing, with Lily adroitly sidestepping an exchange of e-mail addresses due to their uncertain, uncharted and unknown travel plans. Nicole was certain Priya had known it was a smokescreen, but Rajesh had seemed oblivious. Even the server had been watching with a wry smile. Nicole had caught her rolling her eyes at Lily, who'd winked back.

She went back to the paperwork she'd spread out on the narrow table bolted to the floor in front of their seats. The train was far more comfortable than an airplane. But before she could pick up the threads of the report, Lily spoke.

"May I make an observation about the presentations you've been making?"

Nicole raised an eyebrow. "You seem trepidacious."

"I'm not sure what I'm going to say will go over well."

"I'm out of practice at receiving feedback," Nicole said. "The hazards of tenure. But go ahead. I'm listening."

Lily was clearly choosing her words with care. "The first few minutes of your talk you spend explaining what your book isn't, what your study doesn't prove and what your audience won't learn from it. It seems—a bit—defensive. Isn't there a way to turn all those statements to positives?"

Nicole ran over the first paragraph of her lecture in her mind. It was common practice to let students know the parameter of the day's subject discussion at the outset.

"The women there aren't in class, after all. They are there by choice, taking time from their day, because they want answers. And you might have them."

"Point taken," Nicole said. More slowly she added, "You're quite right. I was thinking of it as an academic lecture."

"Some of the events are definitely going to have some students. Tomorrow at the university in Edinburgh for certain. But bookshops and book clubs will be far more casual and what the audience wants is more specific."

"Such as? My findings only address the probable term and success of relationships with certain hallmarks, based on extrapolated data. It won't tell them how to establish a relationship."

"Any more than a diet book guarantees losing weight. But I think women read to give themselves choices. Dreams. When it comes to love, they're looking for hope."

"Now you've lost me. The last thing I want is someone using research to build constructs that aren't real."

Lily leaned toward her. The green light in her eyes was so gentle that Nicole missed the first few words.

"...Page one-fifty or so. It's the case study about the interracial couple that's in the part of the book that deals with whether race and its genetic markers have bearing on relationship success."

"I couldn't find evidence that they do. You really did read the book?"

Lily nodded. "I finished it last night after we got back from Brighton. You don't feel that a person's race has bearing on whether they can have successful relationships."

"My feelings are irrelevant." Nicole had probably said that sentence a hundred times in her career to students, even other faculty, and now to Lily. "The data plainly says that race is not a factor. We had a good sampling across most races as well as many mixed race participants and interracial relationships."

Lily nodded. "You found that people in interracial relationships were no more or less likely to succeed—be happy—than people who weren't. So when I read that case study what I took from it is that if I am looking to find a mate, there is no reason to narrow the field because I think I might be happier with someone of the same skin color or racial background. There may be unique social pressures, but contrary to social myth, your research says they aren't going to be any more destructive than whatever pressures I might get if I stay with choices within my race." She stopped.

"Go on." She wondered why Lily was restating one of the book's core hypotheses.

"You're frowning."

"I am? I'm sorry, I'm thinking. Go on." She forced her expression to relax.

"If that is true, then if I'm a woman looking to find a life mate, my possible pool just increased multifold. And that gives me hope. It says that it's actually a good idea to look outside my usual paths of life. Go further afield. Open my eyes to parts of the world I'd ignored."

Nicole blinked.

"Have I drawn an incorrect conclusion?"

"No."

"You look...startled."

"I am."

"So," Lily concluded, "I'm not sure that your statement that the book won't help women find a life mate is…fully accurate."

A clatter in the aisle jolted Nicole out of her surprised silence.

"Would you two ladies like something from the trolley?" A plump middle-aged woman paused next to them, her cart laden with snack food.

"Oh! I'll have a packet of chocolate McVitie's," Lily said promptly. "And tea with milk."

"Tea for me as well," Nicole said automatically. Her mind was spinning.

Lily opened her packet of what turned out to be thin whole-wheat cookie sandwiches with chocolate inside. Lily dipped hers in the tea before taking a bite. She said in a crumb-thickened voice, "They're good. Want one?"

"No thank you. Are you saying that I ought to frame my speeches to the general audience in those terms?"

Lily finished chewing and swallowed. One corner of her mouth was streaked with chocolate until she licked it away. "I'm saying that if you consider the good news it might make the bad news more palatable."

Nicole watched, fascinated, as Lily dunked the cookie and took another huge bite. The sound she made was positively lustful. "Can't get those at home?"

"Only in ghastly expensive import stores. I'd forgotten how yummy they are until I saw them on the cart."

"Have you been living on a desert island? You seem starved for experience."

Lily froze and a dark flush crept up her throat. After a long silence, she said, "Do I?"

Surprised and intrigued by the reaction, Nicole nevertheless felt that she'd intruded. "That was an overly personal observation. Have I upset you?"

"No." The denial was automatic. "I didn't realize I gave out that kind of vibe."

"Perhaps I have mischaracterized it. I only note that sometimes you are the epitome of the superego and others the epitome of the id."

"Freud? Really, Dr. Hathaway." The flush receded. "Are you changing the subject? We were talking about the opening of your speech."

"I'm giving your comments a lot of thought."

"Uh-huh."

Aware that it was Lily who was changing the subject, Nicole decided to go along with it. "I'm capable of thinking and talking at the same time."

"I should hope so." Lily finished the second cookie and wiped her fingers on a napkin. "I just think a more positive beginning, followed by the necessary caveats and cautions, will keep your audience with you longer."

"I agree." Nicole glanced at the work she had spread out on the table. She knew she should return to it. These hours should be productive. She put down her pen and leaned back in the seat. "As a scientist I'm wary of practical applications. The desire to find one can lead to bias."

"Isn't the reverse true? The desire to remain purely in pursuit of knowledge for the sake of the knowledge might lead to a bias against obvious practical applications."

"It's probable. However, the funding pressure to seek knowledge only when there are practical applications—space research, for example, only if it cures a disease somehow—is so strong that a bias in resistance to that pressure will help keep the research in balance."

Lily's brow was furrowed. "So why did you start the research for *Love by the Numbers*?"

"It was an outgrowth of a different study on genetic mutations and autism. We had gathered DNA profiles for a wide study, looking for a pattern of mutation and a possible common event that might have caused that mutation—nuclear detonations, vaccine releases, and so forth—and were unable to find compelling loci that called for further study. Colleagues went another direction and are working on an examination of comparative toxin levels in air and water and overlaying it with the rise in reported autism. They will be another three years before they can make conclusions. We had digitized all that DNA data—"

"And you thought you'd just see what you could discover with it?"

"My specialty is the intersection of neurobiology—how our body/brain chemistry works—and biopsychology—why our brain and body chemistry affect our behavior. I'm particularly fascinated by the apparent disconnect between a stimulus and a predictable response."

Lily's puzzlement showed. "Say that another way."

"A battered woman is afraid. He body is pumping hormones and adrenaline into her blood with the electrical signal to run. But she doesn't. She stays. Her brain countermands the powerful signals of her body."

"Oh I see. Soldiers stay in a battlefield. Like that?"

"Conditioning is part of the explanation, yes. The brain can and does countermand our neurobiology all the time. I studied the pool of DNA and I couldn't get a good sample of battery victims or soldiers. But there was one common trait across all of it, driven by the way the samples were taken, classified and the donors interviewed."

"Marital status!" Lily's eyes lit up. "Of course. It's practically on every form anyone ever fills out."

"Even more specifically, married, divorced, widowed, never married, unmarried but in a relationship exceeding five years…these are common intake questions when researchers take samples and add to the registry. Dopamine is nearly as powerful as adrenaline, so I asked myself if I could find a link between the presence of dopamine and relationship status."

"Dopamine?"

Nicole pointed at the cookies. "You're enjoying some dopamine right now."

"Oh, the stuff in chocolate that makes you feel like you're in love?"

"It's not in chocolate. But chocolate causes the body to produce dopamine, in many cases."

"Is that an important distinction?"

"Actually, it is." Nicole looked down at her hands because it was hard to keep looking at Lily. "To a scientist, I suppose."

"So you decided to study love."

"No." Love had been the last thing she'd been curious about. "I decided to study the correlation between the DNA centers controlling social behavior and cognitive reasoning with relationship status. At first the results were too huge to have meaning. Yes some sequences—probably shared by six billion people—were in people who'd had a relationship. That's not useful. But when I narrowed the field to sequences for people who'd been in relationships lasting more than fifteen years, that's when the big patterns began to emerge. After that it was—"

"Child's play?"

"Not exactly."

Lily finished her tea. "I think it's all fascinating."

"You've asked better questions than this morning's radio show host." She kept staring at her fingers. She felt odd, as if the train were making her a little dizzy.

"I don't think he was awake yet. But at least you were. So... Why is it that I can't go have my DNA tested and find out the DNA profile of my ideal mate?"

"Because there's no registry you have access to that would supply you with the names and addresses of those people with that DNA. You'd have a string of numbers and nowhere to look up the meaning."

"But aren't there people saying they can do it for you, for a fee?"

"I don't endorse those theories."

"The fingerprint lady?"

"Pure charlatanism as far as I know. But obviously providing a service people are willing to pay for."

"Couldn't you take samples of friends and see if their relationship history confirms your theory?"

The dizzy sensation faded a little. "Why?"

"Confirmation?"

"Without a rigorous control, it would be pure anecdote. I have plenty of case studies for anecdotes already. And anecdotes flooding my e-mail where people can't wait to tell me I'm a genius or a fraud. Most people don't read the cautions."

"I read them. I know you've proven to your own and your peers' satisfaction that there is a greater than statistical probability that people with compatible DNA sequences are more successful in relationships. But that doesn't mean people with other sequences can't be successful. They can be—just not with the same frequency."

"And that all boils down to the tagline on the book: *Does DNA determine the perfect match?* I couldn't convince the publisher to take that off and, contractually, he had the final say on the cover."

"Damon's good at marketing."

"Damon?"

Lily blushed. "Damon Linden."

"Do you know him well? He said you were a family friend."

"He's my uncle, actually." The flush had receded and she got a sidelong look and smile. "That's right, nepotism in action."

Trying to digest that information and not sure how she felt about it, Nicole said, "He has certainly been successful marketing the book."

"You say that like it's a bad thing."

It wasn't surprising that she would defend her relative. "It wasn't my goal."

"You submitted a book to a publisher but didn't want it to sell?"

"I wanted it to be shelved in research libraries and to be of use to the field. This…" She waved a hand at the countryside skimming past the window. "This wasn't in the plan."

"The best-laid schemes of mice and men gang aft agley," Lily said. She turned to throw away her cup as the trolley woman came through the car with a trash bag. The collar of her shirt flipped up and Nicole watched as her own hand began to lift in that direction as if to adjust it. What was she doing?

She forced her hand down to the table. She picked up the pen. She looked out the window to clear her field of vision of Lily's hair and pale, soft skin.

Your body is churning with chemicals, she told herself, and you can't predict your behavior. What chemicals, though, and why? It wasn't the fear of yesterday on the beach. This was something else.

"Cole?"

She turned back. "Yes?"

Lily started to say something, but paused with her mouth half-open. Finally, she said, "I'm just going to step down to the restroom."

"Okay."

She turned back to the window and wondered what had startled Lily. She looked like herself, didn't she? Lily couldn't know that her palms were damp. Again. That her heart was racing. Again. That there was also a strange shaking inside her stomach that wasn't food poisoning.

It had started when she'd heard Lily's soft voice saying her name, saying *Cole*.

It had started when she realized that she wanted to hear Lily say it again. And again.

CHAPTER EIGHT

Seated on the left side near the front of the University of Edinburgh's largest lecture hall, Lily could hear Nicole's voice as she spoke at the podium as well as her voice over the hall's speakers. The air was also filled with the vigorous tapping of keys as the students around her took notes at their keyboards.

She was gratified that Nicole had made a few changes to the opening of her lecture, even for students. It meant their talk on the train had been useful. That Nicole took her advice…seriously.

Her breath caught at the memory. She'd fallen asleep last night thinking about the look on Nicole's face when she'd turned back from the window. It might be the closest Lily had come to seeing Nicole without her thick air of academic seriousness. Her eyes were dark, but soft, lashes low—the look had roused a very inappropriate response. A response that hadn't stopped.

She tried to look at Nicole as a client, a boss, a professor. Rude, unfeeling bee-yatch, remember? Lily tried to feel like a student, an employee, even a caretaker. None of it worked. She looked at Nicole and saw a woman with a fascinating brain, hidden humor, strong shoulders and beguiling eyes.

Black slacks, white blouse, black socks, black loafers. There was no sexy in that, except Nicole *was* sexy. There was no sign of that alluring woman on stage, but Lily couldn't stop seeing Nicole as she had been in that fleeting moment when all the trappings of the professor had been gone and the woman within had stared back into Lily's eyes.

But she's thoughtless, she told herself. *And could care less about other people unless they're printed out on a report. In nearly every conversation it's clear that if social convention didn't require her to speak, she wouldn't. She fights with her sister and doesn't seem to care that her mother loves her. She's...*

Nicole gestured at a slide on the large screen and Libido— who was not helping Lily's heart rate—sat admiring the gesture, committing the length of Nicole's arms to memory, and considering just how far they would go around Lily to pull her close and tight.

Circumspect crossly pointed out that every single thought in her head was *inappropriate*, as if the word was some kind of anti-Viagra.

Libido pointed out that Nicole biked regularly and probably had firm, muscled legs.

So much for sex in an alley, Circumspect retorted. Fat lot of good that did you, because here you are thinking a woman without a sexual impulse in her soul is some kind of love goddess.

Lily snorted. The young man next to her gave her an odd look.

You should take warning, she told herself, that someone who devoted several years to studying human relationships doesn't have a clue about how to translate that to real human emotions and interactions. Everything people felt was just a biochemical imperative to her. If the data didn't support it, would Nicole even believe love existed?

Libido wanted to know what love had to do with it.

Circumspect wanted to know what love had to do with it.

It was entirely too noisy in her head, and between the keyboards and the loudspeakers, there was no room for Lily to think about anything with any clarity. The continual low thrum centered at the base of her spine that made her skin tingle and thighs clench only got worse.

***

Nicole had been surprised when Lily had pleaded a headache and retired for the evening, which had left Nicole alone to accept an invitation to dinner from the university's event host. Lily looked as vibrant as ever, but there was no reason not to believe she felt unwell. The dinner conversation with the host had been easily managed, much like any dinner with a colleague interested in the same subject. Only their mutual accents had caused any issues, and as much amusement as they had frustration. When they'd left the small café it was in time to appreciate the cool early evening and the growing crowds for something called "Fringe."

Now, standing in her hotel room, aware that Lily was probably asleep, she was considering if Cole might finally take advantage of an evening alone. An encounter would undoubtedly take care of her unruly sex drive.

She hoped Lily was feeling okay. Should she call her—would that be the polite thing to do? But what if she were asleep? It was best to leave her be.

Her phone chirped with a reminder and she realized it was the day and time she'd agreed to call her mother. On the itinerary it had seemed a good opening. Best to get it out of the way. If she didn't call her mother would panic.

"Your sister has been put on bed rest," her mother promptly informed her. "Her amniotic fluid is too low and there has been some pelvic discharge and cramping."

"It sounds very unpleasant." Her mother's anxiety was palpable. "Is the baby in danger?"

"If she doesn't do as she's told, perhaps."

In the background she heard Kate's voice protesting. It included the F-word and Nicole wasn't unhappy that a large ocean separated her from both her mother and Kate.

"I'm sure you'll get her to cooperate somehow."

"The cramping helps—it's a reminder from her body to do as she's told." There was more commentary in the background. "Tell me about your appearances so far. Where are you?"

She launched into a colorful description of London and Edinburgh, and went to great lengths to present tea with the relatives as a great success.

"Rajesh's father is very pompous," her mother said. "He is a man you can't tell anything."

"Then clearly Rajesh is his son. But Priya seemed a very nice woman." Those were her mother's words of highest praise.

"She is a bit forward, but that's her father's opinion. A lawyer—he should be proud."

"They both seemed well and happy."

Her mother sighed and Nicole knew that the news would travel. In spite of Facebook, Twitter, Pinterest and phones that zapped photographs from one side of the world to the other in seconds, a week-old account of having seen Rajesh and Priya in good health was more valued by most of her mother's family. She was glad to have provided her mother with something to share.

They chatted for a bit longer, then her mother handed the phone to Kate.

"I am stuck in fucking bed and not for fun. It's a beautiful afternoon and I can't move."

"I'm really sorry. Did you get Mom to bring in the television?"

"No, but we're discussing alternatives. I can't even sit at the computer and read my e-mail. I want an iPad."

"Good luck with that," Nicole said. Under the circumstances she decided against suggesting that such wants were why people had jobs.

"Mom is driving me crazy."

"This was unexpected?"

Kate's tone grew even more waspish. "I'm pregnant and I'm venting."

Nicole laughed. "I'm sorry, sis. If I were there I'd probably make it worse."

Kate's voice softened. "Yeah, I don't miss you at all either."

They chatted for a bit longer, then she was passed back to her mother for goodbyes. A few minutes later she sat on the bed and realized she didn't know what she felt. Or how she ought to feel about what she'd heard. Kate was making the best of it, but her mother was clearly worried, and for good reason. She knew enough about biology to understand that anything cramping or leaking during pregnancy meant risk to both Kate and the baby.

She put aside the idea that it would help to talk to Lily. Lily was unavailable. Besides, what would Lily advise?

She considered that for a moment, then picked up her phone to call Beekman's. It was early afternoon in New Hampshire. She was willing to bet they could deliver an iPad by the end of the day.

***

Cole fit right in with Edinburgh's Fringe Festival. There didn't seem to be breathing room in the narrow streets and she wasn't alone in her leather. Every corner had some kind of performance underway, all in the shadow of Edinburgh Castle, its ancient ramparts outlined against the night sky by moonlight. Simple floodlights illuminated the keep. Lily had expressed an interest in a walking tour through the castle before they caught their flight to Dublin tomorrow afternoon.

From the open doors of theaters, inns, pubs and shops hawkers shrilled out invitations to see everything from comedy acts to puppetry to musicians. Apparently, it was the final weekend of a month of independent theater, dance and cabaret. Most appeared to be suitable for all audiences, but "Fringe" did include adult topics as well, from a performance of *The Vagina Monologues* to a demonstration on knot tying and leather care.

She kept track of the streets as she walked. About four blocks from the hotel she found an open pub door advertising an "LGBT Mixer." The noise level even at the doorway was deafening. As she hesitated several young women pushed past her to enter.

This is why you brought the jacket. Just like the old days. Just like that conference in Dallas or the one in Seattle. Perplexed by her lack of confidence, Nicole followed the young women through the low doorway.

She was struck first by the fact that the group was more than half male. That changed the dynamic in both subtle and obvious ways. Compared to women, men tended to keep greater distance from the bar and from other men for whom they had no sexual interest. Their stances occupied more floor space. They extended arms while speaking more than women did. More subtle was the shifting of body language in unconscious negotiation of status. As a whole, the men in the pub also occupied the best lit areas where they could more easily see and be seen.

She had to shout her request for a pint of a local brew several times to be understood over the bone-shaking volume of the dance music. All the while she told herself that she could always go back to the hotel. Having looked forward to a night like this for several months with a Pavlovian response almost every time, she didn't understand why her sex drive had suddenly gone into hiding.

She sipped her pale, earthy beer, cool but not cold, and slowly surveyed the room. Based on their cues, there were a number of women interested in "mixing." The sidelong looks, the quick glances at the door when someone new entered, the lowered shoulders and exposed curve of the neck all invited examination.

"See anything you like?"

Startled by the voice suddenly shouting in her ear, Nicole turned to find a woman perhaps slightly older than her, not quite as tall, and also clad in denim and leather. She shrugged by way of response.

"The birds love the leather. They'll come to you. Just wait. You here for Fringe?"

Nicole nodded and took the other woman's expression to be relief. The local lion, perhaps, making sure there wasn't going to be another long-term competitor for the attentions of the local pride.

Every time in her past in a scene like this she would have by now introduced herself at least visually, if not verbally, to at least one woman with whom she'd shared more than a fleeting glance. Once again, as on the beach, she found it hard to make eye contact.

Maybe that was it. Maybe she just wasn't giving herself a chance. How long had it been? Two years? Was she rusty?

After a long swallow from her pint she forced herself to study faces. There were several women looking at her and the woman next to her. A brunette kept up the eye contact while saying something to her friend. She was medium height and her jeans and silky blouse did justice to a lush figure. Her wide smile indicated a familiarity with laughter and pleasure.

All very attractive—and Nicole felt nothing in response.

She was going to have to give that situation serious thought, but clearly the pursuit was a waste of time and energy tonight. With a nod at the other woman, who was sharing winks with the brunette now, she made her way around a group of men and set her half-empty pilsner on the bar. As she turned to leave a petite blonde came in with a group. Fishnet stockings and a short skirt drew Nicole's gaze downward at first. A thin shirt knotted at her midriff left smooth, pale skin exposed. By the time Nicole got to her face the woman was staring at her.

She left her companions to stand within inches of Nicole. Shouting, she said, "Leaving so soon?"

"Not now that there's a reason to stay." The answer was automatic and the best she could do from her suddenly dry throat. Her nerves tightened in a delicious coil, sending a wave of heat coursing from her face to her feet and back, settling in the low places between her hips. Her hands felt as if they were on fire.

The swift, primal magnitude of her physical response stunned her. The other woman turned her head to dismiss her companions for the moment. Then she said to Nicole, "Let's dance."

There wasn't a dance floor, but Nicole let herself be pulled to the far side of the pub where the lights were the lowest. Couples swayed slowly together in rhythms that had nothing to do with the music. The woman's hands ran up and down Nicole's sleeves, then around to her back, fitting their bodies together.

The first kiss increased the familiar hunger in the pit of Nicole's belly. The second set off a high-pitched hum in her ears and she could no longer hear the music. She heard only the soft sigh and the quiet purr, followed by the low laugh after Nicole jerked her head back to avoid having her lip bitten.

She let her head be pulled down to another kiss, then shivered as lips brushed her earlobe. "Hard, fast and now."

"Now?"

"Do you have someplace near?"

Instead of answering the question, Nicole glanced around and said, "What about your friends?"

"They know me. I've found myself a butch and won't be back until morning." The woman leaned back, tossing her blond hair out of her face. "Will I?"

Her eyes were blue. Not green.

All the heat in her body turned to ice.

As they'd kissed Nicole had entertained visions of stripping her naked and holding her down on a bed. Pushing her legs apart to find out if she was as ready as Nicole was. Discovering exactly how hard and how fast would please her. Eventually opening the jacket so their breasts could touch, but only after they were both already drenched and panting. Rolling across the bed for the hours of deep pleasure it would take to finally satisfy.

She had envisioned finally looking down into green eyes and asking, "What more do you need?"

Into Lily's eyes.

"Is something wrong?"

An unbidden voice of clinical detachment said, "Take her back to the room and engage in sexual relations. Once purged of the biological compulsions and resulting emotional chaos, everything will return to its previous state." It was followed quickly by a primal dictate: *Pretend it's Lily.*

She couldn't breathe for a moment. Then her lungs finally filled.

"What's the matter? Let's go."

She caught the woman's hands before they reached her ass. "I'm sorry, I suddenly don't feel well."

"You're having me on!"

"No, I'm sorry. I have to go."

The surprise and disgust in not-Lily's face wasn't a look she'd ever wanted to get from any woman, but it faded from her memory as soon as the music of the pub was lost in the hubbub of the crowded streets.

For several minutes she was too overwhelmed to sort out her feelings. She tried to find her innate fascination at the collision of the academic superego and the carnal id but she couldn't focus when another part of her was fixated on the fact that she'd known Lily less than a week.

Human behavior being what it was, she was certain a number of people followed the urge to use the person they were with as a stand-in for the one they really desired. The problem was, she'd never done that before.

Her memory served her well on autopilot and she found herself outside her hotel without recalling much of the walk. Desperate not to encounter Lily she shed her jacket and quickly crossed the lobby to the stairs. Once in her own room she plunked down on the bed, legs wobbly and head swimming.

She'd never used a stand-in before—the impulse to do so was a first. That was because she'd never desired anyone who had a name before. Never closed her eyes, as she did now, and ached for the feel of a specific woman in her arms.

Why Lily? Wishing she'd drunk the entire beer at the bar, she pushed her jacket into her suitcase, changed into pajamas and crawled into bed. But the dark room lit up with her fantasies.

Nowhere near sleep, she turned on all the lights, opened the folder of her next peer review project and read until her eyes burned.

CHAPTER NINE

Nicole had changed her presentation again. The bookshop was stuffed to its exposed rafters with women of all ages from Dublin and the surrounding villages. Prominent in the front row were five little old ladies in stout shoes who'd explained they were from the local Women's Institute and having a day in the city. They were all single and it was never too late to find love, their leader had assured Nicole.

Lily hoped that the ladies weren't put off by Nicole's choice to focus her talk on sex—specifically, the sexual spark that all of the participants acknowledged existed in both successful and unsuccessful relationships.

"Contrary to romantic comedies, the sexual spark isn't a reliable predictor of long-term success. Every participant in our study had felt it with both positive and negative outcomes. More than half said that while sex was important, it was not the deciding factor in the decision to make a long-term commitment."

One of the old ladies piped up with, "You never miss the water till the well runs dry!"

The room erupted into laughter. Nicole's brows knitted for just a moment and Lily could imagine the smackdown a student who heckled would receive. But the glower turned to a grin. "Seeing water does, in fact, make most people feel thirsty."

"Seeing a good-looking lad with a pint does that for me!"

Lily couldn't help but join the new burst of laughter, but she was glad one of the woman's companions poked her with a grin and said, "Now you hush, Mary."

Nicole resumed her talk with a genuine smile that lingered. "The sexual spark is one of the strongest neurobiological impulses in most people's bodies, powered by a cocktail of serotonin, oxytocin and dopamine. For brevity, these are often referred to as the Love Drug. When respondents were asked to rank the intensity of the Love Drug's effect on their cognitive assessment, it was outranked only by loss of a loved one and imminent fear of death. In short, quoting from the woman in the case study on page two-twelve, 'When my engine revs up I can't hear much of anything, especially all the things that should have told me the guy was all wrong for me.'"

Women all over the audience were nodding. Nicole glanced at Lily, then returned her gaze to her notes.

"So if sexual attraction isn't a good predictor of long-term relationship success, what are some of the things that are? One of the most commonly cited personality traits that participants said they shared with their long-term partner was a self-described 'good' sense of humor. That doesn't mean laughter, however. The predictor isn't that both people can laugh, but that they laugh—and cry, or get angry—at the same things. Their emotional responses to the same stimuli—a pie in the face, the loss of a parent, a national tragedy—are similar."

She turned to another page in her book. "From page two-fourteen. 'I never saw Bill cry but when our first baby was stillborn I knew he grieved as hard and as deep as I did. I knew he understood why I cried.' Compare that to the statistically significant number of participants who said emotional mystery was a relationship killer. Page three-twenty: 'She's the woman I wanted the most ever, but I never knew how Cindy felt and it didn't last two years.'"

She watched Nicole set the book down and smooth the cover with the palm of her hand. A gentle touch, almost as if it were a child.

With a start, Lily realized that Nicole was segueing into her final remarks and she quickly took a couple of pictures. Lupe had e-mailed that they were using photographs to maintain a travel blog for the *Love by the Numbers* tour.

Afterward she handled the queue for signed books as she had in London and Edinburgh, and realized she was already in danger of losing track of where she was. It would be easy to do so over the coming weeks. Better to focus on the pleasure of the Irish accents and turns of phrase than the way her heartbeat seemed to leap into double-time every time she made eye contact with Nicole.

Nicole's switch to talking about how sexual attraction got in the way of good judgment wasn't a warning, was it? Nicole couldn't possibly know...

She passed another book open to the title page to Nicole to sign, taking care not to touch her. She wasn't sure what would happen if their fingers brushed, but she was taking no chances given that Libido was busy committing the shape and length of Nicole's fingers to memory. She wasn't sure what her camera had caught, but the photograph in her mind was of the smiling, relaxed Nicole and the simple look of indulgence, even affection for the jokester in the audience. Maybe her warmer nature only came out for little old ladies. Lily had yet to see a look like that directed at her. That strangely compelling shared look on the train to Edinburgh hadn't been...affection.

***

By the time she was buckled into her airplane seat next to Nicole for their afternoon flight to Frankfurt, part of her mind was reflecting on Ashtown Castle's beautiful gardens, resplendent with late summer perennials and just a hint of turning color in the leaves. The rest of her energy was preoccupied with the demanding itinerary of the next eight days.

They arrived in Frankfurt late in the evening and the following morning reported to the opening day of the massive book festival and a cattle call-type of book signing.

The following day they drove to Bremen where one bookstore and two colleges were awaiting Nicole's appearance. After that, they turned west to Amsterdam, then south to Brussels and onward to Reims. Each day had three to five hours of driving and two if not three appearances varying between academic and bookstore settings. Just thinking about it she could have cheerfully shot the person who had planned such a rigorous schedule without any breaks.

They were supposed to stay overnight in Reims, but Lily was considering changing their plans to drive at least part of the way to Lyon and stopping over in Dijon. Since they didn't have to be in Lyon until mid-afternoon, it would give them one morning to take things just a little bit more slowly. After a university lecture they had a shorter drive to Geneva where two more colleges and a bookstore were on the itinerary. They would spend a second night there and then return to Frankfurt via a long, arduous drive, hopefully arriving in time for the close of the book festival and another large signing.

With so many cities ahead, surely one or two would have back alleys behind bars, Libido suggested. *After all, there's no point to thinking naked time with Nicole will cure anything. Dr. Hathaway thinks sex is an annoying distraction.*

And she's not wrong, Circumspect pleaded. *Go ahead, make a pass at her, see how long you keep this job and your self-respect.*

Feeling cross that she couldn't at least doze on the plane, Lily tried to silence the inner argument. Okay, sex was not just a distraction in life, but it could lead to reckless decisions, she told herself. She wasn't going to be one of those women who later claimed the heat of the moment made her do something astonishingly stupid. She could just picture the look on Uncle Damon's face if Nicole told him Lily had made a sexual overture.

There, a decision made. And one that at least silenced Circumspect. Libido would have been silent as well if not for the fact that Nicole had fallen asleep and her head was on Lily's shoulder.

Yes, she'd seen some beautiful places and yes, she was worried about the coming weeks of tiring travel in places she'd never been. She tried to focus on those things but it didn't work. Instead she was inhaling the scent of Nicole's hair and lost in the pleasurable burning along her nerves as she breathed it in.

***

"Where are we?" Lily's voice from the passenger side of the compact rental car was groggy with sleep.

In the low illumination from the dashboard lights, Nicole watched her cup her hands in front of the air-conditioning vent to direct the flow onto her face. France was baking with a heat wave and even with it on full blast Nicole was still lightly perspiring. "About five kilometers from Dijon. Feel better?"

"Yes, thanks." Lily straightened in her seat.

"I felt a little off too for a while last night, but I still slept well. I'm thinking it was the salad at dinner. Probably what kept you up."

The day had begun with Lily not arriving first for breakfast. Nicole had found herself quelling irrational fears that somehow Lily was missing, and for the first time understood how people jumped to the worst possible conclusions. When Lily had appeared, ten minutes later, Nicole had felt a wave of relief, but her wan face had immediately alarmed her. In the nearly dozen mornings since they'd left Meredith, she'd never seen Lily anything other than bright-eyed and cheerful. An exception was bound to happen, of course, but she had been taken aback at how much she'd already come to rely on Lily's unflagging energy and bright "it's going to be a terrific day" smile over morning tea.

She'd done everything she could remember that her mother would do: offered antacids, club soda and soda crackers. She had stopped short of offering to tuck Lily into bed. The very idea made her throat too tight to talk. Besides, there had been no time for going back to bed. Another city, another event was always ahead.

"I think it was the salad too. I usually have a strong stomach. Thank you for driving." Lily resettled her seat belt and let out a tired breath.

"Kate would be impressed. Though she's not inclined to bicker with me at the moment. I sent her an iPad to help ease the boredom of bed rest." Nicole glanced at Lily but couldn't see much more than the silhouette of hair not quite in its usually tidy style.

"That was a sweet thing to do."

"I was attempting to avert matricide. At the moment I am Kate's favorite sister, she says."

Lily giggled. "My uncle used to tell me I was his favorite niece. It took me years to realize I was his only niece."

"Kate apparently thinks I won't figure out I'm her only sister. She persistently underestimates my deductive abilities."

"You're both your mother's daughter."

Nicole frowned. "What's that supposed to mean?"

"That's why you're so alike." Lily turned slightly in her seat toward Nicole. "You and Kate are peas in a pod."

Nicole couldn't keep her skepticism out of her tone when she asked, "Do you have evidence to support this hypothesis?"

"Purely observational."

"*Briefly* observational."

"You're both stubborn."

"A trait we share with almost all of the human race."

"You both know how to get what you want from life."

"I don't agree." Nicole glanced at the GPS unit's glowing display. She was learning to like the way the yellow map and large pink arrows gave her plenty of warning about the route.

"Don't you have what you want from life? Academic acclaim? Fame and fortune? A quiet place to think and family close?"

She had everything she wanted in life? Her leather jacket had stayed in the suitcase ever since the aborted outing in Edinburgh. No bars for Cole in Frankfurt, Bremen, Amsterdam or Brussels. Amsterdam had seemed an obvious place to make the desired connections, but after spending each evening either shopping, dining or going to the theater with Lily she'd forced herself to focus on neglected work. They'd found Shakespeare in the park in Bremen and the rousing rendition of *Pericles, Prince of Tyre* had been delightful. They'd cheered the hero and booed the villains while picnicking on cut sandwiches of wurst on thick pumpernickel. A dessert of large, sour pickles had proven effective relief from the heat.

So she hadn't gone out alone in Amsterdam, even though she knew that sex would cure her of this unfortunate fixation she had on Lily's body. Knowing what she needed to do but not doing it was a perfect example of the neural-biological disconnect. Psychology might also come into play. Regardless, she was unwilling to examine closely the idea that she might not want to be cured.

As to Lily's observation about the tidiness of Nicole's living arrangements she said, "I could do with my mother and sister just a little farther away. Some of my Indian relatives I would prefer on the moon. They have a long reach."

"They can influence you?"

"Not me—my mother. She'll get a letter or e-mail from one of her brothers, or my father's brother, full of recriminations for failing to hold me to my duty and it makes her manic for days. We have the same conversation we've been having since I was seventeen. I'm not ever going to endure an arranged marriage. I'm keeping my degrees and my work."

"Sounds to me like you've arranged your life the way you want it." Now Lily sounded smug.

"My objection to your premise wasn't about me, it was about my sister."

"Kate has what she wants."

"Kate is mercurial. She doesn't know what she wants. First it's ballet, then it's art history, then it's philosophy. None of it has resulted in a degree. Now she's unmarried, ungraduated and unemployed."

"Did Kate ever want a degree, a husband or a job?"

Nicole blinked. She wanted to protest that the question was absurd.

As if she sensed Nicole's uncertainty, Lily persisted, "You may want her to have those things, but I think what you want matters to her about as much as what your family in India wants matters to you. Like I said, you two are peas in a pod."

"Except when looking in a mirror."

"Superficial, an insignificant part of your DNA. You should know that, Professor Hathaway."

She wasn't used to being found inconsistent. She also wasn't used to being teased, which Lily's tone suggested. She was glad of the darkness of the car though even in daylight Lily would have had no way to see that Nicole had an absurd tingling in the region south of her stomach.

Lily had been rustling in her handbag. "I knew they were in there." She held out a small wrapped packet of crackers from breakfast. "Want one?"

"Sure." Nicole glanced away from the road long enough to reach for the cracker.

Their fingertips brushed.

Nicole swerved the car back into the center of her lane. "Sorry about that." She glanced at Lily.

Lily had an arm protectively over her stomach. "It's okay. You're a very good driver. Adapting to the other side of the road and all the different signage when you don't speak the language isn't easy."

Her pleasure at Lily's compliment left her more flushed— that or the air-conditioning was being even less successful. The GPS warned her about the upcoming turn toward their hotel in Dijon. She'd offered to drive after their bookstore event because Lily looked like she wanted to drop where she stood, but she had thought the drive would be entirely in daylight. She'd forgotten that Lily had warned her of the peculiarities of time zones and their use in Europe, which made clock time seem earlier than the sun's position. The dark hadn't unsettled her, though. If she'd known a GPS unit was so useful she'd have insisted that she really didn't need an assistant for the trip.

But if she had, Lily wouldn't be within arm's reach. Both arms' reach.

Stop it, she warned herself. You're not going to hold her. It's not going to happen.

"Look," Lily said. "To the right—that's a Roman highway, isn't it?"

As she completed the turn onto the road to central Dijon, she was able to give the crumbling structure of arches a quick look. "What's left of one, I'd say."

"Amazing." Lily was definitely feeling better, Nicole thought. She was amused by the little lilt in Lily's voice when she was going to give one of her quick sketches of a region. She'd learned she had no need of a guide book. All she had to do was ask Lily.

"Dijon is a mix of architectures, from medieval to Renaissance to nineteenth century. Our hotel is supposed to be one of the closest to the seat of the Dukes of Burgundy. We can see the ducal palace before we have to leave tomorrow, and possibly walk through the museum of fine arts. The *Musée des Beaux-Arts de Dijon*."

It was ridiculous to want Lily to speak more in French. It didn't matter what she said *en français*, the slightly more husky tone suited her. "I'd like that, though it'll be nice to sleep in."

"Me too. Shall we meet in the lobby at nine? We should leave for Lyon by one."

"We can probably find a quick lunch."

"Who needs lunch?" Lily gestured at the open fields to their left. "This is the French countryside. We'll picnic on bread, cheese and fruit as we drive."

"Sounds charming."

"Are you being sarcastic?"

"No, actually."

"I couldn't tell just from your voice."

"Do I always sound sarcastic?"

"Well, perhaps *sardonic* is a better descriptor."

"I wasn't aware that I tended toward either." She paused. "Okay, I realize that I sounded sardonic just then."

Lily laughed.

Nicole focused on the road and the increasingly narrow street. Lily's silence left Nicole to realize that in just a few minutes Lily had given her a vast insight into her sister, had mocked her for not having seen it for herself, and then pointed out Nicole could be grim and sarcastic, something Kate had accused her of. She'd have resented it from Kate, but why oh why did she not mind it at all from Lily?

It didn't matter what Lily said to anyone, it seemed, she got what she wanted but never gave offense. She'd convinced a surly German shopkeeper to accept her last British pounds for a purchase and by the end of the transaction he'd been one more happy, smiling male conquest. It extended to women as well, with more than one bookseller earnestly expressing an interest to work with Lily and Insignis again for future author tours. Waitstaff seemed to always provide Lily with excellent service. She was never haughty, though she'd chilled that reporter from the local Brussels news with a glance when he'd put his hand on her knee. Nicole had felt an unaccustomed rush of loathing for the man but doubted she could harm him more than Lily's withering glare.

Nicole had begun to wonder if Lily exuded some kind of unique pheromone that amplified the effect of her petite beauty and charming manner. High-powered pheromones might explain Nicole's own preoccupation with her.

They checked in smoothly with Lily speaking what sounded like excellent French to the smiling clerk. Two rooms, two keys and they were off to the lift.

Finally alone in her room, Nicole let tension roll out of her body. It was draining to be on her guard against revealing her attraction to Lily.

She was startled by a knock on the door.

Lily stood there with a sheepish smile. "We forgot to eat dinner. Aren't you famished?"

"Now that you mention it." That explained all the flutters in her stomach. Hunger, not imaginary butterflies.

"The hotel café is still open."

"Let me get my key."

When the elevator arrived it was occupied by a large family. Lily quickly squeezed in. "There's room," she said to Nicole.

Nicole stepped in and the doors closing quickly behind her jostled her into Lily. They stood, breast to breast, during the slow descent. Lily's gaze was on the floor in keeping with crowded elevator spacial dynamics. Nicole realized that Lily's head would nestle perfectly onto her shoulder. She closed her eyes, only for a moment, and imagined dancing with Lily. A long, slow dance that ended in kisses.

Pheromones. It had to be pheromones. Their special properties explained what was causing her physical response to Lily. The explanation failed, however, to give her any clue of what to do about it.

***

"Will this do?" Lily pointed at the displayed menu outside the little hotel restaurant. Anything to keep Nicole's gaze off her flushed face. Next time they were confronted with an elevator that crowded, she was taking the stairs. "Omelets all day, *ragoût de bœuf*, *soupe de poulet, melange…*"

"This will be fine. Something simple and a good night's sleep." Nicole opened the door that divided the restaurant from the lobby.

"*Pour deux*," Lily said to the young woman who greeted them. They were led to a table for two at a window facing one of the entrances to the ducal palace, just across a road paved in patterns of white stone. A few people lingered at a café on the other side, but otherwise the streets were quiet. "Is it Sunday?"

Nicole pulled her phone from her pocket with a look of surprise. "Apparently, travel can inhibit the signals from the hippocampus. Yes, it's Sunday."

Their server spoke more than adequate English but also endured Lily's French with a smile. It was passable for conversation but she knew her accent was distinctly American. Her plans had once included intensive language courses to work on her vocabulary and accent, but that would have to wait. These past two weeks had been engaging, exhausting and a great balm to her spirit, but even with ten more weeks to go she could hear the ticking of the clock. She had no clue what she would do once she returned Nicole to New Hampshire. She didn't want to think about that.

Tap water was delivered and she drank thirstily. Whatever it was that had made her sick the night before was waning, thankfully. Now she was mostly feeling the lack of sleep and looking forward to the simplicity of chicken soup. Whenever there was *salade niçoise* on the menu Nicole ordered it, so Lily wasn't surprised by her choice.

"Stomach okay?" Nicole asked.

"A good night's sleep, as you said. I'll avoid another face plant into bratwurst when we get back to Germany too. That sort of started the whole issue. All that wonderful rich food. So yummy."

"I'm very fond of apple pie and never understood the purpose of strudel when apple pie was already excellent." Nicole was gazing out the window toward the palace. "Now that I've had real strudel I understand the culinary necessity."

"Wasn't that bakeshop fun?" Their meals had been almost entirely comprised of walk-up fare, and eaten while walking or driving. Sitting at a table to eat was a treat. Lily realized how little she and Nicole had been face-to-face. "She told us it was the best strudel in Europe and she may have been right."

"I had presumed it was puffery." Nicole continued to look out the window.

The waitress returned with a small basket of sliced breads. In French she said, "Compliments of the house. I apologize that it's dry, but it's the last of today's delivery. The chef will throw it away tomorrow, but a little stale is very good with soup, *n'est ce pas?*"

Answering in French, Lily thanked her. "It's common in the United States to serve bread with a meal as well."

The waitress tossed back her straight black hair. "Bread and cheese. It doesn't take much more to make a woman happy."

"I can think of one or two things." She forced herself not to glance at Nicole.

"You'll have to tell me all about them." She left in response to the sharp *ting* of a bell from the kitchen.

Lily returned her attention to Nicole, who was still gazing out the window. Lily followed her gaze and could imagine herself sitting across the street in the warm night air, sipping a lovely red wine and nibbling at bread, cheese and fruit served on a well-scrubbed wooden shingle. The waitress was certainly on to something. She had far more grand dreams, but she hoped she never lost sight of how little it took to be happy.

Looking at Nicole's profile she wondered again why she never seemed happy. Or unhappy, for that matter. Was she ever ecstatic? Outraged? Only her intensity for her work, for its accuracy and meaning, proved that Nicole felt passion. She wondered what Nicole had been like as a child. Had she had tantrums, squealed with delight over candy or jumped in puddles?

She looked away before Nicole caught her staring. This café also reminded her of one she'd visited with Jenna and Kirsten. To them it had been slumming and they'd been condescending to the waitstaff. Uncle Damon had once told her that everything you needed to know about a person you could discern from how they treated waiters and clerks. Nicole was polite in a perfunctory, my-mother-taught-me way.

Nicole had turned from the window to sip her water. "What are you thinking about?"

"Not much," Lily evaded.

"You look pensive."

"I was thinking about what makes for happiness."

Absolutely serious, Nicole said, "Serotonin and dopamine, in proper quantities."

Lily smiled at the typical answer. "I don't understand why some people deliberately squelch their serotonin and dopamine, then. By disliking things that could make them happy."

"For example?"

"I was in a place like this once with some cousins and they were determined to find it beneath them. Even the water was unsuitable." Lily smiled her thanks at the server for her soup. She hoped Nicole didn't ask a follow-up—she hadn't meant to bring up family.

Oh, let her ask, she thought. You should just tell her. You ought to trust her objectivity and ability to draw a truthful conclusion by now. "This smells perfect. Exactly what I need."

Nicole wasted no time digging into her salad. "Was it an enforced family gathering?"

"No, I just have some bitchy cousins that I'm glad I won't see more of."

"Not even for weddings and funerals?" Nicole offered her the pepper grinder after lightly dusting her salad.

"Thank you, I love pepper in soup." Over the crunch of the grinder Lily said, "Highly doubtful. Our social circles no longer overlap."

Nicole focused on her salad and Lily thought she was safe until Nicole asked, several mouthfuls later, "What changed?"

She didn't think she could shrug it off. Nicole was studying her face and had probably already taken note of her pupil size, eye movements and number of swallows as her version of a truth detector. She delayed by savoring a spoonful of soup. Just salty enough, fragrant with herbs and a touch of white wine. "At one point my parents had a lot of money. They lost it all and have passed away. I can't afford their circle. How's the salad?"

"Very good. The feta cheese is flavorful and fresh." Nicole speared an olive. "If you could afford their circle would they welcome you? I think not, from your expression."

Lily bit her lip to keep from asking why Nicole posed a question when she already thought she knew the answer. "No, they wouldn't. My parents were less than ethical and their financial dealings hurt other people." Her voice threatened to break, but she forced out the next words. "Some people firmly believe I was part of the swindle."

Nicole's eyebrows went up. "Their belief can't be rooted in fact."

Lily tried to squelch the tears she could feel building. So much for feeling like she was moving on. "It's not, believe me. I wish I could figure out what to say to make people believe it."

"It's not in your words, but in the way you act. Unless you're a masterfully skilled con woman, and they do exist, I've seen too far a range of your body language and casual interactions to believe you could be persistently unethical. I don't mean taking an extra packet of saltines at a restaurant that you don't need until later." Nicole put down her fork. "Though your lowered lashes and slight flush when you do so betrays the chemical shift in your frontal lobe."

Trying for humor, Lily asked, "Translation?"

"Studies of people with damage to their frontal lobe…" Nicole lifted one eyebrow. "You're not interested in all that."

"I'm interested in the short version." Lily knew her innocent blink wasn't up to her usual best, but she tried.

Incredibly, Nicole's lips curved into a wry smile. "You do something that makes you feel guilty and your frontal lobe manifests the confusion with physical cues. I've observed that you give off guilt cues over crackers. I'm doubtful, therefore, that you could mask those cues over large sums of money."

It was disconcerting to find that Nicole had studied her so closely, but she was a scientist. She probably viewed her supportive statement as a product of logical deduction and observation, but Lily was content to take it as a show of faith. "So you're saying I'll never make a good thief."

"I wouldn't say that." She sounded philosophical. "You could be a jewel thief who couldn't lie about her activities. Which means you'd need to be a very good jewel thief to avoid having to answer questions."

"Well, I wish everyone thought the way you do. They don't." Her voice cracked.

There was a long silence during which Nicole ate nothing and Lily stirred her cooling soup and didn't dare look up.

Finally, Nicole said, "Have I upset you?"

"No. It's not you," Lily said immediately. She put her hand to her face to quell her quivering lower lip. "It's just—some people won't move on. And I didn't do anything wrong."

Nicole reached across the small table to briefly touch Lily's arm. "The human attention span is highly personalized, but the majority of people do move on after any and all tragedies."

Unnerved by the contact and the unmistakable kindness in Nicole's eyes—an expression she had thought an impossibility— Lily blurted out, "Uncle Damon probably told you I was doing him a favor but I'm the one who needed the favor. I really needed to get away." She stole a quick glance at Nicole, but her gaze was now fixed on the table. "It was last minute and I did need a job and I think he would have hired just about anyone, but still—this has been a godsend to me."

"You are a vast improvement over the previous choices." Nicole cleared her throat. "I had thought there was no reason I couldn't do this by myself. I'm used to being independent. Given that twenty minutes ago I didn't know what day it was has caused me to reexamine my thinking."

Swamped by too many emotions to sort out, Lily took refuge in mock incredulity. "Are you trying to say you changed your mind?"

"Your tone implies this never happens. I frequently receive new data and revise earlier hypotheses."

"I see." She glanced at Nicole in time to see one eyebrow lifted again.

"I've revised several so far. For example, though I've done lectures for years now, I'm surprised how tiring speaking in public is when the communication is bidirectional. Students take notes and leave. I'm not used…" Again her lips curved into a wry smile. "I had not adequately assessed how draining nonoptional social banter is."

"That's because you're an introvert. I'm an extrovert. Solitude is very hard on me." She cleared her throat and hoped Nicole would take up the red herring.

"Be that as it may, to feel persistently alert and energetic while managing the details that you cover would have been a serious challenge."

It was very Nicole that she didn't quite admit she couldn't have met the challenge. Lily wasn't sure what to say.

"You were an excellent choice," Nicole continued. "If I were running for public office I would want you in charge of events, staging and protocol."

Lily's breath caught. "That was the career I was hoping…Damn it." She wiped away a tear.

Nicole lapsed into silence while Lily stirred her now-tepid soup and forced down a few more spoonfuls. When Lily finally murmured a thank you, Nicole's answering "You're welcome," was equally quiet.

Not much later they rode up in a thankfully otherwise unoccupied elevator to their floor. Lily was certain Nicole knew how hard she was trying not to cry in front of her. She had thought her wounds were healing, but they were still as raw as the day she'd left New York. How could she expect other people to move on when she hadn't done so herself?

***

Standing alone in her room, realizing it was still early, Nicole thought about getting out her work. But she had a feeling all she would do is stare at the pages and think about Lily. Tears were a biochemical reaction, but she had thought her own understanding of their effect on those who saw someone in tears would have reduced her instinct to respond. She was able to withstand the sight of her mother's tears, after all. But Lily's…That she'd managed only to touch her lightly—an appropriate, measured gesture of sympathy, she hoped—had been a victory over a compulsion to pull Lily into her arms and plead with her not to cry and to say how she could help.

Could the impulse be maternal in some way? She had felt intensely protective yet helpless. The clash of emotions had temporarily trumped her logic—she'd been certain that kisses would make everything better, though she knew perfectly well that when kisses affected a hurt person's perception of the level of their pain it was only when the kisses came from a trusted source, like a mother. Like a lover.

Lovers they would never be, and the last thing she wanted was for Lily to see her as a mother figure. She was only six years older. Certainly she had more credentials in a field of study and more years spent in a career, but Lily had an expertise of her own, and the experience of tragedy. The precise nature of that tragedy was an unknown, and she disliked being without adequate data.

The lack of data was something she could easily rectify, she thought.

A search with the browser on her phone turned up so many Lily Smiths that it was hopeless. Trying a different tack, she searched for Lily Smith plus Damon Linden, publisher and uncle. When the picture of Lillian Linden-Smith showed up at the top of the results at first she thought she didn't have the right person. The age was right, though, so she zoomed in and there were Lily's eyes. Lily with luxuriant red hair in a photo from her Wellesley yearbook. Lily beautiful and smiling, voted most likely to negotiate world peace.

She didn't remember sitting down at the desk but when she had finished reading all she cared to, she realized she was leaning heavily on it and holding her phone so tight her hand ached. A measured, well-researched news summary at NPR of the events of Lily's life for the last eighteen months or so had left Nicole stunned. She recalled the financial scandal and the headlines about the suicide-by-pills of the two principals of the fraud, but hadn't followed the case after that. The latest update had covered the dismissal of the case against Lily for lack of grounds to go to trial.

All that was enough to derail a person's life, but Lily's losses on all fronts had been magnified by the intense scrutiny of one particular journalist. Article after article after article at a cable television network reported every new development no matter how minor, recycled known information, and asked questions as if there were no trustworthy answers, creating a persistent and false sense of mystery.

The articles were so full of syllogistic fallacies and cognitive biases that Nicole looked up the reporter's credentials. Strike that, she thought. Merrill Boone was no journalist. She was a lawyer with a degree from a small Alabama college who had made a name for herself with her brand of accusatory fact-finding in high-profile cases. A few clicks down she learned that while a trial attorney Boone had been cited several times by appellate courts for overzealous tactics and a clear disregard for the rules of evidence.

Those traits, Nicole supposed, made Boone perfect for television.

So this television entertainer had decided that since the Linden-Smiths who were guilty of fraud were dead, she would devote her energy to the one who was alive: Lily, whom Nicole had first believed to be a preprogrammed robot. Nicole didn't know when she'd stopped thinking of her as a Stepford Wife in the making nor when she'd realized that she was not traveling with a plastic and inauthentic Barbie clone.

She put down her phone and paced the room, her brain furiously turning over new data. Her physical response was out of all proportion with the situation. Her respiration was elevated. She felt a little dizzy, even, and adrenaline made it impossible to work or sleep. Maybe there was a fitness room in the hotel. Even if it was a lone stationary cycle or treadmill she could work out her stress.

She heard the shower start in the room next door. Had Lily cried herself out? Did she have a headache now? Was she taking off her clothes?

With a wry shrug at her reflection in the tiny mirror over the dresser, she noted that the distance between concern and lust appeared to be a very short one. Staying in her room to fantasize about water cascading over Lily's body would waste what was left of the evening. She needed to rid herself of her misplaced feelings. She'd been a fool to turn down the woman in Edinburgh. It would have been a fair and equitable exchange without all of…whatever this was.

If the tropes of movies that Kate so loved were to be believed, she should buy a quart of ice cream and eat it from the container with an oversized spoon. Or go to a bar and drink too much, then wake Lily up just in time to vomit on her. Or pick out a wildly inappropriate sexual partner—perhaps even one for whom she had to pay—only to be caught *in flagrante delicto* by Lily.

Dijon had not struck her as having a wild night life, certainly not on a Sunday night, so a search for a sexual companion wasn't going to be successful. She didn't feel like a point-and-mime conversation with the desk clerk about a possibly nonexistent fitness room, but she could go for a walk. When she got back she'd call home and top that off with a literal cold shower.

She would sleep. She would find perspective.

Given the heat, she slipped into the gym shorts and the thin T-shirt she'd brought along for exercise. The street in front of their hotel was foot traffic only and the narrow passages leading into the grand entrance of the palace were brightly lit. Following one of them she emerged onto a large plaza that could have easily mustered five hundred men and horses. There were a few people around, mostly seeming to be in charge of children running through two bubbling fountains.

She decided a walk all the way around would be safe and told herself not to wish Lily were with her to exclaim over the classical sculptures and pediments and the remaining gothic tower of the palace's keep. It didn't matter what sights they chose to see, Lily was fascinated by all of them. You didn't come out here to think about Lily, she reminded herself.

She made the complete circuit around the palace grounds at a brisk clip and debated which anecdotes of the trip she would tell her mother. She decided not to mention that Lily had had a touch of food poisoning. It would only make her mother worry. She could talk about the lecture host in Brussels who had been determined to use the first thirty minutes of the time slot for his own presentation, but if she did, she'd have to explain that Lily had intervened, taken him aside and after their conversation he'd been covered in smiles.

She had watched it all from the podium. Was that when she'd realized that Lily was handling situations in ways that she could not?

Stop thinking about Lily, she told herself. You brought work with you—think about that. The study she was reviewing had inconsistencies in its data the authors hadn't highlighted. There were so many that the pages were crowded with her notes. Between signing books and writing notes her left hand was sore. She'd mentioned it yesterday and Lily had returned with a small hot/cold pack.

Well. So much for not thinking about Lily. She had to get the woman back in the proper place in her thoughts.

Leaving the plaza where she was fairly certain she had entered she was relieved to see the sign for the restaurant they'd dined in earlier, with their hotel just beyond. As she passed the street door it suddenly opened and she jumped aside.

The woman who had opened the door exclaimed, "*Pardon!*"

"It's all right," Nicole answered the woman. She wished she'd asked Lily to teach her the French for "I don't speak French."

"*Oh, bon soir*. You are out for a walk?"

She recognized the young woman who had served them. "Yes. It's very warm."

"It's never like this in *Septembre*. The global warming perhaps? Where is your pretty girlfriend?"

"She's not my…" Nicole hesitated. Perhaps the woman only meant friend who was a female, not a paramour.

"*Non?* I could have sworn you were, ah…Couple." The young woman stepped just a little closer, her shoulder-length black hair gleaming under the streetlight.

Nicole laughed. "No, she's not…" She gave what she hoped was an explanatory shrug of exactly what Lily wasn't.

"*Non? Zut*, it is so hot tonight." She undid two buttons on her blouse and fanned the fabric against her breasts. "What a pity. Her French was very good for an *Américain* and she flirts like a *femme Française*. So she is not—" She gave a meaningful shrug. "But you are?"

A frank physical evaluation caught Nicole off guard. She wasn't wearing the jacket. She felt naked. Then her lately sex-obsessed brain provided her with a graphic image of ripping the blouse the rest of the way open.

There was a roaring in her ears. She tried to speak in Cole's direct, confident way, but she sounded too breathless—too needy. "I am."

"*Mon nom est Estelle.*"

Though she didn't feel at all like the persona, she said, "I'm Cole."

"You are staying in the hotel, Cole?"

Nicole nearly said yes, but Lily was right next door and though probably asleep, there was no guarantee.

"Oh, but we would not want to wake your companion, would we? Perhaps you would like a drive? The countryside is beautiful."

***

This is a bad idea. And yet she was doing it anyway.

They hadn't gone more than a kilometer before Estelle turned onto an unpaved road, then glided to a halt under a canopy of trees. She got out when Estelle did, desperately telling herself that thought was so difficult because of the loss of blood to her brain due to swollen genitalia. But that fact did nothing to change her feeling of being out of control. The situation put the lie to the idea that knowledge was power.

Estelle had taken a blanket from the backseat and was walking a little distance under the trees to spread it out. "We can, ah…moon bathe?"

Before Nicole could protest—even if she wanted to—Estelle was naked and seated, legs tucked under her, on the blanket. A pale figure in the moonlight, she was very desirable.

With a beguiling smile, she held up her hands. "Your turn."

She let Estelle pull her down to her knees. "I prefer to keep my clothes on at first."

Jacket or not, the heady mix of lust and confidence sent a flame of pure desire down her spine. She held Estelle tight in her arms and kissed her hard. Estelle let out a welcoming purr as they stretched out on the blanket.

Somewhere in the heated exchange of kisses and caresses, Nicole ended up on top with Estelle arching underneath her.

"*Oui. Ici.*" With a throaty laugh Estelle guided Nicole's hand down her stomach. "Here is where I want you."

Estelle's hair smelled of coffee and lavender and her inner thighs felt like silk. Cole knew what to do. Her fingers toyed and teased, and she liked the way Estelle's voice caught in the back of her throat. "Do you want me to do more than this?"

"No more teasing!" Estelle ground down on Nicole's hand.

"But you like it, I think."

Estelle's nails dug into Nicole's back. She nipped at Estelle's ear in answer. Their mutual arching toward one another moved Nicole's knees between Estelle's legs and she dipped her fingers deeper and deeper. Estelle's tight breathing and rising frenzy were exactly the response she wanted. *There, yes right there*, hummed through her mind.

Regardless of their native language, anyone would have understood the meaning of Estelle's throaty cry just as clearly as Nicole did. Feeling her relax, Nicole let out a pleased laugh and began to raise her head. But Estelle wasn't ready to relax. She yanked Nicole's shorts down with a firm, "Your turn, *cherie.*"

Her face buried in the crook of Estelle's neck, Nicole was stunned by how eagerly she opened herself to Estelle's touch. Her wrist was caught in an awkward bend under her, but she ignored it. Places that hadn't been touched in far too long seemed to melt from a wave of heat.

Cole usually didn't…

Cole isn't here, she thought.

Her mind blurred as nerves she had too long ignored woke and sent tingles along her back and shoulders and set alight sparkles behind her closed lids. It felt so good to be touched and was so much what she needed. The encouraging whispers of "*Oui, oui,*" didn't keep her from imagining a different woman underneath her. Lily spoke French. It could be Lily touching her. She wanted it to be Lily.

When she collapsed on her back, shorts akimbo and T-shirt pulled up above her breasts, the first thing she saw was a bright sliver of moon overhead and a horizon dappled with stars.

People had probably been doing this in these fields for thousands and thousands of years to celebrate the moon, the crops, or simply their bodies. With the exception of her aching wrist, it was supposed to feel this good. Every evolutionary development preserved this system of neural action and response.

Stop that, a voice suspiciously like Lily's whispered in her head. *Enjoy...Can't some things just be simple?*

Estelle rested her head on Nicole's stomach. A warm breeze stirred the trees. "You are thinking of her?"

"Yes." The night was too sultry and beautiful to lie to herself.

"She is for men?"

"Yes. And she thinks I am too."

Estelle's laugh was low and knowing. "She is confused, certainly."

"She's not the only one," Nicole said quietly.

There was no hiding, snuggled on a blanket with a desirable woman, both of them languid in their own afterglow. Were good decisions ever made under the influence of moonlight?

She cradled her slightly swollen wrist and told herself it would heal. Lily was resilient and strong and didn't need her help to get on with her life. Lily didn't need her for anything and, likewise, she wouldn't need Lily once this trip was over. She'd just proven that.

Of course she had.

CHAPTER TEN

Lily leaned sleepily against a file cabinet outside the sound booth and hoped nobody thought she was yawning because Nicole's interview at the English audience radio station was dull. She had heard these questions and answers quite a lot, but her fatigue was about a lumpy mattress and noisy neighbors, not Nicole's talking points. It wasn't much past breakfast and the Global Radio Switzerland offices were stuffy and warm. But for the bright posters of pop stars, it would be as drab as a police station holding room. Aside from Nicole and the interviewer on the other side of the soundproof glass, the only other person in Lily's sight was a nervous-looking woman peering at a computer.

"Pardon me? Could you say that again?" Nicole's tone grew noticeably sharper and Lily shook herself awake.

The unctuous radio host, who'd eagerly asked for Lily's business card and had wanted to write down her name and e-mail "in case he had follow-up questions for the doctor," looked exceedingly smug. "I was asking if your work is of interest to the scientific community and not just women."

Lily frowned. She didn't care for his dismissive tone. She'd written him off as a narcissist and not terribly perceptive. He'd accepted her sly introduction of herself as "Passepartout" without comment. Nicole had had to smother a laugh.

"My book is a scholarly work that women outside the sciences have become interested in."

"It seems to preach the idea that women put forth, that life is about marriage, about going two-by-two into the ark. This makes women happy and sells candy and greeting cards."

"Science is not a religion." Nicole's voice held a waspish undercurrent. "It is a fact that people with successful relationships live longer, men benefitting even more than women."

"The great thing about facts is that there's no one answer."

Lily wanted to smack that superior look off his narrow little face. Nicole looked momentarily speechless, then her jaw set and she reminded Lily of both Indira and Kate.

"Saying a fact is not true does not stop science from working. Saying the sun's rays do not cause skin cancer will not stop melanoma." Lily could hear the drumming of Nicole's fingers over the speakers. "Perhaps you need to experience facts in order to believe them. In this case, however, you would need to enter into a significant relationship again. You've been married three—or is it four times already?"

The little man's sneer increased. Who had booked them on a program with a misogynist? Was this what passed for early morning drive time entertainment in Geneva?

"I'm flattered you looked up my bio—"

"I didn't. Just an educated guess based on biopsychological observation. You would need to have one successful relationship, I think, before you could speak anecdotally to the value of relationships. Until then, your resistance to the data could be too easily dismissed as sour grapes."

The woman at the computer spluttered with laughter and quickly dampened it.

"By your argument, Dr. Hathaway, I would need to try murder to disapprove of it."

"Not at all. That's a populist *reductio ad absurdum*. But it's not unexpected that you would equate your experience of marriage with murder."

This time the woman at the desk laughed outright. Lily caught her eye and shrugged.

"If women had their way, they would run men's lives like Nazis."

"I suggest," Nicole said in low, slow voice, "that Godwin's Law can be applied to a radio interview. You've conceded my point and our time together is over."

Lily wasn't sure what had happened. She replayed that last bit in her head and still didn't know.

Nicole was smiling, though, as she left the booth. "Ready, Passepartout?"

Lily giggled. "Indeed I am. Next stop Frankfurt." Once they were clear of the office she said in a low voice, "There were three more minutes left."

"I'm sure he has more to say. He has accepted the sound of his voice as an ersatz acolyte."

"What is Godwin's Law?"

"Most simply, the first person to invoke Nazis loses the point and the discussion is closed."

"Given the way commentators bandy it about, Godwin's Law isn't universal."

"Invoking a specter of genocide in any situation not involving genocide means logic no longer applies to subsequent debate points." Nicole shifted her satchel from her left to her right hand and winced.

"Is that still bothering you?"

"It's getting better."

"No it's not." Lily watched the indicator lights on the elevator panel. "Here's the car keys. I'll join you in a minute."

"Do we have time to waste?"

"You saved us three minutes already, Phileas Fogg."

With a shake of her head Nicole turned left out of the building onto the still quiet side street. Lily jaywalked to the chemist on the corner.

A few minutes later, Lily leaned across the driver's seat to hand Nicole a white paper bag imprinted with the name of a ubiquitous Swiss pharmacy. "All you have to do is fasten the Velcro. I also got you some Nurofen—ibuprofen—and at night you should ice it. I'm concerned that it's your writing hand."

Nicole rustled in the bag as Lily settled into the driver's seat and started the car. "I could have picked it out myself."

"I put it on Insignis's tab. You've gotten carpal tunnel by relentlessly signing books. Not to mention the smackdown you just delivered on that jerk of a talking head. "

After peering at the picture of the wrist brace, Nicole opened the package. "This will help. But it didn't happen signing books and I took him down with words. I slipped getting out of the shower."

"They don't have to know that. Let's keep it simple. Sometimes, simple is better." She glanced at the GPS and made a quick right turn out of the parking lot. Traffic in Geneva wasn't crowded, but Swiss drivers seemed to have two speeds: stopped and accelerator on the floor. She who hesitated could sit all day trying to make a turn.

She was pleased they were a little ahead of schedule. Switzerland was a beautiful country to drive through and she was glad not to be frazzled for the long drive to Frankfurt. Lake Geneva came into view repeatedly from the A1 until they left Lausanne. After that it seemed as if around every corner was another snow-dusted peak.

They'd agreed on a radio station that played "the best of classic rock and oldies." The selection had been varied and she contentedly hummed along to Seal's "Kiss from a Rose."

When it segued into Cher's "Believe" Nicole said, "I refuse to accept the definition of this song as an oldie. I was in college when it was popular, and that wasn't *that* long ago."

"I was in high school. It was the theme of the freshman prom."

Nicole made a dismissive noise that reminded Lily vividly of Indira Hathaway. "I'm only thirty-two."

"I'm only twenty-six and 'Poker Face' is an oldie to somebody."

"I'm not sure that's a comforting thought." Nicole wrote something on a paper and underlined it. "I am going to simplify my life and reject this one. The authors have forgotten I also teach and therefore can figure out when someone is trying to get me to do their work for them."

"I never tried that on my profs." She stole a glance at another mountain, capped with snow that sparkled under the bright sunlight—majestic was the only word for it.

"You have a brain and you use it. Not all students meet both of those standards." She tied up the papers and slipped them back into the folder.

"I did try it out on a librarian once and got big demerits."

Nicole laughed as she pushed the folder into the satchel at her feet. "Librarians are not to be trifled with. By the way, I have about five inches of papers I could send home, if we can fit a postal service stop in somewhere soon."

"Sure. There's probably time tomorrow morning."

Nicole was looking out the window. "What a beautiful country. I hate to say it, but the Granite State is a little outclassed."

"You might not want to admit to that when you get home."

"Can I ask you a personal question?" At Lily's nod, she went on, "Will you ever let your hair go back to its natural color?"

Lily's hand clenched on the wheel. After their discussion at the restaurant in Dijon she had expected Nicole to figure out who she was—she was a researcher after all. But when Nicole had said nothing for the rest of their time in France or their two days in Geneva, she'd wondered. But it was good they weren't face-to-face because she didn't want Nicole to see her fighting tears again. "I don't know. That depends on other people."

Nicole seemed to be choosing her words with care. "I can't imagine letting other people decide the color of my hair."

She wasn't about to let Nicole pass judgment on her. She retorted, "You haven't had the kinds of people I've been dealing with on your case twenty-five-eight."

"You're quite right. I meant—"

"You let your mother determine some of the things you will and won't do."

"Also true."

"Why do you live with your mother?"

"Is this about me?"

Lily kept her gaze on the rapidly moving expressway. It was going to be a long drive back to Frankfurt. Her anger was close to the surface, she realized. Was she entering a new, clichéd stage of grief? "I'm just—"

"I don't live with my mother. I live in the home that is half mine, according to my stepfather's will. He was afraid that after he died his family—who weren't exactly welcoming of his foreign bride and 'ethnic' child—would try to take the house back. It's been in the family a long, long time. He left half to me and half to my mother. Her half passes to Kate, creating equal inheritances in the end."

"He was a very fair-minded man."

"He was. So I view it as my home, not my mother's house that I continue to live in. Neither of us is a guest of the other. As long as I make no attempt to influence how she keeps the gardens and I have my office at the university to go to, we are successful housemates."

"But all of that is now destabilized."

"Indeed. Kate will be with us for…some time." Nicole sounded nonchalant, a tone so rare for her Lily suspected she felt anything but nonchalant.

"My parents…" Lily swallowed. "If they were alive I don't know that I could live with them. Even if none of that…None of that had happened. I always planned to branch out on my own. Maybe because I was fairly independent growing up. My first complete sentence, according to my mother was, 'I can do it myself.'"

"That doesn't surprise me."

"My parents made sure I went to school, had clothes, food, and that's more than some kids get. But the rest of the time I was an afterthought." She couldn't help the bitter twist in her voice.

"I surmised that due to their treatment of you."

Lily had thought she'd read everything a person could find on the Internet about her, and nothing suggested her parents had been distant—Merrill Boone's narrative went exactly the opposite of that. She was supposedly a much loved and pampered child for whom they had desperately wanted to buy entry into elite society. As that spoiled brat, she had turned a blind eye to her parents' source of income, and/or she was a participant in the whole scheme, groomed to take over the family business. Never mind that a basic robbing-Peter-to-pay-Paul Ponzi scheme couldn't live long enough to become a family business. "Where did you read about this?"

"I didn't read it. You are an intelligent, talented person, and you got those genes from them. Regardless of their innate intelligence they launched a criminal enterprise, the discovery of which was inevitable. Every criminal act they undertook for their greed was a sentence on your head, at a minimum the loss of the family name. I was adopted into the Hathaway family, and I understand what an asset a family name can be. Even crime bosses and serial criminals usually take steps to separate their family from their businesses to preserve value in the family name much the way a corporation seeks to protect its brand."

Nicole's tone was the even, measured delivery of facts that she used in her lectures. "Your parents escaped the inevitable sentence for their crimes and left you to face their consequences. Their fall from grace, loss of assets, property, good name, it was all foreseeable and they didn't protect you from any of it. Unless they were given to vast self-deception that belies their intelligence, they could not have loved you to have left you to such a fate."

Lily was aware of feeling very cold, then her stomach churned with a burning heat.

Nicole made a sound of regret, then from far away, Lily heard her say, "Pull over to the side of the road." A moment later, more forcefully, "Pull over, Lily."

She did as Nicole said and watched Nicole's fingers press the emergency blinker and turn the key. The car went silent except for the sound of traffic zooming past them and the high whine of someone trying to hold in the sound of her heart breaking.

Some minutes later she was aware of something wet against her eyes, but it was at least another minute before she realized that it was the fabric that covered Nicole's shoulder, soaked with her tears.

In spite of the center console, Nicole had one arm around her in an awkward embrace, holding her.

She knew what Nicole said was true, but had never allowed that truth—that her parents had simply not loved her—to form in her mind. She'd been able to describe the relationship as aloof, distant, and even that they loved her "in their own way."

Pushing Nicole away, she said, "We're on a tight schedule. We don't have time for this." She realized then that her face was a mess and she gratefully accepted the tissue Nicole proffered.

"Let me drive for a while."

Looking at the narrow shoulder where they were parked, she shook her head. "There's no room to open the door—and this is a really unsafe place to be. I can drive." She proved her words by starting the car and increasing speed until a considerate driver slowed enough to let her move into the lane.

But her hands began to shake almost immediately so she took the next exit and made a right turn into a petrol station. "You take over and I'll have a snack."

"No problem."

The bracing, cool air cleared her head somewhat. As she passed Nicole at the rear of the car, she was surprised when Nicole pulled her into her arms. She wanted to melt to nothing, lose herself completely in the warmth.

"I'm very sorry." Nicole's words were warm in her ear. "I didn't think I would trigger such an enormous emotional response."

Don't go limp, she told herself. She had thought that if Nicole held her like this she would be overcome with lust, but there wasn't even a hello from Libido. She felt something else and it was as bad—possibly worse. She tried for a joke. "Were you thinking I'd be blasé about the subject?"

Nicole sighed, squeezed her one last time and then let her go. "I wasn't thinking. I was…being curious. I thought you had already sorted out your parents' behavior."

"Sometimes situations aren't ready for science…yet."

Going onward to the driver's door, Nicole said, "We'll debate that another time."

Finally letting herself go limp in the passenger seat, Lily fumbled with the seat belt as Nicole turned them back toward the expressway. "Crying is exhausting."

Nicole touched her lightly on the leg before returning her focus to driving. The feeling of relief and letting go was intense, but it was the gentle warmth of Nicole's touch that was the last thing Lily remembered before she slept.

***

With a long sigh, Lily pulled back into traffic. She glanced in the rearview mirror as much to watch Nicole disappear through the huge doors as to make sure she wasn't going to get ticketed for her brief stop in a clearly marked no parking zone outside the massive convention hall.

Even though they had left Geneva almost an hour ahead of schedule, Nicole was barely on time for her signing slot on the last day of the Frankfurt Book Festival. Sobbing on Nicole's shoulder had turned out to be very ill-timed—she'd woken up a short time later to find Nicole caught in the mother of all traffic jams caused by an overturned vehicle. It had happened just a few minutes before they arrived on the scene. But for her weep-fest they would have been ahead of the crash and on their way.

She quickly stashed the car in a nearby car park and ran back to the venue. Their first stop in Frankfurt, exactly a week ago, seemed more like last year, and her mind was reeling with everything they'd experienced since, from the quiet walled cities of Belgium to the soft countryside of France to the cacophony of the traffic jam that had closed the highway. Though Lily had felt like screaming, Nicole had remained resigned and calm.

Using the gigantic Hammering Man as a landmark, she found the closest side entrance to the exposition building and showed her floor pass. The signing venue was in the far end of the hall and if today's crowd was anything like that on the first day of the festival Nicole was going to be swamped.

Hurrying past row after row of publishers of everything from autobiographies to political treatises to cookbooks to science-fiction epics, she wished she'd worn her exercise shoes. By the time she skirted the long queues of book enthusiasts waiting for signatures from their favorite authors she was in a dead sweat. Not feeling her freshest, she tried to compose her expression and approach Nicole's table with some kind of decorum.

There were four women at the table, all talking at once. A line of seventy to eighty more waited within the stanchions that led to "3:00-4:30—Dr. Nicole Hathaway, *Love by the Numbers*."

"You made it," Nicole said in a low voice.

"Wait until I turn in the invoice for the parking lot. It's going to cost more than the hotel in Geneva did." She pushed her handbag under the table and then inserted herself into the line to create a break. While Nicole finished signing and a brief chat with one woman, Lily spoke to the next in line, asked her to open her book to the title page and when the table cleared, to step forward and tell Dr. Hathaway how she'd like the book signed. With a little delaying chitchat she got the bodies at the table down to one so that Nicole could hear more clearly. A little order went a long way and the line moved more predictably for the next forty-five minutes. It cleared further when the four p.m. scheduled appearance by a megastar horror writer began.

Nicole slumped in her chair and rubbed her wrist. "I think you can sit down now. We've been outshone."

"Do you want some ice for that? I'm sure I can find some."

"No, but if you have some water, I'd be glad of that."

"I'll go get some."

Nicole briefly grasped her arm. "No, don't go—it's okay." She smiled at the next woman, who said something eager in German.

Lily thanked the woman and translated the praise as, "She says that you made her realize she might be happy again. Please sign the book for Elise, spelled like the Beethoven."

"I'm pleased to hear that," Nicole said automatically. Lily translated it back and the woman departed, smiling and nodding.

"None of your predecessors spoke multiple languages. It's been a great help."

"Thank you. I think you could have managed, however."

"Yes, but not easily."

Maybe Nicole was not quite the "moody shit" that Kate had described after all. Her moods were for the most part consistent—steady and stable like oatmeal. To Kate, who was more like a platter of fruit ranging from sweet to sour, Nicole would seem bland. But after the scene in the car, and the insightful, unsparing analysis of her parents' actions, Lily realized that Nicole not only knew more about love as a science, her devotion to truth was a kind of love in itself. Truth was the backbone of justice, she mused. On that basis alone, compared to her parents, Nicole was the grand suzerain of all things love.

She had to grant that Nicole now made more of an effort to talk with people rather than at them, and she'd adapted to Lily acting as a translator, not questioning when Lily had pointed out that Nicole should continue eye contact with the speaker while Lily translated. That way it didn't become a three-way conversation. In English, Nicole had also adapted to "nonoptional social banter." Lily wondered if it was still calculated as an obligation or if that little bit of warmth in her expression was actually real. Had the trip changed Nicole at all? She simply could not tell what the woman was thinking. Red, sore eyes and swollen sinuses didn't help her focus either.

After a stretch of several minutes with no additional readers in line, leaving Nicole to have a prolonged chat with the last reader, Lily realized she'd spent the time staring at Nicole's hands and listening to the rise and fall of her voice. Earlier, with Nicole's arms around her, Libido had been blessedly silent. Now Libido was wide awake and ogling Nicole's fingers, but, Lily informed Libido firmly, she wasn't going to act like one of Nicole's case studies. All that mattered to her was the eventual good reference down the line in some new profession where no one cared that her full name was Lillian Linden-Smith. Certain she'd initially been graded as an academic featherweight, it was a relief to know that Nicole saw her in a more favorable light. No doubt her emotional breakdown had taken away some points, though.

All she wanted was to be "that assistant" in future years. Good driver. Spoke several languages. End of story.

Libido continued to watch Nicole's hands move. Lily crossly reminded herself of the To Do list. Navigate to hotel. Check in. Get good night's sleep. Arrive airport seven a.m. for flight to Madrid. Libido suggested they find the well-documented Frankfurt gayborhood and plan to sleep on the plane.

Nicole had said something and was clearly waiting for an answer. "I'm sorry, I missed that."

"We're nearly done, aren't we?"

"I expect someone to come along and shoo us away any moment. Do you want that water now?"

Nicole smiled. "You are persistently thoughtful."

Was that another compliment? Had she accidentally bought Nicole ibuprofen with happy pill on the side? "I'm not sure how to take the modifier."

"You don't forget details. You remind me of my mother."

Lily managed a pleased smile. Part of her was pleased—Indira Hathaway was a strong, intelligent woman and she didn't mind the comparison on that level. But being compared to a mother that Nicole seemed to see as overbearing? She covered her confusion with a forced smile and, "Still not sure how to take that."

Nicole tipped her head slightly as if consulting an inner Google search for the proper emotional response. "My mother is very careful of details."

She scrabbled her handbag out from under the table and headed for the food vendors. "Back with water shortly," she said over her shoulder.

She heard Nicole say something in answer, but it didn't register. Her emotions were all over the place. *Don't cry*, she told herself. *You silly girl, you have nothing to cry about.*

***

Nicole called after Lily, "Why don't I just come with you?" but Lily sped away. Perhaps she knew where the shortest line might be. She seemed to always know things like that.

A reader rushed up and said in French-accented English, "I was so afraid I'd missed you."

The voice was reminiscent of her roll across the grass in France, but the slight, mid-thirties man bore no resemblance to the sleek and playful Estelle. "You're just in time."

He stage-whispered across the table, "I love the fact that your research covered same-sex couples. You have so many homophobes in America I'm surprised they let you print it."

"In America nobody needs permission from anyone to print a book. Just the means and will to do it. How would you like me to sign the book?"

"To my boyfriend Fritz. We've been together eight years now."

"Congratulations." Out of the corner of her eye she saw Lily approaching with two water bottles, but someone had intercepted her. "Best of luck to you both."

She handed the book to the reader and glanced over at Lily. A middling-height man who nevertheless towered over Lily looked upset. She could hear snatches of the conversation, but it appeared to be in German. Lily had confessed her German was not much better than middle school vocabulary, but the lack of understanding didn't account for how pale she'd become. The quantity of tears shed earlier meant a loss of potassium and it occurred to her that Lily needed food. Instead, she'd driven hours in great stress and then made gracious conversation in several languages with strangers. Then concerned herself with Nicole's comfort above her own.

Nicole gathered up her satchel, growing increasingly concerned that the man was well past standards of privacy distance, even for Europeans, who required less space than Americans. He was almost touching her with his chest.

It sounded as if Lily were saying, *"Nine nine dew erst"* but the man began waving his arms.

Lily said one last thing and the man yelled something back and stormed off just as Nicole reached them.

"What on earth was that about? Are you all right?" Nicole took the water bottles from Lily's shaking hands.

"A fan of the Linden-Smiths," Lily said. Her lips were pale.

Nicole uncapped one of the bottles. "Drink. Let's get out of here."

She drank her own water while she and Lily slowly made their way toward the distant main exit. Though Lily pointed out a booth here and there, it was clear to Nicole that she was not really seeing much of anything. Well, that ass had been physically intimidating and that was enough to shake anyone for a while.

"And here we have biographies, more biographies, memoirs," Nicole said, filling in the silence. They were finally nearing the main doors.

Lily stumbled to a stop in front of a massive publishing house booth draped in red, white and blue. Stacks of new books were arranged in clever displays, featuring faces Nicole dimly recognized from television. The news anchor who had come out recently she recognized easily, but Kate's influence was the only reason she knew one of those faces was a Kardashian.

Lily put the booth to her back and walked rapidly toward the exit. "Thank goodness she was here earlier in the week. I can't even look at that woman's face. I don't want to share the same air as her."

Surprised, Nicole took one last look at a stack of books and realized that Merrill Boone was featured on the covers. "I see," she said, but then realized that Lily was already at the doors.

They had cleared the building before Lily slowed her pace. "That woman is merciless. She lied about so many things."

Nicole hesitated, not wanting to trigger another emotional breakdown from Lily. She'd been thoughtless earlier, delivering her evaluation of Lily's parents as if Lily had the distance and perspective to hear the words. Just because in a professional setting Lily was poised and mature beyond her years didn't mean her private life was as neatly ordered and under control, especially after the traumatic events that had led to her parents' suicides. "Her arguments are logically flawed, and if she restated them in acceptable logical expressions their fallacy would be obvious. She chooses not to do that, so she fails to illuminate the truth."

Lily's lips were in a tight, firm line. "All of which is a high-brow way of saying she tells lies."

Confused by the twisting pain she felt in her chest to be at odds with Lily over something they essentially agreed on, Nicole said, "Yes, you're right."

"She gets rich telling lies. I know I'd do a lot of things for a living, but I would never want to be the assistant who rushes in to tell the boss that a child has been murdered because it'll make the boss *happy*. It's...indecent."

They had finally cleared the crowds around the building and Nicole was glad to see some color back in Lily's cheeks. Her head was down though, as she plowed along the sidewalk.

Nicole was immediately startled by a loud creaking sound overhead. Looking up she realized there was a massive moving sculpture of an iron figure lowering a hammer. "Curious public art."

Lily glanced up, not seeming surprised at all. "We walked under it last week. Do you like it?"

"Public art is well-documented to increase emotional valuation of a city's residents and visitors."

Lily sighed. "That's not an answer."

Nicole replayed her words in her head. "I believe I addressed—"

"That public art has a social purpose and whether you like that sculpture are not in any way the same thing." Lily's lips were in a thin, tight line. "Unless you're saying that you can only like something if it has been proven to be of value."

Nicole was reminded of arguing with Kate, who dragged emotional tangents into any discussion. She didn't want to get... off-track, not with Lily. "I like looking at it," she said. "I also like knowing that it has a purpose. It adds to my enjoyment. And profiting in the misery of others is indecent."

"Oh." Lily took a deep breath and her expression softened. "I wasn't sure you heard me."

"I did. I am—I don't wish to upset you again."

"I understand that. I really didn't mean to go off like I did." Lily's mouth was no longer tight and thin. "I could really use some dinner. And chocolate. Not necessarily in that order."

"Chocolate has been proven—"

Lily pressed her forefinger against Nicole's lips. "I know all about the dopamine and the heart healthy antioxidants and the blahppity-blah-blah. All that really matters right now is that chocolate is a gift from kind gods to save lives. Okay?"

Nicole nodded.

Lily removed her forefinger. Nicole resisted the urge to lick her lips.

"The car is this way."

Nicole fell into step and said nothing. It seemed by far the wisest thing to do. When Lily wasn't looking she quickly licked her lips and was disappointed she couldn't taste Lily's skin.

Perhaps, she mused, she needed chocolate as well. Not to save lives, but to keep her from making a fool of herself.

CHAPTER ELEVEN

"Say that again." Nicole looked up from her breakfast, an *especial de la casa* of eggs with a smoky green tomatillo sauce and fingers of toast smeared with a savory, soft white cheese.

Lily grinned at her over her mug of thick Spanish coffee. "I said that the bookseller for one p.m. has canceled because of the rain last night. They have a leak and repairmen everywhere. That means we don't have to be anywhere, do anything, entertain *anyone* until tonight at seven p.m. when the mayor's wife's dinner-slash-book club convenes."

"I can't even take it in." Nicole finally took a bite of her toast.

"I know what you mean." Lily couldn't have been more relieved. She didn't know if the persistent raw tickle in the back of her throat was a cold or lack of consistent sleep, and Nicole was obviously weary.

All in all, Lily would have liked to have had words with the person who had planned their itinerary. There was no leisure time built in, as if Nicole could be "on" seven days a week, several times a day. Madrid was already just a memory and it was such a beautiful city. If there had been time she'd have found the charming winery that she'd visited with her cousins several years ago. A relaxing meal in the countryside would have been wonderful. Instead, they'd rushed from the airport to a college campus in Madrid, then to another college in Toledo by late afternoon, then driven on to Granada last night to be rested for the bookshop event, now canceled.

"I know Granada a little bit." Lily swallowed another heavenly mouthful of the bracing, aromatic coffee. "My cousins and I drove all over Spain during a college break, and we stayed in this area for several days. What would you say to an hour's drive to a day spa on the ocean? We'd be pampered, you could work or read, a luncheon of tapas and wine...We'd be back here in plenty of time for the event tonight."

"Would we be wrapped in plastic and have cucumber slices on our eyes? That sort of thing?" Nicole looked highly skeptical.

"Only if that's your deal. A hot stone treatment and massage, followed by a couple of hours poolside being plied with *sangría*, *jamón serrano* and *queso manchego* would be my preference. I've been there before and it's set in a naturally beautiful location overlooking a long beach and the Mediterranean. It's too far to see Gibraltar but ..." She took a deep breath. "It'll be the closest thing we'll find to Lake Winnipesauke for restorative powers."

Nicole appeared to be considering it as she ate her eggs. They looked tasty, but at the moment, Lily was far too emotionally involved with her coffee to want anything else. Even the Spanish café in Greenwich Village couldn't match what was an "average" blend in Spain. The little carafe of slightly sweetened and thickened milk was the crowning pleasure of her liquid breakfast.

Not making much of an effort to hide her true feelings, she added, "Or we could stay here. I know a wonderful eatery. But...I did call Un—Damon Linden, and I did perhaps suggest that this itinerary is insanely demanding, which it is, and he did agree that a day's respite at Insignis's expense was more than reasonable."

Nicole actually smiled. "I think I would have liked to have heard that negotiation."

"It wasn't so much a negotiation as I said what I wanted to do and he said yes. It's all in the tone of voice."

Nicole's eyebrow was up, but she was definitely smiling when she said, "You hide your alpha female tendencies well."

"I had an international relations prof who said that women in diplomacy had to be mutable." She fluttered her eyelashes.

Nicole laughed outright, surprising Lily further. Maybe the warm climate was melting her moods. Or perhaps she was simply more comfortable around Lily, which was reassuring. If Nicole suspected the range of Libido's musings she'd not be so relaxed.

"Don't bat those things at me." Nicole waved a hand. "They're too dangerous a weapon to play with."

"So…The day spa is a yes? I talked to the concierge and we can hire a driver for the day."

"Yes, if only for that alone. I don't know how you drive such long stretches. Last night seemed endless."

"It's harder after dark. During the day the changing scenery is nice. I really wish we could have taken a train from Toledo to here. I loved the train in England."

Nicole finished her eggs and sipped from her tea. "What does one wear to a day spa?"

"Something comfortable. They'll provide everything, from a swimsuit to slippers, to a wrap for massage, whatever we need. Pampering with a capital P." She finished her coffee and looked regretfully at the bottom of the mug. Maybe she could get another to go before they left for the spa.

"Very well." Nicole rose. "Shall we meet in the lobby in thirty minutes?"

"Perfect."

She watched Nicole leave the café and turn in the direction of the hotel elevators. Libido said something inane about being happy to see Nicole walk away, and supplied high-speed, high-resolution mental trailers for *The Naughty Schoolgirl Teaches the Professor Something New*.

Lily looked into the bottom of her mug again. Since when was an old wooden desk sexy? She was *not* a sex-starved nymphette.

Libido provided an image of the alley in London. Lily shivered.

Circumspect pronounced that since it was an obvious bad influence there would be no more coffee for anyone.

***

A scant thirty minutes later, dressed in simple cotton shorts and a little white blouse, Lily arrived in the lobby to find Nicole already waiting. Nicole was equally casual in a pair of workout shorts and a T-shirt with the University of Central New Hampshire's logo on the pocket.

Nicole handed her a tall travel cup with a sipping lid. "You looked so sorry when you ran out of coffee that I got you more. I hope I put in enough of the sweet milk. *Leche y sucre* is the milk you like, right?"

Lily hoped that her surprise didn't show. Once again she was flummoxed to realize that Nicole, for all her aloof airs, was taking note of the details around her. "Yes, thank you. How thoughtful."

"Our car is ready," Nicole said. "The concierge introduced me to the driver. I'm sorry, I think his name is Eduardo or Lysander or Hercules or all three…" She waved her hands helplessly.

The first sweet, seductive sip was heavenly. Libido compared it to sunshine on bare breasts. Circumspect warned no good would come of the indulgence. "Right now he could be Sweeney Todd and I wouldn't care." Nicole's eyebrow went up and Lily laughed. "Didn't your mother ever tell you that your face could get stuck like that?"

Nicole turned to the doorway where the driver was lingering and smiling. Over her shoulder she asked, "Are you going to be cheeky all day?"

"Maybe. What are you going to do about it?"

Nicole turned away to accept the driver's help into the car, but not before her gaze locked with Lily's long enough to stop Lily in her tracks.

From any other woman she would have taken that smoldering glance as a promise, but there was no way that Dr. Professor Nicole Hathaway, Ph.D., was giving her a bedroom look.

That's it, she thought. Circumspect was right. No more Spanish coffee.

She sipped again. No more coffee after this one.

***

It was getting to be a bad habit, Nicole thought, watching Lily while she slept. This time it was in the back of a compact but very comfortable touring car as they returned from the warm coast to their hotel in Granada. The problem with being in a car was that to look at Lily required that Nicole turn her head in an obvious way. If Lily opened her eyes, she'd catch Nicole in the act.

But she couldn't look away. Lily still had a slightly red nose from time in the sun, and whatever treatment she'd done in the *relajación gruta* had brought out her sinuous grace. Her cheeks were dusted with faint freckles and her lashes seemed longer than ever. She looked closer to sixteen than twenty-six and far from the cheeky, sassy woman of this morning, who'd seemed drunk on Spanish coffee.

"What are you going to do about it?" Lily had dared.

The entire drive to the spa she'd wanted to show Lily exactly what she'd do if challenged so flirtatiously—kiss her until the laughter was gone, until the poise was gone, until soft sounds of *don't stop* were the only ones Lily could make.

Fortunately, they'd parted ways after entrusting their bodies and auras to aesthetists. Nicole opted for a salt massage simply because she was curious what that meant and knowing her mother would find it interesting as an anecdote. Ninety minutes of a warm room and a woman's strong hands rubbing oil and coarse salt into her shoulders, back, stomach, legs, even her fingers and toes, had been truly relaxing. After that, she'd been happy to lounge next to the pool in the one-piece swimsuit and light robe the spa had provided. She'd brought a book she was reviewing for the *Journal of Applied Neurobiology* and read until Lily had emerged from the actualization sphere—or whatever the Spanish name had meant—to join her poolside in the dappled sunlight.

Though she'd kept the book open on her lap and turned the pages, she'd done no reading after that. Lily had quickly discarded her robe, and the skimpy bikini she'd chosen covered everything, just barely.

Nicole was grateful for the sunglasses that hid the fact that she was helplessly staring.

Declaring herself a new woman, Lily had vigorously swum laps in the long pool, emerging from the water against a backdrop of the blue-green Mediterranean stretching to the horizon. She could have been a nymph or a dryad or a fairy sprite, a demi-goddess who turned the air around her into delirious desire. Nicole now understood those silly quest stories where heroes did stupid and reckless feats, all for a kiss from a divinely beautiful woman.

She made herself turn her head from the pool, finally, and feigned sleep after pulling a towel over herself as if fearing sunburn. She hoped it was thick enough to hide her unruly nipples.

Sex in the French countryside with an alluring and imaginative woman hadn't made a bit of difference. Since when had she *ever* had unruly nipples? Or muscles in her thighs that clenched at the sight of droplets across pale shoulders? With a constant feeling of being flushed and swollen and thirsty? And been so hungry, hungry all the way down into the pit of her stomach and deeper?

Never, that was when.

Never was terrifying. Or would be if Lily were to open her eyes and catch Nicole memorizing the shadow of her lashes on her cheeks.

Lily stirred when the car pulled up in front of their hotel. After confirming when they'd meet to go to their evening event, Nicole made a decorous departure, but she felt as if she were fleeing the scene of a crime.

For the first time she was dissatisfied with her wardrobe for an appearance. It was safe—slacks, blouses and a reliable suit jacket or a jacket-cut cardigan, all of which proclaimed her solidity of personality. While some of her colleagues enjoyed being mistaken for students, she did not. On campus she wanted to be presumed a professor; it was hard enough to be taken seriously in the sciences as a woman, let alone a woman of color.

Cole's jacket was the only the article of clothing that sent a different message. The evening was far too warm to wear it and it would be inappropriate for the patio of a museum, where the event was scheduled. Their host was the mayor of Granada's wife and Nicole felt she ought to look like an appropriate guest for what Lily had described as one of the "hot tickets" of the Granada social season.

She'd noticed how Lily recycled her clothing—but she seemed to have an endless selection of accessories. Lily hadn't worn the same exact combination twice. After considering the time left, she made a quick visit to the hotel's gift shop. She'd seen some jewelry in the display window that would make a nice memento of Spain, and Lily had made tonight's event sound definitely upscale from a bookshop. About to check out, she saw two pretty bracelets that each copied one of the many mosaic patterns from the nearby Alhambra. She knew both her mother and Kate would like them. Grateful for the shopkeeper's English, she arranged to have them sent home.

The moment she saw Lily in the lobby she was glad she'd made a little more effort with her hair and the addition of her new necklace and earrings. Lily had put her hair up with two glittery pins holding it in place. A long, lightweight jacket with the peacock pattern that she frequently wore covered the rest of her attire, and the shoes that Kate had so admired on the night they'd met were part of the outfit. The jacket was thin enough that she could tell the dress underneath was black.

"You've not worn that before," Lily immediately said. "It's a handsome piece—it suits you."

Nicole nervously touched the simple teardrop pendant of topaz-colored glass. "I didn't realize how tiring it would be to wear the same clothes over and over, so I bought something new."

Lily gestured at her jacket as she led them to the waiting taxi. "Peacock feathers were all the rage when I bought my travel wear ensembles. I'm a little tired of blue, green and for a change, blue and green."

When Nicole realized where their taxi was headed she felt a rush of what could only be called stage fright. "We're going to the Alhambra itself? I thought this was a book club with some politicos."

Lily's nose was against her window, obviously entranced by the lush gardens. "Book club, hors d'oeuvres-slash-dinner, local wine tasting and a fund-raiser for the local libraries and schools all rolled into one evening. You're this quarter's invited guest. We're going to the *Paradores Museo*, which was a convent built by Catholic monarchs when they moved into the already existing citadel. The gardens have been written and sung about for at least eight hundred years."

She turned from the window, her face aglow. "I've been looking forward to this event the whole time. I've been to the Alhambra before, but we never made it to the convent. It's like walking the green at the Tower of London, or sleeping in the ruins at Betatakin."

Lily's drop earrings caught the waning sunlight, dappling the inside of the cab with prisms of color. Nicole watched the lights dance across her lap, all the while wondering what potion she'd drunk or cookie she'd eaten to fall so far down this rabbit hole. Realizing she had to find her voice, she managed to say, "I'm pleased we'll get to see it."

They alighted from their taxi in the courtyard of the museum and joined the trickle of people going inside. Thankfully, none of the men were in tuxedos, though all wore business suits. The women were in dresses ranging from short and daring to long and flowing. Just inside the door they went through a cursory security screening and then Lily turned to the coat check. "Be right back."

"*Profesor* Hathaway!" Nicole connected the exclamation to a tall, elegant older woman in a silky garment of black and white that wrapped and layered not unlike one of her mother's saris. She was making the proverbial beeline toward Nicole. "It is *un placer*!"

Nicole shook the woman's hand, already missing Lily at her elbow. "It's wonderful to be here."

"I am Margolis Hierro." Her salt-and-pepper hair was pulled sharply back into a twisting braid, and Nicole would not have been surprised to learn she claimed Moorish ancestry.

"Thank you for hosting this event in such a remarkable and historic place." She caught the scent of Lily's perfume and realized she'd returned. "May I introduce my assistant, Lily Smith?"

She turned with an inclusive gesture and watched as the two women shook hands. They lapsed temporarily into Spanish, which required no response from Nicole. This was a good thing as all the while Nicole struggled to simply breathe in.

She'd have had more success if she could have looked anywhere else, but just like at the pool, she couldn't take her gaze away from Lily. This time she had no dark glasses to hide her fixation. The black cocktail dress Lily wore was stunning, cupping her shoulders and highlighting the curve of her neck, emphasizing her small waist and falling smoothly from hip to thigh. The drop earrings matched the pendant that rested an inch above the fabric covering her breasts. And while the dress clung to Lily in all the best places, it wasn't, as her mother would have said, cheap. Sexy—but not cheap.

With the black patent heels adding inches to her height, her hair up and a bright, relaxed smile, she was elegant, classically lovely. Her mother again came to mind—she'd have compared Lily to Audrey Hepburn, her highest praise.

They had reverted to English as their hostess linked her arm with Nicole's. "Please come and meet our most ardent literary supporters."

Nicole could only hope Lily was following behind them. She was rapidly introduced to a dozen people in the crowd of about thirty, most of whom greeted her in English. She heard Lily laugh and her voice confidently rattling off something in Spanish, but she made herself not look. It would only take her breath away again. No water nymph, no Barbie—the consideration and kind smile wasn't an act. It wasn't something studied and false that Lily had learned. It was who she was. While Cole wanted to devour the water nymph whole, Nicole could scarcely stop herself from dissolving at Lily's feet.

She made herself breathe and listen carefully to the men and women around her. Whenever at a loss for words she offered praise for their location and someone would give her another tidbit of the building's history. Unlike the main building and citadel, the former convent was more stark in its stone design, with a deceptive, graceful simplicity that even a modern architect would envy.

The evening breeze was cool to her cheeks, and dinner was served on one side of the large patio at a curving table. Lily was seated toward one end while Nicole and Señora Hierro were at the center. She knew that the thinly sliced ham and small wedges of cheese with drops of golden honey were probably a local specialty and she missed Lily's wealth of knowledge—how dependent I've become, she told herself.

Ah, she thought. At last her inner tensions made sense. She was allowing herself to feel inadequate, which heightened her vulnerability, increased Lily's power quotient in the relationship and created this sensation of confusion where none ought to exist. She simply had to master her own confidence and the perception of her own loss of control would subside.

When she was back in her real life everything would go back to the way it was. All of this was merely an intermezzo.

When she managed to steal a glance down the table, the gentlemen to either side of Lily seemed openly dazzled, the way that pompous Rajesh had seemed over tea. On top of her own feelings of vulnerability in the foreign setting, it was further undeniable that Lily had sex appeal and much as Nicole might like to think she was immune to it, obviously she wasn't.

She closed her ears to the throaty half-laugh she'd learned meant Lily was genuinely amused and focused on her immediate neighbors. They were all charming, and she didn't need Lily near as they took turns with mixed levels of English to describe the sharp, aged cheeses and meats, the vineyards where the sweet to robust red wines were produced, and the regions that grew and cured the bitter, salty olives. The entrée of prawns with a traditional rice dish was delicious.

"I wish we were staying for several days. Lily and I would love to explore this area."

"There is no place in Spain like Granada," Señora Hierro pronounced, drawing murmurs of agreement from all around her. "Our history, our mixed cultures, our respect for our land makes Granada the jewel of Andalusia."

Realizing too late that she may have had too much wine, Nicole lifted her glass to her hostess. "May I propose a toast, then?"

She had meant it as a gesture between her and those nearby, but a silence fell over the entire table. Not sure how to finish what she'd started, she rose to her feet—the wine definitely was having an effect—and smiled down the table in both directions without meeting anyone's gaze. "As you know, I am a scientist. I use research and scientific inquiry to prove a thing is true. Señora Hierro tells me that Granada is the jewel of Andalusia. Having enjoyed these beautiful surroundings, tasted the splendid wine and the many delicious foods that were produced within just a few miles— kilometers, I mean—from here, I can safely say that my standards of proof have been met. A jewel, indeed." She lifted her glass. "*Viva Granada.*"

Her final words were echoed around the table. She quickly sat down, hoping she'd said nothing foolish, and finally made eye contact with Lily. She received a wide smile and a half-wink that made Nicole's ears burn hot against her head.

She turned down a glass of a yellow after-dinner drink that smelled of liqueur and citrus. Her earlier tipsiness had faded and she wasn't going to indulge further. Most guests had glasses in hand as they all migrated to the other end of the patio where semi-circles of chairs were arranged. There was no microphone, but with a group of less than thirty Nicole wasn't worried about being heard. The fragrant breeze had remained steady and the lights in the gardens around them had switched on. She was grateful to note that Lily was discreetly taking pictures—her mother would be endlessly charmed by the setting, and Nicole didn't want to forget it either.

She began by thanking Señora Hierro for the hospitality, and acknowledged the cause of the evening. "A little more than a week ago a bookseller in Ireland told me that books are never dangerous. Not reading books is what's dangerous. It's clear to me that borders and history are not barriers to values we all hold in common. Indeed, the premise of my work in the fields of cognitive neuroscience and biopsychology is that underneath our skins, beyond our language, we are all much the same."

She paused to assess whether she was losing her audience to the language barrier, but a glance at Lily brought a reassuring nod. "What I discovered in my research of how people find success in relationships is that the factors that contribute to long-term happiness involve a surprising amount of our DNA. Our bodies have about thirty thousand genes in total." She gestured at what looked like a type of oak sheltering their end of the patio. "Before we are overimpressed with the size of our genome, this tree has likely forty thousand or more, and there are probably some insects in the gardens that make us look like single-cell xenophyophores— sea sponges."

There was a polite murmur of laughter that helped her relax. Her nerves were finally settling. "It takes a thousand genes to smell perfume, and as many to hear laughter. The genes that make our senses function, plus those that power the mental electricity to imagine a future or anticipate a conversation, as well as the split-second evaluation of the flicker of an eye or the curve of a smile… There are likely fifteen thousand or more of our genes tied into that process. When people say 'It's all I can think about' there's a good reason why it feels that way." Stop talking to yourself, she cautioned.

She cleared her throat. "We're hard-wired to be creatures of community. It's in our DNA numbers. Fifty percent of our genes help us negotiate safety, actualize compassion, form relationships, and recognize compatibility."

Hoping she'd made a successful segue, she gave her shortest talk, one that focused exclusively on case studies that had been working well in bookstores. Follow-up questions were ones she'd been asked many times. Whenever language became an issue both Lily and Señora Hierro helped out. After thirty minutes, when waiters appeared at the patio entrance with several platters with what appeared to be a final tasty treat for the evening, she thanked the audience and closed.

People came up to ask further questions or to simply thank her for her talk, and Nicole finally relaxed. She realized that her nerves were not unlike those she got when going to cocktail parties with the university's donors, some of whom were very wealthy and had the power to directly affect her department's activities. It wasn't a situation she liked, but sometimes it was necessary to prove oneself an appropriate guest.

With a deep breath she acknowledged the rest of the truth: she hadn't wanted to appear a fool in front of Lily. Since that careful conversation on the train when Lily had gently pointed out that Nicole was talking over the average reader's head, she had wanted to meet Lily's standards. Somewhere along the way she had accepted Lily's expertise in reading a crowd and setting a tone. But there was nothing out of the ordinary in that, she thought. It was merely an academic exercise in growth. It was rational to maximize the opportunity to communicate with laypeople...

She let herself watch Lily for a minute, noting how at ease her body language was with the men still gathered around her and how genuinely interested she appeared to be when they spoke. As Nicole watched, Lily turned from her group of male admirers to say something to a woman who was passing by her. Their conversation was immediately lively as they strolled to the bar. Clearly, Lily was in her milieu.

Even as she cynically noted that the men stared after Lily, she chided herself for being no better. Telling herself that Kate would be interested in Lily's outfit—especially the shoes—she took a photo with her phone, then several others of the gardens. Kate would, of course, be interested in those as well.

Lily had hoped for a diplomat's life, but that dream was on hold because of her parents' crimes. She could do many other things and would, eventually. The faint voice of reason added that whatever path Lily chose, it would not lead to a small New Hampshire town. Lily would never be the content acorn, hunkered within a plain, safe husk, that Nicole was.

Not that Nicole was even thinking...It was an absurdity that she'd even made that comparison. But as she watched one of the bedazzled gentlemen again attach himself to group where Lily was conversing she wanted to say, "Go away. She's mine."

She'd just argued that she was hard-wired to have these feelings, but she didn't accept that truth for herself. She didn't tick the way most people did. Why should she start now?

"She's mine..." Those two words circled her brain for the rest of the evening and were still whispering in her ears back at the hotel when she finally fell asleep.

CHAPTER TWELVE

"I don't know why I let you talk me into this." Nicole adjusted the heavy chain mail across her chest.

"It's whimsical. It's what the natives are doing. It's Italy!" Lily twirled in front of the photographer's full-length mirror. The rustle of her green skirts under the heavy velvet purple gown gave her great satisfaction. "The Insignis blogger will love it. You could have chosen a dress, you know."

"I don't wear dresses. I also could have chosen not to do this."

The clank of Nicole's armor boots gave Lily a pang of guilt. It was hot in the tent and if she was feeling the heat, Nicole had to be feeling it more. She took one last look in the mirror and adjusted the voluminous red wig with its pre-attached bevy of white and green ribbons. "Okay, I'll stop primping. I must have been a princess in a previous life."

She caught Nicole rolling her eyes, but didn't comment. As she settled into the ornate chair, which would pass as a throne in a photograph but was primarily carved Styrofoam and gilt, she said, "Your sword is backward."

"I can't even walk with these fake tights tied up around my knees."

The photographer launched into a series of instructions. Her Italian being limited to only the cognates shared with Spanish and English, Lily hoped she was right when she told Nicole, "You're supposed to frown and look fierce. I'm supposed to look…enigmatic. I think. It's enigmatic or constipated."

Nicole stifled a laugh. "I would like to get out of this outfit. It weighs fifty pounds." Her knight's cape was a cleverly adapted piece of carpet, corded with gold and held into position over her street clothes with Velcro. Chain mail gloves with attached black knit sleeves covered her arms, and a thin cape of black netting fell far enough to meet up with the tights that covered her calves.

"Put your hands on the arms of the sword." Lily gestured.

"Quillons."

"What?"

"The crossguard is called the quillons." Under her breath Nicole muttered, "Finally, some medieval trivia I know that you don't."

"I heard that." Lily crossed her eyes at Nicole in the mirror. "Thank you for the gift of your knowledge."

Nicole pressed her lips together, but Lily was pretty sure it was to fight a smile. "I'm ready when you are."

Lily looked one last time in the mirror positioned directly behind the camera. Her wig was straight and she'd pushed most of the hair behind her shoulders. She looked more like the Scottish princess Merida in *Brave* than she did "Italian Renaissance Bride," which had been the description on the outfit. She had to admit that the knight's garb suited the glowering Nicole.

"Kate will love this," she said.

"It's the only reason I'm doing it. I hope she's feeling better—I want to call home again tonight."

"*Pronti*," Lily said to the photographer. She fought the natural urge to smile and instead thought of commanding, "Off with her head!" to the likes of someone like Merrill Boone. She would be glad of the picture even with the costumes, for the scrapbook she'd eventually put together, she told herself. So far she had no photographs of herself with Nicole. She was always the one taking the pictures.

The photographer muttered, then nodded happily at what he saw in his screen.

"One more?"

The photographer shrugged and pointed at the sign outlining the costs. Lily turned to Nicole. "Your mother will want one of just you, won't she?"

"I suppose. But I can't sit down."

The photographer waved his hands and pulled the chair out of the shot. Cranking a wheel he lowered a backdrop of a medieval armory. Lily tiptoed in to adjust the sword and Nicole's hands on the quillons.

"There. Now you're a proper defender of the weak and innocent roaming the countryside while reading poetry." She stepped back to admire the result. One thing was for certain—it was nice to see Nicole in something other than her habitual black slacks, white blouse, black socks and loafers. With her hair pulled back, Nicole might have been a Moorish soldier though few would mistake her for a man. The severity of the hairstyle highlighted her ascetic profile. "You're bending gender quite well."

Nicole's eyebrows went up. "I'm not sure my mother will be pleased."

"Stop that." Lily tried not to notice that Nicole's eyes looked luminous and her lips more full than usual. "Look fierce. Your mother will love it. "

They left the tent with two prints of each photo and a microcard with the digital images. Nicole immediately turned toward a lemonade vendor. Lily smiled. Nicole might not be all that quick with languages, but once she'd had an Italian lemonade, she'd found stands with *limonata* easily.

She drifted a short distance away, looking again at the courtyard of the *Piazza degli Scacchi*. Her regrets over their rapid movement from Naples to Rome to Florence—experiencing little more of any of those historic cities than the inside of chain hotels and the view from their rental car—were assuaged by the late afternoon and evening in Marostica, about thirty kilometers north of equally historic Vicenza. After the bookseller in Vicenza had raved about the Living Chess Game scheduled for the upcoming weekend Nicole had been amenable to checking out the city's festival.

The piazza where the chess game took place was patterned with red and white squares and was overlooked by a gothic tower hung with heraldic shields and flags of medieval city-states. With so many people in period costume it was easy to see how it might have looked in the Renaissance.

Nicole reappeared with a frosty cup. "This could become an addiction."

Before Lily could answer there was a burst of drums and trumpets, then multiple voices shouting, "*Fare la strada!*"

She dragged Nicole out of the street. They'd just reached the safety of the sidewalk when a parade of men and women in black costumes, two accompanied by miniature horses in black livery, marched past them.

"I think—oh!" Lily grabbed Nicole's arm. "It's the black chess pieces."

"What are they shouting?"

"I'm pretty sure they're talking trash about the white team and inviting everybody to the match on Saturday." She looked at the little horses again and laughed. "Those are the knights. And the pawns—they're the ones using what I think is very colorful language to go with what I know is a very rude gesture."

"What are the queen and king saying?"

The most elaborately gowned figures were waving in a restrained manner and pronouncing something with great solemnity. "I don't know—victory, justice. Nothing about anyone's parentage. The pawns covered that pretty well. *Bastardo* isn't hard to translate."

The parade circled the courtyard with the pawns insolently miming the act of urinating on where the white King would begin the game.

"I wish we were staying." Lily sighed.

"We'll be in Bratislava, right?"

Lily turned in the direction of the inn they'd scouted earlier and picked for dinner. "Bratislava, then on to Vienna, Prague and Warsaw. I've never been to Poland, it'll be new. Then we head to Moscow. Ready for some dinner?"

"I'm quite hungry, yes. Am I remembering correctly that Moscow is universities only—no bookstores?"

"That's right. I couldn't tell you why. St. Petersburg we'll be in three bookstores." She paused to indicate to the inn's host that there were two of them for dinner. "But about Moscow—I'm concerned about the transit plan there. The second day's lecture is scheduled further outside of Moscow, and we have to drive back to the airport in record time to make the flight to St. Petersburg. I think we're going to miss it. I was looking at the train schedules—"

"Sure," Nicole said. "Let's take the train."

The host led them to a small table, and pulled out Lily's chair. She smiled her thanks and accepted the menu. "It's not the Orient Express, but the countryside is beautiful in places. I can finally finish *A Study in Scarlet*."

Nicole scanned the menu. "I like trying new foods but right now I could use a very American burger. Don't tell my mother, but I'd probably welcome her vindaloo."

"We could split a pizza. Might be something like home."

"Deal. Anything but anchovies." Nicole set the menu down and looked at Lily across the table. "Isn't that the same Sherlock Holmes you began when we left home?"

Lily shrugged. "I thought I'd be reading at night, but by the time we get in I just want a hot shower and bed. Thank you for going on that garden walking tour with me in Florence, even though it was getting dark."

Once upon a time Libido had thought she would spend her evenings trolling bars for more casual sex. There was just no energy for it, not when she spent most of her time after dinner with Nicole, for at least a little while. Nicole no longer seemed as eager to retire to her room to work on her peer review projects. Perhaps she'd finished them.

"I slept better for it." Nicole was studying her hands. "This trip really is nothing like I expected."

"It's more grueling than I thought it would be, that's for sure." Lily asked their waiter for their pizza, with a local sausage and mozzarella, black olives and roasted red peppers. She wondered if she looked as tired as Nicole did. "I find myself less patient and certainly more easily annoyed."

"Lack of sleep makes us more resistant to dopamine and sera—"

"—tonin, yes I know."

Nicole's eyebrow lifted as Lily expected it to. "Are you intimating that I've repeated this information before?"

With a sweet smile, Lily answered, "Well, you've said it at least once and I have a good memory."

"In addition to lack of patience and being easily annoyed, you could add 'more cheeky' to your list."

"Is that what you tell your students? That they're being cheeky?"

"No. Students don't get cheeky with me. I'm told they get cheeky with the teaching assistants and administrative staff."

"So I'm a special case, then."

"Yes." Nicole's expression didn't alter but her words seemed heavier somehow. "You're a special case."

Lily opened her mouth to reply but the waiter delivered the tea she'd ordered for both of them and soon after that, their pizza.

Later, trying to punch the hotel pillow into the right shape for sleep, she didn't know what to make of Nicole's tone. What a frustrating woman, hiding every emotion and making her spend her nights pondering the meaning of a word or a look.

She stared up at the dark ceiling and wished she didn't care what Nicole thought. She wished Libido would stop playing graphic minimovies in her head. *This is like some shipboard attachment—we're in each other's company so much and I'm sex-starved and lonely.* Nicole was an accomplished, brilliant scholar, and it was ridiculous to feel proprietarily proud, as if they had some...connection. But there was none, nothing more than moving through the same time and space for a while. Every day a new city and one day closer to parting. It seemed as if the only certainty in her future was that it wouldn't contain Nicole.

CHAPTER THIRTEEN

"You were right," Nicole said. She reflexively braked against the passenger floor as Lily snaked the small rental car over two lanes. None of the signs made any sense to her, but she knew bad traffic when she saw it, and Moscow drivers were like Boston drivers on St. Patrick's Day. It didn't help that it had rained for most of the morning and that the expressway had one lane closed for construction—some things are the same the world over. When they'd left the lecture hall at National Medical Research University the rain had stopped, at least.

Lily's hands were clenched on the wheel. "I was right, yippee for me. Yes, we totally missed that flight. Good thing I picked the train instead of another flight later in the day. Good damn thing, because we're going to miss that train and be totally screwed."

Nicole couldn't remember Lily cursing before. She looked at the arrival time indicator on the GPS mounted to the rental car's windshield. It still said 3:12, which was eight minutes after the express train to Moscow left. "Is there a later train?"

"The one I booked was the last express. If I remember correctly, we can take a local and get there an hour late for tomorrow's first event. I can't believe this idiot box sent us the long way around the city." Her hands clenched again and Nicole could easily envision the GPS airborne into the path of a large truck.

Not wanting to add to Lily's stress, Nicole gently said, "Perhaps we can still revert to an air flight, then. I don't see this traffic offering up a miracle."

After a deep breath Lily said, "You're right. Let me get off the road and try booking a flight online. Even if either of us was getting a signal my Russian's not good enough to do it over the phone without having something to read from. It makes no sense to keep heading for the train station. It's leaving without us."

Nicole braced herself for a sudden turn. "When I upgraded my service I'm certain I told them it had to work in Russia and they assured me it would. Only now do I realize the irony of pressing number one on my phone for help with a lack of signal."

"Is there some kind of law that says the one place we can't get phone service is the one place we're running late for everything?"

"It sounds like a variation on the proverbial Murphy's Law, which is not a law at all."

"These drivers make London cabbies look like lightweights." Lily whipped through another dizzying turn to leave the crowded motorway behind. "This is all my fault. I had to stop and listen to that choir. We didn't have five minutes—"

"I don't regret it—not your fault at all." Nicole braced as Lily abruptly slowed the car and merged into a right turn lane. "I'd never heard Balkan singing live. If we'd kept on walking instead of going inside the chapel we would have missed that beautiful sound and we'd have still missed the train."

Lily briefly took one hand off the wheel to tweak the rearview mirror. "I guess you're right. We live in a world where almost any experience can be put on hold, watched again, shared with people who weren't there. While we were standing there I thought about trying to record it on my phone, but then I decided, you know, I'd have to record it where it counts." She tapped her forehead. "And if I'm not losing my mind, that sign we just passed said food and gasoline this direction."

As soon as they left the expressway and industrial lots behind them, the city streets drew in close. In spite of not being able to understand much of the signage, Nicole recognized the ubiquitous local corner markets that had existed in every city they'd been to, complete with bins of produce just outside the doors. Parked cars added to the narrow conditions. Pedestrians were wearing woolen coats that Nicole envied. She'd not brought anything heavy enough for the climate, thinking they were here so briefly she would just tough it out. Tomorrow was the first day of autumn but at this latitude the temperatures were what she'd expect at home a month from now. Though she knew that it was a myth, she understood why people thought warmer climates thinned the blood—she didn't think her feet had warmed up from the moment they'd stepped off the plane from Warsaw yesterday.

Lily craned her neck to look at storefront signs. "And what's the use of my having a laptop that gets Wi-Fi if I don't know what *Wi-Fi* looks like in Cyrillic?"

"Maybe we can find a Starbucks. They're everywhere."

Lily bit her lower lip. "You're welcome to try to find one with the GPS. It thinks we're passing Red Square and I'm telling you, Red Square is at least twenty blocks that way." She took a hand off the wheel long enough to point. "We're not lucky enough to have gotten lost so we could drive by it at least, or past St. Basil's Cathedral. No, we're lost in the part of the city that looks like every other large city in the world."

Nicole took the unit out of its mounting bracket and activated the search function. She momentarily forgot she couldn't read the street signs and glanced out the window to get her bearings—and saw a most welcome sight. "On the left! It's the green lady logo."

Lily hit the horn and veered across several lanes of traffic. "I see a parking space."

Nicole hoped her voice was steady as she said, "One would think you've been driving here for years."

"Right now it feels like the entire United Nations is between me and my coffee. I'm cold and annoyed and I want Wi-Fi—oh my lord, is that a McDonald's?"

"Golden arches probably mean the same thing here." Nicole braced herself for another change of course. They weren't on two wheels as they bounced into the parking lot, but it felt like it.

"I need a cheeseburger even more than I need coffee." Lily shut off the engine.

Nicole was grateful the car was no longer moving. "So we're going to miss a train—maybe we won't make it to an event on time. The world won't end."

"I know that!" Lily softened her curt tone by adding, "I should have anticipated the traffic. I'm sorry." She glanced at Nicole. "Looks like you could use a cheeseburger too."

"Do I look as pale as I feel?"

"Only around the edges. Sorry." Lily gathered up her purse. "I do mean that. I'm tired and peeved—but that's no excuse for violating a half-dozen traffic laws."

"You did it with the same skill you show toward everything else." Nicole opened the door and promptly shivered as a blast of cold air blew into the car.

Lily gave her a narrow look, then broke into a smile. "Thank you. I think."

"Look." Nicole pointed at a sticker in the window. "*Wi-Fi* is Wi-Fi in any language, I guess."

"I should have realized. A lot of computer tech-speak stays in English regardless of country."

"Stop apologizing for not knowing everything in the world. Why don't I get the food and you get logged on?"

"Are you sure?"

"It's McDonald's." She let her tone go dry. "I'll point at the pictures."

Lily muttered something as she headed toward a comfortingly familiar brown and beige booth.

At the counter Nicole said, "English?" hopefully and the teenager promptly handed her a menu with only pictures of the food. She pointed out cheeseburgers, then at a picture of an onion with a big red X on it, gestured "two" with her fingers and swiped her credit card. Two minutes later she delivered the food and, feeling empowered, left Lily frowning at her laptop. Across the street at Starbucks it turned out that "vanilla espresso latte" was a universal phrase, at least for Starbucks employees. Chocolate muffins, by any other name, still looked delicious, so she got one of those as well. Dopamine to the rescue.

Feeling all the pride of a hunter-gatherer returning to the cave with a wildebeest, she set the coffees down and slid into the seat opposite Lily.

Lily looked no happier. "The airlines have good translation features, so I think I'm right that there are no flights available for online booking. I should have realized—same day online booking isn't allowed. But looking at the schedule, I see only two possible flights to St. Petersburg tonight. We would have to go to the airport and wait at each ticket counter. Unfortunately, I was also right about the trains—a local leaves at nine tonight and doesn't get in until ten a.m. and there are no sleeper cars. We could fly to Australia in that amount of time."

Nicole unwrapped her burger. She didn't eat much fast food but her stomach growled anyway. "So what do you suggest?"

"I think we could go to the airport and not find two seats. I mean—the distance involved is like traveling from New York to Charlotte. At home there would be a dozen flights that would get us there. Here, we have perhaps two choices and we could spend two hours finding out there are no seats."

"No flights and no trains—are you suggesting we drive?" Her heart sank. She'd had no idea traveling by car could get so tedious.

"It's nine hours by car, without hitting any slow downs. Most of it's fairly rural and we can make good time. Kind of like driving across Nebraska and Kansas, I would imagine. We can at least take turns driving too. I am *so* sorry about this."

Nicole glanced at her watch. "So if we don't waste time at the airport, we'd get there before midnight. That's not that bad. There's a good chance of staying awake, but if we waste time at the airport and end up with no flights it will be harder to stay awake for the drive."

For a petite woman, Lily was taking improbably large bites of her burger. After a swallow of coffee she said, "We could be having *blini* or *pirozhki*, but instead I'm blissing out on…" She gestured with her last bite of burger before popping it into her mouth. "Blissing out on whatever that was."

"A taste of home. At least it's hot." Not that her feet felt any warmer. "Can you send my mother an e-mail? Let her know I don't have a signal or she'll worry about why I don't call her on schedule. I should have asked you yesterday."

Lily typed furiously for a moment, then she glanced at the burger in Nicole's hand. "And…" Her fingers typed as she spoke. "Nicole is eating her protein, I promise, and remains healthy as the proverbial horse, though the travel and my driving are wearing her down a little. We should be near phones in twenty-four hours or less when we reach St. Petersburg, finish our events and get to the hotel. I hope Kate is feeling better."

A few clicks later she said, "And away it goes. How is Kate, by the way?"

"Bitchy, the last time we spoke. In other words, much the same. I don't blame her. Inactivity was never her specialty. My mother is more worried than she is."

Lily closed her laptop and wrapped up its power cord. "Some mothers are like that. Not mine, but some are." Her smile was wry, but there was no sign of tears.

"Would you like me to drive at first—you navigate?"

Lily agreed and Nicole braced herself, but it was easier than she had anticipated. When Lily said turn left, she turned left. When Lily said speed up to make an exit ramp, she floored it and veered. When they got lost she waited for Lily to sort it out, then they were on their way again. So much for trying to be less dependent. She supposed that Lily would like knowing that Nicole's survival plan was "Trust Lily." But it seemed like a good idea to keep it to herself.

***

"Now this stupid box thinks we're in Lyubytino." Lily stabbed at the volume control to silence the GPS's repetitive announcement of "Off route. Recalculating."

Nicole slowed as they approached a junction. "So am I going straight ahead or bearing right?"

Lily pored over the paper map they'd bought at the last town they'd passed. There was little daylight left at this point, and the overcast skies weren't helping. "I think you're going straight ahead. To Novgorod—see? We can't be in Lyubytino. The sign says Novgorod is eighty kilometers. When we get there we…" Lily switched on the overhead light. "That's better. When we get there we turn north."

"How long?"

"Less than an hour." She held the map up to the wan light. "Unless…Oh no, wait. I told you the wrong thing. We ought to have gone to the right for a shorter bypass. I think."

"Should I turn around when I can?" Nicole's tone was patient, for which Lily was thankful, given how lost they'd gotten again trying to leave Moscow.

Lily peered out the window at the dusk-shrouded landscape. They'd already stopped twice for more drinks and food. The clouds made the drive dreary and gray and the two-lane road was narrow. Unlike Europe, where a hamlet or village was around almost every corner, Russia did indeed remind her of the western United States with its huge, open spaces and cattle ranges. Out of nowhere a church would indicate where a town had once stood, but all of them seemed abandoned and the dirt roads leading to them looked cracked from drought and disuse. There were patches of what might have once been plowed fields but now were fallow with so little growth that she wondered if they'd been salted during one of the wars.

"Lily?"

"I'm sorry—no, don't turn around. We actually want to go through Novgorod for gas and a break. We'll be about halfway to St. Petersburg."

"Do you find it odd that there've been so few cars on the road?"

At the moment the highway was deserted save for them. A scant forest of thin evergreens faded into the gloom on their left and on their right stray cattle nibbled at what remained of summer grasses. Other than the barbed wire fence keeping the cattle off the road, there was no sign of human occupation. "Not really, but I am wishing I hadn't read *The Gulag Archipelago* in college."

Nicole laughed. "Do you want to see if there's any music on the radio?"

"Let's hope. More Murphy's Law—a long unexpected drive in a rental car without an MP3 adapter." They were initially greeted with a blast of static, but with a few adjustments the radio picked up a thin signal playing a lighthearted Russian pop number. "Is this okay?"

"I'll live. Did you see that sign?"

Lily craned to see behind them. The sign was already lost in the darkness. "No, sorry. What did it say?"

"A list of cities and how far. None of them were eighty kilometers or less. The first city on the list was one hundred twelve kilometers."

Puzzled, Lily asked, "So, Novgorod wasn't on it?"

Nicole gave her a sour look. "I don't know Novgorod from Albuquerque in Cyrillic. There were three lines. The first started with an odd W character. The second reminded me of Ilyria with something like an S for the first letter. That's the best I can do."

Lily switched on the light again. "Novgorod in Cyrillic starts with an H. Maybe we should go back to the other route." She scanned a widening radius on the map for any cities like Nicole had described, regretting that she hadn't seen the sign as well. "There's Shimsk. I can see that being a little like Ilyria. If we're headed to Shimsk then we're going southeast instead of northeast."

Nicole was slowing the car and easing onto the shoulder. "I'll turn around. There's nobody else out here and it's wide enough."

Lily glanced at the GPS to see if the compass would at least help, but was surprised to see it no longer blinking "Lost satellite reception." Its map was steady and clear and looked just like the one on her lap. "Hang on, we may actually be getting something useful here."

"Just in time."

She turned on the device volume again. "It confirms that we're going southeast, so we're definitely off-route." Lily zoomed out on the display and studied the results. "I will take back every bad word I said if this is right. Supposedly, if we go ahead about eight kilometers, we can take a road north. It'll be faster than turning back."

As they drove Nicole reported each passing kilometer and Lily looked anxiously for their turn. At about four kilometers the road pitched sharply downward.

"I didn't expect this," Lily said. "Maybe we're coming down off a steppe or something."

With no other cars, Nicole slowed to a crawl as the GPS announced, "In one hundred meters turn right."

"I'm riding the brakes. I don't want to miss our turn."

"I don't see anything there." Lily hoped she didn't sound as frazzled as she felt. "Let's give it another couple hundred feet before we panic."

Nicole eased off the brakes a little and they quickly picked up speed. "Your statement presumes that panic is inevitable."

"There!" Lily pointed. "No marker—if we weren't going slow we'd have missed it."

"Hang on!" Nicole slammed on the brakes and made the turn. Lily felt reassured as the GPS indicated they were now traveling north. The new road was as wide as the previous one and she was glad they were going in the right direction. The radio signal petered out after a few minutes, but they were making decent time.

After about twenty minutes Nicole pointed at the GPS display. "It stopped updating our position."

As Lily leaned forward to confirm Nicole's words the car seemed to rise off the road. Flooded with terror, she tried to scream, and bit her tongue when the car slammed down on the road so hard she saw stars. The clatter and ping of rocks on their undercarriage was so loud she couldn't hear what Nicole was yelling.

They slewed to the left, and Lily was thrown against the limit of her seat belt as they lurched to a stop.

"What the hell!" Nicole's voice was taut and high.

"Are you okay?" Lily rubbed her shoulder and tasted blood in her mouth. "Are we off the road?"

"This *is* the road. It's not paved."

As the dust settled in the glow of their headlights, Lily saw that it was true. Ahead of them was an unpaved road, full of rocks.

They were lost in Not-Sure-Where, Russia. Don't panic, she told herself. *We can always go back the way we came. We could stay here and wait for daylight.*

She got out of the car even as Nicole protested. "I won't go far," she assured her. "There's nothing out here."

"Better safe than sorry."

"We ran out of pavement." She shivered. The temperature felt like the mid-forties and falling. Thank goodness the car's heater seemed fully functional.

"I knew that from inside the car," Nicole called. "Come back."

Lily walked to the edge of the light cast by their headlights before returning to stand at the driver's door. "I don't see that it resumes, but it might. We can go forward and hope to rejoin paved road, or maybe we should just go back the way we came."

"I vote for back."

Lily nodded. "It's safer. I'll guide you turning around. Not only is it unpaved, I think it's a lot narrower." She backed away, giving Nicole lots of room.

A few seconds later she could hear Nicole gunning the engine, but the car wasn't moving. The engine roared but nothing happened.

Nicole rolled her window down all the way. "Flat tire?"

"The car would still move." Lily slowly circled the car. "I can't see much of anything—Cole, get out of the car! I smell gas."

"What?"

"Gasoline. Like the tank is punctured. And if broken metal has a smell, I smell that too."

A scant two minutes later they stood panting, breath visible in the air, some distance away from the rental car, their luggage beside them on the dirt road. Using the light cast by their cell phones Lily fished out her sneakers while Nicole looked for her warmest attire. Double layers of shirts weren't going to be enough to keep out the seeping cold, Lily thought. We're lost in Not-Sure-Where, Russia and now without shelter. *Don't panic...*

"I think we're going to have to walk or freeze," she said. She tugged her jacket around her. It was only a little warmer than a cardigan. "I knew this would be the coldest place we visited, but didn't see the point of packing along winter gear for just a couple of days, most of which would be spent indoors. Not my best decision."

Nicole had covered her white blouse with a thick sweater and a windcheater over that. "I made the same decision. But any New Englander knows socks make good mittens." She handed Lily one of her ubiquitous pairs of black socks.

Lily gratefully slipped them over her cold hands. Her own thin hose wouldn't make a difference, but Nicole's sturdy knit socks would help enormously. "It's at least fifteen kilometers back to that turning." Lily tugged her suitcases after her. She hit a rock and her carry-on tipped, forcing her to drag it. Telling herself it would be easier when she reached the pavement she plodded onward.

Nicole stumbled, but didn't fall. "Watch out—there's…Oh, I've found the edge of the pavement."

The paved road was at least eighteen inches above the gravel one. Lily discovered that by barking her kneecap on the ragged edge. "No wonder the car died. We were airborne!"

"You were wrong, you know."

Lily wanted to cry. "I don't think this is all my fault."

"No," Nicole said quickly. "I meant you were wrong when you predicted we would panic."

Lily burst out laughing and quickly wiped away the tears that formed. It wasn't as if she felt calm. "How do you know this isn't how I panic?"

"You don't have the physical signs of low dopa—"

"—mine, I know. Neither do you."

"It'll be fine. So we miss an event. It'll be—did you hear that?"

The sharp click with a sliding *shoosh* stopped Lily in the act of stepping up to the paved surface. Twirling around to face where the noise seemed to emanate from, she thought distantly that maybe it was time to panic. It sounded heavy, like a large animal. Were there bears in Russia? *Of course there are, idiot, it's their national mascot.*

She did the one thing that she knew would help. She dropped her suitcase handle and groped for Nicole's hand.

Nicole pulled her close as the noise repeated several more times. It was getting closer. The warmth of Nicole's body was the only thing that seemed real.

Fire, Lily thought. Animals are afraid of fire. They could torch the rental car if only they had matches or a lighter. She couldn't feel her feet but didn't know if that was fear or the cold.

There was a sudden glow of light. Nicole had activated her cell phone.

"There's no signal." Lily hadn't realized she could sound so squeaky.

"I just want some light."

They both jumped as a voice shouted out of the darkness.

"*Merde*." Lily could feel Nicole shaking. It wasn't a wild animal, but that didn't mean it wasn't dangerous. What kind of person would be out and about in Not-Sure-Where, Russia at this time of night?

The voice rang out again and Lily cleared her throat. Still sounding squeaky, she shouted back in her third-grade Russian, "Please help. Our auto is dead."

The click-shoosh sounds came from all directions and she realized suddenly they were hooves on rock and dirt. She added the light of her cell phone to Nicole's and huddled closer.

Five riders abruptly materialized out of the darkness. All she could make out were outlines reminiscent of John Wayne.

There was a sudden flash of sharp light, then it steadied to a bright glow that momentarily blinded her. She didn't let go of Nicole.

Several of the riders laughed as one said something Lily took to be, "God save us from tourists."

She squeezed Nicole's hand. "They realize we're lost."

One rider urged his mount a few feet closer. He said over his shoulder, "You were right, son. But I think the cows are safe." He turned his attention to them. His words were at first too quick for Lily to follow.

"Slow, please."

More carefully he said again, "Why are you here?"

"We are going to St. Petersburg. We are lost. The car is there." She pointed and fumbled through her shaky Russian vocabulary and hoped her gestures helped. "Gas on the ground. Fire? We left it. Can you help?"

One of the riders guided his horse in the direction Lily had pointed, turning on a lantern of his own. He played the sharp beam over the car, and Lily could see that one of the front wheels was clearly bent out of position. He yelled back, "There's a gas puddle."

Nicole said, "I did kill the car, didn't I?"

Lily nodded, unable to follow the comments of the men beyond a general consensus that the car was very broken. "You had help from the ground."

"I hadn't thought of it that way."

The man who seemed to be in charge dismounted and walked slowly toward them. His bulky leather jacket and chaps over dungarees showed years of hard use. His thick, black beard obscured his mouth completely and almost covered his eyes as well. "You can't stay here. Come with us. In the morning we take you to Novgorod."

He sounded nothing like Great-Aunt Lillian Von Smoot. "Not tonight?"

He shook his head. "Too far for horses. Truck comes in morning. Come." He gestured at his horse.

She realized he wanted them to get on the horses. She didn't know anything about horses. She hadn't made any preparations for horses. Nowhere in the itinerary was there *anything* about horses or cowboys or broken cars.

Nicole said, "Does he mean what I think he means?"

Lily took a deep breath and tried to steady her nerves. "Yes."

"I'd rather walk."

"We walk," Lily said in Russian.

He pushed his worn Outback hat away from his eyes and she could finally see his expression. He once again launched into a long sentence, but Lily shook her head. Scowling he simply said, "Too cold. Too steep. Too far."

The other riders circled back from the car and he began handing their luggage up to them even as Lily said, "Wait!" She watched her carry-on settled in front of one rider and Nicole's behind him. Their large suitcases were each lashed expertly across the sturdy rumps of two other horses. Then they ambled off into the night.

When she and Nicole didn't budge their would-be rescuer was clearly annoyed. He stalked back to his mount. "Come."

The only remaining rider, the one who had originally turned on his lantern, said, "They're scared, Father."

His father answered, "Silly women."

Lily said to the boy, who looked no more than twelve or thirteen, "Of course we're scared."

He scowled to match his father. "I'm missing dessert."

Lily's anxiety faded so quickly she felt a little lightheaded. They were still in the real world where a teenager's stomach ruled. "I'm sorry."

Nicole whipped around to face Lily. "What are we going to do?"

"Not ride sidesaddle, I guess."

Nicole's voice sounded very tight. "If you don't mind I'd rather panic."

***

After an extremely uncomfortable twenty minutes on horseback, moving at a steady descent along what was clearly a well-used trail through one of the large pastures, Nicole found herself deposited in front of a small single-story dwelling. Smoke curled from the chimney. The bright, comforting light cast from its windows was sufficient for her to make out a modest, sturdy barn and several riders returning from it. Their suitcases were stacked on the wooden porch.

Lily had spent the journey talking to the boy. He had dismounted first and helped her down and Nicole could only marvel at the sight of his smiles and Lily's remarkable aplomb. Her own thighs were on fire and her underwear felt as if it had been pushed into places it was never meant to go. Lily, surprise surprise, looked as if she did this every day.

An older woman clad in a flannel work shirt and sturdy canvas pants appeared in the doorway, adding to Nicole's relief. An exchange ensued, which Lily joined. She heard Lily say her own name and then Nicole's, and they all went inside.

It was more of a bunkhouse than a family home, Nicole thought. The structure appeared to be constructed entirely from wood, with a well-scrubbed but unpolished floor under a thin carpet that showed the most common paths the inhabitants took from beds to kitchen to the table. Like something out of a Hollywood western, four bunks lined one wall and the rest of the space was devoted to a communal table, fireplace and an ample kitchen. The main room was blessedly warm, both from the roaring fire and the substantial wood-burning stove in the kitchen area. She couldn't help herself and made a beeline for the fireplace. She wasn't sure they would have survived the night, even walking. The very thought made her a little dizzy.

Nicole smelled coffee as the woman set a large kettle with steam rising from its spout on the table next to a mixed assortment of mugs. A covered dish from the oven immediately joined the kettle. The woman didn't look much older than forty, though it was hard to say. Her long, dark hair had no silver strands but her face showed a lifetime of hard work. She gestured at them and Lily translated, "She kept the dessert warm. We're invited to join them."

Whatever it was, it was bubbling hot and smelled sweet. Nicole sat next to Lily at the end of one of the long benches. The coffee was unsweetened and unpalatably strong, but the hot mug felt heavenly in her hands.

Lily translated some of the conversation but admitted she couldn't follow it all. When handed her plate, Nicole automatically said, "Thank you."

The woman looked at Lily, who translated. She said something back and Lily smiled. "She says this is her son's favorite."

"And we just took some of his share. Should I offer it to him?"

"No. We should break bread with our hosts, don't you think? I've got a packet of M&M'S in my suitcase I can give him later. Leonid…" She nodded at the boy. "Leonid told me that his father is in charge of one of the largest herds in the area, and his mother is the best cook in Russia. They do have a truck, but two of the men use it to circle the fences during the night. He'd gone out to close up the barn and saw the lights on the road which, you can imagine, is rare at night because everybody knows the road is only for repair crews."

"Stupid GPS."

"You got that right. So when the car didn't get any closer and the lights went out he told his father. They thought we were rustlers. Yippee ki-yay."

"Yippee ki-yay," one of the men echoed enthusiastically and everyone laughed.

Whatever worked, Nicole thought. She raised her mug. "Yippee ki-yay!" There was another laugh and they all shared a universal gesture of toasting.

"Well, thank you Roy Rogers," Nicole muttered.

Lily nibbled at her cobbler, then said something in Russian that made the woman smile back.

Nicole burnt the tip of her tongue on her first bite, but she immediately felt better for the warmth of it. No doubt she was low in dopamine and blood sugar. She looked at their hostess and said, "This is delicious."

Lily murmured a translation and the woman looked as pleased as Nicole's mother did when complimented for her cooking.

"I don't know her name," Nicole said to Lily.

"Katerina." Going on around the table, without missing a beat, Lily added, "Leonid Senior, Leonid Junior, Bela, Novick and Yusef."

She nodded at them all, feeling less alien. "I'm sorry I don't speak Russian, but I'm pleased to meet all of you and grateful for your rescue and hospitality."

Lily's translation seemed to take a lot longer than necessary.

"What else did you say?"

"I hope I said that you're a very smart doctor who studies brains. I haven't a clue what the Russian is for *neurobiology*." She paused to field a question, shaking her head. "I just explained you're not that kind of doctor. I think."

Dessert was quickly finished, and the three other men retired to their bunks with battered paperbacks and to take turns using the shower. The two Leonids sat down to play a game of cards with a deck that had lost most of its printing on the backs. She thought they might be playing gin, but it was hard to tell. Lily joined them as a spectator, offering a new deck of cards that Nicole recognized as one an airline had handed out on a flight after they'd been upgraded to first class. It was accepted with smiles and promptly put into use. Leonid fell on Lily's M&M'S as if he hadn't been fed all day, making his father smile. There were plenty of basic packaged goods on the open pantry shelves in the kitchen—pictures alone identified pancake mix and canned vegetables—but she was willing to bet store-bought candy was a rarity, and she felt inordinately beholden to Lily for having something to give.

When the last cowboy emerged from the bathroom, she made a grateful visit to it herself. The heavy cast-iron fixtures were something out of the early twentieth century, but their functionality and durability was undeniable. When she returned the table had been shifted to make room for a thin mattress in front of the fireplace. A blanket showing creases from having been unfolded covered the mattress. Its bright red pattern stitched with white roses was incongruously frivolous in a home with no pictures on the walls, she thought, but there were shelves on one wall stuffed to overflowing with paperbacks. She had no issue with those priorities.

Lily was leaning over her open suitcase. "I'm going to change into a T-shirt and keep on my jeans—do you want to change?"

"Yes, actually." She found a T-shirt and her own jeans while Lily excused herself. She tried not to think about the fact that she was about to share a bed with Lily. The mattress wasn't that big. She'd stay near the edge. She told herself crossly it was not the time and place for sweaty palms.

Katerina, dressed in woolen long underwear and a shapeless dressing gown, appeared from the only other room with two more blankets, both substantial wool blends. She offered them to Nicole, who made a stab at saying thank you in Russian. It earned her a giggle and a parting phrase that probably meant "sleep well" or simply "goodnight."

She glanced at the men in the bunks, all now sound asleep. It wasn't a life where sleep was wasted.

Lily returned to pull out a thick pair of socks before zipping her suitcase closed and quietly rolling it out of the way. In a low voice she said, "This is quite the adventure, isn't it?"

"We'll have to take photographs, because no one will believe it." She took her clothes into the bathroom and wished she'd gotten out her toiletries. She didn't want to wake anyone at this point by opening her suitcase again. Fortunately, there was a tube of a minty paste on the shelf above the sink. Hoping she wasn't breaking some kind of international custom, she squirted a little on her finger and rubbed her teeth. The water she scooped up from the tap was frigid but delicious with a slight tang of minerals. Her hands were tingling from the cold when she joined Lily on the mattress.

Lily had wrapped herself in one of the blankets, sleeping bag style, and taken the side further from the fire. Nicole followed suit and realized Lily had fashioned her a pillow from one of her sweaters.

"Thanks for this," she whispered, tugging one corner of the makeshift pillow.

"You're welcome. They took our mattress off their own bed." She ran a hand over the blanket under them, tracing one of the roses. "She said this was a wedding gift."

Nicole digested that, and made a pledge to never complain again about having to share a large house with her mother. She had always accepted that her life was privileged, but this experience was definitely reminding her of how much she had. She felt a wave of gratitude for her mother—what if she'd gone back to India before she'd met Robert Hathaway? As annoying as it was to have her uncles trying to wield influence over her, they had not succeeded. Their interference was nothing more than a petty annoyance in the larger scheme of things.

Lily's breathing steadied but Nicole couldn't quite drop off to sleep. Her awareness of Lily's body, just inches from hers, was a constant drumbeat of desire. The tousled curls were orange in the light from the glowing embers. Her expression had relaxed, though one laugh line showed at the corner of her mouth. Nicole wanted to kiss it softly, whisper goodnight and feel a promising tremor against her. The tenderness that washed over her was surprising—it wasn't something that Cole felt.

Or, she asked herself, was tenderness something Cole wasn't allowed to feel? She hadn't just led a privileged life because of her home and access to education or even due to her own hard work. She'd found a way to be a lesbian but avoid any social consequences. Her arguments for doing so—as she trembled with a longing to touch the woman next to her—no longer made any sense.

They would make sense again, she told herself, when she got home. But with the firelight flickering over Lily's face, she didn't believe it. A half-life wasn't what she wanted. While this experience, lost in the Russian countryside and rescued by cowboys, was easily the strangest of the trip so far, the feeling of being a coward and a fraud on the beach in Brighton was the most unpleasant. She didn't want to go back to that. And if there was no going back, that meant there was only moving forward.

Simple physics, Dr. Hathaway, she told herself. *Entropy works in one direction.*

Lily shifted and opened her eyes. Her voice barely above a whisper, she said, "Cole?"

"Hmm?"

"I can't get warm."

"C'mere." She rearranged their blankets so they were both wrapped together with Nicole spooned behind Lily in what she hoped seemed an impersonal arrangement. Her breasts felt swollen and her palms were damp, and if she shifted just slightly her lips were in Lily's hair. The warmth of Lily's body against hers seeped into places she realized had never felt warmth before. She knew that her brain was sending out massive amounts of oxytocin but that knowledge didn't diminish its impact. Her muscles relaxed, her thoughts slowed and every nerve capable of conveying pleasure sparkled into awareness.

Her hand rested lightly on Lily's hip. It would only take a slight change to move it to a suggestive, intimate position. It's what Cole would do. Cole would delight in the need for absolute quiet.

It was time, she thought drowsily, to let Cole go. She snuggled a little closer to Lily, who made a quiet, sleepy sound. Cole made things complicated. With Lily asleep in her arms, life seemed very simple.

CHAPTER FOURTEEN

Surfacing from sleep Lily was first aware that her hip hurt and her thigh muscles were sore. Had she moved at all in the night? Then the unusual feeling of sharing her bed with another person kicked her brain all the way awake. Blinking, she took in the fireplace, the floor, the vigorous snoring from across the room. When she'd drifted off last night she'd thought maybe it would turn out to be a dream. But she really was somewhere in Russia, warm, and fed on the generosity of cowboys. Yippee-ki-yay.

She was also sharing a bed with Nicole and steeped in the steady warmth. She could feel Nicole's chin against her shoulder and stopped herself just before she snuggled back and drew Nicole's arm closer around her as if it were a protective, warm blanket.

She nearly went back to sleep, drifting on a fantasy of long, slow kisses, but the nerves in her hips woke. Sharp needles lanced down her legs and she had to shift her position onto her stomach.

Nicole moved with her, arm now stretched across Lily's back. Libido began to make pointed suggestions but then her bladder played the ultimate trump card. With a sigh of regret she slid out from under Nicole's arm and escaped to the bathroom.

When she returned she saw that a low light had been turned on. Katerina was in the kitchen, filling the kettle with water and ground coffee. She flipped levers on the stove and the change in heat output was immediately palpable.

Tiptoeing past Nicole, Lily said quietly to Katerina, "Can I help?"

"No, sit. We'll have coffee and milk. Sit and wake up."

Lily definitely felt more comfortable with her limited Russian. Nicole could probably explain why her brain, after sleep, could recall vocabulary more easily. No doubt it had to do with something-nefrin or whatever-tonin. "I slept well. Thank you so much."

"That blanket has always been good for sleep." She smiled and added, "Good thing you are both women. It also helps make babies, so my mother told me."

Lily grinned. "A baby would be hard to explain when we got home."

"Our boy arrived ten months after we married, so I put it in the drawer for two years. Got it out and was pregnant right away, but it didn't last. The doctor said no more, so it has stayed in the drawer."

"I am so sorry," Lily said. Katerina seemed capable of raising a dozen children, and they would have all been loved.

"We have a good life. Busy. Hard, but good. Away from the wars." Katerina brought a cutting board and a bowl of apples to the table. "Do you like apple cakes?"

It didn't matter what apple cakes were, Lily would have said yes. A block of firm white cheese joined the apples, and Lily picked up the grater before Katerina could protest. "Stop me when it's enough."

Over the next twenty minutes, one by one, the other members of the household joined them. Nicole sat between Leonid Junior and the broad-shouldered Yusef, looking only a little bit nervous.

Lily was amazed at how quickly the apples were peeled, chopped and stirred into a sweet batter along with the cheese. The end result was a kind of stick-to-the-ribs pancake served with strips of dried beef. It tasted like manna from heaven to Lily.

They were just finishing when there was a rumble of an approaching vehicle.

Lily explained to Nicole, "That will be our transport, back from their rounds."

The two weary men, heavyset and darkly bearded, were taken aback to find their usual seats at the table occupied. Explanations were shared. One of the two said he'd seen their car and wondered where the occupants had gone.

Lily excused herself to shower and dress. She hoped that they could find a working phone in Novgorod in time to let the bookshop know they wouldn't be making that appearance, and to tell the rental car folks where to find their vehicle. It was a good thing she'd paid for the extra insurance. Hopefully Uncle Damon wouldn't have a conniption.

When Nicole took her turn in the shower Lily stepped outside to take pictures of the house and barn. The horizon was a soft orange with a halo of lavender and amethyst where the sun would soon rise. She took several steps before she realized the crunching underfoot was frost.

Uncle Damon wouldn't believe where they'd ended up. There was not a sound of modern life—no drone of cars, no thudding underfoot of the subway, no clicking of anything mechanical except for her camera shutter.

She inhaled as much of the champagne air as she could and let it out slowly. They were lucky to have survived the night. Looking up she was glad to see that the overcast skies were gone. All the stars had faded save one. Wondering if a wish on the morning star was a Russian tradition, Lily made one quickly, just a silly one, not important really.

The door opened and closed behind her and she thought the light step probably belonged to Nicole. Her suspicion was confirmed when Nicole stopped alongside her and said softly, "How beautiful it is out here."

"So quiet," Lily said. "It's a revelation for this Manhattanite."

"Some winter mornings in Meredith are like this. As if the whole world is asleep and dreaming the same dream."

Surprised by the fanciful words, she turned her head to look at Nicole's profile. The cold air had reddened her cheeks, but the rugged landscape suited her. She wondered how she'd ever thought Nicole looked anything like the prosecutor who had interrogated her. They both had dark brown eyes, but Nicole's could be soft with emotion or sparkling with humor. Without warning, Lily raised her camera to take a picture of Nicole with the barn in the background.

Nicole frowned, but after the camera clicked. "I'm not really awake and you're taking my picture?"

I want to remember her with the sky in her eyes, Lily thought. "For the scrapbook. Two days from now this will be a blur."

Still frowning, Nicole said, "You're probably right. I wish it weren't true. This is a memory I want to keep."

Lily wasn't sure if she meant their Russian cowboy adventure or the ruggedly beautiful countryside in the chilly morning air. "It's funny how an unexpected twist in the road can still lead to something good."

Nicole looked at her, lips parted as if she were going to say something. But she turned away at the sound of the door opening. "Time to be on our way, I think."

Lily took a last look at the morning star, but it had faded into the brightening sky. It didn't seem likely that her wish would come true. She was traveling with someone who had proven that happiness was in your numbers, not in your stars. It had been foolish to wish for magic. Magic wasn't real and there was no future for her feelings.

As the truck rumbled its way to the top of the rise above the house, Lily rolled down the window to give Katerina one last wave. Their temporary escort of mounted riders was led by Leonid Junior.

Nicole leaned across Lily to reach the window. She too waved and called out, "Yippee ki-yay!"

Lily laughed as the men swung their hats over their heads in parting and galloped off to their rounds. For a few wonderful moments she soaked up the warmth of Nicole's body against hers. She was highly doubtful that she'd get another opportunity.

***

"They all look alike." Nicole surveyed the gate area of the international terminal at St. Petersburg's Pulkovo Airport. "Faded cream-colored walls, plastic chairs. A duty-free shop, coffee shop, chocolate shop and—" She shook her head. "A TGIFriday's, even here."

"It's a definite letdown that our last meal before we get back to the US is airport food." Lily paused next to her, then pointed. "I vote for the Siberian Crown or Mom Rush—Mother Russia."

"You pick." Nicole didn't think her stomach would find much difference between the airport salads at either establishment. "There's a bank of pay phones right next to them."

Lily turned in the direction of the Siberian Crown. "There are more tables free in here. Let's go in and order, then you call home."

After ordering an Olivier salad on a bed of greens, Nicole made her way to the pay phones. It was almost five p.m. in St. Petersburg and she was nearly certain that meant it was nine a.m. at home and her mother would definitely be up.

Happily, the phone was answered on the second ring and her mother's immediate relief was palpable.

"I'm using a pay phone," Nicole explained. "I called last night when we got to our hotel and left a message. Did you get it?"

"Yes, I was very worried until then. Kate and I were at her doctor's appointment. Lily sent me an e-mail too. She is very considerate. How did you damage a rental car?"

"I had help from the road." She smiled into the phone, reliving the surreal experience of standing in the dark surrounded by cowboys. She told her mother details of the breakdown—not enough to alarm her again—and went on to describe their rescuers. "It felt as if we'd fallen into a time warp."

"I cannot believe my daughter spent the night with communist cowboys."

"I don't think they were overly much concerned with politics, Mom. And if you put it that way, what would my uncles think?"

She was relieved to hear her mother laugh, miraculously clear after being conveyed through atmosphere and space and back again. "You were chaperoned by Lily. She would not let you get into a compromising situation."

If her mother only knew that Nicole wanted to get *into* a compromising situation with Lily. Desire had become a dull throb that could flare into a melting ache just from the vanilla and cherry scent of Lily's shampoo. She glanced back at the restaurant and realized Lily had changed their seat location. She seemed to be in one of her rare reflective moments, pensive, a little tired.

"I never expected to see my luggage on horseback."

"I can hardly believe it. Your sister says you have made it all up."

Lily sipped her water, glanced at her watch, then looked toward the phones. Over the distance their gazes locked. Nicole realized she could have happily stood there for a long time, just looking at her. While she had been as entranced by the Balkan choir in Moscow as Lily had been, she'd also been transfixed by the sight of Lily, eyes closed, with the music washing over her face. Eyebrows lifting slightly at the high notes, lips parting momentarily at the low tones—she had never looked more beautiful. That is, until the very next morning, standing in the cold daybreak air watching the sunrise.

The pleasure of looking at Lily had her dopamine, serotonin and oxytocin spiraling upward. Together those chemicals created a peculiar dizziness. Excitement prickled along her nerves. Euphoria mixed with yearning. The brain chemical cocktail had a non-scientific name she used all the time in her speeches. She shouldn't balk at using it, except right now she wanted to believe that if she didn't name it, it didn't exist.

The emotion-that-shall-not-be-named...A foolish construct, she told herself. But if she didn't name it and it went away, then she'd be better off.

The phone was suddenly slippery in her hand. Blinking in surprise, she took her pulse. Her heart was pounding. She felt out of breath. Her norepinephrine and epinephrine were surging—as if she were afraid of something. Her ears felt hot and the terminal seemed all at once brighter—her pupils were dilated.

She missed the next bit of whatever her mother was talking about as she sorted out the stimuli. She ought to have anticipated that response. As soon as her mind conceived that there was a source of constant happiness within her reach, her body feared that it would be taken away.

There you have it, she thought. *You're living the emotional teeter-totter the study subjects talked about.* Misleading feelings, ambiguous signals, unreliable ups and downs—ecstasy and terror, wonder and confusion.

Well, she thought dryly, all those students who thought I wasn't human, they were clearly wrong.

"…packages arrived," her mother was saying. "What shall I do with them?"

"The heavy one leave out for one of the graduate assistants to pick up. It's peer reviews I've finished that can be mailed back. The other is for you and Kate to open."

"I'll take it right in." Her mother's voice fell to a near whisper. "Kate is quite depressed. The doctor says her amniotic fluid is marginal—no better and no worse than last time, which is both good and bad. He hoped it would improve."

"How is she physically?"

"She is so swollen, especially her hands and feet. The iPad buttons are big, though, and she can at least play Angry Birds. If she gets out of bed for long she starts to cramp."

Kate confirmed her condition when her mother handed over the phone. "I get up to shower and pee, then it's back in bed. I am so fucking bored. I'm going to be so fat when this is over."

A month ago she might have told Kate she should have thought of those consequences before dispensing with birth control, but she could almost hear Lily whispering in her ear, "Be fair. Kate is a healthy young woman and had little reason to expect a pregnancy to consign her to bed rest."

She shook Lily's voice out of her head. "I'm really sorry you're so miserable. What are you reading?"

"My usual wonderful trash. Books you'd hate. Did you send us a present?"

"I did."

"I'll put the phone on speaker."

She heard the snip of scissors and the pop of tape followed by the rustling of paper. Her mother said, "There are two little boxes."

"You can decide between you who likes which best."

She couldn't help herself, she glanced again at Lily, who gave her a questioning look. She answered it with a grin.

After another rustle of paper Kate said, "Oh! So pretty! Where did you get them?"

She explained about the gift shop and the Alhambra—it seemed so long ago now. "You really like them?"

"It is such a beautiful bracelet." Her mother's voice conveyed the kind of broad smile Nicole remembered from a long-ago Mother's Day morning when she and Kate had brought her a breakfast of rubber eggs and burnt toast. "I will wear it tonight for my garden club meeting."

"It's gorgeous, sis," Kate added with an audible sniff. "Thank you."

"Don't cry."

"It's hormones. I cry over dog food commercials these days."

Nicole held the receiver away from her ear as Kate blew her nose. Across the distance Lily mimed a look of surprised inquiry and Nicole shook her head with a silent laugh. Her observant brain noted that they had become skilled at silent communication.

Kate chatted for a little longer and Nicole was glad to hear less stress in her voice. She had feared Kate and their mother would be at each other's throats, but clearly some dynamic had shifted. She would have some adjusting of her own to do, perhaps, when she got home.

As she walked from the phones to the restaurant where Lily was waiting she realized she was no longer counting the days until this tour was over and she was home again, safe behind the walls of her office. Instead, each new morning she looked forward to the first sight of Lily's welcoming smile even as it filled her with a growing sense of impending loss. She didn't like this teeter-totter of emotions and yet…it was wonderful. Improbably, unexpectedly wonderful.

CHAPTER FIFTEEN

"*Laissez les bons temps rouler!*" Lily gestured broadly at the crowds crisscrossing Bourbon Street. Balconies over their heads with intricate cast-iron railings were thick with even more partygoers pelting beads at the people below them. Heavy rock music blasted down the street, but Lily didn't recognize the song. It was fitting for the raucous atmosphere. And, Lily thought, equally incongruous with the antebellum guesthouses with their Creole windows and French shutters. "Looks a little like Europe, doesn't it? Our bookstore is just two more blocks. I'm glad we walked."

"You're right, it's just like Europe except for the fraternity boys walking around with cocktails in one hand and the beads being flung at our heads." Nicole ducked as a scarcely covered college girl lunged for a purple and gold necklace. "Yes, just like Europe."

Lily tried hard not to smile at Nicole's obvious distaste. No doubt Professor Hathaway kept a good distance between herself and student bacchanals. She'd gone to her share of parties at Wellesley but usually the ones without the drunk frat boys. "You wanted to see it, remember? By midnight this will be a mob. It's not even Southern Decadence, so I don't know what the occasion is."

"Perhaps there's no need for one."

"Like the Jimmy Buffet motto?" Libido pointed out that a lot of the college girls—who weren't a lot younger than she was—were quite attractive. Right, Lily thought. Like she wanted to turn up in some *Girls Gone Wild* video. She could just imagine the Merrill Boone headline.

"You're going to need to clarify that."

"It's five p.m. somewhere, time for a margarita? Apparently in New Orleans it's spring break for somebody, all year round." She broke off as a broad-shouldered young man stumbled to a stop in front of her.

"Hey, babe!"

"Hi!" Lily matched his goofy grin and loud tone. "You don't know me at all! Your friends are over there!" She pointed.

"Oh yeah?" He nearly fell over as he turned, then went green. Lily threw her arm out in front of Nicole, backing her up.

"Oh good heavens," Nicole said. "Two million years of evolution and *homo habilis* still can't hold his liquor."

Lily averted her eyes and tried not to inhale as they stepped around the wretched, retching young man. "Okay, maybe this isn't much like the Europe we just saw, but think Europe circa sixteen hundred. The streets were sewers."

"I am profoundly grateful to be a creature of the flush toilet epoch."

The bells and music of Bourbon Street faded behind them as Lily followed the GPS instructions and turned left on Dumaine Street. As far as she was concerned, the box was still on probation. "The bookstore isn't far from the Ursaline convent—one of the oldest in the United States. Would you be interested in one of those late night walking tours through French Quarter cemeteries? We can probably join one tonight. Spooky stories and voodoo curses."

Nicole hesitated. "I think I'm too tired for superstition, especially after another presentation. I have only myself to blame for not paying attention to the first assistant, who created the itinerary. Otherwise I would have asked to stop off at home for a week, to rest and recharge—and change out my wardrobe. I'm still jetlagged."

They'd arrived at their quaint French Quarter hotel—several blocks from the hubbub of Bourbon Street, thankfully—at midday. Like Nicole, Lily hadn't been able to stay awake. Their shared dinner had been quiet. After that Nicole had been a real trouper, neat as a pin in her black slacks and white blouse, and displaying modest enthusiasm for the first big book club gathering at seven o'clock. It was longer, more personal and ultimately more draining than any of the bookstore signings. She didn't know if Nicole had managed to sleep again after they'd returned to the hotel, but Lily had crashed. Nicole had seemed refreshed when they met up for a short cab ride to Tulane University and her first lecture in the United States. But Lily was also finding it an increasing downer every day to look at the same clothing. Tomorrow morning she'd set aside for laundry before they went to the book festival. Undies could be rinsed in the sink only so many times before a trip through a washing machine was mandatory.

Perhaps she'd suggest a shopping trip. They could both ship home clothing and buy some new things. With two official paychecks now in her bank account, less some payback for the advances Uncle Damon had arranged, she could afford a new suit, if they found an outlet mall.

They reached the Pontchartrain Bookstore and fell into their normal pattern. Lily assessed the crowd and took a few photos—at least thirty-five women, a few men and standing room only at that. The old bookstore smelled like the library at Wellesley. If ideas and creativity and storytelling and knowledge put together had a smell, Lily decided it was a blend of wood pulp and furniture polish mixed with damp sweaters and the tang of ink. She wouldn't be surprised to find the aroma was something that triggered all those brain chemicals Nicole talked about—was it oxytocin? She inhaled deeply and held her breath. Whatever it was, it worked and it was free.

Nicole made her usual opening remarks, markedly more casual and with more humor than that first appearance in London. It was a shock to realize it was more than a month ago now. If practice made perfect, Nicole had had lots of practice. Nevertheless, she was constantly adapting and Lily had yet to be bored.

"As I've talked about my findings all over the world I find that most people want to see relationships as natural combinations. Sometimes they're compatible through similarities, like cheese and cream. Other times they're compatible through their differences, like shrimp and grits." There were chuckles from the crowd. "We can taste when it's right. We can smell when it'll be good. I was raised in New England and we like our seafood, but I'd never had it with grits—apparently I've never had properly made grits in my entire life. Last night I had properly made grits. After a long and tiring journey, they may have saved my life."

Nicole waited while the crowd laughed. She glanced at Lily who nodded back—even with an obviously appreciative crowd, Nicole still looked for reassurance.

"How can people who are, on the surface, as different as crustaceans and corn, meld into a satisfying, enduring relationship? Based on the research it all comes down to chemistry. Today I want to talk about how our DNA determines our brain's response to the chemicals of passion and love."

Lily eased into a position where she could lean on a bookcase. She didn't know this material.

"A complex and uniquely tuned mixture of chemicals is pumping through all of our brains right now. No two people, the world over, have the same mixture. We can, however, have similar mixtures. When we feel attraction or experience good sex our brains load up on oxytocin, serotonin and dopamine. Even scientists refer to the mixture as the Love Drug, and it's powerful stuff. No doubt all of us know someone who, under the influence of the Love Drug, did something they would have never otherwise contemplated." Nicole nodded along with many in the crowd. "But we also know people who didn't lose their mind—literally—when they were obviously pumped full of the Love Drug. Researchers have determined that specific strands of DNA sequencing are what control how our brain handles the Love Drug cocktail. What I found in my study is that people with the same type of response had relationship lengths at least twenty percent longer than those with different responses to the Love Drug's effect."

There was a low murmur in the crowd and a woman near the front raised her hand. Nicole said, "Go ahead."

"Does that mean if I'm crazy about a guy and get all googly and flushed when he's around, and he says he's crazy about me but is cool as a cucumber that we're not really compatible?"

"Good question—that's an easy leap of logic to make, but it would be an incorrect one. Physical manifestation of the Love Drug in our system is only one indicator of its presence, and perhaps of how much of it is present, but it's not a consistent measure of what's actually going on in our brains. Sexual attraction can evidence itself in a telltale blush, a shaky voice, averting of eyes. But another person with the same amount of the Love Drug releasing in their brain may look nonchalant. On the inside, by their own standards however, they may feel as if they're going insane with these foreign feelings. That person might have…" Her voice trailed away. She glanced at the lectern as if to consult notes.

"That person might have…The person you describe might have a higher resistance to the physical impact of the Love Drug, that's all. But I want to clarify that the exterior response to our brain chemicals varies both because of biological reasons—it's in our hard wiring—and for social reasons. For example, most men feel the urge to cry as often as women do, but social conditioning has taught them to tamp down the physical response. So it would be a mistake to think that just because we're hardwired to respond in a certain way that we don't have some measure of control. It's equally a mistake to think that because we have a measure of control we're not sometimes incapable of mastering our hard wiring." She glanced at Lily, then back at the audience. "An example from my own life would be that my mother's hard wiring is to shriek, loudly, at the sight of a spider. When I was little and she did that it frightened me and when I was in my twenties I realized that she had learned how not to scream for my sake."

A young woman in the back raised a hand and Nicole again paused. She was being unusually indulgent, Lily thought. Usually she asked people to hold their questions.

The young woman said, "So if my girlfriend says she's just not the type to cuddle and, you know, get all emotional when I get home from work, that's something she can't help?"

"That's very difficult to say on a specific case. My background in biopsychology says there's a fine line between *can't* and *won't*. We do train our brains to shut down responses. *Won't* can easily become *can't*. We live our own limitations with a staggering amount of success." Nicole paused again, this time with her mouth not quite closed. Her gaze met Lily's for a split second and then she fumbled with the copy of her book that she always took on stage.

After a long, deep breath she went on, "Another key consideration about the Love Drug is that for some people it can prove highly addictive. People who have many relationships over a lifetime may be always looking for a new relationship to get another swell of the Love Drug, and leave relationships when the chemicals fade. In other words, they love falling in love." Nicole paused to let a ripple of agreement die down. "Questionnaire results from our long-term successful participants were highly indicative that they continued to produce the Love Drug over the long-term. As the octogenarian in the case study on page one-twelve puts it, 'Hank and I stayed high on love. Don't know how we did it, but from the day we met until the day he died I got a flutter when I looked at him and I could tell he felt just the same about me.'"

That was Lily's favorite case study. She heard her little sigh echoed around the room and felt a little foolish. In this day and age, being romantic at heart seemed hopelessly old-fashioned. That ass of an interviewer in Geneva wasn't alone in his thinking that romance and love were fairy tales perpetrated on society to sell diamonds and candy. But she was romantic at heart, she realized. Some classmates in college had been obsessively focused on getting married—not so much on finding a mate or romance. They would go to great lengths to discuss wedding dresses and places to have a ceremony while Lily felt too shy to even begin to admit she wanted someone in her life who made her heart miss a beat. So she was capable of a quickie in an alley. But that's not how she wanted to live.

Lily lost track of time, mulling over what Nicole had said. There was no doubt in her own mind that when she looked at

Nicole her brain was cranking out chemicals. But it couldn't be the Love Drug. More like a Lust Drug. Because if it was a Love Drug, then why did she feel so bleak? She wanted, even now, to nuzzle at Nicole's neck as she unbuttoned her blouse. She felt a little faint remembering how waking up in Nicole's arms had made her feel warm and sheltered and deliciously aroused.

But her feelings were running headlong toward a cliff. If she didn't stop she was going to fall, and it was going to hurt. It was futile to feed the situation with wishes on stars. She didn't need magic that led to a lifetime of regret.

Applause jolted her back to the room. Nicole was giving her a quizzical look and Lily realized she was scowling. She immediately sent a smile, but Nicole's eyebrow went up. Busted not paying attention, she thought. She'd tell Nicole she was thinking about their flights or something. Little white lies were preferable to the big ugly truth.

***

The New Orleans Festival of Books was nowhere near the size of that in Frankfurt, but it attracted crowds of readers interested in the new fall books. Nicole noted that, as in Frankfurt, the lines for fiction writers were long, and lines for celebrities signing memoirs were equally popular.

"This is still a great turnout," Lily said when Nicole commented on the size of the crowd. She craned her neck to look at the marquee that listed that hour's appearances and which line they were listed to appear in. "You can't compete with a tell-all by someone who claims he was the rent boy for every gay actor in Hollywood during the sixties. But it looks like you have more people than a Supreme Court Justice."

"I think that's a sad commentary on our times."

"Oh, I don't know. The Supreme Court Justice is an anti-woman homophobe." Lily shrugged. "The gay guy says he went out gambling in Monte Carlo with Marlon Brando. I'd rather hear about that." She gave Nicole a cross-eyed look. "Or get advice from Love Doctor Nicole Hathaway."

"Stop that nonsense."

"Or what?"

Nicole answered her with a look that was challenging and almost feral, then gone so quickly that Lily wasn't sure what she'd just seen. She had goose bumps and her heart was pounding.

She forced herself not to take a step back. "I promise not to say it in front of readers. But they're still thinking it."

"Oh piff." Nicole turned to the next person in line.

"How scientific," Lily muttered under her breath.

Out of the corner of her mouth Nicole said, "It's a technical term."

They fell into their usual pattern without further discussion. It was certainly easier to handle a crowd when she didn't have to translate. The cavernous convention floor was increasingly crowded as the festival planners brought in roving street performers to entertain the many readers waiting in the long lines for the biggest titles of the season. Jugglers had their line in a cheerful mood, and that was welcome.

Their allotted ninety minutes passed quickly. Then Lily was sliding her camera into her purse and thinking about their flight to Atlanta in the morning and the lecture at Georgia State University.

As they left their table Lily noticed that one line snaked almost twice as long as any of the others, leading up to the author of the summer's surprise erotica best seller. Some of the fans were even dressed in fetish wear—full body latex suits, dog collars and chains were on display. A couple of women wore thigh-high leather boots with heels so high that Lily knew they were on tiptoe. Libido found it *very* interesting, but Lily decided it was best to avert her eyes. Circumspect advised that she not bring it up unless Nicole did.

The subject was unavoidable when their path toward the exit passed a group of leather-clad women Lily thought had to be dominatrices. Nicole raised an eyebrow with a glance at Lily, who shrugged by way of an answer.

"To each her own," Lily said when they were out of earshot. "I like high heels, but otherwise, not really my scene."

"Nor mine."

Lily wondered if there would ever be a way to get Nicole to admit just what her scene might be. On the other hand, she reminded herself, it wasn't as if she'd been busy telling Nicole about her alley tryst or even that she was a lesbian. It wasn't as if they were girlfriends gossiping over coffee, sharing diet tips and *Cosmo*'s latest sex secrets. *Inappropriate, remember?* "Those are fantastic boots, though."

Nicole smiled. "I don't disagree, not that I would ever consider wearing any like that."

Nicole in high heels? No, that was simply wrong. About to answer, Lily dodged around a fast-moving woman barreling through the venue, obviously in a huge hurry.

She was two steps past the woman when her heart stopped.

She couldn't breathe.

Nicole stumbled against her. "What is it?"

Lily told herself not to look, to keep walking. But couldn't make her feet move and she had to know. She turned her head—and met Merrill Boone's inquiring gaze.

***

Surprised by Lily's sudden stop so close to the exit doors, Nicole followed her stunned look. For a split second she was flummoxed by how forcefully her fight-or-flight reflex kicked in, then she took Lily's arm and dragged her toward the doors. She'd think about the fascinating chemical reaction later. All that mattered right now was that Lily seemed incapable of moving on her own.

From behind them she heard Boone call out, "Lillian Linden-Smith!"

Lily stumbled and made a sound like a hurt bird.

Nicole bumped open the exit door with her shoulder. "Just keep moving."

Boone was taller than either of them, but heavier, and in a footrace they would both easily outdistance her, Nicole analyzed. Did she have assistants somewhere, with cameras? The last thing Lily needed was footage of her running for her life.

Lily had done nothing wrong, she reminded herself. It went against her personal grain to be the ones forced to run.

"Is that hair supposed to be a disguise?" Boone had followed them out the door.

Nicole dodged along the crowded sidewalk. A streetcar was getting ready to depart just a few hundred feet up the street, but they wouldn't get there in time.

The woman's drawl was penetrating. "What are you running from? They're still investigating you. They're going to reopen your trial! Do you have a comment about that?"

Lily gasped for breath and shook off Nicole's hand. "I can't do this. I won't. I just won't."

Nicole didn't know what Lily meant until Lily turned to face Boone, who was bearing down on them like a hurricane.

"I have nothing to say to you." Lily's voice was thin and high.

Boone, her face flushed from the pursuit, was digging frantically in her briefcase. "Why don't I have a damn camera! You're not running away from me. People want answers. Where's their money? What about that e-mail where your mother said she was leaving everything to you? What about the key to a safety deposit box that's still unidentified? Have you no remorse about the lives you ruined? About the people who lost their homes? If you don't have the money how are you still wearing Givenchy?"

A lone tear rolled down Lily's cheek. Tension, Nicole thought, as she watched Lily dash it away. Her voice was steady, however, when she asked, "Are you even aware that you're addicted to serotonin?"

Nicole blinked.

"What?" Boone stopped a scant foot from Lily, using her height to tower over her. She hadn't yet looked at Nicole, but Nicole was certain Boone knew she was also standing there.

"Serotonin," Lily repeated. "You're addicted to it."

Actually, Nicole thought, Boone was likely addicted to a norepinephrine and adrenaline cocktail. An urgent voice asked her why that even mattered. Lily had answered Boone's questions with a question, and was standing her ground.

"That's slander. Don't tempt me to sue you. I can't wait to have the power of discovery to find what the prosecutors in New York missed."

"There's nothing to find. There was *never* anything to find. Defending myself bankrupted me, which ought to make you happy. I have paid for the sins of the father and mother. All I have left fits in a small storage locker and a suitcase. Go ahead, find a pile of cash everyone has missed—my lawyers would like to know about it too!"

"You are one of the best liars I've ever seen. That innocent act almost works."

"Now that's actually slander." Lily was pale, but her voice was rock solid. "I think I could prove malice too. I'm done being your punching bag for ratings."

Boone inched even closer and Nicole stepped in the way.

Boone glared down at her, layers of blond hair not moving an inch in the wake raised by a passing bus. "Who are you?"

"Ms. Smith's friend."

"It's Linden-Smith. Lillian Linden-Smith." She pulled a cell phone from her case and frantically tapped at its tiny buttons.

Lily's head was up but she seemed momentarily at a loss for words.

Nicole casually observed, "You must be a middle child."

"What does that have to do with anything? Who *are* you? Why are you protecting her?" Boone used her cell phone like a pointer. "Are you getting a cut?"

Nicole shrugged. "Middle children tend to use shorter sentences and smaller words because of their acute awareness that parental attention spans are limited. They also tend to ask many questions in the hope that a parent will answer at least one and acknowledge they exist. *Invisible* is a common descriptor middle children use to describe their familial standing. These feelings lead to increased production of serotonin inhibitors." Nicole lifted her chin. There was no research basis for anything she'd said, but the important thing was to give Lily a chance to recover. "Hence, resistance to feeling the effects of serotonin and your body's output of far more than you need. Your pupils are dilated in a situation that is not threatening. You were eight or nine when your parents divorced?"

Boone's mouth gaped slightly as she took a step back. "I don't know how you know that, but you have no idea who you're messing with."

Nicole was on comfortable ground with this line of argument—truth was easier than bullshit, a fact she'd tried to impress on her students as often as possible. In Spain or Italy she'd peer-reviewed a study about the body language of bullies and their potential biopsychological roots. "Just a conclusion based on observation of your combative stance, tendency to lean forward at the ends of your sentences, and, of course, the classic overcompensation for fear of being devalued as a woman the way your mother was."

"Be careful. Be very careful." The steely gaze with eyebrows low was practiced and looked good for the cameras, but Nicole wondered if Boone could actually raise her eyebrows if she wanted to. Her range of expressions did seem limited. Perfect for the camera. Icy in person.

"It's merely a working hypothesis." Nicole cocked her head. "Clearly, your addiction to serotonin and adrenaline hasn't harmed you insofar as it built your marketable reputation for being relentless." She made another educated guess. "With your ratings slipping—"

Boone jabbed at Nicole with her cell phone. "My change of networks had nothing to do with ratings. How dare you insult—"

"Merrill." Boone stopped talking at the sound of her own name the way most people did. Skilled debaters learned to ignore the impulse which Nicole interpreted to mean that Boone had constructed her life so that no one argued with her. "Of course your ratings are slipping. You just published a memoir."

Lily's voice was steady and clear. "Rock bands release a greatest hits album because their agent insists the time is right. Sales are slipping, business partners are leery of further investment, time to make some easy cash for no work. Next thing you know, they've disbanded." Her tone became increasingly helpful and upbeat. "The Foo Fighters are an exception."

Boone was wide-eyed. "What in God's name has that to do with me?"

Nicole was intrigued that Boone's honeyed accent diminished under stress. Was it an affectation? If so, it was a transparent declaration of not feeling her authentic personality was adequate to get her through life. "When your agent suggested you write a memoir, you're too intelligent not to know it was a warning. Your neurobiological reaction was to sublimate your panic by producing greater extremes of work product...And resorting to Botox."

Boone gasped, confirming Nicole's theory. "I don't know who you are, but I'm going to find out. And I'm going to nail your friend Ms. Linden-Smith to the wall while I'm at it."

"No, you're not."

All the money and time that Boone put into her face was ruined by the sneer on her lips. "Listen, honey, nobody tells me what I will or won't do."

When it came down to basic debate tactics, Boone was either rusty, or she'd ignored the fundamentals of the practice of law. Nicole sighed. "I think you meant to say that very few people tell you what you will or won't do."

"This conversation is over," Boone snapped. "Now get out of my way. I don't have time for you. Lillian?" She tried to step around Nicole, but Nicole moved into her path again.

"Or what? You'll prove to your corporate handlers that you're the bloodhound they think you are? Isn't that your nickname?" Nicole hoped she remembered that tidbit correctly. "The Bloodhound?"

"You make that sound like an insult."

Nicole didn't smile though she wanted to. Boone was thoroughly engaged now. It was fortunate that her entourage was nowhere to be found. It occurred to her that Boone had been rushing into the venue to meet up with her staff, all waiting wherever Boone was supposed to be signing her book. "Is being compared to a canine a compliment?"

"Now you hate dogs? Bloodhounds are amazing."

"Of course they are. Highly skilled and very reliable dogs bred to perform a task. They receive stimuli and act on it." She saw Lily give her a quizzical glance that quickly transmuted to her usual air of aplomb and confidence. She didn't think anyone but her could read the flutter of fear clouding the green of Lily's eyes. "What they do is programmed into their DNA."

Boone's hostility had taken a backseat to puzzlement. Nicole knew she'd touched a nerve. She pressed her advantage. "By comparing you to a creature whose success is purely instinctive, people are really saying that you run prey to ground because you don't know how to do anything else."

At a momentary loss for words, Boone finally spluttered, "That's ridiculous."

"Your constricted pupils and slight perspiration at the neck says you know otherwise. As I said, you're an intelligent woman. You already know everything I'm telling you, but you've chosen to live in denial. You're chasing foxes because you don't know how not to and you wrongly believe cornering more foxes will prove you are capable of better than that."

"Doing the same thing over and over and expecting a different outcome is a sign of mental illness," Lily offered in her helpful-docent mode.

"According to Albert Einstein," Nicole added.

"Actually, it was Rita Mae Brown."

"Really?"

"Absolutely." Lily nodded with conviction.

Boone seemed to come out of her stupor. "You can spare me your psychobabble. You can't manipulate—"

"Merrill." Again, Nicole successfully interrupted her. She had graduate students who could best this woman in any kind of discussion. What kind of editing must they do to her interviews to make it appear that she could win a throw down with Daniel Webster? "We're going to leave now. Enjoy your evening."

Boone's cell phone chirped and Boone reflexively glanced at the display.

"You're late, aren't you?" Lily gave Boone a steady look. Nicole marveled at her now clear eyes and fearless stance. "You are a smart woman, I agree. You've spent so much time and energy on me and found nothing. Accountants who work for lawyers know that I am broke. There's no money to find. If you keep at it and still find nothing they might stop calling you The Bloodhound."

Nicole held up a hand to draw Boone's gaze back to her. "Ms. Smith may be without resources, but she still has friends. Given your ratings issues and the personal makeover you're attempting with your memoir, consider the damage a lawsuit for stalking, harassment and malicious libel would do. How long do you think it would take me to find a lawyer who would be happy to take a retainer for the pleasure of embarrassing you? To find a sympathetic talk show host who'd be pleased to help you fall further from grace?"

Boone's gaze had narrowed and Nicole was willing to bet she had already drawn up a mental short list of enemies who might be willing to take her on if the price was right.

"If I have to I will find those people you just thought of," Nicole said in a low voice. "You are too smart not to know when the only winning hand is not to play."

The phone chirped again and Boone stood like a woman pulled in two directions at once.

"This conversation is over," Lily said, then she turned on her heel and walked away with Nicole in her wake.

CHAPTER SIXTEEN

Lily's ears told her that Nicole was behind her, but she couldn't turn her head to look. She didn't see anything but the pavement ahead of her next footstep. They reached a corner. She turned randomly, crossed the street, turned again.

Nicole finally slipped a hand gently around her arm and pulled her to a stop. "She's not following us."

"I know." They were standing in the shade of an antique shop near Bourbon Street. It wasn't that hot, but the asphalt seemed wavy.

She vaguely heard Nicole snap, "You are *not* going to faint!"

She did anyway, or something like it. Disoriented, feet not on the ground, she heard Nicole's voice somewhere above her saying, "Not even a blink when Cossack outlaws ride down on us in the middle of the night... You're not giving that bitch the satisfaction..." To someone else maybe, "Thank you. Yes, in here."

There was a hubbub of surprised voices and a scratching of stools on a wood floor. Lily found herself sitting upright at the edge of a booth seat, Nicole's hands clamped on her upper arms.

Over her shoulder Nicole said, "Just the heat, I think. Thank you so much."

A woman with bob-cut gray hair peered at Lily from around Nicole, her dark face creased with concern. "You okay, honey? Here's your purse. I know you wouldn't want to be parted from it."

"Thank you," Lily managed. She included a bartender in her grateful look as he set down a frosty glass of water.

Nicole relaxed her grip, then slid into the booth across from Lily.

The other woman regarded them both with beaming approval. To Lily she said, "That was like something out of *Gone with the Wind*. She just scooped you right up and carried you right in here." She turned her bright gaze to Nicole. "You must work out or something."

Nicole nodded at Lily without looking at her. "Her purse is heavier than she is and you did that part."

"That is the truth about purses, now ain't it? You sure you're okay, honey?"

"I'm fine." Even to herself, her voice sounded close to normal after a couple of swallows of the cold water. "Thank you again."

Left alone, they fell silent. Lily didn't know why it felt awkward. Maybe because other people in the bar were still stealing glances at them. Maybe because she had a mental picture of herself in a fabulous Scarlett O'Hara gown with a ripped bodice and Nicole in a raffish Clark Gable suit, carrying her up a curving staircase to their bed...

"Are you really feeling better? Can I get you something stronger than water?"

"I would love a vodka and cranberry juice." She watched Nicole go to the bar and considered that it was the second time this trip she'd been held off the ground by another woman. The two experiences threatened to merge in her memory with the confusing, exquisite blend of being held close and safe while being enjoyed and savored.

She felt faint again.

Nicole returned with two identical looking cocktails and a bowl of pretzels and peanuts. It was a neighborhood bar, Lily gathered, with worn, not quite level floors and the lights just low enough to imply anonymity, but not so low the bartender couldn't see a signal for another round. "Thank you." She meant for more than the drink.

"You're welcome."

She didn't meet Nicole's gaze until after a refreshing sip. The tart cranberry woke up her brain and the vodka slightly burned her throat. "You know where I made my big mistake?"

Nicole shook her head. Her dark gaze never left Lily's face.

"I didn't know that with my life in a shambles, planning a funeral for both parents and realizing that they'd lied to me just like everyone else, that the sudden wealth and travel and rich cousins on speed dial was all based on a fraud—what I really needed more than anything else was a publicist. They don't teach you that in school." The vodka took some of the tension out of her shoulders.

"What would that have done?"

She couldn't keep the bitterness out of her voice. "I'd have never given interviews, those first few days. Someone would have told me that words and pictures can be chopped up and repackaged. That I could say 'people think I'm rich and I'm not' and the headline would be 'I'm not that rich says Ponzi heiress.' I needed a publicist more than a lawyer. Hell, I didn't even realize I needed a lawyer until they arrested me."

"You were innocent."

"Naïve. I thought being innocent was enough. With people like Merrill Boone, innocence is meaningless. I was good ratings, nothing more." After another hefty swallow, Lily noted, "You called her a bitch."

"Not to her face. I would have though, if it might have helped."

"I've never heard you swear."

"It seemed appropriate to the situation."

"You didn't have to get in her way. She could come after you. It wouldn't take her long to come up with your name. She'd milk the notoriety of *Love by the Numbers* for her own publicity." Lily shivered at the idea that Insignis would somehow get dragged into her problems. Uncle Damon had stood by her, and he and his small company didn't need Merrill Boone camping in his office.

"Let her."

Lily shook her head. "You don't get it."

"I do."

"She could decide to look into the mystery of your mother's immigration status. The puzzling questions surrounding your birth certificate. The unfortunate stigma of your sister's unwed motherhood."

Nicole's expression hardened. "I know. I don't relish the idea."

"Then why did you do it?"

She sipped from her glass and gave it a surprised look. "That tastes better than I thought it would."

"You're from New England and you've never had a Cape Cod?"

"I don't tend to drink."

"Are you changing the subject?"

"Why would I do that?" Nicole was looking anywhere but at her.

"You did a nice thing and I think you're embarrassed."

Their gazes met for a moment, then Nicole's smoky brown eyes seemed to darken even more. "I dislike bullies and she's not very good at it, in spite of her publicity. Her vulnerabilities were obvious. You got off to a great start with serotonin addiction. Incorrect, but inspired."

Lily still felt like Nicole was trying to change the subject. "I couldn't think of any of the others. But you put your biopsychology chops to work."

"She was remarkably easy to read."

"She's a dipshidiot." Lily blew out air before having another sip. "I doubt she'll leave me alone, but I stood up to her and as far as I know, it won't be on YouTube by morning. I sat in my condo for months and months, afraid to go outside. I thought if I ever had the chance I'd slap her, or scream, or something like that. Not...blind her with science." She giggled.

The corners of Nicole's mouth twitched. "I wouldn't say it was science, but it was a reasonable facsimile."

Lily decided a pretzel was a good idea. Around the crumbs she said, "You've worn off on me."

"I refute that claim." Nicole's attempt to look stern failed. "From our first meeting it was very clear that you are gifted at making suppositions sound like facts."

"You mean I'm a bullshit artist." Lily's grin widened as Nicole, of course, lifted one eyebrow.

"You are a diplomat at heart."

"Some people would say it's the same thing." She waved a hand at her drink. "It might have been smart to get something to eat before this, but I certainly feel better."

Nicole shrugged. "What are we supposed to be doing tonight?"

Startled, Lily searched her memory. "Nothing—our flight is at nine thirty tomorrow morning, so it means leaving the hotel by seven." Clearly, their bar bonding time was over. She'd been about to suggest finding some dinner.

"I think I'd like to have room service and try for an early night," Nicole said. "If that's okay with you."

"Sure. I'll probably do the same thing." Even as she said it, Lily knew she didn't want to be alone. She'd brood and raid the mini bar for more alcohol and twenty-dollar cashews. With all the fabulous food in New Orleans she could at least find a relaxing meal.

***

She'd liked the cocktail but hadn't finished it. Sitting at the desk in the hotel room, staring at the untouched room service menu, Nicole felt numb, not tipsy. The scene with Boone had been surreal. She'd only been frightened for Lily's sake—there was nothing she had that Boone could take away. Though Nicole had refined her arguments with academic resources, she'd learned how to argue a point from her mother. Let Boone show up at their house and try to question Indira Hathaway, or Kate, for that matter.

She smiled at herself in the mirror over the desk. Arguing to win was in her DNA. The smile faded as she recalled the image of Lily, pale and shaking with tension, standing her ground against the tank-like Boone. Lily was so small, seemingly so fragile. Profound trauma had not broken her, though. Again, Nicole thought of her mother, who hadn't been broken by life either. For a moment she was tempted to call home, just to talk, an urge as unusual as the one that had prompted her to help Lily by distracting Boone.

Kate was the impetuous doer of good. Kate rushed into things without thinking first. Kate had been in the seventh grade, and Nicole a college sophomore, when they'd come upon boys throwing rocks at a cat in a tree. It was an uncomfortable memory because she'd stood frozen wondering why anyone would practice cruelty and thinking how to summon help. But Kate had launched herself screaming at the boys, knocking one down before Nicole could even move. The boys had run off when they'd realized Kate wasn't alone—they didn't realize Kate was the one they had to fear. Kate had refused to leave the scene until the cat moved and appeared to be just fine.

That was Kate. Not her. She could hear her own lecture in her head, talking about the fine line between *won't* and *can't*. That we argue for our limitations with spectacular success. But today Lily had been just like that cat and Nicole hadn't hesitated to protect her. Was that what love did to a person?

She looked into her own dark eyes, seeing no sign of her turmoil in her somber expression. Love, she thought again.

But for her knowledge of psychology, she'd call it insanity. She felt utterly unlike herself. The clamor and noise in her head was something she could no longer ignore.

Love? Her?

It only took minutes to change her clothes.

***

Lily hadn't gone as far as getting out the seamed stockings she'd worn in London, but if she was going to find a club and dance to release her tension, she had thought the little black dress and the Manolos were the least she could do. She liked wearing them. But, she told Libido firmly, there would be no alleyways, no trysts. That wasn't her mood.

After a quick, delicious dinner of Creole shrimp on mustard greens with a sweet pecan dressing, she backtracked toward the hotel. There had been a club with a promising level of dubstep thumping out of the open doorway and a rainbow sticker in the window alongside various other symbols from university logos to "Who Dat?" for the Saints football team.

There was no bouncer to navigate or even a cover charge. The crowd was mixed in gender, but most pairings appeared to be same sex. She felt right at home wriggling her way onto the crowded dance floor. She wanted to move, stretch, twirl, spin like Julie Andrews on a mountaintop. Maybe Boone would come back. Maybe she wouldn't. But Lillian Linden-Smith was no longer *afraid*.

She wasn't running away anymore. She was running toward life again.

She found herself dancing to Deadmau5 with two young women, as impersonal as hip to hip could be in the boisterous crowd. She didn't think they were old enough to drink but that wasn't her problem. Eventually they danced away and Lily just kept moving.

When arms wrapped around her from behind she was reminded of that attractive Welsh butch. But it wasn't her mood and she slipped out of the other woman's grasp. When she turned around to wag a finger at the other dancer she saw a chunky brunette with a cheeky grin giving her an inquiring, hopeful look. She had the shoulders of a long-distance swimmer.

Lily smiled and shook her head.

The other woman took advantage of the song lyrics to mouth, "Then I'll be on my way."

Lily laughed as the brunette sidled up to another woman. To each her own. A few weeks ago she might have said yes. But even the flicker of the thought brought the image of Nicole's smoky eyes, and even more powerfully, the conviction and strength of Nicole's voice as she picked at Merrill Boone.

The music changed and softened its pace to what passed as a slow dance in a club. Her energy drained, she now felt tired—and was glad. It was possible she'd sleep, even though her heartbeat felt a little unsteady when she recalled the petrifying moment she'd recognized Boone. That had been the worst of it, as it turned out.

Perhaps it was time to go back to the hotel. A frozen margarita to sip from on the walk would be refreshing. Reaching the bar she ordered one virgin, to go, and relaxed while she waited.

A voice suddenly boomed into her ear, making her jump. "My buddies said we were in the wrong kind of place to meet a woman like you."

She gave the sandy-haired jock in the LSU T-shirt a narrow look, then turned her back on him.

He sidled around to the front of her. "Now, you're not gonna tell me that you're not into men are you?"

Unsmiling, she shouted back at him. "I'm not into men and I'm certainly not into boys."

He scowled and said something that was lost in the music, though it looked to Lily liked it had included *queer*.

She waved her hand dismissively in his face. "Run along."

The woman from the dance floor was suddenly next to her, leaning in between them. "This asshole bothering you?"

"He's not succeeding," Lily said. "I don't need a rescue, thanks."

She exchanged cash with the bartender for the frothy green margarita in its clear plastic cup and pushed away from the bar. The jock elbowed the brunette who staggered and trod on Lily's foot. Lily dropped the glass, lunged to scoop it off the floor before all the contents spilled and butted heads with another woman who'd been standing right behind her.

"Damn it!" She could only see stars.

***

Nicole put down her fork with a satisfied sigh. It had been a walk to get to the café where she and Lily had eaten last night, but worth every step. She would tell her mother all about shrimp and grits. If she was lucky, it might mean less vindaloo.

Thoughts of what life would be like when she got home were disjointed. She couldn't predict with any certainty what changes it would take to add Kate and a baby more or less permanently to her life.

She paid the bill and picked up her leather jacket from the back of the chair. The white UCNH T-shirt tucked into her jeans had much in common with most of the other diners, college-aged kids. Did they think the jacket added something else or was that all in her head? Slipping it on, she relaxed into its warmth, welcome after the chill of the restaurant air-conditioning.

Pausing to look at a display of Mardi Gras masks in a window, she confronted her reflection. She liked the way she looked in the jacket. But like looking at her reflection, putting the jacket and her entire sexuality into a box so she could study it was how she had kept from actually dealing with its meaning. An all-too-easy mental sleight of hand.

Putting the jacket on had felt different tonight. Not like a mask she was donning temporarily, as she had in the past. Tonight the jacket felt like an amplifier, an announcement. On a metaphoric level, she might never take it off again. It felt as if everything the jacket represented now fed a part of her she'd kept starved. She would not go back to ignoring the hunger. But how could she conquer all the barriers she had created and accepted as necessary without turning upside down the life that made her so content?

Some of those barriers guaranteed a future without Lily. She walked for a while, riding the edge of all the fear that surrounded any vision of the future without Lily in it. All possible futures had no Lily, she tried to tell herself. Lily collected male hearts and attention like breathing and one of theses days Lily would like one of them back. Nicole would receive Christmas cards and announcements of life events, such as "And baby makes three."

If there was no Lily, there was no reason to change. Simple, then, she could go back to her life. But she knew it would not be the same. The difficulty there, however, was that she had already changed. She was in a middle place, still trying to go backward and knowing full well that forward was the only direction physics allowed.

Love.

Her of all people, in love and changed by love.

Curious, the way despair felt through the denial and distance necessary to keep her norepinephrine and epinephrine at bay. Equally curious how admitting that her brain was high on the Love Drug left her feeling oddly relieved. Was this how she handled euphoria and panic? Push the fear away, and wallow in false contentment?

Lily listening to music. Lily laughing at a billboard. Lily reveling in a horseback ride in the middle of Russia, and sleeping like a baby on a mattress in front of a fire. Lily was everywhere in her memories. Would she, for the rest of her life, feel the pulse of excitement in her blood and the thick sensation of arousal whenever she smelled the vanilla and cherry blend of Lily's favorite shampoo?

Her wandering path had turned back in the direction of her hotel. Music poured out of a little club that reminded her of the one in Edinburgh, though the volume was not as painful. She wasn't ready to settle in for the night, and a frozen drink like the ones she saw other pedestrians enjoying was appealing. Dr. Hathaway knew that alcohol was not the most useful sleep aid, but Nicole, woman in love, thought it might help. She couldn't afford to lay awake, fantasizing about the impossible beauty of Lily's hair on the pillow next to her.

Her drink ordered—the house's specialty Hurricane—she surveyed the dance floor. There were several petite blondes in the crowd. If she didn't look too closely she could pretend they were all Lily. Lily, Lily everywhere, but not a drop to drink, not for her. There, she could imagine the one in the black dress and stilettos, dancing with her back to the bar, was Lily. Or the one in the green-sequined sheath—Lily could easily wear something like that.

Her gaze went back to the black dress, taking in its details. It had the same sleeves that cupped around the shoulders, was the same length...Her hair was blond, but at the roots much darker—a shade that could have been red.

Coincidence.

When a brunette embraced the intriguing blonde from behind, Nicole relaxed. It couldn't be Lily, then. She turned to take her bright red drink from the bartender, then realized it was in a tall pilsner-style glass.

"Sorry—I should have said I wanted to carry it out." It was easier to make herself heard now that the music had changed to something quieter.

The bartender shrugged his broad shoulders and quickly poured the contents into a standard plastic cup. She sipped from the straw. Fruit punch and several types of liquor—it was too sweet for her taste, but very cold. She relaxed for a few more sips.

She was about to leave when a male voice to her left said what she thought was, "Fucking queer."

Startled, she couldn't help but look. All in a rush she saw the back of the petite blonde in the black dress, the brunette from the dance floor, a football player with gigantic shoulders and all the makings of a hostile situation. There was a jostle and the blonde's drink hit the floor. Nicole went to grab it before somebody slipped in the spreading liquid and collided with the blonde.

"Damn it!"

Nicole was seeing stars. That accounted for being certain that she'd heard Lily's voice. She made a second grab at the cup, bonked heads again and gave up.

"It's on my shoes—can you hand me a napkin?"

The brunette said, "Sure thing, sweetcakes."

The foul-mouthed jock looked like he wanted to spit but he stepped back when Nicole pointed at him and said in her firmest professorial voice, "Go away!"

The blonde froze in the act of dabbing sticky liquid off one of her shoes.

Nicole met the familiar, green gaze.

Curious the way her auditory nerves blanked out the music and hubbub of voices. She heard instead Lily's quick intake of breath. A pulse fluttered in Lily's throat.

The brunette eyed Nicole and said to Lily, "Is this dyke bothering you?"

"No," Lily said automatically. She blinked, glanced down at Nicole's clothes.

Nicole realized she was still no more skilled at reading Lily's expression than she had been on the day they'd met. She had only the usual cues. Lily's heart rate was up. Her eyes were bright with what might have been tears of tension or shock.

"I don't need a rescue, really," Lily said to the brunette.

The brunette looked a little put out. She once again eyed Nicole. "You're into leather daddies?"

Lily burst out laughing. She teetered on one foot while slipping her shoe back on. She gave the brunette an indulgent look, but shooed her away with a gesture. "This is a friend."

The brunette stared for a moment longer, then shrugged and headed back to the dance floor.

For some reason Lily continued to smile at Nicole. She made a point of looking down at Nicole's boots and her gaze seemed to take in every detail of the leather jacket.

Finally, she said, "Dr. Hathaway, is there anything you'd like to tell me?"

Abruptly released from her own shocked review of all the cues she'd taken as indicative of Lily's heterosexuality and wondering how on earth she'd been so wrong, Nicole thought the only thing to do was feign nonchalance. "I think…" She hoped her voice sounded more cool than it did to her own ears. "I think we may have equal confessions to make."

"It never came up."

"True." Were they equally to blame or had her own desire to avoid the topic been internalized by Lily? "I keep parts of my life separate to maintain balance."

"I thought it would be inappropriate to bring up." Lily seemed eager to make that point. "I didn't want to make you uncomfortable. Not knowing how you might react, you know, it's an odd world, people don't always take it well and we were going to spend so much time together it would have been weird maybe, so I didn't think—why create undue tension—"

Nicole watched her own hand rise and was as surprised as Lily seemed to be when she pressed her fingertip to Lily's lips to silence her. "I understand. I had some of those same thoughts myself." There was no point in explaining that in retrospect she'd been attracted to Lily the moment she'd met her, and hiding that fact had been her biggest motivation.

Lily's lips were warm against Nicole's fingertip. Nicole took a deep breath and made herself pull back even though she felt as if she were standing in quicksand. "You decided to come out dancing tonight?"

"I didn't think I could sleep. It's exercise," Lily added quickly.

"You wouldn't lack for partners I would think."

Lily flushed a deep red. "Uh, not tonight, I mean, that's not what I was doing."

"None of my business," Nicole said hurriedly. Had Lily been out before this? Were they talking about dance partners or sex partners? "You can have a private life."

"So can you," Lily assured her. "The, uh, this look suits you. It's just different from your day-to-day. Until right now you didn't ping my gaydar at *all*."

"Nor you mine."

They stared at each other. Nicole was profoundly grateful she was wearing the jacket—her rock hard nipples didn't show. She hadn't given her feelings away and wasn't about to start. "Would you like to go back to the hotel?"

Lily glanced at the puddle on the floor. "I wasn't destined to have that drink, so maybe I should. But you don't have to. I mean— do you want to find someone to dance with?" Something about her body language didn't ring true with her smile, though. "I could be your wingman."

"Not necessary. I came in for a cold drink, not to dance. I...I, uh, have to be in a particular mood to dance with strangers."

Lily shifted her body toward the door but she was watching the dancing. "We should go then."

"Unless you want to dance." Nicole surprised herself with the offer.

Lily stammered something about maybe it being time to leave, but her body turned back to the dance floor. She does want to dance more, Nicole thought. I'm cramping her style, perhaps.

She gestured "After you" at Lily, who moved to the edge of the parquet before beginning a low-key, simple side-to-side step. Nicole didn't know the song, and knew it was coincidence that the predominant lyric was repetition of the word *madness*. The bass beat was low and throbbing. Nicole doubted she would remember it later, because all she could feel was the excruciating almost-brush of Lily's arms against hers. She resisted all her practice at dancing to seduce. Didn't inch closer, couldn't keep eye contact. She was aware of all the people around them, men and women, but couldn't keep her eyes on Lily for fear of what might show.

It was Lily who shifted closer with a quick half-step, then leaned in to shout over the music, "By the way, I don't think you're a leather daddy."

Nicole rolled her eyes. "I just like how the jacket makes me feel."

Lily pointed downward. "My shoes. Same thing I think."

Except, Nicole might have said, the shoes had been part of what had fooled Nicole. Shame on her for thinking a lesbian wouldn't wear such sexy, seductive shoes.

The song ended and she wanted to leave. It hurt to dance, it hurt to be so close. She was only now sorting out how likely it was she'd deceived herself about Lily's sexuality because it made spending time with her safer. What would keep her hands in her pockets, her eyes in her head—how would she damp down the idiotic, inappropriate impulses that her brain generated now that she knew the truth?

The brunette who had been lingering earlier suddenly reappeared. She bumped her hip against Lily's. Lily looked annoyed by the contact and danced away, but the brunette gave Nicole a challenging glance before following Lily.

It was tediously predictable body language from the brunette. Completely ignoring Lily's very obvious cues of dismissal, she tried to pull Lily against her by tugging on her arm. Lily's rigid posture reflected her outrage. Nicole edged between them, and without thinking wrapped Lily close against her side with one arm while giving the brunette a one-fingered salute that would have made Kate cheer.

The brunette reacted by using both hands to shape a W on her forehead. Lily seemed to melt into Nicole and they rocked together. For a long, peaceful moment, Nicole held her close and acknowledged that nothing in her life had ever felt quite so right.

The moment shattered when Lily pushed her away and then stomped with all her might on Nicole's foot.

"What the hell!" Fortunately the boot saved her from a stiletto-sized hole in her arch, but Nicole was still limping as she hurried after the rapidly departing Lily. She forgot all about her drink on the bar as she chased Lily out to the street.

Lily didn't slow down when Nicole called her name, but the stilettos slowed her pace and Nicole was catching up without having to run. The evening was still warm and the streetlights had come on while they'd been in the bar.

They rounded a corner and were in sight of their hotel.

"What did I do?"

Lily stalked onward.

Finally, Nicole drew alongside her. "I think I deserve an explanation of the physical assault."

"You were the one who manhandled me first!"

"You wanted that woman to keep pestering you?"

"Of course not—but that was for me to decide. You may have been very helpful earlier today, but I do not need rescuing from you or anyone in a bar. I can handle myself."

"I just thought—" There was no point in continuing as Lily pushed her way through the revolving door and into the hotel lobby.

They walked in silence to the stairs, Lily maintaining a half-step lead. Their boutique hotel was only three stories and their rooms were across the hall from one another on the second floor. Lily took the stairs at a rapid pace, perhaps under the mistaken idea that she could outrun Nicole.

At the top of the flight Nicole tried again. "I was sure you could have handled it without me, but I thought it would get rid of her more quickly."

"Really?" Lily wheeled around. "That's why you did that? Hold me like we were...You know? Like I was some possession?"

"I'm sorry it felt that way. I just wanted that woman to go away."

Lily gave her a strange look, then stared down at her hands. "So did I. It, well…It's…I…You can't just grab me like that."

"I'm sorry."

Sounding puzzled, Lily went on, "I mean, you could have told her to go away without doing *that*."

"Was it that awful for me to touch you?" Stop talking, she told herself. Shut up and go to your room.

"No, I mean, it's not that…"

"Then what are we arguing about?"

"You…I mean." Lily clenched her fists, arms rigid at her sides. "Why did you do that? It wasn't necessary. You don't do things that aren't necessary. Your whatever-tonin is never unbalanced. You picked me up nearly off the street this afternoon and didn't even look like it was a strange thing to have to do."

"You were fainting. It was necessary."

"Well grabbing my ass in a bar wasn't."

"I did not grab your ass!"

"I beg to differ. It was my ass, after all." Lily's hands were on her hips as she tapped the toe of one stiletto.

"If my hand ended up on your ass I'd remember, believe me. It's not something I would be likely to forget!"

"Is that supposed to be a compliment?"

"Yes. Your ass is terrific!"

"Okay then," Lily snapped. "Good night." She pivoted expertly on her heels and stalked to her door.

Nicole knew that an escape to her own room was essential as the enormity of what she'd just said sank in. But in all defiance of the desperate messages from her brain, her feet wouldn't move.

***

So much for an elegant exit, Lily thought. Her key card didn't work on the first try, and she wasn't sure at all why she was so angry, she just was. And she was scared, scared that on the dance floor she'd *cuddled* with Nicole and inhaled the surprisingly arousing scent of leather and really liked it, that is until she'd realized that Nicole was just rescuing her again. She'd let down her guard and the highly observant Nicole could figure out that she felt...more than she should.

And Nicole was a lesbian! Dr. Nicole Hathaway, Ph.D., all-around emotional freezer, was a lesbian who danced in bars and could flip someone the bird. And looked neck-snapping hot in a snug T-shirt and jeans. It wasn't fair.

It was kind of a lot to take in, Lily fumed. Better to escape and figure out how she was going to go eight more weeks not seething with desire for this infuriating, attractive-all-the-time plus sensuous-in-leather woman who liked her ass.

She swiped the key card again and this time it worked, thankfully. Half inside the door her brain finally caught up with Nicole's words. She spun around. "You think my ass is terrific?"

Nicole started and sidled toward her own door. She mumbled, "It conforms to the standards of what is generally regarded as attractive in western society."

The flipped-up collar of the jacket brought out Nicole's strong shoulders. Libido had soared into the stratosphere with glee—so not fair. She didn't want to be at the mercy of an equation of brain chemicals. She put her back to her door and pushed it further open. Circumspect was wailing and wringing her hands every second that Lily delayed her escape. "That's not an answer."

"Yes it is."

"No—the question isn't how society feels about my ass." Lily stopped as an older couple exited their room and walked down the hallway toward the stairs. She gave them a bright smile and waited for them to disappear from view.

"It's not about how society feels about my ass," Lily resumed. "I asked how *you* feel about my ass."

"I've already stated my thoughts."

"You think it's terrific?"

"Do I need to say it again?"

"No." Oh, but Lily wanted her to. She wanted to be sure—of what, she didn't know. But after weeks of having no clue if Nicole even saw her as anything more than a sometimes helpful nuisance, it was strange and wonderful to think Nicole was aware of her as a woman. She couldn't admit that. She floundered for an exit line. "But you don't get to grab it unless I say it's okay."

Nicole stopped fumbling in her jeans pocket for her room key. "Are you saying it's okay to grab your ass?"

"No, you can't *grab* my ass." This wasn't where she'd meant the conversation to go. "I don't like being grabbed. I mean—wait. Do you…"

All in a rush Nicole crossed the hallway, was standing in front of her. "What if I don't grab?"

Lily tried to form phrases like, "That would be inappropriate Dr. Hathaway" or even, "We'll talk about it in the morning" but all that came out of her mouth was a shaky, "Well, that's a different matter."

Nicole lifted Lily's chin with one fingertip. Lily gasped at the naked expression of desire on Nicole's face. She'd never seen her so unguarded, so exposed. For her? Was that possible? The wonder of it set off a chain reaction flush that prickled her scalp and simultaneously tightened her nipples and threatened to buckle her knees.

Nicole slowly stooped close enough to kiss the corner of Lily's mouth.

She tried not to moan and failed completely. This wasn't some anonymous tryst. Tomorrow would arrive with a suitcase full of consequences if Nicole realized that it meant more than sex to Lily. But she hadn't a clue how to pretend otherwise. She tried one last time to save herself from the inevitable regrets. "Cole, what are you doing?"

"I'm kissing you and *not* grabbing your ass."

Lily couldn't help a short laugh. That Nicole had a sense of humor continued to surprise her. "Is that a good idea?"

Nicole drew back far enough to look Lily in the eye. "I'm not capable of higher reasoning at the moment."

Keep it light, she told herself. Don't let it mean anything. "Chemical soup for brains?"

"Something like that." There was a slight wry twist to her lips as she added, "Based on your pupil dilation and perspiration on your upper lip, I would guess that you're equally chemically challenged."

"That's just from dancing earlier."

"There you go denying what exists again."

Lily shivered as Nicole brushed her lips close to her ear. "It's a coping mechanism."

For a scant moment, not even as long as a heartbeat, she hoped Nicole might laugh and back away, but Lily's undoing was the deep, quiet noise that Nicole made as she inhaled the scent of Lily's hair.

She grabbed Nicole by the lapels of her jacket and yanked. They stumbled into Lily's room, finding the wall just inside the door.

"I think, Dr. Hathaway, we should examine our symptoms. Make a complete diagnosis."

Nicole did laugh at that, just long enough for Lily to feel the smile against her lips as Nicole kissed her, this time aggressively. Lily shivered against Nicole's lean, strong body and opened her mouth with a throaty groan she didn't try to hide. If this was about chemicals and neurobiological imperatives for Nicole, so be it, Lily thought. It was a coping mechanism, after all.

But it was unnerving not to see Nicole's face. She fumbled for the switch and light blossomed from the bathroom. As Nicole pressed her lips to the tender skin below Lily's ear, Lily tried to pull down the zipper on the side of her dress and felt Nicole's fingers join hers. The soft burr as the zipper gave way sent another thrill down Lily's spine. After another breathless kiss Nicole stepped back enough to let Lily shimmy out of the dress.

Nicole made a helpless, appreciative sound. Then one arm coiled around Lily's bare waist, pulling her into a tight embrace. A finger slipped first under a bra strap, then trailed down her ribs to ease just under the top of Lily's panties. She tightened her grasp, nearly lifting Lily off her feet.

She instinctively wrapped her arms around Nicole's neck and her legs around Nicole's waist.

It was only a few steps to the bed with its neatly turned down sheets. Nicole set her gently on the edge. For a breathless moment Lily was washed over with shyness. She looked up at Nicole, not sure what to do next. She put her fingers to the front clasp of her bra, but Nicole pulled them away.

Her eyelids were heavy with desire. "I'll take that off of you when I'm ready."

Lily exhaled in surprise and a hot shock of pure arousal. When Nicole yanked her bra straps down her shoulders she pulled Nicole's mouth to her breasts. The dopamine made her do it, that was the answer.

They rolled across the bed and Lily found herself on her back, her panties down to her knees and Nicole's denim-covered thigh hard against her soaked and aching flesh. She moaned, then couldn't hold back a yelp as the jacket zipper dug into her pelvis.

Nicole shrugged out of the jacket and awkwardly pulled off one boot, then the other, tossing both to the floor. Then the smooth cotton of her T-shirt was against Lily's stomach and breasts, warm and soft, but only increasing Lily's desire to feel Nicole's skin against hers.

Lily ground against Nicole's thigh and felt as if she were going to break apart. She tried to speak but her throat was parched from panting. After a swallow she managed to ask, "Do you want me to take off my shoes too?"

"God no." Nicole leaned down to tease Lily's nipple through the pale pink fabric of her bra, first with her tongue, then with her teeth. "I want you just like this."

Lily gave up what restraint she had left. *I'm doing this because it feels good, not because I'm in love with her. It's just my brain, not my heart.*

Pinned by Nicole's weight and a restraining hand on her arm, she coiled her free hand in Nicole's hair and pulled Nicole's head away from her breasts.

Through parted lips Nicole asked, "Did I hurt you?"

"No. I just want your mouth somewhere else."

Nicole's hips jerked involuntarily and her eyes narrowed with lust. Lily felt a heightened chill of awareness. She might be the one on her back but she had some control over Nicole.

Nicole shook Lily's hand out of her hair, then leaned her thigh deliberately into Lily so firmly that Lily whimpered in need.

"I want to feel your skin," she pleaded.

"We'll get there," Nicole promised. "But I believe you had a request first."

Lily's head swam at the whisper of Nicole's breath across her stomach. "Yes."

"You of all people should know how to ask."

She returned Nicole's not-quite-teasing look with a wry smile. "Please?"

Nicole let out a low laugh as she kissed Lily's inner thigh. Lily tried to lift her hips to complete their contact but Nicole lifted her head. "Now say it like you mean it."

Lily's already pounding heart thudded against her ribs. She knew she should laugh it off, somehow regain safety in the distance a show of amusement would bring. A prickle of fear that she was giving up too much ran down her arms, but there was no strength in her for anything more than a ragged, breathless, "Please, Cole."

The first touch of Nicole's mouth on her drew out a sharp cry. The raw pleasure of it was intense but her fear surged as well—until she heard Nicole's groan and realized that Nicole was trembling as she deeply tasted Lily, then retreated to tease and savor. With an earthy groan she finished peeling off Lily's panties. Moments later her bra joined the panties on the floor.

Deliciously naked, Lily spread herself on the bed. Nicole's T-shirt was soft against her legs as Nicole settled again, this time between Lily's legs. When Nicole's tongue flicked over her swollen flesh all of her nerves ignited in a frenzy of sensation that left Lily gasping for breath.

Already overwhelmed, legs shaking, she felt the teasing pressure of Nicole's fingers. She wrapped her arms around herself as if that would somehow save her. She arched up to Nicole's mouth, then ground down on her fingers while the bed seemed to spin and quake under her.

Shuddering with release, she wanted to cry when Nicole's clothed body covered hers. She felt wanton and exposed, and aftershocks of pleasure kept her hips moving, begging for more. Nicole's long, sensuous kisses, sharing the taste of Lily's saltysweet essence, brought Lily's desire to a raging boil.

She pulled at Nicole's T-shirt with her hands. "I need to feel you. Please, Cole."

It might have been a trick of the light, but for a moment Nicole looked shy. But the look was gone after she unceremoniously stripped off her shirt and bra. Lily couldn't help her hands—she filled them with the small, soft wonder of Nicole's breasts.

Lily swept her hands to Nicole's back, enjoying the feeling of taut muscles under her fingertips. Nicole didn't resist as Lily pushed both hands down the back of her jeans, and the guttural moan she made was very satisfying.

Her skin was hot against Nicole's. She tried to stay rooted in what her body felt, to revel in the physical, but with every touch, every kiss, it felt as if Nicole was caressing her heart.

Too late, she thought, too late. The damage was done. Nicole was everywhere inside her that mattered, in places that would be cold and empty in future days.

She begged for more and Nicole gave it to her. She said earthy, needy words that Nicole answered. For hours her body rose to Nicole's touch, possessed with a wild, unleashed abandon.

CHAPTER SEVENTEEN

Nicole stirred in the night to find Lily curled against her. In the low light from the bathroom her features were exquisite and fragile, though Nicole knew now how strong Lily was as well. She held her breath as she memorized the lines and curves of Lily's face from this intimate angle. A coil of Lily's hair tickled at her nose and she exhaled, finally, and felt all over again the swell of euphoria, of tenderness and desire.

She hadn't known she would need so many words to describe her emotions. This was unfamiliar territory. Kate—with whom she shared half her DNA—was comfortable feeling emotions and equally comfortable talking about them and, in the case of an older sister who refused on principle to give her answers to her science homework, express them at the top of her lungs. Nicole had kept her emotions tucked in the pockets of Cole's jacket. She had thought letting them out was too risky.

She gently ran her fingertips across the silky hair on the pillow. Risky to let feelings out, but this was the reward. A reward, she mused, until the consequences that would surely follow turned the reward into a penalty. So they were both lesbians, surprise, surprise. So they enjoyed the same kind of sex, obviously. The magnitude of Lily's surrender had been deeply arousing and she'd felt almost drunk.

With a shock she realized that Lily's eyes were open.

"It's not morning yet," Nicole whispered.

"Good." Lily lightly touched Nicole's cheek with her fingers. "I don't care what the theories of time are. I don't want this night to end."

Lily's kisses were searchingly gentle, but the intent in her eyes was clear. An answering tremble in her belly made Nicole moan softly and Lily smiled against her mouth.

"To help you get back to sleep," Lily said as one hand lazily brushed over one nipple, her ribs, then across her hips. "Please let me."

Unable to speak, Nicole rolled onto her back, cradling Lily's head between her breasts. Lily's touch was so gentle that it seemed to slide past Nicole's primal needs to stroke something else inside her, something that didn't seem to have one physical location.

She closed her eyes, fighting the feeling of being lost. She told herself none of her feelings made sense. This was not the first time she'd done this, so why did she feel as if it were?

She couldn't catch her breath. The pressure of Lily's fingers ought to feel like every other woman's touch, but it didn't. Why were her eyes swimming with tears? Why did Lily's light kisses across her chest make it so hard to inhale?

She shuddered against Lily, who whispered something soft in response. Muscles knotted, clenched, relaxed as Nicole clamped one hand over her mouth. She couldn't afford the words that would only confuse tomorrow.

Her body was melting into afterglow. Dopamine was flowing through her blood. Meanwhile her brain raced with panic: the numbers no longer added up to anything she was willing to admit might be real.

When Lily stretched out alongside her Nicole hoped she looked as composed and sleepy as a woman could be after a powerful orgasm in the middle of the night.

Lily's smile was drowsy as she tucked one hand under Nicole's shoulder and sighed with contentment. "I don't know that I'd call us even, but at least I've put something more on my side of the scales."

"Thank you." Nicole was surprised her voice was so steady. Her throat felt choked with tears and an ineffable anguish. She pulled the sheet over them only to realize it was unanchored and now their feet were exposed.

Lily wriggled until they were covered again and her eyelids promptly drooped. "If your feet get cold you can cuddle up to me."

Nicole didn't want to close her eyes. She wanted to go on remembering the shadows on Lily's cheeks, the curl of her lashes. If she didn't sleep then tomorrow might not come.

There, she thought. She was officially in denial of scientific law. She was now worthy of being in one of her own case studies.

The thought was not comforting, but the scent and warmth of Lily's body was enough to lull her back to sleep.

***

When Lily woke again, her arms still feeling like melted butter, she thought at first the clamor was the alarm clock. But it was actually the phone on the bedside table. Nicole was stirring as Lily muttered a bad word and scrabbled the receiver off the base.

"Is this Lily?" The clipped voice was stretched thin with stress.

Lily sat bolt upright, clutching the sheet over her breasts. "This is Lily, Indira. What's wrong?"

Nicole surged out of the sheets with a gasp.

"I need to find Nicole. It's Kate—"

"She's right here." Lily realized too late that Nicole might not want her mother to know she was in Lily's hotel room at four thirty in the morning, but Indira was clearly distraught.

Nicole, who had been rummaging through her clothes on the floor, was staring at her phone display in dismay. Pointing at the display she handed it to Lily and took the desk handset.

"Mom, what happened?"

The latest text message received on Nicole's phone read, "Kate still in surgery. Where are you?" The missed call alert held a dozen or more from Indira, starting just after midnight.

Lily wrapped herself in the sheet, went to the desk and opened her laptop. Every minute might count in getting Nicole onto a flight home.

"Mom, slow down," Nicole said. "I'm sorry, I was asleep. I didn't hear the phone vibrate. What's happened?" There was a long pause, then Nicole said, "A girl? Is she okay?"

Lily's heart stopped for a moment as she looked at Nicole in a panic. Kate wasn't due for more than a month, she'd thought. Had Kate lost the baby? Nicole gave what seemed like a reassuring smile, but she was getting more pale by the moment. Lily fetched a glass of water from the bathroom which she pressed into Nicole's hand.

"So after the C-section—they tried an angiogram? Mom, an angiogram is a test, not a treatment. She went in for high blood pressure? But the baby's okay?" Nicole stared at the glass of water as if she didn't know how it had gotten in her hand, then sipped. Lily took the glass just before Nicole sank down on the bed, cradling her head in her free hand.

"Those were the exact words? The doctor actually said to prepare for the worst?"

Lily wanted to smash her sluggish laptop keyboard. She wasn't even past the hotel's log in yet.

"I can be home later today," Nicole was saying. "As soon as I can. Is there a doctor I can talk to? Kate is too strong, the doctor is just being cautious."

Nicole didn't sound as if she believed it. Lily gave up on her computer and began grabbing things off the dresser to stuff into her suitcase. They needed showers. A cab to the airport would be easy to order. Nicole could be home by afternoon.

"I'll call again in about thirty minutes, Mom. If you can find a doctor who will talk to me, that would be good. Lily will get me there, it's okay."

The moment she clicked the phone off Lily said, "It's best to get ourselves to the airport as soon as possible."

Nicole was staring at the handset, frozen except for the slight trembling in her hand.

"You're right, Kate is very strong. The baby is a girl?"

Nicole's nod was distracted. "A girl. Kate had cramps last night after dinner and started to bleed, so my mother drove her to the hospital. Her blood pressure was very high but the baby wasn't in distress. It sounds like they planned to have Kate stay in the hospital for every possible extra day for the baby to be in utero, but the baby's vitals suddenly dropped and they took them into emergency surgery. The baby's in perinatal care. Kate lost a lot of blood and my mother wasn't very clear about exactly what's wrong now. She's on a ventilator, they're trying to get blood back into her, but the doctor said to expect the worst—" Nicole's voice broke.

Lily abandoned the modesty of the sheet to join Nicole on the bed. She wanted in the worst way to pull Nicole into her arms. Instead, she said, "Let me help."

Nicole scrubbed her eyes, nodding slightly as if making notes in her head. Lily wasn't surprised when Nicole resumed gathering her clothes. "Thirty minutes?"

"Yes, I can be ready by then," Lily promised. "In the cab we can both start calling airlines."

Nicole was out the door and inside her own room before Lily's door clicked shut. Lily surveyed the wreck of the bed, her panties and bra on the floor next to her stilettos. She wadded her undergarments and the shoes into a corner of her suitcase and ignored the echoes of her broken pleas and gasps of unrestrained pleasure. But every time she stopped moving, even for a moment, she felt herself under Nicole's body and relived the sensation of Nicole's kisses.

In the shower Lily fought the urge to cry as she stood under the hot water. She wished there had been a chance to say "Thank you" or even "Wow that was fun."

Her suitcase was just about packed when she realized that Nicole's leather jacket was half-rolled up in the comforter she'd tossed back onto the bed. She indulged herself for five seconds, holding it against her face and inhaling the scent. It wasn't one she'd associated with Nicole until last night, and now she might never be able to forget it.

Telling herself to focus, she folded it into her suitcase. She'd return it when they got to Nicole's house.

Everything stowed and her carry-on and purse stacked on top of her big suitcase, she opened her door to find Nicole already in the hallway.

"I talked to my mother again," Nicole said. "No new news. She sounded like she was about to break. I called one of her friends to go to the hospital. She was on her way before we hung up."

"I'm glad she has a friend like that."

"Several. They're organizing support—typical of my mother not to call anyone for help. She's the first person there when someone needs a helping hand, which of course comes with plenty of free advice." Nicole's expression was rueful. "Anyway, someone will meet us at Logan."

"Terrific."

The cab ride seemed to take twice as long as when they'd arrived, even though the early morning traffic was light. They took turns calling airlines only to be told there were no flights until the afternoon. Lily thought it best not to book and try their luck in person.

Ticket counters were just opening up when they rolled their suitcases into the terminal at six a.m. When they'd arrived two days ago Lily had been appreciative of the whimsical sculptures and photographic tributes to the airport's namesake, Louis Armstrong. Now she hardly saw them as she made a beeline for the departures display. "There's a nonstop that leaves in less than an hour," Lily announced. "Maybe too close to book over the phone, but they might ticket it in person."

"We won't make it."

"The ticket counter is over here—no line. It can't hurt to try."

Within a few minutes Nicole had explained the need to the sympathetic ticket agent, but Lily's heart sank when the young woman shook her head.

"It's past the time when we can check your luggage."

"It can be on a flight later in the day," Nicole said.

"Due to security, it has to go on the flight with you. The flight is full, too—well, there's one first-class seat left."

"We'll take it," Lily said. She plunked down Insignis's credit card, knowing Uncle Damon wouldn't hesitate.

Nicole began to protest, then swallowed hard. "Thank you, Lily."

"You'll be in Boston by noon. I'll get there as soon as I can, bags and all."

The ticket agent quickly scanned the card and tapped at her keyboard. "No bags, here's the boarding pass. Security is usually light at this hour. Good luck." She handed a sheaf of papers to Nicole. "I hope your sister and the baby are doing well by the time you get there."

"Thank you."

"Now, let's get you and the suitcases on the next possible arrival," the agent said to Lily.

Lily handed her ID to the agent, aware that Nicole was hesitating. She looked up long enough to say, "Go. You don't have time to waste."

Nicole's eyes were dark. For a moment Lily thought Nicole might kiss her, but she nodded instead. "Thank you."

She willed herself not to tear up. There was no time for it. "Don't miss the flight—text when you're in your seat, okay?"

She watched Nicole half-run toward the security screening, her carry-on roller bouncing over ripples in the carpet. The agent asked for her credit card again and when Lily glanced one more time in the direction of security there was no sign of Nicole.

She walked away from the counter with a ticket for a flight that didn't leave for nearly four hours—she'd be in the air when Nicole landed. Her flight stopped in Charlotte before going on to Boston and it would be mid-evening before Lily reached Meredith.

There was no sign of Nicole at security, which was a good thing, Lily told herself. Thankfully, everyone in line seemed to be too sleepy to take any notice of Lily and her increasingly red eyes. Maybe, too, her famous face was finally passing out of short-term memory.

She was putting her shoes back on when her phone chirped.

Nicole's message read, "In my seat. Thank you. For everything."

You're welcome would seem glib, so Lily texted back, "Will arrive Meredith 8 tonight. See you then."

She didn't expect an answer. Nevertheless she got one more chirp. The message only said, "Please."

Puzzling over the meaning, Lily realized she was ravenous, and she finally had the time to blush over why. All that physical activity last night had her stomach growling over airport food. A Starbucks kiosk was the only thing open, but it would do for a start. She smiled into her latte, remembering the crazy drive through Moscow and their great relief at finding a Starbucks there. And blushed again remembering Nicole's mouth on her.

Fortified by caffeine, she found a comfortable electronics workstation and booted up her laptop and plugged in her phone to charge, blushing once more as she recalled why she'd forgotten to do so last night. Headset in place she called Uncle Damon's home number, figuring he was up and partly caffeinated as well.

"Lily? To what do I owe this early morning pleasure?"

"We've got a major wrinkle," Lily answered him. She explained about Kate and that Nicole was already in the air on her way home. "I thought it best to start canceling. We were supposed to be at Georgia State tonight. I thought I should at least cancel the next four days, and more tomorrow, after there's some kind of news— hopefully good news."

"That's probably prudent. It can't be helped. Are you okay? You sound shaky."

"Do I? I guess I am." Lily wanted to confess to all her confusions, but at the moment she felt she was talking to her boss, not her uncle. Though he and David had, of course, been the ones she'd first told about her crush on a female classmate, convincing him over the phone that she'd fallen for a woman he considered a pain in the ass didn't seem like a good idea. "Everything is so uncertain. Nicole was frantic—for her, that is."

"That's hard to picture, but under the circumstances understandable. Pumpkin, if she is going to be at home for an extended time my door is open—the guest room is yours and I can keep you on the payroll for a little while. I can think of one or two projects no one ever seems to find time to do to justify it to the other partners. You'll figure out your next step."

"Thank you. That helps," Lily said vaguely.

"I am still hopeful that you'll become a diplomat and live in exciting places and I'll visit you twice a year."

"So am I, I guess. I could stay in New York. After all, New Yorkers will take you back after a scandal." She knew she had to make a plan, and that plan couldn't include Nicole. If the worst happened Nicole would probably cancel the rest of the trip to be with her mother and new niece…She knocked on the faux wood surface of the work desk. "I'm not going to think that far ahead. There's time."

"The trip has been good so far? Other than getting lost in Russia? Did you see the blog we wrote up about that adventure?" Lily heard what sounded like the espresso maker sputtering and pictured her uncle's cheerful, tidy kitchen.

"I did. Nicole said it made the situation seem more dangerous than it was."

"Dr. Hathaway isn't very imaginative."

Lily flushed as she relived the sensation of Nicole pulling her bra straps down. "I wouldn't say that."

"Really? Well, you know her better than I do."

He had no idea. "Oh! Really—this proves my point. Guess who we ran into yesterday?"

"Do tell."

Lily related the encounter with Merrill Boone. "So the very imaginative Dr. Hathaway asks Boone if she was eight or nine when her parents divorced—and apparently she was close enough that Boone went into a defensive tailspin."

"My opinion of her has gone up twenty points. I'm glad she was there for moral support."

She wasn't about to tell him that Nicole had flipped off another woman for getting too friendly with Lily in a gay bar, even though he was likely to find that a positive character trait as well. "I don't know if Boone is going to leave me alone. If she doesn't then I know it'll still be hard to find the kind of work I was hoping to get. But so what? I can be a hotel concierge in Spain and live on bread, olives and cheese if I have to. I do have choices."

"So when you get back we'll talk about your choices. It's not so bleak as it was, is it?"

Lily agreed even as she was thinking she could also wait tables in Meredith. Get a teaching certificate for languages and find her way into the school system somehow, even though she'd never wanted to be a teacher. She could cobble together a living in the area, couldn't she?

Circumspect had no patience for Libido's hopeful, wishful thinking. *How does it feel, after a night like that, to still not know if the woman can even feel love? She clearly wanted you, but for what?*

Libido was happy with the answer of, "Great sex."

Focus on what matters right now, Lily thought.

"Let's just take it day-by-day," she said to Uncle Damon. She had work to accomplish in the next several hours. Before she began she sent one more silent prayer winging heavenward for Kate and her little girl. Priorities.

CHAPTER EIGHTEEN

Nicole was only a few steps inside the doors of Meredith General Hospital when she was reminded why she'd opted out of pursuing a career in medicine. The smell of antiseptic left her nauseated, and even though she knew it highly unlikely, she thought she smelled blood. She'd attempted to overcome the response with standard desensitization techniques, but after a course of volunteering in the hospital she'd been as queasy on the last day as the first. Her neural pathways were stubborn.

Her stepfather had died in this particular hospital, and that association from her childhood only added to her anxiety for Kate. She'd spoken with her mother twice on the drive from Logan, and knew Kate was still in intensive care and listed as critical. The latest description of her vital signs from a doctor was, "Thready but steady."

She was glad Betty Creedy, who had met her at the airport, had insisted on some food during the drive. It had steadied her nerves. She was carrying a frothy chai tea for her mother, having asked Betty to stop at the Meredith Grinder. It was all she could think to do, and she thought that Lily would approve.

She missed Lily. She missed Lily with every step. Every heartbeat. She told herself that she shouldn't rely on someone else to make her a better woman and a more thoughtful daughter, but it seemed that she wanted more on the resume of her life than "excellent researcher" and "consistent professor."

Her mother broke down the moment she saw Nicole. She wanted to cry too, but her mother had been bottling up her fear all night. Nicole could wait. She rocked her mother while she wept, not certain that her fervent, "It's going to be okay," was heard.

The storm abated after a few minutes and the eagerness with which her mother drank half of the tea without pausing proved that she'd not eaten much. Her color improved, and Nicole went with her to the restroom to wash her face and stood helpfully by while her mother repaired her makeup.

"There," she pronounced, looking at her mother in the mirror. "Kate will know you when she wakes up."

Her mother blew her nose. "Waiting is hard. I have been praying. One loses one's parents, that is natural. Losing my husbands was not easy, but I had my daughters. But losing a daughter—"

"Kate's going to be okay," Nicole said firmly. "And now you have a granddaughter."

The words brought a slight smile to her mother's lips though her brow remained creased with worry. "Kate won't have another baby. One of the things they had to do in the surgery was remove her uterus. I don't understand what went wrong."

After five minutes with the ICU resident, Nicole understood. Kate's blood pressure had set off a cascade of bad outcomes, including a massive loss of blood during the C-section. When the doctor said Kate had flatlined twice for sixty seconds before responding to electric shock the surgeon had deemed it more important to stop the bleeding and stabilize Kate's heartbeat than to try to save the uterus. Nicole completely agreed.

The ICU nurse let them both in to see Kate for only a minute. Nicole swallowed queasily and kept her arm around her mother. Kate's face was waxy and pale and her skin seemed to hang off her chin and hands. The tape holding the breathing tube in place would leave marks for several days. She wanted Kate to wake up and complain about the tape, how boring it all was and to beg someone to turn on the TV.

When they both touched her hand her vital signs didn't change.

"The baby is doing fine." Nicole squeezed Kate's fingers. "Her APGAR score was six. That's good for a pre-term delivery, Kate, more than good. She's going to be fine, but she needs you."

"You need to pick a name." Her mother patted Kate's arm. "I know you couldn't decide between Aliyah or Juliet for a girl."

"We'll be back. We're going to go look at Aliyah-Juliet now."

It became the pattern of their afternoon. A few minutes with Kate, twenty minutes peering through the glass into the nursery, then back to the waiting room to decide nothing in the vending machine was edible. Betty Creedy dropped by, bringing some freshly baked pumpkin chocolate chip muffins for both of them and the nurses. Nicole did her best to express her gratitude and it wasn't lost on her that Mrs. Creedy was a little surprised by her effusiveness.

Through the thick plexiglass window Baby A-J looked healthy considering her rushed arrival into the world. Even though they could see only the tiniest bit of the little girl's face, it was obviously pink and she knew how to cry. Her tiny mouth was already trying to suck even though feeding by mouth would wait while the intravenous feeding tried to load her up with nutrients she'd missed by arriving early. The signs were all good. The nurse had said the baby would be in the perinatal unit for at least three more weeks. What effect would it have, Nicole wondered, to start life separated from the world by barriers and the faces of those who loved you indistinct, and the sounds of affection muffled?

With an inward wry laugh, she touched the glass. It wasn't all that different from the way she'd been living. Separated from other kids by her skin color and "strange" mother, and a brain that understood math and science problems long before her peers did, she'd always been behind a wall of her own and other people's making. Having learned that barriers could help the pursuits of a scholar she'd made good use of them to keep people out—and her emotions in.

But for now her personal glass seemed to be gone. She was grateful to have her mother's hand to hold. Whether her barriers had been melted by Lily or shattered by her fear for Kate didn't matter. The muffins were delicious. Her mother was beautiful. The nurses were kind. All of these things she would have deflected before, but now they washed into her senses, leaving her a little dizzy.

She knew she would go back to the university and back to dealing with frustrations of academia and students. But she didn't want to go back to a state of perpetual annoyance that filtered out all the positives. She chuckled to herself again. She wouldn't go so far as loving vindaloo, however.

Her mother heard her little laugh. "What is funny? I need to smile."

"Just thinking about Kate coaxing Baby A-J to eat strained peas. You know how she hates gooey things."

Her mother did smile at that. "I have been warning her about diapers. When you were born I was sure I would be ill wiping up poo and spit-up. But motherhood changes everything, overnight. There is nothing that comes out of a baby's body that bothers me now. I would rather not touch some of them, but…" She shrugged. "A baby needs. A mother gives."

Nicole was startled by the sudden chirping of her phone. She glanced at the display and felt herself flush with pleasure. She forgot her mother was there as she answered, "Where are you? When will you get here?"

Lily's voice was a little garbled. "I'm in Charlotte, waiting for the next flight. I talked to Uncle Damon—he said you're not to worry about anything. The coordinator at Georgia State was very understanding, and I've e-mailed or called the contacts for every event for the next four days to cancel."

"You've been productive."

"I've had a lot of coffee."

Nicole laughed. "I'm up to my eyes in really bad tea."

"How about when I drive into town I stop at that café next to Beekman's and get some real food?"

"Mom's friends are bringing some dinner in a while, but thank you." She turned to look at her mother and found herself the subject of an intense maternal stare. "It's Lily," she explained. "She's halfway here."

She watched her mother raise one eyebrow and for a moment she had a clear idea of what she would see in her own mirror in another twenty years. What had she said to deserve that look?

"My flight is starting to board," Lily was saying. "When I land I'll get a rental and drive out. Don't worry about anything, okay? Just Kate. How is she? How is the baby?"

Nicole gave her a quick update and wished her a safe flight. "We'll be here at the hospital unless I call. You'll come directly here?"

Lily's voice grew soft. "Yes. Of course."

Nicole couldn't help her equally quiet, shy response. "Thank you."

She disconnected the call and turned back to her mother. "She'll be here tonight. It was good of her to keep my suitcase so I could make the earlier flight."

"Lily is—"

They were interrupted by the perinatal nurse, a solid, round-faced young woman. "I hate to be a pest, but state law requires we file a certificate of live birth within twenty-four hours. It's better to have a name than putting 'refused to state' on the form."

Her mother was shaking her head. "Kate must decide. She will wake up and decide."

Nicole sighed. "So at about twenty-three hours you're going to file one anyway?" The nurse nodded regretfully. "So regardless, Mom, Kate will have to file for an amended certificate to change the name. We could make a guess—if we get it right then she won't have to go through the bother. If we don't she's no worse off."

"Let's wait until tonight to do that," her mother said. "But we'll give you a name. 'Refused to state' is not acceptable, I agree."

The nurse smiled. "I'll let the night nurse know to ask again. Your beautiful granddaughter could be president some day and you wouldn't want anyone questioning her birth certificate."

They all laughed and Nicole was glad of the released tension as she walked with her mother back to the beige and gray waiting room. She decided, finally, that a vending machine bag of M&M'S looked good to her touchy stomach. Tearing the packet open she popped a couple into her mouth, recalling young Leonid's ravenous consumption of the bag Lily had given him. From there her mind called up the image of Lily getting out of the pool at that spa in Spain. She'd held that lovely body against her last night, had found ways to make Lily quiver and cry out.

Her pulse rate went up and Nicole didn't mind. Right now it was just good to know Lily was on her way. She was smiling when she sat down next to her mother and offered some of the candy.

"No. I will grow fat sitting in this room," her mother said. "So. Tell me about Lily."

Nicole popped more candies into her mouth. "She's been a great assistant."

"No," her mother said.

Nicole gave her a quizzical look.

"Tell me about Lily. The truth."

Nicole choked in midswallow.

"Don't tell me you don't know what I mean. You were in her room at four thirty in the morning. She had obviously been asleep just before she answered. You said you were asleep and didn't hear the phone. I had thought perhaps there weren't enough rooms at the hotel so you were sharing, but just now, when you spoke—I am your mother."

"I know," was all Nicole could think to say. There was not a chance she could meet her mother's gaze. Heat radiated from her cheeks.

"I know you well, Nicky. You spoke in a way I have never heard you speak before."

She could feel herself turning into a little girl, swamped with the fear of discovery of a misdeed. But she wasn't a child. She would not die because of the truth. There was nothing wrong with how she felt. "I feel more than friendship."

"Does she?"

"I don't know. But she's not even as old as some of my graduate assistants and Meredith is too quiet, too small for her."

Her mother made a sound of distress and Nicole stole a glance. The frown was deep, but not necessarily angry.

"Mom, you have so much on your mind. Let's talk about this later."

"No. We'll talk about it now. It's a relief."

"Explain?"

"You are over thirty and alone. That's not natural."

"For some people it is."

Her mother shrugged—an eloquent statement of "You may think that but you are of course wrong" that Nicole had never mastered. "I did not expect this to be the reason why you refused to marry, or even dated. But I am glad there *is* a reason. Glad that you haven't been lonely, even if you felt you had to keep some of your life from me."

"I've been devoted to my work, mostly. You know that, right?"

"Yes. Your success is clear, Nicky, and I am proud of you." Her mother's eyes were suddenly filled with tears. "I hope that you don't think that's all I wanted for you. Success and money. I want you happy and happiness comes from other people."

"There are monks who would dispute that."

Her mother's eyes turned into laser beams. "We are not talking about monks, Nicky."

With a quaver in her voice she couldn't control, Nicole said, "I knew I liked women. I've always known. But Lily is the first time I've felt this way."

Her mother's expression eased. "I will tell my brothers to give up all hope."

"Well, that's a relief." Nicole tamped down on the urge to laugh hysterically. From about age sixteen she'd expected this conversation to include recriminations, yelling, despair and dire predictions of social, financial and moral ruin. "None of that matters, does it?"

"It matters. I will worry."

"Of course you will." That would never change.

"But I am sitting in a hospital waiting to hear if one of my daughters will live. My brothers and their far-away concerns are the sands of a desert I do not need to cross."

Her mother took her hand and seemed content to be silent for a while. After a few minutes, Nicole realized that there was not really anything more to say. Just like that, she was on the other side of yet another barrier, one that she'd thought impenetrable and only now realized was made of bricks she'd created all by herself.

***

The miles from Logan to Meredith were long and lonely. Lily recalled her first drive to Meredith, filled with uncertainty and running for cover. Now she couldn't wait to get there. Her world was on a tilt and wouldn't be right until she saw Nicole again.

If nothing else, she needed closure. It was possible—though, for Kate's sake and her own, she prayed not—that she and Nicole would part in a few days, tour canceled and the need for Lily's services at an end. If that happened she would accept it, of course. Nothing else to be done. So they'd had great sex.

Really great sex, okay, obviously their chemicals were resonating or congruent or compatible when it came to sex.

Impatient with the painful merry-go-round of her thoughts, Lily turned up the radio. Last trip she'd soothed her ragged soul with Beethoven. Right now she needed loud. She pushed the buttons quickly past the sound of Adele's haunting voice—like that would help—and settled on what sounded like some new Green Day. But the next song up was Muse's "Madness" and that put her right back into the bar in New Orleans, getting erotically high on the scent of Nicole's jacket.

She turned the radio off and endured the silence. The sleepy lights of Meredith finally appeared around the next corner, and she consulted the GPS on how to get to the hospital.

She made her way to the visitor's parking lot, not full, and realized once inside the door that she didn't know if Kate was in maternity or the ICU. She texted the question to Nicole and stepped into the little gift and flower shop in the lobby while waiting for an answer.

She was inhaling the rich, velvety scent of a dozen roses when a peculiar, pleasant tingling told her that Nicole was behind her. Without looking up she asked, "Does Kate like roses?"

"Yes, but they're not allowed in the ICU."

"Pity, these are gorgeous." She straightened up and turned with nonchalance, an air that fled the moment she saw Nicole's eyes. The rest of her face was as composed as ever, if a little pale, but her eyes were red and glistening with tears. "Is there news?"

"No, nothing new. I'm glad your drive was safe."

"How is your mother doing?" They fell into step on the way to the elevator.

"She's as good as one might expect. Better in some ways than I expected, even." Nicole's voice was laden with something Lily couldn't identify. "Baby Aliyah-Juliet is doing fine."

"Is that her name?"

"One or the other. Kate can't say so we're going to pick her two top choices for now." Nicole looked up at the indicator. "It takes forever to arrive. It's only two flights. Take the stairs?"

"Sure."

Nicole looked down. "Even in those?"

Lily tried not to flush. She'd grabbed the Manolos because they were the first pair she'd found in the hurry to leave for the airport. She had had ample time during the wait and then the drive to change into something more practical. But Nicole had obviously liked her wearing them…"I'm fine."

The stairwell was drab and cold and they were passed by several nurses and a doctor hurrying downward. It was deserted when they reached the third-floor landing. Nicole paused with her hand on the door handle.

Lily looked at her inquiringly. Nicole seemed about to say something but all she did was reach up to touch Lily's hair.

There didn't seem to be the right words in Lily either. She turned her head to kiss Nicole's fingertips.

"This isn't a good time," Nicole whispered.

She didn't resist when Lily pulled her close for a quick, hard kiss. The tight-wound knot in her stomach relaxed, finally, relief and arousal mixing in equal measures. Nicole's quick intake of breath seemed to echo her feelings even as Lily wondered exactly what it wasn't a good time for. Kisses? Talking? Being together?

A slamming door below them forced them apart. How Nicole managed to look so composed so quickly was beyond Lily. Her own cheeks were hot and her lips felt bruised and swollen.

It didn't help that the first thing she saw as they stepped out of the stairwell was Indira rushing toward them.

"She's awake! She's breathing completely on her own now. They might remove the tubes. They're checking her vital signs and then we can go in for a minute."

Nicole embraced her mother tightly and they rocked together. Lily dug in her handbag for a tissue, handing it to Indira, who gratefully dabbed at her eyes.

"I'm so glad to hear Kate is improving," Lily said. "It can only get better now."

"It is a pleasure to see you again, Lily. Nicky says you have been an excellent assistant."

Lily fixed her gaze just above Indira's eyes. She felt as if her feelings for Nicole were etched on her forehead. It was a first, being in the company of a lover's parent. Lily had put that on a personal To Do list—like, never. She controlled the urge to blurt out that it wasn't just sex for her. "We've had some adventures, that's for sure."

They all turned at rapid footsteps and a man's voice saying, "Mrs. Hathaway? You can go in now. The baby is already with her, so you'll need masks."

"I'll wait here," Lily said before the nurse could discourage her from crowding the room. Kate needed the comfort of those she knew, not making polite conversation with a virtual stranger.

She watched the two Hathaways follow the nurse down the hall. It was probably a good idea to squelch the flicker of hope that perhaps, in a week, their tour would resume. Libido was pleased with the idea, but Circumspect woke up Common Sense and they both reminded her that "assistant with benefits" wasn't going to feel good when it was over.

***

Nicole heard the baby's weak half-cry as they opened the door. The head of Kate's bed had been raised so she was slightly elevated, and the baby was cradled on her chest. One hand rested on the tightly wrapped bundle and Kate's eyes were closed.

"I think she's asleep," she said to her mother. She pulled her mask more firmly into place even as she thought that the damp constriction was another thing that would have made a profession in medicine impossible for her.

Kate's eyes blinked half open. She slurred, "No, she's drugged and not with the really good stuff."

Nicole laughed. Her worry that having lost her heartbeat twice would leave her with brain damage dissolved. Kate was still very much Kate.

Her mother's eyes were dry and bright. "Don't tire yourself out. And now you've met your daughter."

Kate's hand tightened on the blankets. Even considering that Kate was still seriously ill, Nicole was caught off guard by how much Kate suddenly resembled their mother in the set of her jaw and the watchful glimmer in her eyes. "She's been a real pain up until now. But she stopped wailing the moment the nurse put her down."

"It's only the beginning."

"You came back," Kate said. "Like you care or something."

"Or something," Nicole teased. "I care about my niece, that's for sure."

"What is her name to be?" Her mother dabbed the corners of Kate's mouth with a wet tissue smeared with lip balm, easing off the remnants of tape.

"Juliet."

"I was calling her Aliyah-Juliet," Nicole said. "She could be A.J. for short."

"No," Kate and her mother said simultaneously.

"Just a thought," Nicole muttered. "I like Juliet."

The door opened behind them and the male nurse said kindly but firmly, "The baby needs to go back to the nursery and new mom needs her sleep now."

"Of course," Nicole said automatically. She hesitated long enough to get out her phone and take a picture.

"Stop that! No pictures, Nicky." Kate glared. "You better fucking delete that."

"No such language in front of the baby, Kate," her mother snapped. "I'll be back in the morning, and we'll talk about getting you strong and ready for when Juliet comes home."

Nicole made a hasty retreat and wondered, now that there was a baby to be protected, if her mother's hearing would extend to Kate's voice and often colorful choice of words. She couldn't help a little schadenfreude at the thought.

Lily was leafing through a magazine when they returned to the waiting area.

Nicole held out her phone. "Mother and child."

Lily gazed at the picture then looked at Indira. "They're both beautiful."

"The women in my family have all the looks."

Lily's agreement sounded perfunctory, but her color was high. Nicole suddenly woke up to how Lily must be feeling. She wasn't aware that her mother knew about them. Maybe, just maybe, there were some social situations that Lily didn't know how to handle. Even as she tried to think of how to ease Lily's anxiety she felt a wave of panic that her mother would tell Lily that Nicole had admitted to feelings.

"I think we should go home," her mother said. "Lily, the guest room has baby gifts in it, but otherwise, it is yours to make use of."

"I was planning on a hotel—"

"No. You shall stay with us."

Lily made no further argument, but the decision left Nicole even more flustered. At the parking lot she turned in the same direction as Lily, just as she had for the last five or so weeks, but stopped short. Her mother was drooping with weariness.

"I'll drive, Mom." She held out her hand for the keys.

"I'll follow you," Lily said. "If we get separated I know the way."

"You can always use the GPS."

"And end up in Lyubytino."

They shared a fleeting smile and parted ways.

Nicole was backing out of the parking space when her mother said, "Why did you tell me that you didn't know if Lily had feelings for you?"

"I don't know if she does."

"No. You refuse to see."

"Why wouldn't I want to know?" She glanced at her mother then turned onto the Daniel Webster Highway.

"I am not the one with degrees in what makes minds work the way they do. But Lily cares very much about you. It's plain as day."

"Mom, she's sweet and kind and nice to everyone."

"You are just another woman to her?"

"That's not what I meant. Lily isn't…She doesn't…I don't think I want to have this conversation now."

"You have studied love to death and still don't know what it is."

The words stung. She realized her mother was very tired, so she clamped down on the urge to retort something she'd regret. "I do know what it is, Mom. But as with the marriage proposals conveyed by my uncles, this is my life."

"Lily is a beautiful, talented girl."

Nicole tightened her hands on the wheel. "I know."

There was no point in telling her mother that unless Lily could find some kind of fulfillment through the university or the Meredith tourism industry, there was nothing in Meredith to interest a beautiful, talented girl. Her mother had no idea the depth of Lily's gift with languages and that Lily ought to be working in an embassy, planning cultural exchanges, celebrating the arts and spreading peace through food and laughter.

The headlights from Lily's rental stayed in the rearview mirror for the entire drive. At home Nicole hurried down the driveway from the garage to help get the suitcases out of the trunk. Lily was already tottering to the house with one of them, those absurd, sexy shoes not helping her keep her balance. A sharp, cold wind blew across the house.

Lily returned. "It's cold out here."

"Not as cold as Russia—but it's good to be home." Nicole eyed the thin sweater Lily wore over her blue and white striped dress. "You'll need something heavier."

"I know. There was a cute little boutique in the village near Beekman's. I thought I could likely find something there."

It was a surreal feeling and not one she much liked, thinking of Lily, her Lily, walking through the Meredith stores, and talking to shopkeepers, walking the same sidewalks and looking in the same windows that Nicole did. Lily would be around every corner of town for her after this.

The feeling got worse when Lily rolled her suitcase into the guest room and reappeared in comfortable jeans. Watching her drink tea with her mother was as disconcerting as it had been on the day they'd met. She'd thought her some Barbie doll and now knew exactly how hot-blooded, spontaneous and wickedly intelligent Lily was. But her mother's insistence that Lily had feelings for her? She didn't see it. It was all about sex, an intense physical connection, something her mother wouldn't understand. Or, if her mother did, Nicole certainly didn't want to know.

She was used to living inside her own mind, most of the time, but it was now absurdly crowded. There were too many pictures in her head to keep clear. Too many impulses pumping through her muscles, too many chemicals mixing and changing her ability to reason, to react.

Everywhere she looked there were green eyes and elegant fingers and in every quiet pause she heard Lily's laughter.

CHAPTER NINETEEN

Lily knew that if she could have forgotten where she was, she would have loved waking up in a real bed in a real house with real sheets and blankets. But even as the pleasure of it made her smile into the soft, downy pillow, the recollection that she was a guest in Nicole's home caused her a pang. Libido loved being close. Circumspect insisted she find a way to avoid throwing herself into Nicole's arms when they were alone. Common Sense made a short appearance, advising her to get far away and make it a clean break now before she made it into more than it would ever be.

She snorted and sat up. It was too late to run away. Besides, she still needed this job. She wasn't out of the woods of infamy yet.

The alarm clock showed it was nearly nine—she'd slept hard after worrying she'd be awake half the night. The house was very quiet. Hoping it met Indira's standards to be seen in her pajamas she peeked out the door of her room but still heard nothing. Perhaps they had both gone to the hospital.

She tiptoed to the breezeway that led to where she'd seen Nicole park the car in the garage last night. She braved the sharply cold morning air and peered into the garage through the window. One car, not two. Yes, the hospital made sense.

The house phone was ringing when she went back inside. She heard the distant clicking of an answering machine, then it was quiet again. In the kitchen the teakettle was still warm and came to a boil quickly. On the kitchen table was a bowl of oatmeal sprinkled with brown sugar and a note with her name on it. A few seconds in the microwave brought it back up to steaming and she settled in to enjoy every bite. It was vastly superior to anything they'd have found in their hotel's dining room in Georgia.

Back in the guest room she fiddled with the clock-radio until she found some innocuous pop music. Unpacking only what she needed to shower, she made her way to the bathroom across the hall and took advantage of the excellent lighting to peer at her hair. It was looking worse and worse every day with very red roots and a sharp line where blond began. She ought to wear a hat all the time.

The shower was hot and refreshing. She wrapped herself in a towel and went back to her room only to discover Nicole in the act of turning off the radio. Her pulse leapt to a painful throb and she couldn't swallow.

"You're back. I hope it was okay I took a shower, and thank you for the oatmeal, it was really good, not mushy." You're babbling, she thought. What exactly was the right thing to say? She was wearing only a towel and they were standing entirely too close to the bed and its tousled covers. She could only hope that the flush she felt washing down her cheeks and shoulders could be attributed to a postshower glow.

"I was looking for you," Nicole said. Her voice was almost distant as she added, "Dear heaven."

"What?"

"You." Nicole reached for her.

Lily couldn't help a reflexive glance over her shoulder.

"My mother is still at the hospital. Kate is doing better. We'll go back in a while." Nicole still sounded distracted though her eyes were dark with desire.

"In a while," Lily echoed. She watched Nicole unknot the towel and was in a moment naked in her arms, then pulling Nicole down to the bed.

"You feel delicious," Nicole whispered.

They shouldn't, Lily thought. She tried to say it, even, as she pulled Nicole's T-shirt over her head. But Nicole's kisses took her breath away and the only words she could say were *yes* and *please*.

What seemed like only minutes later, as the world around Lily shifted from a shining gold glow to the soft reflections of morning light off the red and white wallpaper, Nicole wrapped Lily close in her arms and said quietly, "I'm sorry if that was abrupt. I can't seem to help myself."

That was a doubled-edged compliment, Lily thought. It was nice to be irresistible, but knowing as much as she did now about biological imperatives and Nicole's deeply held belief that every impulse in the human psyche and body were powered by them, she wasn't keen on being the bell for Nicole's Pavlovian urges.

If we keep doing this I'm not going to like myself much. She couldn't help but stretch into Nicole's warmth, and she undeniably liked the heat that was growing again in her fingers and toes.

"I need you to help me find something," Nicole said.

Lily closed her fingertips around Nicole's small, erect nipple. "Found it."

Nicole laughed, but Lily also felt a shiver. All in a rush they were kissing again, rolling across the bed, this time with Lily landing on top and Nicole making breathy pleas for attention. She took her time, teasing and kissing away ragged requests for more. She finally let Nicole guide her hand where she wanted it and a few minutes later muted Nicole's shout of climax with her lips.

With a shiver of delight she relaxed into Nicole's arms, half-laughing.

There was an answering ripple of amusement from Nicole. "Now that we have that out of the way…"

"Yes? You wanted me to find something?"

"It's called a bed jacket. Kate says she has three and if I don't return with at least one of them I am no longer her sister."

"I'm sure we can find one."

"You haven't seen her room."

Though she hated to move, she shooed Nicole out of the bed. "You go look for something that's a lot like a long, silky sweater and I'll get dressed."

"But I want to stay here."

"If you do we'll not get up. We have things to do." Lily began inching toward the side of the bed.

Nicole slowly sat up. "You're bossy, did you know that?"

"You like it, admit it."

Nicole caught her hand and pulled her close for a kiss. "Sometimes."

"Stop that," Lily said when she was able. She couldn't take her eyes off Nicole's mouth.

"Oh, that was convincing." Nicole kissed her again, then let her go. "They moved Kate out of the ICU this morning. They're now watching for postsurgical infection. The doctors are very pleased. She could come home in two or three days."

"I'm glad." Lily paused in the act of pulling clean pants and a top out of her suitcase. "I really am."

Nicole was buttoning her jeans again, her expression pensive. "I don't know how soon I can resume the tour. But perhaps in a week? Truly, I could use the break at home. It took me forever to fall asleep last night but once I did I think I didn't move."

"It's been a tiring trip. I understand." Lily buttoned her only sweater over the plain white shirt. "I'll take care of everything. Let me go dry my hair and I'll join you."

She surveyed herself in the mirror, amazed at how the last few minutes of eager passion didn't show in the least. She took her time with the hair dryer because of the temperatures outside—no point in going out with a wet head.

She finally felt it was dry enough and had just finished taming the tendency to curl and snarl with hair spray when Nicole appeared in the bathroom doorway holding two garments, one black and translucent, the other pink and opaque.

"Which?"

"Silly—which do you think?" Lily pointed at each. "That's a negligee and would shock the nurses. The pink is a bed jacket."

"I have little experience of either."

"I can give you experience with negligees, if you like." I'm a dipshidiot, Lily thought—Libido had complete control of her brain.

Nicole's eyes took on the dark fire that brought Lily's blood to a boil. She tossed both garments over her shoulder into the hallway. "I'd like."

Backed up to the sink, Lily shivered into Nicole's kisses and helped get her jeans unbuttoned. Nicole's slender hand slid under Lily's panties, fingers seeking and finding a slick welcome that Lily echoed with a sharp cry. She panted into Nicole's shoulder, bewildered and amazed that she could come again, so soon, and still feel like her desire had not even begun to be satisfied.

Nicole laughed low in her ear as she rocked Lily against her. "I'm so glad you like that."

"I'm feeling things I didn't even know I could." An unwise admission, Lily thought.

"I don't want to leave until I'm sure my mother can cope with Kate being at home, and transporting her to the hospital to be with Juliet every day. But I can't wait…" Nicole tightened her arms around Lily. "I can't wait to spend the nights with you."

Lily closed her eyes and tried not to again hear a double-edged compliment. Only the nights? And yet what possible basis did Lily have to expect more?

***

"Give me a few minutes to make up some sandwiches. Mom is sick of hospital food already and Kate insists she can eat peanut butter and jelly." Nicole managed to disentangle herself from Lily's arms, though even those few inches of separation felt like a dash of cold water.

How was she ever going to look into the guest room or the bathroom and not remember Lily in her arms? How was this house ever not going to seem as if it were throbbing with the memory of Lily's cries?

"I'll go finish getting ready," Lily murmured. "I need earrings. I feel half dressed."

A flash of Lily, blouse open, chest flushed with desire, left Nicole disconcertingly breathless. She resolutely went to the kitchen and set about making PB&J sandwiches. She packed them in a paper bag along with a couple of bags of Cape Cod chips and an orange for her mother, who didn't think a meal was complete without a fruit. Task completed, she also felt a welcome calm. Lily had still not appeared, so Nicole went in search of her. A cold draft from the sitting room French doors drew her in that direction.

The back garden, even this late in the New England season, was still beautiful and lush. Mums showed yellow, brown and white under the evergreen bushes. The apple tree leaves were golden and orange. In the middle of the riot of color stood Lily, simply gazing around her. Her hair lifted in the wind. Abruptly she smiled for no apparent reason.

The remaining rational part of Nicole that could still think about tomorrows wondered how she would ever sit at her desk in her bedroom again, look into the garden and not see Lily there. She wouldn't merely remember Lily in the gardens at the Alhambra, against the chessboard in Italy or shivering in the cold Russian morning. Every vista in her daily life, inside and out, was filled with green eyes and those beautiful curving lips. Her ears were full of passion and laughter that reflected the quick curiosity of Lily's mind.

So many futures ahead of her, Nicole thought. She brutally reminded herself that Lily was young enough to be one of her graduate students.

Lily turned and saw her in the doorway. "Your mother is a wonder."

"In a few more weeks it'll be covered in snow and ice and still look beautiful. Crocuses come up in January." Nicole didn't leave the doorway. "We should go."

"Can we stop and get a sweater or light jacket in town? I'll be very quick."

"Sure." Yet another place that would be full of Lily in the future.

As Lily walked past her Nicole smelled the familiar vanilla and cherry scent of her freshly washed hair. She felt her stomach tighten, this time not with arousal but with resignation.

***

"I can't believe you survived so many weeks with that one and can still stand to be in the same room with her." Kate's words were softened by an indulgent look at her sister that surprised Lily to no end. Post-partum feel-good hormones? The snipe level did seem to be diminished. But Kate had been greatly cheered by the arrival of the bed jacket to wear over her hospital gown and had crowed when Nicole had put her iPad on the bedside table and explained that she'd already transferred photos of Juliet to it.

"We were both focused on the grueling schedule. Hardly time to read the signs welcoming us to town before it was time to leave." She took back the hairbrush Kate handed to her, dropping it into the little travel bag with Kate's name on it. Kate was definitely the kind of girl who felt better for some blush on her cheeks and snarls out of her hair.

"You don't look like you just had a baby and major surgery," Lily pronounced.

"Really?" Kate looked doubtful.

Lily patted her hand. "More like you just had the flu—but you're on the mend."

Kate gestured at the paraphernalia lining one side of her bed. "I can't wait until they take away the IV and monitors and I can walk to see Juliet."

"Tomorrow maybe, depending on how your sutures are holding," Indira reminded her. "If you don't have a relapse for eating solids when the doctors said to wait."

"Peanut butter and jelly. Seriously, Mom. It's not going to hurt me."

Lily truly admired the economical shift of Indira's shoulders. She was going to try to learn that. It so clearly said that pity was the only reason Indira wasn't arguing the point. She tamped down a grin as both Hathaway daughters rolled their eyes in precisely the same manner. Though Nicole didn't want to believe it, they were very much alike. Juliet was going to grow up just as strong-minded, and so utterly loved.

The control it had taken to keep from grinning helped her hold back sudden tears. One of these days she'd stop tripping over her parents' lack of affection. She could still hear Nicole's pronouncement, "They could not have loved you."

What she felt in this room was palpable. Love washed in through her eyes and ears to warm her bones, heart and soul.

"I think I'll go for some coffee. Does anyone want anything?" She put Kate's travel kit in the drawer labeled "Patient's Belongings."

Assured no one could stand the thought of hospital coffee she made her way to the cafeteria. She didn't much want coffee but the warm paper cup felt good in her hands, and her absence would give the Hathaways more time together.

The second-story windows had a lovely view of Lake Winnipesauke. The onset of cold weather made its waters seem a darker blue even though a brilliant sunshine shimmered off its rippling surface. She pulled her new bright blue cable-knit sweater more tightly around her shoulders. It wasn't hard to imagine the lake with snow-covered shores and ice where people had been wading in the water on her first visit. For now, the green-crusted islands were dotted with golds and oranges as the leaves turned. A week from now it would be even more stunning, she thought. She would love to watch it change, bit by bit.

The coffee grew more bitter as it cooled so she wandered back to the condiment station to add more half-and-half. It was peaceful but for the drone of the television which suddenly penetrated her pensive distraction. It was a measure of how far away her thoughts were that she hadn't recognized that woman's voice sooner. It was a commercial for her program, which began in another few minutes.

Against her will she paid attention to the words.

"Today I'll be interviewing the Jefferson County police officer at the center of the controversial handling of evidence from the Kitty Reilly kidnapping. Procedures appear to have been followed, but who wrote those procedures? Was it the now discredited chief of police who left office abruptly three years ago? We'll find out. We'll also have the promised exclusive update on the whereabouts of the rich girl everybody wants to find."

She resisted throwing the contents of her cup at the screen. So she wasn't going to be left alone. Fine. Whatever. Merrill Boone wasn't going to find her anytime soon, and so what if she did? She had nothing to fear. She left the cafeteria and briskly circled the floor in an attempt to clear her head of the woman's voice and the poison it spread.

When she returned to the room it was to find that little Juliet had been brought in. A double-masked Nicole shooed an understanding Lily back out the door. Once in the hallway she pulled down her mask to reveal a grin.

"When the nurse found out I'd just returned from abroad she just about banned me from the hospital, but doubling up got me a waiver. Later I might have to submit to a hazmat scrub down."

"Oh—I hadn't even thought of that. A good precaution. I totally get it," Lily assured her. She hoped to make little Juliet's acquaintance some day, but germs were germs and there was no telling what they'd dragged home with them. "I can happily do some more shopping and return later."

Nicole seemed to accept that, though she asked quietly, "Are you sure?"

"Of course. There's a shoe store."

Nicole heaved an indulgent sigh. "See you after a while then."

Lily waved her phone as she headed for the stairs. "I'll text if I need to."

Several minutes later a wrong turn happily landed her in front of the public library. Now that she was on her own, her curiosity was getting the better of her. Her little laptop negotiated with the library's wireless service and she reluctantly went to the Boone website. Better to read the dirt than have to listen to Boone say it.

Well, it was something that she wasn't the featured story on the page. But she was the story with the banner "Exclusive" across it at the bottom of the page.

MERRILL BOONE has learned that runaway heiress LILLIAN LINDEN-SMITH has relocated to New Orleans under disguise of a new blond haircut and in the company of people who may not be Americans. Looking remarkably refreshed and well-dressed for someone who cried "I'm broke!" to the

court, Linden-Smith was the picture
of leisure while sightseeing with
her new playmates. Anyone who spots
Linden-Smith should call the show.
Cash reward for photographs.

So a person free to travel anywhere in the world was now a "runaway"? She shouldn't be surprised, but she was a bit baffled why Boone had chosen to say she was with "playmates," plural. Had she been unwilling to tell her staff she'd been flummoxed by a woman who "may not be American"? What a racist assessment, Lily fumed.

She disconnected and found herself in no mood for shopping. A hike in the woods would be glorious and clear her head, but she lacked anything close to decent gear. She had no boots, no warm coat should she get lost or the weather turn. No way was she going to do something stupid and then need to be rescued by Nicole again.

A power walk down the greenway that sprawled alongside the city government buildings helped to calm her nerves, but her mind was still spinning in circles when she returned to the rental car. Part of her still wanted to get away from Nicole and their damned chemistry that made it so hard to think. She knew her heart was going to get broken, and yet she couldn't make herself leave just to save herself. Now she knew that Boone was still on the hunt. What about Nicole—and Indira, and Kate and even little Juliet—if someone decided their houseguest might be worth some money, just a photo? If she stayed for the week they were at risk of harassment when they needed to be left alone.

All at once Lily was back on the subway with the man and woman jostling her with their briefcases while they pretended she didn't exist, then following her from car to car. People were more vicious than Nicole could know. Indira, as an immigrant, had no doubt spent a lot of her life staring down unwelcoming locals, but why should she have to do that again on Lily's behalf?

Nicole had said she couldn't wait to get back on the road so they could spend their nights together. That wasn't exactly a declaration that she wanted Lily around all the time. That her day didn't begin until Lily said "good morning" and couldn't end until they kissed good night.

That was how she wanted to be needed. All the time. She wasn't going to stick around to be a Passepartout with Benefits to Nicole's science-above-all Phileas Fogg. But if she was with Nicole again and again and again, that was what she'd be. With a cold shiver she wondered what Uncle Damon would say if he knew. A bewitching night was one thing, but an affair for the duration of the job? That was something else.

Going on six weeks ago she'd been desperate for an escape. Nothing had really changed. This job was temporary and that bitch Boone was still determined to keep her name in the public mind. She'd had time to heal a little, that's all. She'd had the pleasure of doing a job well, and regained some confidence. What professional prospects she had were improved.

Personally, though, she'd really screwed up. How was it that sex with a stranger had seemed a safe declaration of freedom, but sex with Nicole was a danger to her future?

She lost track of time, replaying those fantastic, passionate hours in Nicole's arms. Words of desire, kisses of pure fire and a clear, physical connection were brilliant in her mind.

Ultimately, however, she could not recall one word of affection or one whisper of love.

CHAPTER TWENTY

Nicole looked at Lily's text message in disbelief. She fumbled with her phone buttons and scrolled up to read it again.

"Must go back to New York. Side door was unlocked, got my things. Will be in touch about tour changes. Hugs to all."

Had Lily been offended that she couldn't come into Kate's room with Juliet there? No, her eyes had been clear, her skin color unchanged. Nicole would swear that Lily had had no intention of leaving town two hours ago.

Whatever the reason for her abrupt departure, the result was clear. She would not see Lily later today. Wouldn't hear her laughter fill the house or see her delicate hands holding one of the university's coffee mugs. She'd been dreading memories of Lily further intruding into every aspect of her life and now it wasn't going to happen.

Why was it so hard to breathe? The chemical smell of the hospital room seemed suddenly overwhelming.

"What is it, Nicky?"

Her mother had to repeat the question before Nicole could lift her gaze from the stark words on her phone display. "Nothing."

Kate snorted. "You look like you're going to faint."

"Lily had to go back to New York."

"Chalk up another one," Kate said. "How many assistants is that now?"

"Kate, hush," her mother said. "Did you have a fight?"

"No. She went shopping."

Kate tapped her iPad one more time and rested back on the pillows with a sigh of relief. "There, baby announcement all formatted. So Lily took one look at Meredith stores and ran for Fifth Avenue? I don't blame her."

"Kate, please." Her mother gave Nicole a searching look. "Did she say why?"

"No." Damn it all, her voice broke the word into three syllables. Kate waved a hand. "Wait a minute—are you shitting me?"

"Kate! Language! And this doesn't concern you."

"Maybe it doesn't, but this is a newsflash from the Department of Shit That's Obvious." Kate put a hand on her belly as she laughed with triumph. "I warned you that you were in big trouble with this one, Nicky. Have you finally seen the rainbow that's tattooed on your forehead?"

The physical urge to throw her phone at Kate was so strong that Nicole began to cock back her arm. But she was able to calm herself enough to pocket the phone and say through stiff lips, "I don't want to talk about it."

"I have all the time in the world to talk about it," Kate said. Her tone softened slightly as she added, "Sometimes, talking about stuff helps. Hey, I'll start. I like men in bed, but they are a pain in the ass the rest of the time. If it weren't illegal, I'd want to do a harem-in-reverse thing. Live exclusively in the company of women and keep the guys around for sex."

Her mother spluttered an outraged, "Kate!"

"You don't know the right men," Nicole said.

"My sister the lesbian is telling me the right man is out there for me? What would you know about it?"

"I know *everything* about it!" Nicole was glad Juliet had gone back to the nursery. She hadn't meant to shout. She supposed she'd just come out to her sister, but apparently, as usual, Kate knew it all along. She'd been going to tell her, but in her own time, not because Kate was a little snot. "You look in the wrong places."

"Show me the ideal man in the flesh, not on a graph." Kate shrugged. "People are not an accumulation of numbers. I'm betting you can't even begin to express what you feel right now in an equation."

"Of course I could, but not with you jabbering on about it. All I need is measurements to fill in the variables."

"How fucking romantic." Kate gave her a hard, unamused look. "Just what every girl wants to hear."

Nicole was kept from responding with a hearty suggestion that Kate go fuck herself by their mother's shrill, "Enough!"

"I am what I am, Kate," Nicole muttered.

"You are what you want to be," Kate muttered back. "Everybody is."

"You two are like dogs that cannot stop barking. Kate, we are going to have a new rule. There will be no cursing of any kind, at any time, for any reason. Do not test me on this. You will not like the consequences."

Nicole drew in a deep breath. When their mother didn't even bother to define the threat it meant it would be bad. The memory of a day without any books to read for having wadded her dirty laundry under her bed instead of putting it into the hamper as instructed was suddenly foremost in her mind. It had been one of the most agonizing days of her teenage life.

Kate seemed likewise chagrined, but couldn't seem to resist saying, "She started it."

"No. She did not start it. You are a mother now. You must see these things more honestly." She turned to Nicole. "As for you, if you did not make Lily go away, then why do you look so guilty?"

"I didn't—"

"Your face knows something your brain does not."

"I need some air." It was the only exit line Nicole could think of, and it was the truth. She swallowed down nausea and hurried for the stairs. Moving helped. The sharp, cold air outside settled her stomach. Truly, she detested the way hospitals smelled. Perhaps that accounted for all of these feelings. Her biochemical response to the antiseptic had gotten the better of her will to ignore it.

Liar, liar, pants on fire, she could hear Kate chanting.

She wasn't ready to face Kate or her mother again. She felt as if she'd been turned inside out, and everything she'd guarded all her life was on display where anyone could poke at it. Kate, in particular, knew just where to stick her needles. She couldn't bear the thought of anyone seeing her with emotions naked on her face.

She found herself in her mother's car and following the familiar route to the university. To her surprise she realized it was a Saturday, explaining why the faculty lot had plenty of empty spaces. The hallway of the science building was nearly deserted and the sound of her footsteps on the marble reminded her of the sharp tap of Lily's heels that had so annoyed her.

She unlocked and then shut the office door behind her, glad to see that it apparently had not been loaned out to anyone. Her desk was precisely as she had left it. As she sat down she waited for the arrival of the familiar sensation of being safe in her work cocoon.

Several minutes later she was still waiting, but the calm focus she associated with her office didn't develop. It was a small space, and she liked that, but today it seemed almost claustrophobic. Turning on the desk lamp seemed to further darken the room.

Lily had sat in the side chair, the epitome of an automaton. Her impressions of Lily at first had been so wrong, and she'd been so focused on shutting out Lily's presence that the memory was tissue paper. Lily wasn't why her office felt two sizes too small.

Unsure of how to alleviate her anxieties, she turned to work to settle her nerves. Her computer login still functioned and e-mail had stacked up. It was reassuring to see that her settings to sort the incoming mail into folders had worked well. Student e-mails had received automated responses explaining about her sabbatical and providing alternate contacts. Colleagues at the university had sent only a few messages, knowing she was unavailable. Announcements of meetings and so on she could ignore. The folder for administration missives was full of the expected reminders about grant application deadlines, the need for economy, the urgency of securing donors and so forth.

Finding nothing mentally engaging in anything so far, she turned to the folder where e-mail from other colleges had been shunted. As she expected, there were a couple dozen calls for papers at conferences and requests to speak at other institutions. There were also several thank yous from various colleges where she and Lily had been over the last few weeks.

The last item she opened she presumed was another thank you, this time from one of the universities outside Geneva—she couldn't picture the facility. They had all started to look alike, and the only one she remembered clearly was in Moscow where Lily had paused to listen to the Balkan choir.

The e-mail wasn't a thank you.

She read it twice and then answered.

***

I just need to think.

Lily had told herself that for the entire drive back to New York. She needed to breathe away from Nicole's pheromones so her own brain chemicals would get back into balance. After all the evidence Nicole talked about, this seemed imperative. Uncle Damon's guest room would be just the place. So she was a coward. Running away by text message. It wasn't as if she was abandoning the job. She would see Nicole in a week, probably.

She wondered why she didn't have a text reply from Nicole. Was she angry? She'd have a right to be, Lily supposed. Maybe she was distracted with Kate and the baby. As the hours passed without any kind of response she decided, however, that the silence was a sign. Nicole felt so little emotional connection with her that she didn't even rate a text message. There, that was clear enough. She might get a message around bedtime, when Nicole finally missed her. Imagining a booty call from Nicole, however, was so funny that she smiled most of the way across Connecticut.

As she went through the rigmarole of returning the rental car near the Newark airport and taking the train into Penn Station, she debated on how to send another text, worded perfectly naturally, nothing out of the ordinary. She didn't come up with any brilliant ideas.

Emerging at street level above Penn Station, Lily was comforted by the familiar Manhattan smells—damp sidewalks, car exhaust. A hot dog from a steam cart in one hand, she hailed a cab.

When the cab dropped her off she wasn't surprised Uncle Damon was home. She'd warned him she was on the way. After a bear hug he proffered apricot rugelach from the bakery on the corner and a piping hot espresso.

"So what made you bolt for here? Hathaway is going to be sidelined longer than you thought?"

"I think she'll be ready to resume in about a week." Lily tried for a nonchalant shrug. "We're both pretty beat. Like I said, whoever thought filling every single day with a commitment was crazy."

"You could have stayed up there for the week—you've earned the rest."

"I wanted to come home…I need winter clothes. And I need a break." She nibbled at her pastry, then had to take a huge bite. Sweet and flaky and buttery.

"From Hathaway? That I believe."

"Yeah. That's it." Maybe not for the reasons Uncle Damon thought, though. She noticed he was in beautifully creased black slacks and a gorgeous pullover. The multicolor wool weave reminded her of El Salvadoran textiles. It was a little upscale for an evening at home with his niece. "Do you have a date?"

"Just meeting a friend for drinks."

"Don't come home early on my account." She was much happier to talk about his life than her own. He still wore David's ring on his finger, and he'd been lonely for years now. After listening to Nicole for all these weeks, she had to believe that the numbers were in his favor—not to find another David, but find someone who could make him happy.

"My club days are long behind me, pumpkin. We are going to see if we can get into a piano bar featuring a young woman who plays like Marian MacPartland. You don't know who that is, but trust me, if it's true I will be a very happy man."

"I hope she's all that and more, then."

"You should go out clubbing. After weeks of a deadly dull academic for company you should go where the young people are. Act your age." He gave her a twinkling smile.

"I'm too tired, I guess." She shrugged. "I was thinking I'd go into the office with you on Monday. I do have a lot more cancellations to make and other adjustments."

He agreed and left her to finish off the rugelach. It was a little bit of a relief that she could settle in on her own. He was too perceptive and she didn't want to answer any more questions, not when her voice wasn't as steady as she hoped whenever she said Nicole's name.

Was Nicole sorting through her papers and deciding which studies she'd look at next? With something like détente between the two sisters was she telling about their travels and travails to alleviate Kate's boredom? Lily tried not to wish herself there. She would be swooning at the sound of Nicole's voice and drinking in every smile and laugh. Uncle Damon wouldn't believe her if she told him that Nicole's sense of humor was an endearing quality.

Before she settled in for the night she sent a second text to Nicole saying she'd arrived safely and would get the itinerary updated with a copy to her on Monday. It was very businesslike. Nicole's reply was a sparse "Thank you."

It wasn't until she unpacked some of her suitcase contents that she realized she still had Nicole's leather jacket. She held it against her face like Linus holding his blanket and told herself firmly that she would not cry.

A few days of something like normal and Nicole would be out of her system. The chemicals would fade and she'd get her brain back. Once her brain was working again she could put the feelings in perspective and move on.

She inhaled the scent of the jacket again.

**

The revised itinerary Lily had sent proposed that they would meet up the following Saturday at a hotel in Chicago. That night they would resume their events with a bookstore appearance. They'd be in Chicago for three days before leaving for St. Louis.

Studying it over breakfast on Tuesday morning, Nicole appreciated that Lily had canceled at least one event each of the remaining weeks to give them longer breaks.

Nicole pondered how to word her e-mail reply, then simply said she appreciated the effort and would see Lily Saturday evening. What else was there to say?

She refreshed her inbox again and resisted the urge to retreat to her bedroom to use the computer there, just in case her phone was somehow blocking the e-mail she really cared about. Two long days of waiting had led to being chided by her mother for her restless pacing. She supposed her mother thought it was due to missing Lily. Fortunately, Kate was coming home tomorrow and the installation of a temporary hospital bed had given her mother delivery people to fuss at and arrangements to make—in other words, her mother was preoccupied, blissfully so.

She was glad of the break from the endless speeches, but unable to wrap her mind around any of the peer review work she ought to have tackled, or at least staged so she could take papers with her. Instead she had packed and repacked her suitcase for Saturday. Her leather jacket had gone missing. Recalling how it had fallen to the floor in that New Orleans hotel room, landing next to Lily's panties and stilettos, didn't help her composure.

She mourned the loss of the garment, but not the way she would have even a few weeks ago. It was no longer the representation of her identity. Not when her sister casually referred to her as the "lovesick lesbo" at every opportunity.

Studying the new itinerary didn't trigger a bout of Cole planning which bars she'd prowl, not this time. Now she looked and wondered where she and Lily would have dinner, if there was a place where they could dance together, if they could fit in a movie or a concert.

Her phone buzzed in her hand and she quickly keyed up the new e-mail window even as she told herself not to hope.

It was the one she wanted.

It was the answer she wanted.

She really ought to think it over. Ask some questions, consider the pros and cons in light of the best interests of her career. But she tapped out her answer without doing any of those things, and sent the correspondence to the printer the household shared.

After a quick, hot shower she stood gazing at the only photograph she had of the two of them together—Lily in the garb of a Renaissance lady and Nicole the silent, dour knight at her side. They were like opposite sides of the moon, only meeting at the edges.

She packed up her toiletries and stuffed them into her suitcase.

As she rolled the case to the garage her mother came out of Kate's bedroom looking dismayed. "I thought you weren't leaving for your tour until Saturday."

"I'm not."

Her mother waited until Nicole was making her final trip for the carry on and her satchel. "New York?"

"Yes."

Her mother shook her head with a long maternal sigh. "You know that I am worried your position with the university will be compromised. Worried that the next election these hateful people will pass some law or another that hurts you."

"I know." Nicole remembered the last departure and her dread of her mother's inevitable histrionics. There were tears in her mother's eyes now, to be sure, but it didn't appear they would spill over.

"I worry about other people. But I am not worried about you."

What was the world coming to, Nicole thought, when she was the one who did the crying? She sniveled into a tissue for several miles and hoped she didn't get lost. Getting lost by herself would be unpleasant. If she were with Lily she didn't care at all where the road was leading.

Thankfully, the signs to New York were self-explanatory and she only turned wrong once trying to get onto the Henry Hudson Parkway. She didn't recall much of the drive—really, it was fascinating that her brain simply wasn't processing input the way it should.

Fascinating, perhaps, if it were happening to someone else.

She turned her car over to a valet at a Midtown parking garage and told the receptionist in the Insignis Publishing House lobby that she did not have an appointment.

Just a few moments later, looking as if he'd hurriedly rolled down his sleeves, Damon Linden appeared. "Nicole, what a surprise."

"I was in the neighborhood."

He raised his eyebrows at that and ushered her down the hallway to his office. The midday sun was peeking through afternoon clouds, but as striking as the view was, it was not what she'd been hoping to see. Nor did the quiet, purposeful sounds of the office include Lily's voice or laughter.

After waving her to one of the chairs at the small conference table in his office, Damon said, "Congratulations on your new niece."

"Thank you. My sister loved the fruit basket and sends her thanks."

"What brings you to New York? Lily tells me you were eager for a break, which I completely understand. All the feedback we've received so far has been stellar."

"I want to talk to Lily."

His expression shifted enough to signal puzzlement, so Nicole presumed that Lily had not discussed anything about her with him. "She's not answering her phone?"

Nicole felt a vivid blush heat her cheeks. She'd not even tried. What a colossal idiot she'd become.

Giving her an odd look, he picked up the phone on his desk, pressed a few buttons, then said, "Hi—just making sure your phone works. Thanks."

She said nothing after he'd disconnected. This is what all the seratonin and dopamine plus the heaps of oxytocin had gotten her into. Utter humiliation and reckless decisions. She was literally madly in love. "I just want to see her."

Damon's voice took on a protective tone that sounded more like an uncle than an employer. "Then may I respectfully suggest you do what I just did?"

She found there was nothing remotely dignified to say to that. She might have sat there for several more minutes, mute and crimson, but for the opening of the office door.

There was a flash of blond hair, a glimpse of a leather jacket. And green eyes.

"What was that all about—oh!"

Nicole got to her feet though her knees felt like jelly. Lily's hair was cut pixie short and the blond wisps with vivid red roots looked stylish and attractive. And even though it was a little long in the sleeves and wide in the shoulders, she was wearing Nicole's leather jacket and looking as impossibly sexy in it as she did in everything else. In her jeans and a pair of ankle boots she looked every inch a Manhattan girl, used to bright lights and a fast-moving life.

"You changed your hair."

Lily flushed. "Yes—I had to do something about it."

There was a long silence. Nicole stole a glance at Damon, who looked understandably curious.

Finally, Nicole said, "My jacket looks good on you."

Lily's gaze was fixed somewhere over Nicole's shoulder. Her cheeks remained bright red. "I should have told you I had it. Do you want it back?"

"No."

"Was there something about the itinerary that was wrong?"

"No."

Finally, Lily met her gaze. "So…?"

Nicole didn't know what she'd expected to happen. She supposed she'd hoped that the sight of her would have Lily throwing herself into her arms, but words were apparently going to have to do.

She got no further than, "I feel—"

"You *feel…*" Lily echoed.

"I would like to talk to you."

Lily blinked. "Talk to me about your feelings?"

"Yes."

Lily's confused expression was softened with a smile. "Did you know that right now you are frowning as if someone has asked you to do their research conclusions for them?"

"No." Her heart felt like it was trying to turn inside out. "I would like to buy you a cup of coffee."

"I see. Just a casual cup of coffee."

"*Casual* is the last word that describes me at this moment, Lily."

Damon abruptly stood up. "I think *I'll* get some coffee. You two can talk."

When the office door was closed and they were alone, Nicole decided that putting her hands in her pockets would keep her from reaching for Lily. She'd no sooner done that than she realized Lily was in motion. She was hastily grabbed, kissed and released. Lily then retreated behind Damon's desk.

"I wasn't going to ask," Nicole said.

"That's why I did it."

This woman will never make any sense to me, Nicole thought. There was surprising comfort in the idea that she could rely on Lily's ability to confound her. After all, in equations consistent uncertainty was treated as a constant.

She no longer felt as if her heart were coming apart in her chest. The lingering warmth of Lily's lips filled her with a heady sense of well-being. It felt ridiculously wonderful.

The only honest course was to admit that Kate had been right: there was no way she could, at this moment, put any of what she felt into an equation.

***

Cursing herself for not being able to keep her hands off Nicole for even thirty seconds, Lily retreated to the window and turtle-hunched the leather jacket up around her ears. She'd been busted in the act of wearing it, but it wasn't as if she'd thought in a million years that Nicole would drive all the way to New York. She was dizzy with pleasure at the sight of her, but couldn't help but wonder what was so urgent.

"How is Kate?" She already knew the answer—if Kate weren't doing well, Nicole would have never left.

"Coming home tomorrow. Juliet is thriving. The doctors and my mother are all ecstatic."

Lily nodded and lapsed into silence. It was typical of Nicole to describe other people's emotional state but not her own. But she'd said she was here to talk about her feelings, hadn't she?

She wanted to look into Nicole's eyes, to search for clues there, but couldn't make herself do it for fear of what she herself might reveal. Instead she stared at Nicole's loafers. Comfortable, basic professional footwear, chosen precisely because they would not cause comment. She had three similar pairs and Lily had seen all of them, every single day of the tour. No surprise there...except...She narrowed her eyes and peered carefully.

Both socks were black, as usual, but the left was a jacquard weave of black-on-black and the right a simple knit.

Even when they'd gotten lost or been running late, even when they'd used socks as mittens and even when they'd had to bolt out of the hotel in New Orleans Nicole's socks had matched.

Her foolish heart wanted to declare that Nicole was so distracted by her inner turmoil that she was, for her, disheveled. But it could be a simple mistake. Even Nicole could make a mistake, couldn't she?

Nicole opened her satchel and pulled out several papers, wordlessly holding them out toward Lily. Her expression was carefully blank, but Lily thought she heard a catch in Nicole's breathing.

She reached over the desk to take the papers. It was good to have a large wooden obstacle between them because the brief touch of their fingers sent sparks down Lily's spine.

The pages appeared to be a series of e-mails. The most recent said, "I accept your offer with pleasure." It had been sent from Nicole to someone Lily didn't know at an e-mail address for the University of Geneva.

She read down. And found an offer to Nicole to act as Distinguished Visiting Professor of Neurobiology effective for the semester that began in January.

"You're...you're moving to Switzerland?"

"For five months."

"Why?"

"It is an excellent opportunity."

"Okay." Lily tried to take it in. "And this is what you drove all this way to tell me? That you have an excellent professional opportunity?"

"No. I mean, yes, it is an excellent professional opportunity, but that's not why I drove all this way."

Nicole had arranged her home, her office, her entire life to suit herself. She was throwing that all aside to go to Switzerland?

Libido donned lederhosen and began a striptease.

Lily put the papers on the desk. "Your socks don't match."

Nicole looked down with a frown. "I didn't notice."

"When was the last time you wore mismatched socks?"

Both of Nicole's eyebrows went up. "You consider that important? Right now? I've just told you I'm going to live in Europe for five months and you want to know about my socks?"

"Yes."

Nicole took a sudden step forward. "Does this get easier?"

"Does what?"

"This!" Nicole gestured at herself and then at Lily. "Us."

"I just want to know about your socks!"

Nicole heaved a large sigh, both eyebrows raised as high as they had ever gone. "I do not recall ever wearing mismatched socks. You'd have to ask my mother if I wore mismatched socks as a child."

"So, let's say from age seven on, that's about twenty-five years, for ease call it three-hundred-sixty days a year, that's…"

"More than nine thousand days."

"More than nine thousand days. Would you consider one event out of nine thousand to have statistical relevance, or is it an anomaly outlier?"

"What on earth?" Nicole gazed at Lily, then broke into an outright grin, one so infectious that Lily smiled back. "Are you trying to use science to prove that I love you?"

"You use science to talk about love. Rather spectacularly well, I might add. Fans all over the world line up to hear you talk about the science of love." Had Nicole just said she was in love? No. Not really…Well, sort of…

"Clearly, I don't know much about practical application of the research." Nicole gestured at the e-mails. "I thought that was a romantic gesture. But you're fixated on socks."

"I'm fixated on the part of you that didn't stop to think." Lily swallowed around what felt like a boulder in her throat. "I admire Dr. Hathaway, and I am respectful of the alphabet soup after her name. I think Dr. Nicole Hathaway Ph.D. is a brilliant researcher, and I enjoy our conversations on almost any subject. Dr. Hathaway decided to move to Switzerland for, I'm sure, very sound reasons. But I went to bed with Cole. Cole's the one who put on the wrong socks."

Nicole abruptly sat down in the nearest chair. "You're wrong."

Lily bit her lip. "Which part?"

Nicole looked up at her. Her dark eyes were glistening with tension. "I didn't accept the position in Switzerland for sound reasons. I haven't even cleared it with my own department head, because I don't care what happens, I'm going."

Lily shook her head, but the words still didn't make sense to her. "I don't understand."

"I can't offer you the world unless I live in it. I can research and teach anywhere, I think. At least I am willing to try. But you can't be *you* in Meredith."

Lily tried one last time not to believe it. I can't trust my heart, she told herself. My heart thought my parents loved me. My heart thought Merrill Boone would give up eventually. "But I like Meredith. If I had a reason to live there I'm sure I would adapt."

"I don't want you to adapt. If you adapt to my limitations, you won't be you and we won't survive." Nicole scrubbed at her face with both hands before looking up at Lily again. "So maybe I was thinking about equations and case studies, but I don't recall doing so. I saw the offer and knew it was our way forward. I just...*knew*. You and I have a chance if we start fresh together."

Together. Nicole wanted a together beyond the end of the tour, a together beyond the bedroom. Lily didn't know if she should laugh or cry and ended up in between with a half-hiccup. "I'm more than an equation or a bunch of chemicals. I'm not just Passepartout with Benefits."

Nicole fixed her gaze just over Lily's shoulder. "You are an excellent Passepartout. And the benefits, as you call them, are quite wonderful. But I do not want an assistant for life."

"This is a lot for you to give up." Lily touched the e-mail printouts. "I know this was hard."

Her eyes burning like topaz fire, Nicole said fiercely, "I was thinking only of how I could be with you, and it was *easy*."

"But..." Lily didn't know why she was arguing so hard against something when she wanted to shout *yes* and then do things on Uncle Damon's desk that would get her fired and possibly disowned. "I won't forgive myself if Merrill Boone ruins your life. She could come after you."

"Let her come to Switzerland to do it, then. My mother likes you and I cannot stress enough that her goodwill alone nullifies any and all harm Boone may ever do me."

"What if you hate how I brush my teeth? What if you're a cover hog? What if I can't make eggs you like? What if my shoes take up too much room? I don't have a lot of shoes right now, but I will get more. And clothes. I don't know what a standard statistical deviation is and you can pronounce words with fifteen syllables and what if it doesn't work out?" Shut up, you idiot, she told herself. Why give her reasons to turn around and leave?

Nicole's face abruptly shuttered as she leaned heavily on the arm of the chair. There was no sign of emotion beyond the bright shimmer that remained in her eyes. "Maybe we could agree to a trial then. For the five months."

Common Sense pointed out that Lily could get her master's degree and Switzerland was an excellent place to study international relations. Circumspect suggested she should get a job to avoid being a kept woman. Libido replayed the night in New Orleans with the volume on Dolby Surround Sound.

A trial arrangement would give her a chance to settle. She studied the detached expression on Nicole's face. On the day they'd met she would have said Nicole was an aloof snob. She'd have thought that Nicole didn't care about Lily's answer.

But this wasn't the day they'd met. She knew she was looking at Nicole with love-soaked eyes and a brain chock-full of the most powerful drugs the body could produce. For most people, according to Nicole, that meant their powers of observation were limited and their judgment impaired.

But what if she wasn't most people? What if her eyes were finally telling her the truth? All at once she saw that the uncaring detachment was a fraud—Nicole did care about the answer. Through the subtle layers of her expression Lily could see clearly that Nicole was definitely *not* interested in living together to see if it would work out.

Well, neither was she.

"No. No trial." Through a sudden rush of tears in her eyes, Lily could see that Nicole had lifted one eyebrow. "If you think you're going to get off that easily, you're wrong, Dr. Hathaway."

One corner of Nicole's mouth twitched. "Then perhaps you should tell me where my offer is inadequate."

"I'll tell you where it's inadequate. You're going to marry me, Nicole Hathaway. You're going to marry me and your mother and sister and niece and my uncle and everyone else we care about is going to be there to watch. I'm going to wear white and really high heels, and you're going to wear whatever the hell you want, though I recommend a tuxedo because you would look totally hot in one, and people can shake their heads and say we rushed it and it won't last."

Nicole was openly smiling now. "And then you and I are going to prove them wrong?"

"You bet your ass we're going to prove them wrong."

"So I'm going to marry you."

"Yes." Lily left the safety of the desk and dropped to her knees in front of Nicole. "And I'm going to marry you. My future is the only thing I have left in this world, and I want to share it with you."

Nicole swept her up into her arms for a laughing, tear-streaked kiss that was quite possibly the best one ever. Until the next kiss, Lily thought.

She found herself nestled on Nicole's lap. Nicole's fingers were in her hair, softly stroking it. Fighting a shiver of desire, Lily murmured, "I'm sorry I wore your jacket."

"Keep it."

"As if."

Nicole leaned away enough to look into Lily's eyes. She traced the corner of Lily's mouth with a fingertip. "Call it an engagement gift."

Lily began to melt into another kiss but the sound of the office door opening had her scrambling to her feet.

Uncle Damon gave her a stern and worried look. "I think perhaps explanations are in order."

"I don't know…" Lily gestured at Nicole. "It's actually inexplicable."

He blinked at them, then said slowly, "We've sold nearly a million copies now of a book that says it can be explained."

Nicole rose to her feet and held out her hand. "Mr. Linden, my name is Nicole Hathaway, and I'm planning to marry your niece."

Lily couldn't have loved Uncle Damon more than she did at that moment. His discomfiture was obvious, but so was his attempt to take the situation in stride. He gave Lily a searching glance and said carefully, "This is very sudden, isn't it?"

"Yes," Nicole said. "But it'll work out."

"It's in the numbers?" He was almost smiling.

Lily looked at Nicole and lifted an eyebrow. "Is it?"

She placed Lily's hand on her heart and covered it with her own. "Right now the only number I care about is when two becomes one."

Bella Books, Inc.

Women. Books. Even Better Together.

P.O. Box 10543

Tallahassee, FL 32302

Phone: 800-729-4992

www.bellabooks.com